The Dead
Lie Down

SOPHIE HANNAH

The Dead
Lie Down

PENGUIN BOOKS

PENGUIN BOOKS

Published by the Penguin Group
Penguin Group (USA) Inc., 375 Hudson Street, New York, New York 10014, U.S.A.
Penguin Group (Canada), 90 Eglinton Avenue East, Suite 700, Toronto,
Ontario, Canada M4P 2Y3 (a division of Pearson Penguin Canada Inc.)
Penguin Books Ltd, 80 Strand, London WC2R 0RL, England
Penguin Ireland, 25 St Stephen's Green, Dublin 2, Ireland (a division of Penguin Books Ltd)
Penguin Group (Australia), 250 Camberwell Road, Camberwell,
Victoria 3124, Australia (a division of Pearson Australia Group Pty Ltd)
Penguin Books India Pvt Ltd, 11 Community Centre,
Panchsheel Park, New Delhi – 110 017, India
Penguin Group (NZ), 67 Apollo Drive, Rosedale, North Shore 0632,
New Zealand (a division of Pearson New Zealand Ltd)
Penguin Books (South Africa) (Pty) Ltd, 24 Sturdee Avenue,
Rosebank, Johannesburg 2196, South Africa

Penguin Books Ltd, Registered Offices:
80 Strand, London WC2R 0RL, England

First published in Great Britain under the title *The Other Half Lives*
by Hodder & Stoughton 2009
Published in Penguin Books 2010

PUBLISHER'S NOTE
This is a work of fiction. Names, characters, places, and incidents are either the product of the
author's imagination or are used fictitiously, and any resemblance to actual persons, living or
dead, business establishments, events, or locales is entirely coincidental.

ISBN 978-1-61664-504-5

Printed in the United States of America

For Jane Fielder

I didn't want to go first.

Three seconds ago—four—I had said, 'All right.' Now Aidan was watching me. Waiting. I bit back the words *Why me? You suggested it—why don't you start?* To ask would have made him think I didn't trust him, and I didn't want to sully the moment by saying something petty.

The air around us felt charged, taut with anticipation. Energy radiated from our clammy, clasped hands. 'It doesn't have to be everything,' Aidan whispered. 'Just . . . as much as we can . . .' Unable to finish the sentence, he decided he already had. 'As much as we can,' he said again, stressing the last word. His warm breath settled on my skin every few seconds, like a tide of air that kept sucking out, then blowing back in. We hadn't moved from our spot at the foot of the bed, in front of the mirror, but it seemed, suddenly, as though everything was speeding up. Our faces gleamed with sweat, as if we'd run for miles, when in fact all our movements—through the hotel's revolving glass door, towards reception, into and out of the lift, along the narrow spotlit corridor to the closed door with a gold '436' on it—had been slow and deliberate, a thousand heartbeats to the footstep. We both knew something was waiting for us inside the room, something that could only be put off for so long.

'As much as we can,' I echoed Aidan's words. 'And then no questions.'

He nodded. I saw his eyes shining in the dimness of the unlit room and knew how much it meant to him that I'd said yes. My fear was still there, sitting hunched inside me, but now I felt better able to manage it. I'd secured a concession: no questions. I was in control, I told myself.

'I did something stupid. More than stupid. Wrong.' My voice sounded too loud, so I lowered it. 'To two people.' Saying their names would have been impossible. I didn't try. Even in my thoughts I cannot name them. I make do with 'Him' and 'Her'.

I knew then that I was capable of giving Aidan no more than the bare bones, though every word of the whole of it glowed in my mind. Nobody would believe how often I tell myself the story, one unbearable detail after another. Like picking at a scab, except it's not. It's more like taking a sharp fingernail and gouging out raw, runny pink flesh from a spot I've never left alone long enough for a scab to form.

I did something wrong. I keep hoping I'll find a new way to start, at the same time as knowing there isn't one. None of it would have happened if I'd been blameless.

'It was a long time ago. I was punished.' My head throbbed, as if a small, hard machine was rotating inside my brain. 'Excessively. I never . . . I still haven't got over it. The unfairness of it and . . . what happened to me. I thought I could escape by moving away, but . . .' I shrugged, trying to affect an equanimity I did not feel.

'The worst things stow away in the hold, follow you wherever you go,' said Aidan.

His kindness made it harder. I shook my hands free from his and sat down on the edge of the bed. The room we'd booked was awful: it had the tall, narrow proportions of a telephone box, and there were green and blue checks everywhere—the curtains, the bedspread, the chairs—with a grid of red lines separating each square from its neighbours. When I stared at the pattern, it warped in front of my eyes. I didn't need to see all the other rooms in the Drummond Hotel to know they were identical. There were three pictures, one above the television and two on the hollow wall that separated the bedroom from the bathroom; three insipid landscapes that begged to be ignored, with colours that were as close to colourless as it was possible to get. Outside, through the thick, rectangular slab of multi-layered glass that made up one side of the room, London was a restless yellow-streaked grey that I knew would keep me awake all night. I wanted to be in the pitch black, blind and unseen.

Why was I bothering with this pretence of a confession? What was the point of telling the only version of events that I could bear to utter out loud—an abstract shadow, a template that could have applied to any number of stories?

'I'm sorry,' I told Aidan. 'It's not that I don't want you to know, it's just . . . I can't say it. I can't say the words.' A lie. I didn't want him to know; I had wanted to please him by agreeing that we should tell one another, but that wasn't the same thing. If I'd wanted him to know, I could have promised to show him the file under my bed at home: the trial transcript, the letters, the newspaper clippings.

'I'm sorry I've told you so little,' I said. I needed to cry. The tears were there; I could feel them inside me, blocking my throat and chest, but I couldn't squeeze them out.

Aidan knelt down in front of me, rested his arms on my knees and looked at me hard, so that I couldn't look away. 'It isn't so little,' he said. 'It's a lot. To me, it's a lot.' That was when I realised that he wouldn't go back on the deal we'd made. He wasn't going to ask me any questions. My body sagged, limp with relief.

I showed no sign of wanting to say more. Aidan must have assumed I'd reached the end of the non-story I had not quite told him. He kissed me and said, 'Whatever you did, it makes no difference to how I feel about you. I'm really proud of you. It'll be easy from now on.' I tried to pull him up onto the bed. I wasn't sure what the 'it' was that he thought would be easy; he might have meant making love for the first time, or the rest of our life together, all of it. I had left my last life behind, and now

I had a new one with Aidan. Part of me—a big, loud, insistent part—couldn't believe it.

I wasn't nervous about the sex, not any more. Aidan's idea had worked, though not in the way he'd hoped it would. I'd confided a little, and now I was desperate to do anything but talk. I wanted physical contact as a way of warding off words.

'Wait,' Aidan said. He stood up. It was his turn. I didn't want to know. How can the things someone has done in the past make no difference to the way you feel about them in the present? I knew too much about the worst human beings can do to one another to be able to give Aidan the reassurance he had given me.

'Years ago, I killed someone.' There was no emphasis, no tone to his voice; it was as if he was reading from an autocue, each word appearing on its own and out of context on a screen in front of him.

I had a terrible thought: *a man. Please let it be a man.*

'I killed a woman,' Aidan said, in response to my unasked question. His eyes were flooded. He sniffed, blinked.

I felt my body begin to fill up with a new sharp sadness, one I was sure I wouldn't be able to stand for more than a few seconds. I was desperate, angry, disbelieving, but not frightened.

Not until Aidan said, 'Her name was Mary. Mary Trelease.'

1

Friday 29 Feb 2008

Here she is. I see her face in profile and only for a second as her car passes me, but I'm sure it's her. Detective Sergeant Charlotte Zailer. If she drives past the part of the car park that's reserved for visitors, I'll know I'm right.

She does. I watch her silver Audi slow down and stop in one of the spaces marked 'Police Parking Only'. I reach into my coat pockets, allowing my red-cold hands to rest in the fleecy warmth for a few seconds, then pull out the article from the *Rawndesley and Spilling Telegraph*. As Charlotte Zailer gets out of her car, unaware of my presence, I unfold it and look at the picture again. The same high cheekbones, the same narrow but full mouth, the same small, bony chin. It's definitely her, though her hair is longer now, shoulder-length, and today she isn't wearing glasses. She isn't crying, either. In the small black and white picture, there are tears on her cheeks. I wonder why she didn't wipe them away, knowing the press were there with their cameras. Perhaps someone had told her it would go down better with the public if she looked distraught.

She hitches her brown leather bag over her shoulder and starts to walk towards the looming red-brick building that casts a long, square shadow over the car park: Spilling Police Station. I instruct myself to follow her, but my legs don't move. Shivering, I huddle beside my car. The winter sun warming my face makes my body feel colder by contrast.

There is no connection between the building in front of me

and the only other police station I have been inside—this is
what I must tell myself. They are simply two buildings, in the
way that cinemas and restaurants are also buildings, and I am
never stiff with fear when I walk past Spilling Picture House or
the Bay Tree Bistro.

Detective Sergeant Zailer is moving slowly towards the entrance: double glass doors with a sign saying 'Reception' above
them. She fumbles in her handbag. It's the sort I like least—long
and squashy, with a silly number of zips, buckles and protruding
side pockets. She pulls out a packet of Marlboro Lights, throws
it back in, then pulls out her mobile phone and stops for a moment, jabbing the keys with her long-nailed thumb. I could easily catch her up.

Go. Move. I stay where I am.

This time is nothing like last time, I tell myself. This time I
am here by choice.

If you can call it that.

I am here because the only alternative would be to go back to
Mary's house.

Frustrated, I clamp my mouth shut to stop my teeth chattering.
All my books advocate the technique of repeating encouraging
mantras in your head. *Useless.* You can issue yourself with sensible instructions endlessly, but making those words take root in
your mind and govern how you truly feel is another matter. Why
do so many people believe that words have an innate authority?

A lie I told as a teenager pushes to the front of my mind. I
pretended I'd said something similar to my father about the Bible, boasted to my friends about the terrible row it caused. 'It's
only words, Dad. Someone, or maybe lots of people, sat down
thousands of years ago and made it up, the whole lot. They
wrote a book. Like Jackie Collins.' The lie was easy to tell because those words were always in my head, though I lacked the
courage ever to speak them aloud. My school friends knew
Jackie Collins was my favourite writer; they had no idea that I
hid her books under my bed inside empty sanitary-towel packets.

Disgust finally gets me moving: the realisation that I'm thinking about my father in order to dishearten myself, offering myself an excuse to give up. Charlotte Zailer is heading towards
the doors, about to disappear inside. I start to run towards her.
Something has found its way into my shoe and it's hurting my
foot. I'm going to be too late; by the time I reach reception,
she'll be in an office somewhere, making a coffee, starting her
day's work. 'Wait!' I yell. 'Please, wait!'

She stops, turns. She has been unbuttoning her coat on her way
up the steps, and I see she's wearing a uniform. Doubt stills me, like
an invisible blow to the legs, then I lurch forward again, staggering.
Detective sergeants don't wear uniforms. What if it isn't her?

She is walking towards me. She must think I'm drunk, sway-
ing all over the car park. 'Are you after me?' she calls out.

Other people are looking at me too, those getting into and
out of their cars; they heard me shout, heard the desperation in
my voice. My worst nightmare, to be seen by everybody. Strangers. I can't speak. I'm confused, hot and cold at the same time,
in different parts of my body. I can't work out any more if I
want this woman to be Charlotte Zailer or not.

She draws level with me. 'Are you all right?' she asks.

I step back. The thing in my shoe presses into the skin between my little toe and the next one as I put my weight on my
left foot. 'Are you Detective Sergeant Charlotte Zailer?'

'I was,' she says, still smiling but more guardedly. 'Now I'm
just plain sergeant. Do we know each other?'

I shake my head.

'But you know who I am.'

I have rehearsed what I will say to her countless times, but
not once did I think about what she might say to me.

'What's your name?'

'Ruth Bussey.' I steel myself for signs of recognition, but there
are none.

'Right. Well, Ruth, I'm part of the community policing team
for Spilling now. Do you live in Spilling?'

'Yes.'

'This isn't a community matter, is it? You wanted to speak to a detective?'

I can't let her pass me on to someone else. My hand closes around the piece of newspaper in my pocket. 'No, I want to talk to you. It won't take long.'

She looks at her watch. 'What's it about? Why me in particular? I'd still like to know how you knew who I was.'

'It's . . . my boyfriend,' I say in a monotone. It won't be any easier to get the words out once we're inside. If I tell her why I'm here, she'll stop asking how I knew her name. 'He thinks he killed somebody, but he's wrong.'

Charlotte Zailer looks me up and down. 'Wrong?' She sighs. 'Okay, now you've got my attention. Look, come inside and we'll have a chat.'

As we walk, I move my foot around inside my shoe, trying to dislodge whatever's digging into the pad of soft skin beneath my toes. It won't budge. I can feel a sticky wetness: blood. *Ignore it, block it out.* I follow Sergeant Zailer into the reception area where there are more people—some in uniform, others in blue Aertex tops with the words 'Police Staff' printed on them. There's a lot of blue here: the herringbone carpet on the floor, two suede-effect sofas forming a right angle in one corner. A long counter of pale, varnished pine with a semi-circular end protrudes from one wall like a breakfast bar jutting out into the middle of a kitchen.

Sergeant Zailer stops to speak to a middle-aged man with a pot belly, a dimpled chin and fluffy grey hair. He calls her Charlie, not Charlotte. I press down on my coat pocket with my right hand and listen to the faint rustle of the newspaper, trying to remind myself of the connection between us—between me and Charlie—but I have never felt lonelier in my life, and only the pain charging up from my foot through all the nerves in my body stops me from running away.

After what I've told her, she would run after me. How could she not? She'd chase me and she'd catch me.

'Come on,' she says to me when she's finished talking to the grey-haired man. I limp after her. It's a relief once we're alone, in a corridor with uncovered brick walls that looks much older than the reception area. There is a background noise of running water; I look around, but its source isn't obvious. Along the walls on both sides, against the brick, are pictures at eye level. On my right is a series of framed posters—domestic violence, needle exchanges, building safer communities. Opposite these are framed black and white etchings of different streets in Spilling. They're atmospheric in a jagged sort of way, conveying the narrow, claustrophobic feel of the interlocking roads in the oldest part of town, the uneven house- and shop-fronts, the streets with their slippery cobbles. I feel a pang of sympathy for the artist, knowing that his or her exhibition is displayed here purely for its local relevance; no one values these pictures in their own right, as works of art.

'Are you all right?' Charlie Zailer asks me, waiting for me to catch up. 'You're limping.'

'I sprained my ankle yesterday,' I say, feeling a flush spread across my face.

'Did you?' She turns and stands in front of me, forcing me to stop. 'Sprained ankles generally swell to twice their size. Yours doesn't look swollen. It looks to me as if it's your foot that's sore. Has someone hurt you, Ruth? You seem very far from all right to me. Has your boyfriend hurt you, maybe?'

'Aidan?' I think about the way he kisses the straight line of pink scar tissue that starts below my ribcage and runs down over my stomach. He's never asked what caused it, neither on that first night in London nor since.

He is incapable of harming anybody. I know he is.

'Aidan?' Charlie Zailer repeats. 'Is that your boyfriend's name?'

I nod.

'Has Aidan hurt you?' She folds her arms, blocking the corridor so that I can't pass her. I don't know where we're going anyway; I have no choice but to wait.

'No. I've got a . . . a bad blister on my foot, that's all. It hurts when my shoe rubs against it.'

'Why not say so, then? Why pretend a blister's a sprained ankle?'

I can't understand why I'm out of breath. I clench my teeth, against the pain in my foot and against her attitude. Knowing what she's been through, I expected her to be kind. Understanding.

'Here's what we're going to do,' she says in a loud, clear voice, as if she's talking to a small child. 'I'll settle you in one of our reception rooms, sort us out with some tea, see if I can find a plaster for your foot . . .'

'I don't need a plaster,' I say. New beads of sweat prickle my upper lip. 'It's fine, honestly. You don't need to—'

'. . . And then we'll talk about your boyfriend. Aidan.' She starts to walk again. I have to half run to keep up with her. Is it a test? The pain is constant now; I picture a wide, weeping gash beneath my toes, with whatever caused it embedded in the wound, pushing its way deeper in with every step. The effort I'm making not to think about it is like a tight thread in my mind, winding tighter and tighter. My eyes ache to close. I'm aware of the sound of my breathing, of the air rushing out of my lungs and having to be dragged back in.

I follow Charlie Zailer round a corner and we are in another corridor, colder than the last, with windows all along one side. No pictures here, only a row of framed certificates, all with some sort of official-looking stamp on them, but they're high up on the wall and we're going too fast for me to read the writing.

I stop when I see a pale green door ahead. I've done this before: walked down a long passageway towards a closed door. *Green. Dark green.*

'Ruth?' Sergeant Zailer is calling me, snapping her fingers in the air. 'You look as if you're in shock. What's wrong? Is it your foot?'

'Nothing. Nothing's wrong.'

'Are you asthmatic? Have you got an inhaler?'

Asthmatic? I don't know what she's talking about. 'I'm all right,' I tell her.

'Well, come on, then.' When I don't move, she doubles back on herself, takes my arm and, with one hand on my back, steers me down the corridor, saying something about tea and coffee that sounds more complicated than a simple either-or offer. I mumble, 'Thanks,' hoping it's the right answer. She unlocks the green door, directs me to a chair, tells me to wait. I don't want her to leave me alone but I'm unwilling to ask her not to, knowing how pathetic I'd sound.

The room contains two chairs apart from the one I'm sitting on, a waste-paper basket and a table with a white-flowered cyclamen on it. The plant is too big for its pot. It must have been for some time, yet someone has been watering it regularly, or else its foliage wouldn't look so lush. What fool would water a plant day after day and not realise it needed re-potting?

Green. The door of our room at the Drummond Hotel in London was green. One night of my life, one night out of thirty-eight years, but part of me is still there, trapped in the night that Aidan told me. Part of me never left that hotel.

All my books say there's no point wasting your energy on 'if only's. They offer no advice about what to do if you're hooked on them. There are no patches available in chemists' shops that an 'if only' addict can stick on her arm to help break the destructive habit.

If only Aidan and I hadn't gone to London last December, the nightmare I'm living now would never have started.

'My boyfriend told me he killed a woman, but he didn't.'

'I need the woman's name, and details of where we can find her,' says Sergeant Zailer, ready to write down whatever I say. When I don't answer immediately, she says, 'Ruth, if Aidan's beaten somebody up so badly that—'

'No! He hasn't touched her.' I have to make her understand.

'She's fine. Nobody's hurt. I . . . He hasn't been anywhere near her, I'm sure he hasn't.'

'Nobody's hurt?' Charlie Zailer looks stumped.

'No.'

'You're certain?'

'Yes.'

She thinks for a few moments, then smiles at me. 'All right. Let's come back to your boyfriend and this woman later,' she says. 'I'm going to take a few basic details first, if that's okay.' Suddenly, she has an entirely different manner; she is no longer impatient, suspicious. She's ditched her too-loud patronising voice and is acting as if we're friends; we might be at a pub quiz, on the same team—she's writing down the answers. 'Name? Ruth Bussey, right? B-U-S-S-E-Y?'

'Yes.'

'Middle name?'

Does she really want to know? Is she joking? 'Zinta.'

She laughs. 'Really?'

'My mother's Latvian.'

'It's a great name,' she says. 'I've always wanted a more interesting middle name. Mine's Elizabeth. And your address?'

'Blantyre Lodge, Blantyre Park, Spil—'

'You live in the park?'

'In the lodge house, just inside the park gates.'

'That funny little house with the black and white top?'

Timber-panelled gables. I don't correct her. I nod.

'I see that house every day on my drive to work. That's yours?'

'I rent it. I don't own it.'

'One thing I've always wondered: how do you get those red leaves to grow down the roof like that, like a fringe? Did you plant something in the chimney? I mean, I can understand a plant growing up the side of a house, but . . .'

'Why does any of this matter?' I blurt out. 'I'm only the tenant. I didn't plant anything anywhere.'

'Who's your landlord?'

'The council.' I sigh, recognising the need to be patient, however impossible that might seem. If I try to speed things up, she will make sure to slow them down. Her cheery determination is like a restraint around me, pinning me in my chair for as long as she wants me there.

'How long have you lived there, Ruth?'

'Nearly four years.'

'And no trouble paying your rent on time during those years?'

Another odd question. There must be a reason for it. 'No.'

'Not tempted to buy a place? Get on the property ladder?'

'I . . .' *This is ludicrous.* 'I'm not ready to . . .'

'Commit to home-ownership? Put down roots?' Charlie Zailer suggests, still smiling. 'Fair enough. I felt that way for a long time.' She taps her pen against the hard cover of her notebook. 'What was your address before Blantyre Lodge?'

'I . . . Could I have a drink, please?'

'Tea's on the way. Where did you live before Blantyre Lodge?'

With my eyes fixed on the table in front of me, I recite my old address: '84 Pople Street, Lincoln.'

'Also rented?'

'No. That house was mine.'

'So you'd put down roots in Lincoln. Why did you move?'

I open my mouth to lie, then remember what a hash I made of my last attempt at dishonesty: my fake sprained ankle. I rub the palms of my hands against my jeans, wiping off the sticky dampness. 'Why are you asking me all these questions? What does it matter why I moved? I'm here to talk about my boyfriend . . .'

The door opens. A tall, thin man who looks too young to have left school comes in holding two mugs of tea. Proper mugs that look like bone china, one with green stripes and one with brown. Mine is chipped at the top. 'Perfect timing.' Sergeant Zailer smiles at her colleague, then at me. He mouths something at her, pointing at her notebook. She says, 'Apparently nobody's hurt,' and gives him a look I can't decipher. 'Thanks, Robbie.' Once Robbie has left us alone, closing the door behind him, she says, 'Drink your tea and relax, Ruth. There's no hurry. I know you've got something you want to tell me, and we'll get there, I promise. The questions I'm asking—they're all standard. Nothing to worry about.'

In other words, there is no way I can avoid answering them. What a fool I was to imagine Charlie Zailer would be more sensitive than any other police officer. After what happened to her, she probably resolved to fill the space her feelings used to occupy with sheet metal. I tried to do the same thing myself for a long time; I understand the logic behind it.

To my relief, she doesn't ask again why I left Lincoln. Instead, she wants to know if I have a job. I lean forward. Steam from my tea wets my face. Somehow it's comforting.

'I work for my boyfriend,' I tell her.

'What's his name?' She watches me carefully.

'You know his name.'

'Aidan?'

'Yes.'

'Surname?'

'Seed.'

'And what does Aidan do?'

'He's got his own picture-framing business, Seed Art Services.'

'Oh, I've seen the sign. You're by the river, aren't you? Near that pub, what's it called . . .?'

'Yes.'

'How long have you worked for Aidan?'

'Since last August.'

'Where did you work before that? When you first moved to Spilling?'

I tell myself this will be over soon. Even the worst things end eventually.

'I didn't, at first. Then I worked at the Spilling Gallery.'

'As a picture-framer?'

'No.' The word comes out like a cry of pain. It feels like a punishment, this long, drawn-out, pointless interrogation. 'I didn't know how to frame pictures then. My boss did the framing. I was a sales assistant—a receptionist, but I also sold pictures to customers. Aidan trained me properly, when I went to work for him.'

'So now you know how to frame pictures.' Charlie Zailer sounds pleased with my achievement. 'Did you work when you lived in Lincoln?'

'I had my own business.'

She smiles encouragingly. 'I'm not psychic.'

'I had a garden design business. Green Haven Gardens,' I say quickly, before she can ask me.

'Quite a change, then—garden designer to picture-framer. Your boss at the Spilling Gallery, what was his name?'

'Saul Hansard,' I say weakly.

She puts down her notebook and pen. She watches me, the bony fingers of her right hand playing with the ring on her left. It's a single diamond—a small one with gold claws around it, sticking up from the gold band it's attached to. *She's engaged.* I feel excluded from her private happiness, and know I have no right to. It's a sign of how far back I've slipped since London.

The better you understand yourself, the easier it is to change, my books say.

'So, you and Aidan Seed work together, framing pictures by the river. Ever been flooded?' Sergeant Zailer asks brightly. 'I know the pub has. Oh—the Star, that's what it's called. I've seen your sign—"Seed Art Services, Conservation Framing"—but I assumed you'd shut down. Whenever I look, there's a sign in the window saying you're closed.'

I stare at her. I can't do this any more. I stand up, knocking my legs against the table, spilling tea. More from her mug than mine. 'Aidan believes he killed a woman called Mary Trelease,' I tell her again. 'I know he didn't.'

'We'll be getting to that in a moment,' she says. 'Sit down, Ruth. I asked you a question: Seed Art Services is still up and running, is it?'

'Yes, it is,' I snap, feeling humiliated. 'Aidan and I work there, six days a week, sometimes seven. The sign in the window says "Closed except for appointments and deliveries". We're too busy to have people dropping in with little odds and ends. If someone only wants one picture framed and they spend half an hour choosing the frame and the mount, we make a loss on that job.'

Charlie Zailer nods. 'So, who are your customers, then?'

'*Why?* For God's sake, why does any of this matter? Local artists, museums and galleries, some corporate customers . . .'

'And how long has Aidan been in business? His workshop's been there for as long as—'

'Six years,' I cut her off. 'Do you want to know where we both went to school? Our mothers' maiden names?'

'No. I'd like to know where Aidan lives, though. With you?'

'As good as.'

'Since when?'

'Two, two and a half months.' *Since our night in London.* 'He's also got his own flat, attached to the framing workshop. It's more of a storeroom than a flat, really. It's got a tiny kitchen in one corner that barely works. You can't have the gas rings and the oven on at the same time.' I stop, aware that I've told her more than I needed to.

'Most single men could live in a grimy bucket and not no-tice.' Sergeant Zailer laughs. 'So does he own or rent his . . . premises?'

'He rents.' I brush my hair away from my eyes. 'Before you ask, yes, he also pays his rent on time.'

She folds her arms, smiles. 'All right, Ruth. Thanks for your patience. Now, tell me about Aidan and Mary Trelease.'

Unsure whether I've passed or failed whatever bizarre test she has just inflicted upon me, I try to compose myself and say clearly, 'He didn't kill her.'

'Let me clarify this point one more time: to your knowledge, nobody—neither Aidan nor anyone else—has hurt or killed Mary Trelease. Correct?'

I nod.

'She's unharmed?'

'Yes. You can check . . .'

'I will.'

'. . . you'll see I'm right.'

'Then why does Aidan think he killed her?'

I take a deep breath. 'I don't know. He won't tell me.'

Her eyebrows shoot up. 'Is this some sort of joke?'

'No. It's ruining both our lives.'

She slaps the palm of her left hand flat on the table. 'I need a bit of context here. Who is this Mary Trelease? What does she do? Where does she live? How old is she? How do you and Aidan know her?'

'She lives in Spilling. She's an artist. A painter. She . . . I don't know how old she is. I think maybe about my age. Thirty-eight, forty. Maybe older.' None of the answers I know are the answers we need. Charlie Zailer hasn't realised this yet, but she will. I'm terrified that, as soon as she does, she'll give up on me.

She looks the way I am sick of feeling: at a loss.

Eventually she says, 'Well, this is a new one. You're saying that Aidan—how long has he been your boyfriend, by the way?'

'Since last August.'

'Okay. So pretty much since you started working for him?'

I nod.

'Aidan believes he's killed Mary Trelease, yet you know for a fact that she isn't dead or even injured?'

'That's right.' I flop back in my seat, grateful to be understood, finally.

Charlie Zailer's eyes are narrow.

'Forgive me if this seems like a stupid question, Ruth, but . . . have you told Aidan that Mary Trelease isn't dead?'

'Yes.' I start to cry. I can't help it. 'I've told him over and over. I've told him until my throat's sore and my voice is gone.'

'And how does he respond?'

'He shakes his head—he looks so *certain*. He says she can't be alive, because he killed her.'

'You've had this conversation many times?'

'Hundreds. I've told him where she lives. He could go to her house and prove to himself that she's still alive, but he won't. He won't go and see for himself, he won't take my word for it—I'm getting desperate.'

Charlie Zailer taps her pen against the side of her face. 'What you're telling me is very odd, Ruth. Do you realise how odd it sounds?'

'Of course I do! I'm not stupid.'

'How do Aidan and Mary know each other?'

'I . . . I don't know.'

'Brilliant,' she mutters. 'Are you sure Aidan isn't having you on? He didn't tell you on April Fool's Day, did he?' Seeing my expression, she straightens her face and says, 'When did he tell you? Where were you, what was the situation? I'm sorry, Ruth, but this story is too way out for me.'

'We were in London. It was last year, December the thirteenth.'

'Any particular reason you were in London that night?'

'We . . . we went to an art fair.'

She nods. 'Carry on.'

'We were in our hotel. It was late. We'd been out for dinner and got back about half past ten. We went straight up to our room and . . . that's when he told me.'

'Out of the blue? With no warning, just, "Oh, by the way, I've murdered someone"?'

'He didn't say murdered. He said killed. And, no, it wasn't out of the blue. Aidan was upset. He said he didn't think our relationship was going to work unless we . . . unless he confided in me, but he obviously didn't want to. I could tell he was dreading it. I was too.'

'Why?' Charlie Zailer leans forward. 'Most people don't dread being confided in by their partners. Most women, especially, would be gagging to know. Did you have reason to believe Aidan might have committed a violent crime?'

'No, I . . . no. None.' *Most women.* She is talking about people for whom the word 'secret' means a tantalising prospect, not a source of anguish.

'What exactly did Aidan say?'

I close my eyes. 'He said, "Years ago, I killed someone. I killed a woman. Her name was Mary Trelease." '

' "Her name was Mary Trelease"?' Sergeant Zailer looks puzzled. 'So he said it as if she was someone you'd never heard of, then? He didn't know you knew her?'

I should have anticipated this question. My mind starts to churn. 'I don't know her.'

'*What?*'

'I don't know Mary Trelease.'

'Then . . . Again, Ruth, you'll have to forgive me if I'm being slow here, but if you don't know her, how did you know she was still alive when Aidan first said he'd killed her?'

She wouldn't believe me if I told her. Still, I'd risk it if I thought I could say the words without bringing my first meeting with Mary to life again, as if it was happening now. Even thinking about telling the story makes me feel hot and panicky. I stare into my half-drunk tea, squirming, wishing she'd ask another question, but she doesn't. She waits. When I can no longer bear the silence, I say, 'Look, all you need to do is check that she's alive. She lives at number 15 Megson Crescent . . .'

'On the Winstanley estate?'

'Yes, I . . . I think so.' I can't appear too certain, having claimed not to know her.

'Megson Crescent is a contender for the title of roughest

street in Spilling. Most of the ground-floor windows are boarded up.' Sergeant Zailer raises an eyebrow. 'Ms Trelease is a struggling artist, I take it? She can't be making much money from her painting if that's where she lives.'

I feel a hysterical laugh rising inside me. 'She makes no money from it.'

'Does she have a day job?'

'I don't know.'

'Don't you?' Charlie Zailer says smoothly, as if passing comment on the weather. 'Do you think I don't know when I'm being lied to, Ruth? Do you think I don't meet liars every day? I do—liars of the highest grade. Shall I tell you about some of them?'

'I'm not a liar. I *don't* know Mary, and I hadn't heard of her when Aidan told me . . . when he told me . . .'

'When he told you that he'd killed her, years ago.'

'That's right.' My words sound like someone else's, as if they're not coming from inside me but from somewhere far away.

'You're panicking, Ruth, and you're spewing up lies faster than the magic porridge pot spewed up porridge. Remember that story from when you were a kid?' Sergeant Zailer yawns, leans back in her chair. 'Is it possible Aidan killed another woman with the same name?' she says, as casually as if she were suggesting the answer to a crossword clue. 'I know Trelease isn't a common surname, but . . .'

'No,' I say, my voice cracking. 'I could see the details were familiar to him when I told him. That she lives on Megson Crescent, that she's an artist, forty-ish, with long black curly hair, silver streaks in it where she's starting to go grey.' *His face: the absolute recognition, the fear, in his eyes.* 'It's the same woman, the one he's sure he killed. I'm not making this up! Why would I?'

'Silver-grey hair and she's only forty? Still, they say people with very dark hair go grey youngest.' Charlie Zailer drums her fingers on the table, raises an eyebrow at me. 'So, you've seen her, then? If you know what kind of hair she's got, you must have seen her, even if you don't know her personally.'

I say nothing.

'Or perhaps you've seen a picture of her? No, I think you've seen her in the flesh. A picture wouldn't have put your mind at rest. Aidan told you he'd killed her, and you needed to see her in person, see for yourself that she was still alive. Undeterred by the sheer unlikeliness of anyone pretending they've killed someone when they haven't, you set out to find this dead woman and, lo and behold, she wasn't dead at all. Is that how it happened?'

The silence between us is unbearable. I try to pretend she isn't here, that I'm alone in the room.

'Curiouser and curiouser,' she mutters. 'Okay, here's a question you might be happier about answering: what are you doing here, apart from wasting my time?'

'What?'

'Why are you here? Aidan hasn't killed anyone—fine. Mary Trelease is alive—hooray. What do you want from me, exactly?'

Now I can talk freely. 'I want you to check that what I'm saying is true. If it is, you could . . . convince Aidan. I've tried and failed. You're the police—he'd listen to you.'

'*If* it's true? So you're not a hundred per cent sure Aidan didn't kill this woman who's alive. Make up your mind.'

'I'm as sure as I can be, but . . . what if the woman I think is Mary Trelease isn't? What if . . . I know it sounds insane, but what if she's some other woman who fits Mary's description, a relative or . . . or . . .' *Or someone pretending.* I don't say it; it would make me sound paranoid. 'There are things the police can find out that I can't.'

Charlie Zailer sighs. 'The police *find things out* in the process of investigating crimes. Nothing's happened here, according to you. There's no crime to investigate. Correct?' She opens and closes her lips several times, making a popping noise. She appears to be thinking. Perhaps she's bored, daydreaming. After a few seconds, she says, 'From my point of view, there are three questions. One: did Aidan kill the woman you're talking about, the person you know as Mary Trelease?'

'He didn't. He can't have. She's alive.'

'All right. Then did he kill another person called or known by the name of Mary Trelease? And lastly, question number three: did he kill or injure anyone? Is there a body somewhere, waiting to be found? Not that it'll still be a body by now, if the killing happened years ago.'

'Aidan couldn't hurt anybody. I know him.'

She puffs her cheeks full of air, then blows it out in one breath. 'If you're right, you should be consulting a shrink, not me.'

I shake my head. 'He's sane. I can tell from the way he reacts to other things, normal things. That's why this makes no sense.' It occurs to me that perhaps Sergeant Zailer asked me all those pointless questions about my job and my rent for the same reason: to test my reaction to ordinary enquiries. 'Have you heard of the Cotard delusion?' I ask her.

'No. I've heard of *The God Delusion*.'

'It's a mental illness, or a symptom of mental illness, usually associated with despair and an extreme lack of self-esteem. It's where you believe you're dead even though you're not.'

She grins. 'If I had that, I'd worry less about smoking fifteen fags a day.'

I'm not interested in her jokes. 'As far as I know—and I've looked into it—there's no mutation of that syndrome, and no other syndrome that I could find, where sufferers believe they've killed people who are still living. I ruled out psychological explanations a while ago. I *don't* think Aidan's committed any violent crime. I know he hasn't, and wouldn't, but . . . I'm worried something's going to happen, something really bad.' I didn't know I was going to say this until the words are out. 'I'm frightened, but I don't know what of.'

Charlie Zailer looks at me for a long time. Eventually she says, 'What has Aidan told you about the details of what he did?

What he says he did. When, why and where did he kill Mary Trelease, by his own account?'

'I've already told you everything he told me: that he killed her, years ago.'

'How many years?'

'He didn't say.'

'How, why and where did he kill her?'

'He didn't tell me.'

'What was their relationship? When and how did they first meet?'

'I told you already, I don't know!'

'I thought Aidan wanted to confide in you. Did he change his mind halfway through? Ruth? What did he say, when you asked him for more details?'

'I didn't.'

'You *didn't*? Why not?'

'I . . . I did ask him one question. I asked him if it was an accident.' I can't bear the memory. The way he looked at me, as if I'd stamped on his heart. *No questions.* He stuck to the deal we made; I broke it.

'Right,' says Sergeant Zailer. 'Because you couldn't believe he'd harm anyone deliberately. What did he say?'

'Nothing. He just stared at me.'

'And you didn't ask him any more questions?'

'No.'

'Frankly, I find that impossible to believe. Anyone would ask. Why didn't you?'

'Are you going to help me or not?' I say, mustering what's left of my hope and energy.

'How can I, when you're withholding at least half the information you know is relevant, assuming you're not making all this up. A strange way to behave if you want my help.' She straightens up in her chair. 'Aidan made this confession to you on the thirteenth of December last year. Why did you wait until now, two and a half months later, before coming in?'

'I hoped I'd be able to make him see sense,' I say, knowing how feeble it sounds in spite of being true.

'I see conspiracies everywhere, that's my trouble,' says Sergeant Zailer. 'What I don't know is, who's on the receiving end of this one: you? Me? One colossal piss-take—that's what this sounds like to me.'

I feel as if I might pass out. There's a sharp pain between my shoulder-blades. I picture myself pressing a big red button: *stop.* I imagine my finger holding the button down—it's supposed to make the bad thoughts go into retreat. Whichever book said it worked was lying.

Conspiracies: they're what I fear most. I was wrong before. My nightmare didn't start when I went to London with Aidan. It started earlier, much earlier. The list of possible starting points is endless: when Mary Trelease walked into my life, when I met Him and Her, when I came into the world as Godfrey and Inge Bussey's daughter.

Sergeant Zailer holds up her hands. 'Don't worry—if there's any chance a crime's been committed, I'll do whatever it takes to bottom that out,' she says. Her words are no comfort. *Aidan and Mary Trelease, conspiring together against me.* If it's true, I don't want to know. I couldn't bear it. Is that where he's been, all the nights he hasn't been with me?

I stand up, wincing as my weight lands on my injured foot. 'I made a mistake coming here. I'm sorry.'

'Don't be. Have a seat. If I'm going to take this forward, we need to sort out a proper statement . . .'

'No! I don't want to make a statement. I've changed my mind.'

'Ruth, calm down.'

'I know the law. You can't force me to be a witness. I haven't done anything wrong. You can't arrest me—that means I can leave.'

I limp to the door, open it, hurry down the corridor as fast as I can, which isn't very fast. Sergeant Zailer soon catches me up.

She strolls alongside me, saying nothing as we pass reception and head out into cold air that's like a slap in the face. She whistles and examines her long fingernails, as if our walking side by side is a coincidence. Eventually she says, conversationally, 'Do you know what's happening tomorrow night, Ruth?'

'No.'

'It's my engagement party. You wouldn't . . . this whole thing wouldn't by any chance be related to that, would it? You aren't going to pop out of a cake tomorrow night and say "Surprise!", are you? And if you are, it wouldn't be anything to do with a certain Colin Sellers, would it?'

I stop, turn to face her. 'I don't know who or what you're talking about. Forget everything I said, all right?' And then I start to run, properly run, grinding the pain further into my foot, and she doesn't follow me. She shouts after me that she'll be in touch. I pull open my car door, feeling her eyes burning into my back.

She knows where I live; she won't let this drop. But she isn't coming after me now. For the moment, that's all I care about. If I can just get away from her for a few moments, I'll be okay.

I lock the car doors as soon as I've turned on the engine. My tyres screech as I reverse too quickly, then I'm on the road and I can't see her any more. *Thank God.*

It's a few minutes before I realise I'm shaking from the cold. I haven't got my coat. I left it in the room at the police station, draped over the back of my chair. With the article about Charlie Zailer in the pocket.

2

1/3/08

Somebody needs to say something, thought Charlie. A speech. *Oh, God.* It was too late; it had only occurred to her now, this second. She hadn't prepared anything and she doubted Simon had either. Unless he was planning to surprise her. *Of course he isn't, fool—he's as clueless as you are about engagement party protocol.* Charlie laughed to herself as her mind filled with the image of Simon clinking a fork against his glass, saying, 'Unaccustomed as I am . . .' And what better way for his imaginary speech to begin; the word 'unaccustomed' might have been invented for Simon Waterhouse.

I'll make him do it, thought Charlie, running through a list of possible threats in her head. The party had been his idea. *I'll force him to stand up in front of nearly a hundred people and declare his undying love for me.* Charlie turned away from the packed room, the shouting, dancing and mingled laughter. What right did her guests have to be happier than she was?

She filled the last of the champagne glasses, lifted the yellow tablecloth and bent to put the empty bottles out of sight. Crouching by the table leg, she wished she could stay there for ever, or at least until tonight was over. She didn't want to have to stand up and face everyone with a this-is-my-special-night smile.

Not that they were her guests, or Simon's—that was part of the problem. Neither of them had been willing to host the party at home, so they, their friends, relatives and colleagues were all—for a price, of course—guests of the Malt Shovel in Hamblesford for the evening, a pub that, as far as Charlie knew, was known and loved by nobody present. It was the first place she'd phoned and been given the answer 'yes' to the question 'Do you have a function room?' Too busy to research the matter further, Charlie had decided it would have to do. Hamblesford was a pretty village with a green, a memorial cross and a church at its centre. The Malt Shovel had window boxes stuffed full of yellow and red flowers, a white-painted stone exterior and a thatched roof. It was advantageously positioned opposite a stream and a small bridge; it looked the part.

Because tonight was all about faking; Charlie knew that even if Simon didn't. She couldn't understand why he'd insisted on having an engagement party; it was so unlike him. Did he really want to make their relationship the centre of everybody's attention? Apparently so, and he'd clammed up whenever Charlie had asked why. 'It's normal, isn't it?' was all he was willing to say on the matter.

It couldn't be a bid to please his mother. Kathleen Waterhouse rarely left the house, apart from to go to church and to the care home for the elderly where she worked part-time. It had taken Simon weeks to persuade her to come tonight, and even when she'd agreed it had been with the proviso that she would only stay for an hour. Would she really leave on the dot of nine? She'd arrived at exactly eight, as Simon had predicted she would, clutching her husband Michael's arm, white-faced, saying, 'Oh, dear, we're not the first, are we?' Simon and Charlie had enthused about how nice it was to see them, but they hadn't responded in kind. Nor had they brought a gift. Charlie had waited for them to say, 'Congratulations', but all Kathleen had said to her, shrinking against her husband as if she wanted to dissolve into him, was, 'Do you know we're only staying for an hour, dear? Did Simon tell you? I don't like to be where people are drinking and getting rowdy.' Her eyes had widened in horror as they took in the array of bottles and cans on the table at the entrance to the room. At the moment, Charlie thought, I'm not linked by marriage to a rabidly devout teetotaller, but all that's about to change.

Something shiny appeared beside her arm as she rummaged under the table. She turned and saw a silver shoe with a heel so high it bent the foot it was supposed to support into a right angle, and, above it, an expanse of spray-tanned ankle. 'Hiding, are you?' DC Colin Sellers' wife Stacey nudged Charlie's shoulder with her leg, nearly making her lose her balance. 'Yum!' she said. 'Lovely jubbly bubbly. You're going to love the prezzie me and Colin got you.'

Charlie doubted it. Stacey had a sticker on her car saying 'Honk if you're horny'. Her taste in most things was poor. Husbands especially; Colin Sellers had been screwing a singer called Suki Kitson for as long as Charlie had known him. Everyone knew but his thick-as-a-brick wife.

Charlie waited until Stacey had moved away before coming out from under the table. She looked at her watch. Quarter to nine. Only fifteen minutes left of Kathleen's hour. If Simon's parents left promptly, as promised, the volume could go up again. As it was, Charlie could barely hear the *Limited Sympathy* CD that was playing in the background. Kathleen had asked for it to be turned down, claiming loud music gave her a migraine.

Charlie looked round the room, through the gaps in the clusters of sweaty bodies that surrounded her on all sides, trying to catch a glimpse of her future mother-in-law. *Ugh, what a thought.* Her next one was even worse, and made her eyes prickle with tears: *It won't happen. Simon doesn't really want to marry me. He'll pull out, when it's almost but not quite too late.*

Did she want it to be too late? she asked herself, not for the first time. Did she want to see Simon trapped, by his own foolishness and lack of self-knowledge, in a marriage that she wanted and he didn't? She dug her nails into the palms of her hands to put a stop to the nonsense in her head. It *was* nonsense; of course it was. The one thing about Simon that was beyond dispute was his intelligence. Clever people didn't propose marriage over and over again to people they didn't want to marry. Did they?

Am I as stupid as Stacey? Charlie wondered.

The function room was like a sauna—a split-level, squalid one with mustard-coloured wallpaper in a geometric pattern of diamonds within diamonds, and sash windows with grease-smeared panes that were so original their frames were rotting. All the money that had been spent on the Malt Shovel in recent years had been spent on its exterior. *Here's to deceptive appearances*, thought Charlie, raising her glass in a private toast. She looked around for a member of pub staff, someone who could turn off the heating.

Simon was over by the window, talking to DC Chris Gibbs and his wife Debbie. Charlie couldn't catch his eye. She tried to beam the word 'speech' into his brain using telepathy. When that failed, she tried the word 'parents'. Where were Kathleen and Michael? Charlie was annoyed, convinced she was more worried about them than Simon was. *Please let them be having a pleasant chat with someone respectable.* Inspector Proust and his wife Lizzie—that might not be a total disaster. On the other hand, Proust, though not a drinker, could be relied upon to open any conversation with a remark that would offend his interlocutor to the core. But then he generally let Lizzie do the talking when they were together, so maybe it would be all right.

Charlie liked the inspector's wife a lot. Lizzie was petite with cropped white hair and a surprisingly youthful face for a woman in her late fifties. She was down-to-earth, socially adaptable, a pacifier rather than an agitator. Charlie felt guilty for calling her Mrs Snowman behind her back; it wasn't fair to extend Proust's nickname to his wife, whose warmth was one of the few things that could thaw her husband's freezer-compartment demeanour.

Charlie spotted Giles and Lizzie Proust talking to Colin Sellers by the buffet table. Sellers was visibly drunk already, red in the face and dripping sweat. Proust looked unimpressed, but then that wasn't unusual for the Snowman. He looked that way most of the time, even when not faced with a moist inebriate. Something jarred in Charlie's mind: a twitch of discomfort beneath the surface of her thoughts. What was it? Something to do with Sellers . . . The woman yesterday, the one who'd called herself Ruth Bussey. Charlie had asked her if Sellers had put her up to telling that preposterous story about her boyfriend killing someone who wasn't dead, as a prank to be revealed here at the party. *If only.*

Charlie didn't want to think about her, whatever her real name was. She'd got the innocent waif look down to a T: waist-length golden wavy hair, flared faded jeans, cheesecloth shirt embroidered with flowers round the neck, irritatingly feminine shoes with ribbons wound round her ankles. *No socks or tights—no wonder she couldn't stop shivering. Unless that was all part of the act.* Her pleading eyes, her helpless shrugs . . . Charlie had almost been convinced she was genuine. Then she'd found an article about herself in the pocket of the coat the woman had left behind. She'd needed to sit down and close her eyes for a few seconds until her panic subsided. She'd hardly slept last night, wondering, worrying. One more reason why she was in no mood for a party.

She heard her mother's laugh and turned. Oh, no. Simon's parents were talking to her own. Listening to them, rather. Kathleen and Michael Waterhouse cowered against a wall the colour of bile; they appeared to be huddling together against the onslaught. Charlie's father, Howard Zailer, was telling one of his stories. Linda, her mother, emitted loud, theatrical chuckles in all the right places. Neither of Simon's parents cracked a smile.

Charlie couldn't bear to watch. Clutching her glass of champagne, she pushed through the mass of people towards the door that led to the stairs. *The escape route.* Before leaving the room, she turned and caught Simon watching her. He looked away quickly, nodding at whatever Debbie Gibbs was saying. Debbie was looking elegant in a long, high-necked black dress that was clingy without being at all revealing. Her hair was pulled back in a chignon. 'Thanks a lot, thanks ever so fucking much,' Charlie hissed as she stomped downstairs, splashing champagne on her clothes. She knew that she and Simon were the hosts—sort of; insofar as the landlord of the Malt Shovel wasn't. She knew they had to mingle, pay more attention to their friends than to each other, but would it have killed him to smile at her?

She went outside into the cold night, found a wall to sit on, started to feel pleasantly cool, though she knew it wouldn't be long before she was freezing. She'd lit a cigarette when she heard footsteps approaching. Kate Kombothekra. Kate's husband Sam—dubbed 'Stepford' by Sellers and Gibbs because of his pleasant, polite manner and his desire to please everybody—was Charlie's replacement in CID, Simon's new skipper. Like Debbie Gibbs and Stacey Sellers, Kate was dressed for the special occasion to end all special occasions. Her shimmery green off-the-shoulder number was the exact colour of the Mediterranean sea under a warm summer sun, and swished around Kate's full figure as she walked. A gold shawl and gold pumps provided the perfect top and tail to the outfit.

Had the CID wives got together and resolved to take the piss out of Charlie's pathetic engagement party by overdressing, show it up for the farce that it was? Charlie wished she'd worn her only dress instead of a cerise V-necked top, black trousers and black pumps. The thin strip of velour around the V was her outfit's only fancy touch, one tiny concession to the celebration tonight was supposed to be; without it, she would have looked as if she was off to a committee meeting.

'If you can't stand the heat . . .' said Kate, wiping her forehead. 'I'd have had to pour one of your ice buckets over my head if I'd stayed in there.'

'Not my ice buckets. The pub's.'

Kate gave Charlie an odd look, then smiled knowingly. 'I met your in-laws-to-be. No wonder you're looking deathly.'

'Thanks a lot.' Charlie took a long, deep drag of her cigarette, sucking hard, trying to give herself proper pulled-in skull-cheeks.

'You know what I mean. Deathly of mood, not deathly of appearance.' Kate's blonde hair and glowing skin always looked as if experts had finished buffing them only seconds earlier.

'It's funny how meeting someone's close family can bring into focus everything that's wrong with them,' said Charlie. Kate had insulted her; being made privy to one of Charlie's more obnoxious thoughts was her punishment. 'You suspect there's something deeply amiss about a person, and then you meet their parents and think, "Now I understand." I wonder if Simon, having met mine, can see clearly everything that's wrong with me. And bound to get steadily wronger as I get older.'

Kate chuckled. 'Sometimes it's possible to defy both nature and nurture,' she said. 'Look at Sam—he's the kindest, most considerate man alive, and his parents are lazy, selfish tossers. His brothers and sister too—the whole Kombothekra clan. When we have them round they sit immobile in armchairs like the human equivalent of a druid stone circle while Sam and I wait on them hand and foot. They do nothing for themselves. They're worse than my boys have ever been, even as toddlers.'

Charlie couldn't help smiling. It was reassuring to know that even women with silky blonde hair had problems.

'They're going to get what's coming to them,' said Kate, her eyes narrowing. 'I'm not inviting them for Christmas dinner this year. They don't know it yet. I do, and I've got nine months to gloat in secret.'

'It's only the first of March. Please don't put Christmas in my head.' What would Charlie and Simon do? Would he want to spend Christmas Day with her? Would it be a merging of the Zailer and Waterhouse families? Charlie felt her blood temperature drop by several degrees.

The situation with Sam's folks had to be dire, she thought, if

Kate was planning to withdraw her hospitality. She was the sort of person who seemed to want nothing more than to drag strangers in off the street and cook for them, then insist they stay the night. Charlie had been a virtual stranger when Kate had first started to demand her presence at Kombothekra family meals; now, after countless such occasions, Charlie supposed she had to regard Kate as a friend. It couldn't hurt to have a friend who made staggeringly good apple and cranberry crumbles, could it? Kate always said that whisky was the crucial ingredient, but in Charlie's view it was even more crucial to start off as the sort of person whose notions of pudding extended beyond unwrapping a Cadbury's mini roll.

'Did you and Sam have an engagement party? Of course you did,' Charlie answered her own question. 'I bet it was at one of your houses.'

Kate dragged herself out of whatever revenge fantasy had temporarily consumed her. 'My mum and dad's. Huh! Sam's parents wouldn't . . .' She stopped. 'But you didn't want the party at yours, you said. Simon didn't want it at his.'

'Exactly,' Charlie said quietly. 'What's wrong with us?'

Kate shrugged. 'Simon wouldn't have been able to relax with people all over his house, would he? And you're in the middle of decorating.' She grinned. 'Though I'm not sure something that never ends can be said to have a middle.'

'Don't start.'

'I did try to tell you that an undecorated house was the ideal party venue—no expensive wallpaper for people to puke on.'

'And you were right,' said Charlie. 'But I still went ahead and booked a dingy room in a pub, because I'm not like you and Sam. Neither is Simon. We're incapable of making anybody feel welcome. If we have to pretend to like the people we know, we'd rather do it on neutral territory.' For some reason, Charlie enjoyed being vicious about herself; she felt it compensated for those occasions on which she was vicious about other people. 'Did anyone give a speech?' she asked.

'At our engagement party? Sam did. It was earnest and end-less. Why, are you going to? Is Simon going to?'

'Of course not. We don't do anything properly.'

Kate looked puzzled. 'You can give a speech if you want to. It doesn't matter if it's off the cuff. Often a spontaneous—'

'I'd rather dip my face in a tray of acid,' Charlie cut her off. 'Simon would feel the same.'

Kate sighed, gathering her shawl more tightly around her shoulders. 'I bet he wouldn't if he was certain of being able to give a really good speech. Confidence, that's all he's lacking. This is unfamiliar territory for him.'

'Sounds like you know more about him than I do.'

'I know he adores you. And before you say "Why doesn't he show it, then?"—he does. If you don't see the signs, it's because you're looking wrong.'

'I thought I was looking deathly,' said Charlie through clenched teeth.

'Simon does things his own way. He needs time, that's all—time to get used to being a couple. Once you're married you'll have plenty of time. Won't you?' Kate sounded as if she was proposing something unutterably wholesome: a brisk walk in the fresh air. 'Stop worrying about what you ought to be doing and stop comparing yourself to other people. When are you go-ing to set a date?'

Charlie laughed. 'I hope you know what a lone voice you are,' she said. 'You're the one person who doesn't think me and Simon getting married would be the biggest mistake since the dawn of time. Including me and Simon, that is.'

Kate pulled Charlie's cigarette out of her mouth, threw it on the ground and stamped on it with a gold pump. 'You should give up,' she said. 'Think of your future children, how they'd feel having to watch their mother die.'

'I've no intention of having any.'

'Of course you'll have children,' Kate said with authority. 'Look, if you want to feel sorry for yourself, let me make it worth your while. Do you know what everyone's saying in there?' She pointed at the pub. 'Almost every conversation I've been party to has centred around whether you and Simon have *done it* yet. I've heard two people predict that you'll be divorced within a year and a good five or six say they doubt there'll be a wedding at all. Do you know what Stacey Sellers has bought you as an engagement present?'

Charlie had a nasty feeling she was about to find out.

'A vibrator. I heard her laughing about it, telling Robbie Meakin and Jack Zlosnik that Simon probably wouldn't know what it was. "He'll run a mile when he finds out," she said.'

'Don't tell me any more.' Charlie jumped down from the wall and started to walk towards the bridge. She lit a fresh cigarette. Dying wasn't an altogether unappealing prospect, unobserved as she would be by her own non-existent children.

Kate followed her. 'Then she said, "Oh, well—at least Charlie'll be able to get her rocks off after Simon's scarpered in terror." '

'She's a cockroach.'

'More of a slug, I'd say,' Kate amended. 'She's all squish and no crunch. And she's going to have a field day if you walk out of your own engagement party and don't come back. Do you want her to think you're ashamed of your relationship with Simon?'

'I'm not.' Charlie stopped. 'I don't care what anyone thinks.'

Kate grabbed her arms, wrinkling her nose as cigarette smoke wafted in her face. 'You love him more than most people love the people they're married to. You'd die for him without a second thought.'

'Would I?'

'Take it from me.'

Charlie nodded, in spite of feeling as if she ought to argue. Why should she take it from Kate? Was it possible to measure the levels of love present in one's guests while serving up baked Alaska?

Kate released her grip. 'Look,' she said, 'unless all the gossip I keep hearing is completely off the mark—and gossip rarely is, in my experience—then you and Simon have got some kind of problem with your sex life.' Before Charlie could tell her to mind her own business, she went on, 'I don't know what it is and I'm not asking to be told. But I do know one thing: there's more to love, and to life, than sex. Now, the only way to put a stop to what people are saying in there is to go back and interrupt every conversation. Address your guests. Don't leave them to speak to each other—they can't be trusted. Stand on a chair—you've got flat heels on—and give a speech.'

Charlie was surprised to hear herself laugh. *You've got flat heels on*—had Kate really said that?

'Char, wait for me!' The voice came from the knot of trees by the side of the bridge.

Charlie closed her eyes. How much had Olivia overheard? 'My sister,' she said, in answer to Kate's raised eyebrows.

'I'll see you inside in no more than three minutes,' said Kate.

'Who was that?' Olivia asked.

'Sam Kombothekra's wife. You're late.'

'It's not a concert,' said Olivia. It was a saying she'd picked up from her and Charlie's father. Howard Zailer said it about all the things he didn't care if he was late for. He never said it about golf, which he played at least five days a week. Howard's passion for golf had been forced on his wife, though they both pretended Linda's sudden enthusiasm for the game had been arrived at independently, by a huge stroke of luck.

'So, are you giving a speech?' asked Olivia.

'Apparently.'

Olivia was wearing an ill-advised tight skirt that bound her legs together, and could only take tiny steps towards the pub. Charlie had to restrain herself from screaming, 'Get a move on!' She would march back into that room and beat the shit out of anyone who looked as if they might have been predicting the demise of her and Simon's engagement. *How dare they? How dare they drink champagne we've paid for and slag us off behind our backs?* Her speech—forming in her mind as she walked with feigned patience beside her shuffling sister—would be a verbal thrashing for all those who deserved it. Not exactly party spirit in the traditional sense, thought Charlie, but at least she was fired up.

Once inside and upstairs, she stood on a chair. She didn't need to bang anything or call out to get attention. All eyes were on her, and people quickly shushed one another. 'Can someone turn the music down?' she said. A man in a white shirt and a black bow-tie nodded and left the room. She didn't know his name. She wondered if he knew hers, if word of her unsatisfactory sex life had spread as far as the Malt Shovel staff who were helping out for the evening.

A quick scan of the room confirmed that Kathleen and Michael Waterhouse had left. Simon, in a corner at the back, was looking worried, no doubt wishing Charlie had conferred with him before opting to make a tit of herself in front of everyone they knew.

The music stopped mid-song. Charlie opened her mouth. Two seconds ago she had known what she was going to say—it would have left no conscience unflayed—but she kept looking at the wrong people. Lizzie Proust was beaming up at her, Kate Kombothekra was mouthing, 'Go on,' from the back of the room and Simon chose that precise moment to smile.

I can't do it, thought Charlie. I can't denounce them all. They don't all deserve it. Possibly less than half of them deserve it. Kate might have been exaggerating. It struck Charlie that denouncing was probably the sort of thing that ought to be handled with a bit more precision.

You're standing on a chair in the middle of the room. You've got to say something.

'Here's a story I've never told anyone before,' she said, thinking, *What the fuck am I doing?* She hadn't told the story for a very good reason: it made her look like a world-class moron.

She saw Olivia frown. Liv thought she knew everything about her older sister. It was almost true. There were only a couple of stories she'd missed out on, and this was one of them. 'When I was a new PC, I went into a primary school to give a talk about road safety.'

'The headmaster had never seen you drive, then!' Colin Sellers called out. Everyone laughed. Charlie could have kissed him. He was the perfect undemanding audience.

'In the classroom, apart from me and the thirty or so kids, there was the teacher and a classroom assistant—a young girl—'

'Woman!' a female voice yelled.

'Sorry, a young *woman*, who was working as hard as the teacher was—wiping noses, helping to draw pictures of highway code symbols, ferrying kids to the loo. The teacher had introduced herself to me at the beginning of the lesson, and she'd made all the children tell me their names, but she never introduced the assistant, which I thought was a bit rude. Anyway, when I'd finished doing my bit and the bell was about to go, the teacher stood up and said, "Can we all please give PC Zailer a huge round of applause for coming to visit us and giving us such a fascinating talk?" Everyone clapped. And then she said, "And now, let's put our hands together for Grace." '

Charlie cringed at the memory, even at a distance of several years. She saw Sam Kombothekra laughing next to Kate, the only person who seemed to have anticipated what was coming next.

'Thank goodness, I thought to myself: finally the poor classroom assistant—Grace—is getting some acknowledgement for all her hard work. I started clapping vigorously, but nobody else did. All the little kids were staring at me as if I was a nutter. And then I realised that they all had their palms pressed together, praying style . . .'

A tide of giggles rose in the hot room. Charlie heard her father's throaty guffaws. Her mum and Olivia were on either side of him, watching him to assess how much he was enjoying himself and infer from that how much enjoyment they were entitled to.

Think nice thoughts.

Kate Kombothekra was giving Charlie a thumbs-up sign from across the room. Stacey Sellers had a smear of guacamole in the corner of her mouth.

'That's right,' said Charlie. 'That's when I remembered that I was in a *Catholic* school, and that Grace, as well as being a girl's name, was also the name of a prayer. The fact is, I knew nothing about Catholicism, having been raised by atheist hippies whose idea of a deity was Bob Dylan.' Linda and Olivia Zailer looked worried momentarily; when Howard laughed, they smiled, but turned warning eyes in Charlie's direction. 'If I had any ideas at all about Catholics, I probably imagined they were all repressed weirdos who think they're right about everything all the time.' Charlie gave it a few seconds before saying, 'And then I met Simon.'

Laughter broke out. Stacey Sellers' tittering was audible above the general noise. Too late to back out now, thought Charlie. 'Simon, a good Catholic boy, is bound to have had preconceived ideas about the children of atheist hippies: foul-mouthed, loose-living, promiscuous, bent on annihilating themselves and everyone around them.' *One, two, three, four.* 'And then he met me.' This time the laughter was deafening. Charlie tried not to feel hurt. 'And, in fact, he's now looking at me as if I've sprouted horns, so maybe the engagement's off. I hope not—if it is, all prezzies will be returned.' As an afterthought, Charlie added, 'Which means, Stacey, that you'll get your vibrator back, though I doubt you'll manage to get much purchase on it, having had two children the natural way. Anyway, moving swiftly on . . . Thanks so much for coming, everyone. There's plenty of booze left—have a great evening!'

Charlie saw Simon marching towards her while she was still climbing down from the chair.

'What the *fuck* . . .' he started to say, but his words were drowned out by Lizzie Proust who appeared between him and Charlie, dragging the Snowman behind her. 'That was absolutely the best speech I've *ever heard*,' she told Charlie. 'Wasn't it, Giles?'

'No,' said Proust.

'It *was*. You were terrific!' Lizzie hugged Charlie with one arm, keeping hold of her husband with the other. By the time she'd managed to struggle free, Charlie couldn't see Simon any more.

'I don't think it was the best speech your intended has ever heard either,' said Proust, giving her a wintry look.

'Most people seemed to like it, sir.' Charlie smiled resolutely. She wouldn't let him ruin her mood, so recently improved. Her speech *had* been good. But now where was Simon? He couldn't really be angry, could he?

The music came back on, louder than before, and a different CD: Wyclef Jean's *Carnival II*. Charlie noticed Proust's instant displeasure, and wondered fleetingly if he'd ever been open-minded even in his youth. She felt a hand close around her arm: Debbie Gibbs. 'I wish I could laugh at myself the way you laugh at yourself,' she said. Her eyes looked wet.

'I can laugh at you if you want,' said Charlie. Debbie shook her head, not getting the joke. You're a cop, not a comedian, Charlie reminded herself.

Once Debbie had moved away, Olivia pulled Charlie to one side. 'Mum and Dad were never hippies.'

'Well, whatever they were, then—champagne socialists. People with wooden floors who go on CND marches and eat pasta a lot—but that would have taken too long to say. Much easier to summarise now Dad's a golf bore.'

'Don't start, Char.'

'Interested in his golfing stories, are you?'

During Olivia's treatment for cancer, Howard Zailer had been fully involved. As much as Linda and Charlie were. It was when he'd retired that his horizons had started to narrow. By

2006, when Charlie's name had been splashed all over the papers, he had been willing to talk to her only briefly about what she was going through; it wasn't life-threatening, after all. Howard couldn't be late for his day's play, or, if it was evening when Charlie happened to ring, for a drinking session with his friends from the club. 'I'll hand you over to Mum,' he said whenever she phoned. 'She can fill me in later.'

'You'll have to forgive me if I'm determined to like my family in spite of their faults,' Liv said huffily, looking Charlie up and down. 'It's not exactly an abundance of riches scenario, is it? I don't have any relatives who *aren't* a pain in the arse in some major way. I suppose you'd like me to cut all ties, take myself off to the pound to sit in a mesh-fronted cage until some perfect new family comes to claim me.'

Charlie decided it would be unwise to pursue the point.

Olivia had no such reservations. 'Do we all get to say exactly what we think, or is it just you? I wasn't going to say a word about how ridiculous this whole charade is, your loony engagement . . .'

'That policy has subsequently been revised, I take it?' Charlie snapped.

Liv didn't get the chance to answer. Shouting was coming from the bottom of the stairs near the presents table. *Simon's voice.* Everyone who could hear it was shifting in that direction, not wanting to miss out.

Stacey Sellers was crying. Simon was holding a large vibrator, wielding it like a truncheon. 'This is what you thought we'd want, is it?' he yelled, throwing it on the floor. It landed amid strips of wrapping paper, next to what was left of its cardboard and plastic box.

'There's nothing wrong with sex toys. They're not dirty,' Stacey screamed back at him. 'Haven't you ever watched *Sex and the City*? Don't you know *anything*?'

'She's got a point,' Olivia whispered in Charlie's ear. 'A libido might not be essential but a sense of humour is.'

'Liv says she'll have it if we don't want it,' Charlie shouted down the stairs.

Simon looked up at her. 'Get your stuff,' he said. 'We're going.'

'Going? Simon, it's only ten past nine. We can't leave—it's our party.'

'I can do whatever the fuck I like. Give me your keys. I'll see you later.'

Keys? Did he mean he planned to spend the night at her house? *He had to mean that—it was unambiguous.* Charlie looked around to see if anyone was smirking. Most people seemed more interested in Stacey's weeping. There was no way anyone could know that Charlie and Simon had never spent the night together at either of their houses or anywhere else, that she'd feared it might never happen, even after they were married. 'I'll come with you,' she told him, grabbing her coat and bag from the stand at the top of the stairs.

Olivia was waiting to pounce. 'I've only just got here. Can't Simon wait?'

He certainly can, thought Charlie. Let no one say of Simon Waterhouse that he couldn't wait. He could wait so long that Charlie's heart was in danger of fossilising. She was the one who couldn't stand it any longer.

'So. Are you going to tell me?' Simon sat on Charlie's lounge floor, knees pulled up to his chin, an unopened can of lager in his hand. His skin looked grey and grainy. Charlie could see specs of grit in the parting in his hair. Hadn't he showered before coming out?

She stood in the middle of the undecorated, unfurnished room, trying not to howl. They were missing their engagement party for this, to be mired in this grim atmosphere, this stilted conversation. 'It doesn't matter, Simon. For Christ's sake!'

'So you're not going to tell me.'

Charlie groaned. 'It's a TV programme. About four women

who live in New York, all right? They're friends, they screw lots of men—that's about it.'

'Everyone's seen it. Everyone except me.'

'No! Probably there are loads of people who have never even heard of it.'

'Repressed weirdos. To quote your brilliant speech.'

'It *was* brilliant.' Charlie tried to harden her misery, turn it into anger. 'I've explained why I did it. Kate Kombothekra told me everyone was taking the piss out of us. I thought I'd steal their thunder by doing it myself.'

Simon sprang to his feet. 'I'm going home.'

Charlie put her body between him and the door. 'You came back here so that you could ask about *Sex and the City* and then leave? Why are you here, Simon? Did you overhear someone at the party talking about our sex life, or lack of? Kate says they were all at it. Maybe you wanted everybody to see us leaving together and draw the wrong conclusion.'

'It's what I heard *you* saying that's the problem!' Simon shouted in her face. 'Foul-mouthed, loose-living, promiscuous, bent on self-destruction. Lucky for me my parents had left by then.'

'Scared of Mummy and Daddy finding out, are you? What I'm really like?'

'You'd still have done it, wouldn't you? Even if they'd been there.'

'They *weren't* there! You're being ridiculous. This is all about your vanity.'

'It's about your distortions, your . . . exhibitionism! That story about the primary school—was it true? Since the rest of what you said was a load of shit, I have to wonder.'

'You think it was just an excuse, a convenient way into slagging off Catholics?'

'Oh, you don't discriminate—you'll slate anything that moves. The more defenceless the better!'

Charlie stepped back, away from his anger. Stacey Sellers got off lightly, she thought. 'Who's defenceless, Simon?'

'So it really happened? The teacher said, "Put your hands to-gether for Grace," and you didn't know what she meant? Sorry, but . . .' His words tailed off. He turned away, rubbed his face with his hands.

'Sorry but *what*?'

'Do we have anything in common? Do we even inhabit the same world?'

This can't be happening. It can't be. 'Do what you have to do,' Charlie said. 'I'm not going to talk you out of it.' She left the room and went upstairs.

In her bedroom, she decided not to slam the door. Instead, she closed it carefully. She wasn't a child; she wouldn't be treated like one and she wouldn't behave like one. Lizzie Proust had liked her speech. Debbie Gibbs had liked it. Her awful speech. What had possessed her? *Foul-mouthed, loose-living, promiscuous* . . . Simon had misremembered the last bit: *bent on annihilating themselves and everyone around them.* 'Oops,' said Charlie out loud. The sound fell heavy in the silent air. She wondered what Kate Kombothekra had thought of what she'd said; would it be a thumbs up or a thumbs down from the per-son who'd put her up to making a laughing-stock of herself in the first place?

The door opened. 'Talk me out of what?' said Simon. He didn't look happy. He never looked happy.

'Dumping me. Here's your ring.' Charlie dragged it off her finger. 'I'm not going to haggle over the world's smallest dia-mond.'

'I'm not . . . that's not what I'm trying to do. Look, I'm sorry. I got angry.'

'Really? I must have missed that part.' Charlie would sooner have died than let him see how relieved she was. She was furious with herself for being relieved at all. How many men might she be engaged to at this very moment who would have found her Grace story hilarious? Billions. Dozens, at least. Most of whom would probably want to have sex with her.

'I had a bad day at work,' Simon told her. 'I had to tell a man—'

'Oh, diddums! Did the canteen run out of steak and kidney pie before you got to the front of the queue?'

'Shut the fuck up and put your ring back on,' said Simon.

'I had an evil day yesterday, as it happens,' Charlie snapped. 'It totally fucked up my day off today, in fact, but in spite of that, I seem to be able to behave like a civilised human being. Or rather, I *seemed* to be able to, until you started on me!' She blinked away tears as she slipped her ring back on. *The world's smallest diamond.* She shouldn't have said that. It wasn't true and it was an unforgivable thing to say. 'I'm sorry. I love this ring. You know that.' If our marriage is going to happen, she thought, if it's going to work, he'll ask me about my rotten day before telling me about his.

'I spent all afternoon with a man who's confessed to a murder,' said Simon. 'Trouble is, the woman he reckons he murdered isn't dead.'

Charlie's mind flattened out; all other thoughts fell away. 'What?'

'I know. Strange. Actually, it gave me the creeps—he wasn't someone I enjoyed being in a small room with.' Simon opened his can of lager. 'Do you want a drink, or is this the last beer?'

'Tell me,' Charlie heard herself say. It was as if the party and their row had never happened; she was back in the reception room at the nick, trying not to stare at the ribbons Ruth Bussey had wound round her thin ankles. Ruth Bussey with her limp and her frail, reedy voice, who was frightened something was going to happen, but didn't know what . . .'

No, no, no. I can't have got it all wrong, not again.

'I wasn't there for the beginning,' said Simon. 'I only got dragged into it today. When he came in yesterday, Gibbs talked to him.'

'Yesterday? What time? What's his name, this man?'

'Aidan Seed.'

'I don't believe it.'

'Do you know him?'

'Not exactly. What time did he come in yesterday?'

Simon screwed up his face, thinking. 'Must have been some time between one and two.'

Charlie let out the breath she'd been holding. 'At ten to twelve, his girlfriend was waiting for me when I turned up for my shift.'

'His girlfriend?'

'Ruth Bussey, she said her name was.'

Simon nodded. 'He mentioned her. Not her surname, just as Ruth. What did she want?'

'Same as him, by the sound of it. Told me her boyfriend was adamant he'd killed a woman called Mary Trelease . . .'

'Right.' Simon nodded.

'. . . but that he couldn't have, because Trelease is still alive. I thought she was deranged at first, so I asked a few background questions. The more she talked—'

'The more you thought she seemed sane?' Simon cut in. 'Preoccupied, upset, but sane?'

'Preoccupied's an understatement. I've met human wreckage before, but this woman was in a worse state than anyone I've seen for a long time. Shaking with fear, crying one minute, then staring into the distance as if she'd seen a ghost, telling pointless lies that made no sense. She had something wrong with her foot, and claimed at first that she'd sprained her ankle. When I said it didn't look swollen, she changed her story and said she had a blister.'

Simon paced the room, chewing his thumbnail as he often did when he was concentrating. 'Seed was the opposite—not changeable at all. He was very controlled. At first I thought he had to be asylum material, but . . . he didn't seem it, even though he was insisting on the impossible and wouldn't listen to anything I said. Twenty-eight times, he told me something I knew couldn't be true; tried to use logic, even, to make me believe it.'

'How do you mean?' asked Charlie.

'I asked him to describe the woman he killed, which he did in great detail. Point for point, his description matched the woman I saw and spoke to this morning.'

'You've met Mary Trelease?' The idea made Charlie feel funny; she wasn't sure why.

'I have and Gibbs has. We've both seen her passport, her driving licence. Today she showed me the deeds of her house with her name on, all the paperwork from her solicitor from when she moved, her bank statements . . .'

'Why so much?' said Charlie. 'Passport and driving licence should have been enough.'

'I think she was worried one of us was going to turn up every day and ask her to prove all over again that she's who she says she is. She gathered together a stack of stuff to show me how absurd the whole thing is. She acted like . . . like she was afraid I was trying to steal her identity or something.'

'Afraid, literally?'

Simon considered it. 'Yeah, underneath her chippiness, I reckon there was some fear there.'

Two frightened women. Charlie didn't like the feel of this at all. 'So how did you get dragged in? You said Seed saw Gibbs first?' She waited to be told that Seed had at some point requested Simon's involvement, asked for him by name. She wasn't quite ready to believe this wasn't all a cruel hoax aimed at her. If Ruth Bussey and Aidan Seed knew she and Simon were engaged . . .

'Kombothekra said Gibbs was needed elsewhere,' Simon told her, 'Reading between the lines, he didn't trust him with it.'

'He doesn't think Gibbs is capable of checking if someone's alive or dead?'

'Mary Trelease wouldn't let him in,' said Simon. 'He didn't see the house. Most importantly, he didn't see the master bedroom, the one facing the street. According to what Seed told Gibbs yesterday, that's where he left Mary Trelease's dead body, in the bed in that room . . .'

'Hold on. When did he say he'd killed her?'

'He wouldn't say. Nor why, though he did say how: he strangled her.'

'Ruth Bussey said Seed had told her he'd killed Mary Trelease years ago.'

Simon blinked a few times. 'Sure?'

'Me or her? I'm sure she said it, and she seemed convinced that was what he'd told her. I think she quoted his exact words as, "Years ago, I killed a woman called Mary Trelease."'

'Makes no sense,' Simon muttered, turning to face the window. Which was why Sam Kombothekra hadn't wanted Gibbs on it, thought Charlie. Most of what CID were called upon to investigate had some logic behind it. People hurt or killed each other over money, or drugs, usually some combination of the two. They stole from shops, disturbed the peace or terrorised the neighbourhood because they saw it as the only way out of a hopeless life—it was grim, but you could see the reasoning.

Charlie was about to ask Simon what he'd meant about Seed trying to use logic to convince him Mary Trelease was dead, but Simon was already saying, 'He killed her years ago, left her body in the front bedroom at 15 Megson Crescent, and expects it to be there, undisturbed, for us to find several years later when he decides to confess? No.' Charlie watched him junk the hypothesis. 'Trelease didn't live in that house years ago. She bought it in 2006, from a family called Mills.'

'That's two years ago,' she pointed out, knowing what the response would be. Would she ever be able to hear '2006' without experiencing a small earthquake in the pit of her stomach?

'The phrase "years ago" implies longer,' said Simon, on cue. 'You know it does.'

She couldn't argue. Ruth Bussey had said Seed had confessed to her last December, at which point 2006 would only have been 'last year'. 'What else did he tell you, apart from that Trelease's body would be on the bed in the master bedroom and that he strangled her?'

'In the bed, not on. He said she was naked, she'd been naked when he killed her. And her body was in the middle of the bed, not on one side or the other—he made a big point of that. Apart from saying several times that he didn't rape her, that was all he told me.'

'Ruth Bussey mentioned none of this.' Charlie pulled a cigarette out of a packet on the window-sill. She had nothing to light it with. 'Was he in the bedroom with her when she took her clothes off? Had they gone to bed together?'

'He wouldn't say.'

'Did he have his clothes on when he strangled her?'

'Wouldn't say.'

Charlie doubted she'd be able to come up with a question Simon wouldn't have put to Seed. Everything Gibbs would have neglected to ask, Simon would have asked several times over.

'He answered some questions willingly and in great detail—others, he wouldn't open his mouth.'

'His girlfriend was exactly the same,' said Charlie.

'I've never come across anything like it before.' Simon shook his head. 'You know what it's like normally: people talk or they don't. Sometimes there's nothing doing at first, then you twirl them and they spill the lot. Other times they spout crap until you point out to them how they've landed themselves in it, at which point they clam up. Aidan Seed: none of the above. It was like he had this . . . this checklist in his head. Two lists: the questions he was allowed to answer and the ones he wasn't. When I asked him the questions on the first list, he went out of his way to be informative. Like I said, I got every detail of Mary's appearance, from the tiny caramel-coloured birthmark beneath her lower lip—he actually said "caramel-coloured"—to her small earlobes, her wiry, curly hair, black with the odd strand of silver.'

'Is she attractive?' Charlie asked. 'Don't look at me like that. I'm not asking if you fancied her. I just wondered.'

'She's not pretty,' said Simon after some thought.

'But striking? Sexy?'

He shrugged. 'Dunno.'

Aidan Seed's not the only one with a list in his mind of questions it's not safe to answer, thought Charlie. 'Did he say if he killed her in the bed or moved her body there later?' she asked, a question she knew would be on Simon's acceptable list. *Is there anything I wouldn't do to please him? Would I take early retirement and roam the country with a set of golf clubs, wearing dreadful sweaters?*

'She was in the bed when he killed her, he said. But . . . listen to us.' Simon took a swig of his beer. ' "Did he move the body?" If Seed and his girlfriend are mad, we've nearly caught them up. What body? Mary Trelease is alive.'

'You said "the questions he's *allowed* to answer",' said Charlie. 'Who's doing the allowing? Ruth Bussey? She also seemed eager to talk, but only in response to certain prompts. And then I'd ask her something else—in most cases, the obvious next question—and she'd button it. Not a word, not even, "Sorry, I can't answer that." '

'Could there be a third person involved, someone who's telling them what they can and can't say?'

'Mary Trelease?' Charlie suggested.

Simon waved the idea away. 'Why would she tell them both to go to the police and pretend Seed believes he killed her? Why would they go along with it?' He didn't wait for an answer, knowing she didn't have one. 'Gibbs asked Trelease if she knew an Aidan Seed. She said no, but he thought she was lying. I asked her again today, told her he was a picture-framer, how old he was. She said no. Seemed genuine enough, but then she'd had a day to polish up her act. Seed, though—he wasn't acting. He feels guilty about something, that's for sure. Whatever's in his head, I wouldn't want it in mine. He kept saying, "I'm a murderer." Said he'd felt like he was dying himself when his hands were round her neck, the nail of his left thumb pressing into his right thumb . . .'

'He said that?'

Simon nodded.

'But he hasn't strangled her. Nobody has.' Charlie shuddered. 'This is starting to do my head in. I've heard plenty of people confess to crimes they haven't committed, but they're always crimes *someone's* committed. Why would anyone confess to the murder of a woman who isn't dead? According to Ruth Bussey, Seed didn't tell her any of that stuff about the bedroom, or strangling Mary—why not?'

'You wouldn't want to put that sort of image in your girl-friend's head,' Simon suggested.

'What did Seed say his relationship with Mary Trelease was? How did he know her?' Seeing Simon's expression, Charlie guessed the answer. 'He wouldn't say.' She cast around for something else to ask, as if the right formulation of words might shed sudden light. Nothing came to mind. 'We should be doing the pair of them for wasting police time,' she said.

'Not my decision. For once, I'm glad. Seed's not like any bull-shit artist I've ever seen. Something was bothering him, something real.'

Charlie had felt the same about Ruth Bussey until she'd found the article.

'Kombothekra's got to decide where to go next with it,' said Simon. 'If it was my call, I don't think I'd want to risk not tak-ing statements from everyone involved. From Seed at the very least. Though I've no idea what I'd do with his statement once I had it.' He frowned as a new thought occurred to him. 'What did you decide to do? After you spoke to Ruth Bussey?'

Charlie felt her face heat up. 'Err on the side of negligence, that's my motto,' she said bitterly. 'I wasn't planning to follow it up, even though she told me she was afraid something really bad was going to happen, and even though a fool could have seen she was seriously fucked up. I hadn't even checked, like you and Gibbs did, that Mary Trelease was alive.' Charlie put the ciga-rette she was holding in her mouth: comfort food.

'I don't get it,' said Simon.

She left the room, started to go downstairs.

'What?' He followed her. 'What did I say?'

'Nothing. I'm getting a lighter.'

There were a few to choose from on the mantelpiece in the lounge, all plastic and disposable. 'What aren't you telling me?' Simon asked.

'That's a question from the wrong list. Sorry.' Charlie tried to laugh, lighting her cigarette. The wonderful tranquillising power of nicotine started to do its work.

'You said before that Ruth Bussey was waiting for you when you went into work yesterday.'

'Did I?' *Too clever for his own good. And everyone else's.*

'Why you?'

Charlie walked over to her handbag, which she'd left dangling from the door handle, and pulled out the newspaper article. 'She left her coat behind. This was in the pocket.' Did he have any idea how hard it was for her to show it to him? Chances were he hadn't seen it at the time; Simon didn't read local papers.

She left him alone in the lounge, took her cigarette through the kitchen and out to the backyard, even though it was cold and she had no coat or shoes on. She stared at what Olivia called her 'installation': a pile of broken furniture, things Charlie had dismantled and thrown out two years ago. 'How hard is it to hire a skip?' Liv said plaintively whenever she visited. Charlie didn't know, and didn't have the time or the inclination to find out. *My neighbours must pray every night that I'll move,* she thought. Especially the ones who'd replaced their neat, paved yard with a little lawn and flower-beds as soon as they moved in. Now they had colour-coordinated borders: red, white and blue flowers in a pattern that was overbearingly regular. *What a waste of time, when your garden's the size of a fingernail.*

Charlie felt something touch her and cried out in alarm before realising it was Simon. He put his arms round her waist.

'Well? Did you read it?'

'Slander,' he said. 'Like the way you described yourself to-night.'

'It wasn't negligent, to take no action over Ruth Bussey?' She knew he was talking about the party, but chose to misunderstand.

'I'm not sure,' said Simon. 'As we both keep saying, no crime's been committed. Bussey told you Trelease was alive and well—turns out she is.'

'So Sam Kombothekra will tell you to leave it. It's not a police matter. Just three oddballs behaving oddly, none of our business.'

Simon sighed. 'Are you happy with that explanation? Seed and Bussey come in on the same day, separately, and tell two versions of almost the same story? You want to let it lie?'

'Ruth Bussey said she was frightened something was going to happen.' That was the part Charlie kept coming back to in her mind, now that she knew the whole thing hadn't been about her.

'One thing's going to have to happen if we want to take it any further,' said Simon.

'What?'

He's still touching me. He didn't have to, but he did, he is.

He started to hum a tune, Aled Jones' 'Walking in the Air'.

'You, not we,' said Charlie. One of the advantages of leaving CID—the only one—was that she no longer had to negotiate with the Snowman. She tried not to sound as if she was crowing when she said, 'I don't work for him any more.'

3

Sunday 2 March 2008

A noise startles me: my house, breaking its long silence with a sharp ringing. The woolly feeling in my head clears. Adrenalin gets me moving. I crawl into the lounge on my hands and knees to avoid putting weight on my injured foot, and manage to grab the phone on the third ring, still holding the blanket I've been using as a shawl around my shoulders. I can't say hello. I can't allow myself to hope.

'It's me.'

Aidan. Relief pours through me. I clutch the phone, needing something solid to hold on to. 'Are you coming back?' I say. I have so many questions, but this is the one that matters.

'Yeah,' he says. I wait for the part that comes next: *I'll always come back, Ruth. You know that, don't you?* For once, he doesn't say it. The thudding of my heart fills the silence.

'Where have you been?' I ask. He has been gone longer than usual. Two nights.

'Working.'

'You weren't at the workshop.' There's a pause. Does he regret giving me a key? I wait for him to ask for it back. He gave it to me when I first started to work for him, the same key for Seed Art Services as for his home. It was a sign that he trusted me.

I spent parts of both Friday and Saturday nights in his messy room behind the framing studio, crying, waiting for him to come back. Several times, drained and exhausted, I fell asleep, then came to suddenly, convinced that, if Aidan returned at all, he would go to my house. I'm not sure how many times I drove from one end of town to the other, feeling as if wherever I went I would be too late, I would miss him by a fraction of a second.

'We need to talk, Ruth.'

I begin to cry at the obviousness of it. 'Come back, then.'

'I'm on my way. Stay put.' He's gone before I can reply. *Of course I'll stay. I've got nowhere else to go.*

I crawl back to the hall, where I was before Aidan phoned, where I've been sitting cross-legged since six o'clock this morning, staring up at the small monitor on the shelf above the front door. My body is stiff and sore from being in one position too long. The underside of my damaged foot looks like decayed puff pastry. I don't feel strong enough to clear up two days' worth of mess, but I must.

The remote control: if Aidan sees it on the floor he'll know I've been watching the tapes. He'll be angry. I glance up at the screen, scared that if I take my eyes off it, I'll miss something. The image changes a second later: a grainy black and white picture of the path outside my house, with English yew hedges sculpted into rounded abstract forms bordering the grass along one side, is replaced by the cluster of poplars on the other side of the house and a clear view of the park gates. *Nobody coming in or out. Nobody.*

I pick up the remote control, try to stand at the same time, and knock over the stinking, overflowing ashtray that's been keeping me company lately. 'Shit,' I mutter, wishing I'd thought to ask Aidan how far away he was. Will he be back in five minutes or two hours? As well as the upturned ashtray and its contents, there's an empty wine bottle next to me and an empty packet of Silk Cut. My blood-soaked shoe lies on its side by the front door, where I dropped it on my way to the bathroom to clean myself up on Friday.

If I'd told Charlie Zailer I'd got something in my shoe, she'd have said, 'Take it out, then.' How could I have explained why it was so much easier to pretend it wasn't there?

There's still some blood in the bath. I should have given it a proper scrub on Friday afternoon, but I couldn't face it. It was hard enough to hobble down the hall, put my foot under the tap and turn it on. I'd come home to find my boiler had packed in again. The house was as cold as the park outside, and the water coming out of my taps was colder. I kept my eyes closed as I rubbed the torn, pulpy flesh with my hand, shivering, trying to dislodge the thing that had cut me. My foot throbbed as liquid cold flowed over it. I felt sick when I heard something hard hit the enamel.

Walking on my heel, I throw my ruined shoes in the outside bin, along with the wine bottle and cigarette packet. Moving thaws my chilled bones a little. I sweep up the ash and cigarette butts, put them in the bin too. Then I give the bath a good going over, stopping now and then to get my breath back when dizziness threatens to lay me low. I've eaten nothing today but a Nutri-Grain cereal bar and a packet of Hula Hoops.

We need to talk, Ruth.

I have to keep moving, or I'll imagine all the worst things Aidan might say to me. I'll panic.

I'm about to pick up the remote control and put it on the shelf next to the monitor when I hear a noise outside, a movement in the trees close to my lounge windows. I stop, listen. Almost a minute later, I hear another sound, louder than the first: branches moving. Someone is standing next to my house. Not Aidan; he'd come straight to the door. I sink to my knees in the hall, slide across into the lounge and position myself behind an armchair.

Charlie Zailer. I left my coat at the police station. She might have brought it back. I pray it's her—someone who won't hurt me—even though on Friday I couldn't wait to get away from her.

Then I hear laughing, two voices I don't recognise. I edge out from behind the chair and see a teenage boy framed in my lounge window. He is undoing his flies, turning back towards the path to shout at his friend to wait for him while he has a slash. A shaving rash covers his neck and chin, and he's wearing jeans that reveal a good three inches of the boxer shorts beneath. I close my eyes, steady myself on the arm of the chair. *It's nobody, no one who knows about or is interested in me.* I hear the more distant voice, the friend, calling him an animal.

As he walks away, I watch to check he doesn't look back. He adjusts his jeans and scratches the back of his neck, unaware of my eyes on him. If he turned round now, he would see me clearly.

It was one of the things I liked most about this little house, the way the lounge stuck out like a sort of display box at the front of the park, with large stained-glass-topped windows on three sides. Malcolm told me he'd had trouble finding a tenant after the last one left. 'No privacy, you see.' He pointed as we approached the park gates, keen to list Blantyre Lodge's flaws before I crossed the threshold: there were bollards I'd have to lower and raise every time I drove my car into or out of the park. The lounge and bedroom weren't perfect squares—each had a corner missing, as if a triangle had been cut out of the space. 'I might as well be honest,' Malcolm said. 'It's not as if you wouldn't notice.'

'Privacy's the opposite of what I want,' I told him. 'If people can see me and I can see people, that suits me fine.' I was surprised by my own words, unsure if this was the truth or the exact reverse of how I felt. I remember thinking, if I'm invisible, nobody will be able to help me if I need help.

'Get yourself some good net curtains,' Malcolm said, and I flinched, imagining faces obscured by densely-patterned white material: His face and Hers.

'No,' I made a point of saying, and making sure Malcolm heard me. I doubt he cared one way or the other, but I needed to assert myself. 'I want to be able to see the park, if it's going to be my garden.' I was happy to share it with children, joggers, passers-by. A garden I wouldn't have to touch but that would always be well maintained because it was a public resource; a beautiful green space that was neither secluded nor enclosed—it was ideal.

'The last tenant had some big Japanese screens,' said Malcolm, apparently oblivious to what I'd just said. 'You know, the sort people use for dressing and undressing. He put one at each window.'

'I won't cover the windows with anything,' I said, thinking that I might even take down the curtains, assuming there were some. I'd spotted two large square lights attached to the side of the house facing the wide path that cut the park in half. 'Do those come on automatically when the natural light falls below a certain level?' I asked. Malcolm nodded, and I thought, *So they'll show colour, even in the darkness*. At night, each of the lodge's windows would be a stunning still life of trees, plants and flowers: rich, deep greens, reds and purples, all bathed in a gold glow. Whoever was responsible for planting in the park knew what they were doing, I thought, looking at the blue hobbits and astilbes that circled a large pink-edged phormium. 'When can I move in?' I asked.

'You're keen. Don't you want to see inside first?' Malcolm laughed.

I shook my head. 'That's my house,' I said, standing back to take a mental photograph of the small building in front of me with feathery red Virginia creeper leaves all over its roof. I could have gazed at it for hours. Its pleasing aspect was bound up, in my mind, with the idea of getting better. It was seeing a beautiful object—a painting—that had first tripped something inside me and made me realise I could rejoin the world if I wanted to. Blantyre Lodge wasn't art; it was a place to live: something functional, something I needed. Yet to me it was also beautiful, and I felt at the time that each beautiful thing I saw and felt a connection with—made a part of my spirit, however pretentious that sounds—took me one step closer to recovery.

That's why I stood still and carried on staring, even when Malcolm started to walk on ahead without me: whenever I experienced that sensation of suddenly being one step closer, I felt, perversely, that there was no hurry. I could afford to take a few seconds to appreciate the moment.

I haven't felt that way since London. The pictures on my walls that took so long to collect, all the wire sculptures, the carved wood, the pottery, the abstract metal forms that I've stuffed my house full of—they don't work any more. Until I know what's wrong with Aidan, until I can make it right, nothing will work.

I am bending to pick up the remote control when the front door opens. It's him. He's wearing the shoes he had to wait two years to have made—one of the first stories he ever told me—and his black jacket, his only jacket. It's got shiny patches on the shoulders and makes him look like someone who empties dustbins for a living, or who did, in the days before everyone started to wear fluorescent yellow jackets to perform any sort of public service.

I am about to speak when I see that he's noticed what I'm holding. He walks over to me, takes the remote control from my hand. 'Not again,' he says, and sounds as if he is talking about the future: he will not let me watch again. He presses a button and the screen goes black.

People wouldn't see the monitor and VHS player above the door if they came into my house and walked into any of the rooms, only if they turned back on themselves, or perhaps on the way out. There are no people, anyway. No one comes here apart from me, Aidan and Malcolm. It's a strange thought: the Culver Valley's area manager for parks and landscapes could probably draw every inch of my home from memory, while my own parents have never seen it and never will.

'He's been back,' I tell Aidan. 'This morning. He walked up the path and stared at the house, like he always does.'

'Of course he's been back. He walks his dog in the park.

Don't do this.' His expression is pained. This isn't what he wants us to talk about.

'Where have you been?' I ask.

'Manchester.' He pulls off his jacket. 'Jeanette had some pieces that needed reframing. Had to be done on site.'

He's taken his jacket off. He's staying. 'It's like the Arctic in here,' he says. 'Is the boiler knackered again?'

I stare at him, wanting to believe his story. Jeanette Golenya is the director of Manchester City Art Gallery. She's used Aidan before, used both of us. It's at least a three-hour drive from Spilling to Manchester, but Jeanette's always happy to pay for our travel and accommodation. Aidan's the only conservation framer she knows who never cuts corners. He's the best at what he does. He told me that too, the first time we met.

'Ask her if you don't believe me,' he says.

'Why didn't you ring me? I've been going out of my mind.'

'I'm sorry.' He wraps his arms around me. 'Before I went to Manchester, I went to the police,' he whispers in my ear, his voice uneven.

The shock is like a cold wall in my face. 'What?'

'You heard.'

I pull away, look at his eyes and see that something in him has changed. He looks . . . I can't think how to describe it. Settled. The silent war that's been playing out in his head since London has stopped. I steel myself, scared of what he will say next. I don't want anything to change.

Then why did you wait for Charlie Zailer outside the police station?

'They'd have caught up with me eventually. They always do. I couldn't stand the waiting, so I went to them.'

'So did I,' I blurt out. He can't be angry, not when he's done the same thing.

'You went to the police?'

I could tell him I waited for Charlie Zailer, but I don't. It would feel too much like confessing to an illicit attachment.

Aidan smiles, his eyes gleaming the way they always do when anger or some other emotion overpowers him. 'You believe me,' he says. 'Finally. You believe I killed her.'

'No!'

'Yes. You wouldn't have gone to the police otherwise.'

'I don't. I don't! Aidan, what's going on?' I sob. 'How *could* I believe you killed her when I've seen her with my own eyes, alive and well?'

He doesn't answer.

'What did the police say?'

'The same as you. I had a visit yesterday from a detective, Simon Waterhouse . . .'

'Yesterday? You mean here, a detective came here?' While I was at the workshop trying to do the work of two people alone, looking in every hiding place I could think of for Mary's picture. 'I thought you were in Manchester yesterday.'

A long pause. Then Aidan says, 'Don't try to catch me out, Ruth.' He makes no attempt to reconcile what he's telling me now with his earlier lie.

I know I ought to let it go, but I can't. 'Where's the painting? What have you done with it? Where did you spend last night? At Mary's?'

His face pales, freezes. 'You think I could go there even if I tried? I'd wipe that shit-hole off the face of the earth if it was up to me.'

I couldn't go there either. Last night, when Aidan didn't come back, after I'd been to the workshop and not found him there, and waited and waited, I decided I had to go to Megson Crescent again. At two thirty in the morning I got into my car, using the heel of my wounded foot to work the clutch, and told myself I had to drive to Mary's. I'd done it before, and anything you've done once you can do again. But I couldn't. When I turned on to Seeber Street and saw the Winstanley estate's mesh-fenced playground in front of me, the decades-old paint peeling off the swing, slide and roundabout, my good foot slammed down on the brake. I had to turn round and drive home. However infinitesimal the chance, I couldn't risk finding Aidan at Mary's house. I couldn't have stood it.

'Why would I go back to the place where I killed her?' he demands, his face crumpling in pain. 'Why would I?'

'But . . . didn't this detective tell you she isn't dead? Didn't he see her, speak to her?' I ask, feeling my hold on the situation start to unravel. I've felt this way so often lately, I've almost forgotten there's any other way to feel.

'He says he did.' Aidan paces the room, back and forth. 'Whoever he saw claimed she didn't know me. She'd never heard of me.'

'What do you mean, "whoever he saw"?' A cold ripple of panic passes through me. 'Didn't he check . . .?'

'She showed him her passport and driving licence. The woman he spoke to was Mary Trelease. His description of her fitted the one I'd given him, detail for detail.'

'Aidan, I . . .'

'So, that's it.' His voice is loud and forced. 'They don't believe me. It's over as far as they're concerned.' He lets out a humourless laugh, jeering at himself. 'No one's going to come and arrest me in the middle of the night, no one's going to cart me off to jail. We should celebrate.'

'Aidan . . .'

'Three cheers for me.' He looms over me, a droplet of his saliva landing on my face. 'Why don't you crack open a bottle of champagne? It's not every day your boyfriend gets away with murder.'

I didn't meet Aidan by chance. I planned it, though it took all the self-discipline I could muster to put the plan into action. On the twenty-second of August last year, I got up, threw on the T-shirt, jeans and flip-flops I'd worn every day for the past two months, and got into my car without giving myself time to think or change my mind.

I had Aidan's details written on the back of a receipt in my jeans pocket. I knew where Seed Art Services was, didn't need reminding, but having the address with me, written in black and white on a piece of paper, made it harder for me to avoid what I knew I had to do. A positive prescription, my books call it. I'd tried the technique a few times and it seemed to work.

I parked at the bottom of Demesne Avenue, where it gives way to the unmade road that runs alongside the river, and walked under the overhanging trees, counting my footsteps to take my mind off the task ahead. I'd got as far as forty when I reached the small, flat-roofed grey-brick building, with a wide wooden door that had buckled at the bottom where the wood was cracked and blistered, flaring out like a skirt. The door stood slightly ajar. On its inside were two large iron hinges and two even bigger bolts. Rust clung to them, looking like an exotic species of chestnut-coloured moss. Had the door been closed, I'm not sure I'd have been brave enough to knock.

Saul Hansard, my boss at the Spilling Gallery until two months earlier, had promised me Aidan would be pleased to see me. He could have told me thousands of times and I wouldn't have believed him. Wherever I went, I felt unwelcome. I stared at Aidan's open door and listened to the music that was coming from inside the workshop: 'Madame George' by Van Morrison. I knocked and waited, feeling my heartbeat in my throat, staring in through the long rectangular pane of PVC-framed glass on my right—the only window, as far as I could make out. It ran the length of one side of the building. Through it I saw neon strip lights, a concrete floor, dozens of planks of wood, some plain and some painted, leaning against a wall; two large tables, one covered with what looked like velvet cloths in different colours, a small radio with a paint-spattered aerial. On the other table there was an enormous roll of brown paper, scissors, a pair of pliers, a Stanley knife, lots of what looked like catalogues in a pile, a few bottles of glue and tins of paint.

No Aidan Seed.

I shivered in spite of the heat, jumpy and nauseous, every nerve in my body on alert. Why was nothing happening? Where was he? Aching to run away, I told myself I had the perfect excuse. If I knocked and no one came, what was I supposed to do? I couldn't walk in uninvited. My fingers closed around my car keys, tightening their grip. I flexed my toes, ready to move at speed once I gave myself permission. *Go, then.* I never wanted to set foot in another picture framer's studio as long as I lived. I could leave and no one would know; Aidan Seed, whoever and wherever he was, wouldn't know I'd been here.

Saul Hansard would know.

I stayed where I was and knocked again, louder and more insistently. Saul would never let it lie. I didn't want any more messages from him, any more fatherly concern. Even thinking about him made me feel ashamed. I had to convince him I was all right, and there was only one way to do that.

That's a negative reason. Think of a more positive one.

If I go through with this, I told myself, if I'm brave and ask Aidan Seed for a job, I'll start to earn money again. I'll be able to afford to stay in Blantyre Lodge, to buy more paintings to put on the walls. I needed to be able to do that. The book on my bedside table at the time was called *What if Everything Goes Right?* Its blurb promised to train me to make decisions based on hope, not fear.

I knocked again, and this time an impatient voice, deep and male, shouted, 'Coming,' as if I'd already been told several times and was being unreasonable. Aidan appeared in the doorway, holding a threadbare blue towel. His rough hands looked red and damp; he'd been scrubbing at them. 'Yeah?' he said, looking me up and down.

More vividly than anything else about that day, I remember my utter surprise at the sight of him. It had nothing to do with attractiveness, though I registered that he was unusually attractive. This is the man, I thought. I'd never seen him before, but I recognised him as being the right person. Right for what, exactly, I couldn't have said. All I knew was that I wanted to keep him there, keep myself there with him for as long as possible.

'I'm busy,' Aidan said. 'Do you want something?'

I'd almost forgotten, in the shock of seeing him, why I'd come. 'Um . . . Saul Hansard from the Spilling Gallery told me you're looking for someone to work for you,' I mumbled, taking in the shiny shoulder patches on his black jacket, the dark stubble on his chin and above his mouth. His hair was so dark it was almost black. It hadn't been combed recently, if ever. A scar formed a lopsided cross with the line of his upper lip, cutting his stubble diagonally in half. When he moved nearer, I noticed his eyes were dark blue with flecks of grey around the pupils. I guessed that he was in his early forties.

He was inspecting me closely too. 'I'm not looking for anyone,' he said.

My spirit withered. 'Oh,' I said faintly.

'Doesn't mean I don't need someone. Just haven't got round to looking yet. Been too busy.'

'So . . . does that mean you'd be interested in . . .'

He gestured towards the workshop. 'I can't do it all myself,' he said, as if I'd told him he must. 'Why, are you looking for a job?'

'Yes. I can start straight away.'

'You're a framer?'

'I . . .' The question had floored me, but I did my best not to show it. I wasn't a framer—in all my time working for Saul I hadn't framed a single picture—but I sensed that 'no' would be the wrong answer. I was as eager to prolong my conversation with Aidan as I had been to leave a few moments earlier. I couldn't let him dismiss me. It scared me to feel such a strong, irrational need for a stranger who owed me nothing. 'At the moment I haven't got a job,' I said. 'I used to work for Saul at the Spilling Gallery, but I didn't . . .'

'How long were you there?'

'Nearly two years.'

'Right,' he said. Was he grinning at me or sneering? 'What did you think of Hansard's framing skills?'

'I . . . I don't know. I . . .' *Surely one picture-framer's methods would be much like another's*, I thought. Again, I sensed this would be the wrong thing to say, so I kept quiet.

'Did he train you?' Aidan asked.

'No. I never actually did any framing.' Better to admit it straight away than be caught out trying to wing it, I decided. 'Saul took care of that side of things. I did some admin for him, answered the phone, took care of sales . . .'

'In two years, you never framed a picture?'

I shook my head.

Aidan jerked his in the direction of his workshop. 'If I put you in there and told you to get started, would you know what to do?'

'No.'

He pushed his fringe out of his eyes with his paint-spotted right arm. 'In that case, you're no use to me. I'm a picture-framer. I need a picture-framer to help me. Frame more pictures,' he said slowly, as if I was stupid.

'I can learn,' I told him. 'I'm a quick learner.'

'You're a receptionist. I don't want a receptionist. Hansard doesn't listen. No surprise there—his head's all over the place. You must know that if you've worked for him.'

Was he testing me? I wasn't about to be disloyal to Saul, who had always treated me well.

'You can't be a picture-framer and run an art gallery at the same time,' said Aidan. 'Hansard spreads himself too thin, ends up making a hash of everything. That's why I asked what you thought of his framing. I've seen his work—it's shoddy. He doesn't use acid-free tape or backing card.'

I must have looked mystified, because he sighed heavily and said, 'The essence of conservation framing is that it's all reversible. You've got to be able to undo everything you do, and end up with the picture exactly the same as before it was framed, however long ago that was. That's the first thing you need to learn.'

'You mean . . .?' It sounded as if he was offering me a job, unless I'd misunderstood completely.

'You're Ruth, right?'

I felt my confidence start to drain away, as if there was a hole in the pit of my stomach, and thought back to the last message Saul had left on my voicemail. *I gave you a glowing reference—Aidan'll snap you up if he knows what's good for him.*

'Why do you want to work here?'

Was this my interview? 'It sounds corny, but I love art.' I spoke quickly to hide my nerves. 'There's nothing that's more . . .'

'The way I heard it, you're a liability,' Aidan talked over me, his voice hard and cold. 'You upset one of Hansard's clients, lost him a lucrative source of business.'

I tried to keep calm. 'Who told you that?'

'Hansard. Who do you think?'

I didn't see why he would lie. Fury sprang up out of nowhere, crushed me like a lead weight. Saul had encouraged me to come here, without saying a word about how he'd pre-empted me and sabotaged my chances. I stared down at the dirt path, mortified, trying not to explode with defensive rage. This wasn't an isolated incident: in my mind it acted as a magnet, attracting, like iron filings, memories of all the terrible moments in my life so far. *Same horror, different incarnation.* After what I'd been through, no bad feeling ever seemed new to me: I had already felt them all, recognised them like familiar relatives each time they paid a visit.

'Sorry I bothered you,' I said, starting to walk away.

'Can't take criticism very well, can you?'

His mocking tone made me want to kill him. If I hadn't been furious with Saul, I wouldn't have dared to do what I did next. *Most of the word 'courage' is the word 'rage'*—which book was that in? I turned and walked back to Aidan, counting my steps.

'The essence of asking a conservation framer for a job is that it's reversible,' I said in a deliberately pompous voice. 'You've got to be able to undo everything you do. I'm undoing asking you for work, and I'm undoing coming here at all. Goodbye.'

I ran back to my car, and this time he didn't call after me. I slammed the door and sat in the driver's seat, panting. I tried to brainwash myself: I'd been wrong about Aidan. I'd seen nothing in him, nothing at all. And I'd been wrong about Saul; I'd thought he cared about me, but he'd set me up for a fall.

Where else could I go? What could I do? Nothing that brought me into contact with pictures or artists, nothing in a gallery. The Spilling art world was too small; this latest humiliation had brought that home to me in the most painful way. If Saul had told Aidan, who else had he told? I could go to London, but then I'd have to give up my little house that I loved. Something told me that if I lost that, I'd lose everything.

I could get the sort of job anyone could get—serving fast food or cleaning toilets. Even as I had the thought, I knew I couldn't. However much I needed money—and I did, urgently—I wasn't the sort of person who would do anything to get it. I didn't see any point in prolonging my life purely for the sake of it; if I wasn't able to do something that mattered to me, I'd rather stop doing altogether.

I turned on the ignition, then turned it off again. Carbon monoxide poisoning. Probably the easiest way, I thought. After all, I had a car. I was in it now. If I had a length of rubber hosepipe with me, I could do it right here, get it over with.

My mind started to wander aimlessly. Him and Her came into my thoughts, but for once there was no friction. I wondered idly if, by ending my life, I would alter the balance of blame between us. I was so tired of blame—of hoarding it all for myself, of giving it out. Someone else could take over the precise measurements, the minute calculations, that were necessary for its correct distribution.

A knocking sound near my head made me jump. My vision

was blurred. I felt dizzy, and couldn't see what was outside my car at first. Then I recognised Aidan; he was tapping on the window. Funny, I thought. I'd almost completely forgotten him in a few seconds; he'd drifted far away, along with the rest of the world I was preparing to leave. I ignored his knocking.

He pulled open the car door. 'What's wrong with you?' he said. 'You look terrible.'

'Leave me alone.'

'Are you sick? Do you need help?'

I needed a drink. I'd eaten and drunk nothing all day; I'd been too nervous. I imagined a hot cup of tea, fizzy Coke, even flat Coke. I started to cry. How could I want to die and want flat Coke at the same time? 'I'm a stupid fuckhead,' I told Aidan.

'You can talk me through your CV later,' he said. 'Look ... you don't want to let the likes of me upset you. My interview technique's a bit rusty. I've never had anyone work for me before. It's always just been me.' He shrugged. 'If you still want the job, it's yours.'

'I don't want it,' I whispered, trying to wipe my face.

Aidan crouched down beside the car. 'Ruth, Hansard hasn't been bad-mouthing you. Far from it. All he said was that you offended one of his regulars without meaning to, and lost him a client he was happy to see the back of. If someone as mild as Saul Hansard says something like that the way he said it to me ... Look, we've all got nightmare customers. Hansard, me— any picture-framer'd tell you. There's the ones who can't choose and force you to make all the decisions for them, then kick off when it's done and they decide they don't like it. The ones I hate most are the neurotics who spot tiny specks of dust on the inside of the glass, and insist on having the whole thing opened up and the glass cleaned, and then you have to reframe it, but they don't pay for the second framing.'

I felt myself slipping, my hand moist on the wheel, my head

lolling. Aidan caught me. 'What's wrong with you?' he asked. 'Do I need to take you to a hospital?'

'I'm fine,' I said, rousing myself. 'Just tired, hungry, thirsty. I'll go home and—'

'No, you won't. You're in no state to drive. You're coming with me.'

He helped me out of the car, supporting me with both his arms. I felt my skin fizz, like a sort of electrical charge, when he touched me. He turned me round, pointed me in the right direction, and I stumbled back to the workshop, leaning on him. 'Have you got any flat Coke?' I muttered into my hair, which was falling in front of my face. I started to laugh hysterically. 'My interview technique's even worse than yours,' I said. 'This is me applying for a job.'

'I've already told you, the job's yours.'

'I don't want it.'

'Yeah, you do,' he said mildly. He paused when we reached the door of the workshop, looked at me. 'You want it and you need it. And I'm not only talking about money.'

'I don't—'

'I'm the best at what I do. This is where you want to be working. I'm stubborn, too. See these shoes?' I looked at his feet. 'I waited two years for them. Someone recommended me a guy in Hamblesford, makes his own shoes. A proper craftsman. I went to the shop and he told me he had a two-year waiting list. I put my name down and I waited. I could have gone to an-other shoe shop and bought some mass-produced crap, but I didn't. I waited the two years, because I knew what I'd be get-ting was the best. Rain and snow and mud were pouring into my old boots, but I still waited.'

Aidan looked embarrassed for a moment. Then he went on, 'Hansard told me you were first-rate. He's crap at framing pic-tures, but I trust him where people are concerned.'

I made the crassest, most idiotic comment: 'Pity your shoe-maker didn't have any elves to help him.'

Aidan completely ignored it. Maybe he never read *The Elves and the Shoemaker* when he was little. 'What were you going to say before?' he asked. 'About art?'

'Nothing.'

'You started to say, "There's nothing more . . ." '

'It'll sound stupid.'

'So?' he said impatiently. 'I want to know.'

'I'm . . . kind of obsessed with art,' I told him, blushing. 'That's why . . . that's how I came to be working for Saul.'

Aidan's eyes narrowed. 'You a painter yourself?'

'No. Not at all. I'd be hopeless.'

He nodded. 'Good,' he said. 'Because it's a framer I need.' He led me through his messy workshop to an even messier room at the back. My eyes passed quickly over the unmade bed, the mounds of clothes, books, CDs, unwashed cups and plates. I forcibly silenced the voice in my head that was saying, 'Okay for a bloke in his early twenties, not so okay for one in his forties.' That was the sort of opinion my father might hold, and I didn't want to share anything with him, not even an opinion about something trivial.

I smelled fruity soap, or shower gel. I scanned the room for a basin, but couldn't see one. Where was Aidan's bathroom? I wondered. On the other side of the workshop? I was about to ask when I noticed the walls, and as soon as I did, I couldn't believe it had taken me so long to spot the only truly bizarre thing about this room. Three of the four walls were covered with what I imagined was Aidan's handiwork: extravagant frames—one had a carved wooden crown attached to its top edge—as well as lots of ordinary ones, pale or dark wood, flat or slightly curved.

One thing was not ordinary: none of the frames had anything in them.

Aidan was squatting in front of his miniature fridge. 'Cheese sandwich do you?' he said. 'Think it'll have to. I've got a carton of orange juice.' He sounded surprised.

When he stood up, he saw me staring. 'I told you I was the best,' he said. He crossed the room and started to point out individual frames. 'This one's a palladian,' he said. 'With the sticky-out corners. It's based on the pattern of a Greek temple. This one's called egg-and-dart, for obvious reasons. Can you see the pattern?'

'Why's there nothing in them?' I blurted out. 'Why have you framed . . . *nothing*?'

His expression hardened. 'These are highly collectable,' he said. 'It's not nothing, it's black card. It's a statement. The artist wants to make you think.' His mouth twitched. Then he started to laugh. 'I'm having you on,' he said. 'It's just backing card.'

I don't like being tricked. The joke over, he didn't explain. I didn't find out why he'd put frames on his walls with no pictures inside them. I didn't particularly care. All I wanted was the orange juice and the cheese sandwich he'd offered me. I was so hungry that I was finding it hard to keep thoughts in my head. I was also worried my breath stank. Had I even brushed my teeth?

Standing in Aidan's one-room home, the stark fact of how low I'd sunk in two months hit me like a boulder in the chest. What was wrong with me, that I'd let it happen? I could have reacted differently. Better.

'What are you thinking?' Aidan asked, cutting cheese with a paint-spotted Stanley knife.

'Nothing,' I said quickly.

'Yeah, you were.'

He hadn't answered my question about the frames, so I didn't have to answer his. I knew he was as aware of this as I was.

He gave me my sandwich and a glass of orange juice. I sat cross-legged on the floor to eat it. It tasted divine. 'Want another one?' Aidan said, watching me devour the sandwich as if I'd never seen food before.

I nodded.

'Want to tell me the story of why you left Hansard's place?'

'There's nothing to tell. An artist brought in one of her paintings to be framed; I asked her if I could buy it; she said no, it wasn't for sale.' I recited woodenly. 'I asked her if I could buy any of her other pictures, and she said none of her work was for sale.'

'That's crazy,' said Aidan, his back to me as he foraged in the fridge again. 'An artist who won't sell any of her work? I've never heard of that before.'

I shivered. *Crazy. Like having empty frames all over your walls, with no pictures in them.*

'So? What happened?' Aidan asked.

'She accused me of harassing me.' I took a sip of my orange juice, hoping he would leave the subject alone.

'Sounds like a standard shit day at work,' he said. 'Why did you leave? Hansard weighed in on your side, didn't he?'

He sounded as if he was guessing. *Saul hadn't told him.*

Aidan handed me another cheese sandwich. It had dents in the bread from his thumb and forefinger. He looked down at me, frowning. 'You'll have to toughen up,' he said. 'I'm not having you resigning on me after the first visit from some awkward bugger artist.'

I ate my food to avoid having to answer.

'There's something you're not telling me,' said Aidan, watching me carefully. 'Isn't there?'

I nodded.

For a second he looked wary, perhaps even afraid. 'You're just like me,' he said. 'I knew it, soon as I saw you. That's why I gave you a hard time.' He put his hand on my shoulder. 'It's okay,' he said. 'I won't ask again.' He stared at the empty frames on his walls, as if making some kind of silent pact with them.

I was smiling at him when he turned to face me, and he smiled back. Having established the ground rules, we could both relax. From that point on, we talked about art, framing—things we were happy to talk about. Aidan started—immediately, while I was still eating—to tell me everything he knew about his craft, everything he thought I should know. He told me that all the concepts and designs in picture-framing come from classical architecture. He dug out dusty hardback books from under piles of black T-shirts and faded jeans, and showed me photographs of tabernacle frames and *trompe l'oeils* and cassettas, explaining what each one was. He railed against people like Saul, who didn't read up on the history of picture-framing, whose libraries on the subject were less extensive than his own, and against all the art books that contained photographs of unframed pictures, free-floating against a black background, as if the frame were not crucial to the work of art.

I remember being struck by his anger, his apparent determination to make my brain a replica of his, containing the same information. Apart from the bits that were missing, that is. He didn't tell me, not then and not ever, why he had framed emptiness and hung it on his walls. And I didn't give him the missing details from the story about why I'd left my job at Saul's gallery. I'd made what had happened sound so straightforward, but it wasn't at all—my reaction to the picture, my conviction that I had to have it, all the different ways I'd tried to persuade the artist to sell me some of her work, hounding her so that she had no choice but to lash out at me . . .

My fault. My fault, again.

And of course, the main thing I didn't tell Aidan, because I didn't know it at the time, I only found out months later: that the artist's name was Mary Trelease.

4

3/3/08

'Have you been bullying DS Kombothekra, Waterhouse?'

'No, sir.'

'Filling his petrol tank with porridge, putting laxatives in his coffee?' Proust pressed his hands together church-and-steeple style, index fingers protruding.

'No.'

'Then why is he afraid to give you a simple instruction? You might as well spit it out, Sergeant, while you've got me here to protect you.'

Beside Simon, Sam Kombothekra shuffled from one foot to the other, looking as if he would prefer to be in an abattoir, a skip full of rubble—anywhere but the Snowman's office. 'I'm assigning you the statements in the Beddoes case,' he muttered.

'What?' For a second, Simon forgot Proust was in the room with them. 'You told me you'd given that to Sellers and Gibbs.'

'Sergeant Kombothekra changed his mind,' said Proust. 'He decided it was a task best suited to a pedant with a keen eye for detail. That's you, Waterhouse. As it happens, I agree with him.'

Simon knew what that meant. There was no way this was Kombothekra's initiative. 'I don't mind doing my share if we're all chipping in,' he said, doing the calculation in his head as he spoke. Kombothekra would have to do his bit too if he was making Simon do it; he wouldn't dare not to.

'Good.' Proust smiled. 'Tell him what his share is, Sergeant.'

Kombothekra looked as if someone had inserted a hot poker

into a tender part of his body as he said, 'I'm giving you all the statements.'

'All of them? But there are two hundred-odd.'

'Two hundred and seventy-six,' said Proust. 'In this instance, no one will be chipping in apart from you, Waterhouse. This is something you can make your own. I know that's important to you. You'll have no one interfering, no one to cajole or negotiate with. From here on in, Nancy Beddoes is your exclusive territory. You can plant your flag unchallenged.'

'Sir, tell me you're joking. Two hundred and seventy-six people, all living in different parts of the country? It'd take me weeks!'

The Snowman nodded. 'You know I'm not one to gloat, Waterhouse, or push home my advantage, should I be so lucky as to find myself in possession of one, but it would be remiss of me not to point out that if you were a sergeant, as you certainly should be by now and could be in a matter of months if you put in for your exams—'

'Is that what this is about?'

'Don't interrupt me. If you were a DS, you'd be the team leader. You'd be the one assigning the actions.'

'To a different team, maybe hundreds of miles away!' Simon struggled to compose himself. Charlie was in Spilling, his parents were here, everything he knew was here. Proust couldn't make him move, couldn't force a promotion on him that he didn't want.

'You need to broaden your horizons, Waterhouse. Another good reason to give you Nancy Beddoes. As you say, taking all those statements will involve a fair amount of travel. Aren't you even a bit curious about your native land? Have you ever left the Culver Valley for any significant period of time?'

Simon wanted to kill him, mainly for staging this production in front of Kombothekra, who knew Simon had been to university in Rawndesley but not that he'd lived with his parents for all of his three years as a student. Proust, unfortunately, knew everything—all the sad details of Simon's life so far. Which of them was he about to mention now? The age at which Simon left home? The Sunday mornings he'd spent at church with his mother rather than upset her while his university mates had been in bed sleeping off hangovers?

'I can't believe you're serious, sir,' he said eventually.

Proust grinned. Unlike most of his good moods, this one didn't have a provisional, threatened-with-imminent-extinction feel about it. It seemed to have taken root, possibly for the whole day. 'Waterhouse, explain something to me. Why do you respond with such . . . bamboozlement, if that's a word, when all I'm asking you to do is your job?' Giving Simon no opportunity to respond, he went on, 'I'm not ordering you to dress up in a gorilla costume and distribute free bananas on public transport. I'm asking you to take statements from the people to whom Nancy Beddoes fraudulently sold items of clothing on eBay, clothing she'd stolen from high-street shops. Is it my fault there are so many of them? Did I ask Mrs Beddoes to put in the hours of a hedge-fund manager in pursuit of her criminal activities? The woman's an exceptionally motivated and diligent lawbreaker—you don't see her complaining about having two hundred and seventy-six people to deal with. Think of it this way, Waterhouse—she did it for the money, and so will you be, because it's your job.' Proust beamed, pleased with the neatness of his conclusion. 'I trust that, by the time you've finished, you'll have had your fill of taking statements. You certainly won't want to bother taking one from an irresponsible timewaster about a murder that never happened.'

'So this is about Aidan Seed,' said Simon angrily. He should have known. He looked at Kombothekra, who'd agreed with him no more than an hour ago: they ought to take Seed's statement, make sure all bases were covered. Had Kombothekra broached the subject with the Snowman? He must have. It made perfect sense: Simon's punishment was Nancy Beddoes, Kombothekra's was having to participate in this excruciating scene.

'It's a shame, in a way,' said Proust. 'Mr Seed's statement is one I'd have enjoyed reading. Pity we can't get it just to entertain ourselves. "I do not intend to explain why I killed one Mary Trelease. I do not intend to inform the police of the date on which I killed Ms Trelease. I do not intend to offer details as to the nature of my relationship with Ms Trelease prior to my killing her . . .'

'Sir, Simon and I both think . . .'

' "I do NOT" '—Proust's voice rose to a crescendo as he drowned out Kombothekra's words—' "have any comment to make regarding the claims made by DCs Christopher Gibbs and Simon Waterhouse that they, on the twenty-ninth of February 2008 and the first of March 2008 respectively, found Ms Trelease alive and well at her home, 15 Megson Crescent, Spilling, RY27 3BH, and were shown by Ms Trelease several items of identification that confirmed her identity as Mary Bernadette Trelease, aged forty . . ." ' '

'If a situation being at all unusual prevents us from taking a statement, sir, we might as well all give up now,' said Simon. *Cunning bastard.* Proust had to prove he'd memorised the relevant facts before dismissing them.

'Tell me why we aren't charging Mr Seed with wasting our time,' the inspector snapped. So the good mood was finite after all. Even so, Simon was sure Proust had broken his record; usually the ice storm was much quicker in coming.

'Trelease told Gibbs she didn't know Seed, but he thought she was lying,' said Kombothekra. 'What if Seed beat her up, left her for dead, and now she's too scared to tell us in case he does it again?' It came out sounding awkward because they weren't his words. He was quoting Simon, trying to make amends for Nancy Beddoes.

'Did Ms Trelease look as if she'd recently been attacked? Any scars, bruises, cuts? Any sign of limited mobility, hospital notes lying around the house, wheelchairs parked on the front lawn?'

'No, sir,' said Simon.

'We've been able to find no evidence—substantial or circum-stantial—that Aidan Seed's committed any crime,' Kombothekra told Proust. 'That's if we leave aside the verbal evidence . . .'

'Verbal evidence?' the Snowman intoned flatly. 'You mean lies?'

'I spent most of last night going through our unsolveds, just in case anything from any of them chimed in with what Seed and Bussey had told us.'

'Chimed in? Are you a bell-ringer, Sergeant?'

Kombothekra smiled in deference to Proust's witticism. 'I found nothing that might fit the bill, however wide a margin I allowed myself: no suspicious deaths where the victim's name or appearance or address was in any way similar to Mary Tre-lease's. Nothing. We've put all three names—Seed, Bussey and Trelease—into Visor, Sleuth, the PNC, NFLMS. None of them have got form.'

'Yes, yes, Sergeant.' Proust waved his hand dismissively. 'And you failed to find mention of them in the cast list of Rawndesley Opera House's production of *West Side Story*.'

'Simon and I think that, all this notwithstanding, we ought to take a statement from Aidan Seed,' said Kombothekra. Ner-vousness about the brave stand he imagined he was taking made his voice louder than it normally was.

'Not only Seed,' said Simon. 'Bussey and Trelease too.'

'If only we could amuse ourselves by doing as you suggest,' said Proust with feigned wistfulness. 'Had we but world enough and time. Imagine Mary Trelease's statement: "On a date that a man I don't know called Aidan Seed refuses to divulge, he did not murder me." ' Proust banged his fist down on his desk. 'What's wrong with the pair of you? Did you share a beefburger of questionable origin in the mid-nineteen-eighties?'

'No, sir.' Kombothekra took a step back. The brave stand was over, then.

'I've heard as much as I want to about Aidan Seed, and seen more than I want to of your pathetically expectant faces. I'm sorry Santa didn't bring you both what you wanted, but there's only so much tat you can force down one reasonable chimney. Are we clear?' Proust stopped, red in the face.

Reasonable chimney? Was he talking about himself? The Snowman had trouble recognising his opinions as opinions, had for as long as Simon had known him. He regarded himself as the embodiment of universal truth. It wouldn't for a moment have occurred to him, in constructing his metaphor, that he was closer to being a chimney than he was to being reasonable.

'Yes, sir,' said Kombothekra, who would probably have been bowing by now if Simon hadn't been there.

'Good. Now get out there and do your perishing jobs.'

Kombothekra made a run for it, no doubt assuming Simon was close behind. Once the sergeant had gone, Simon pushed the door shut.

'You're still here, Waterhouse.'

'Yes, sir.'

'Since you've gone to the trouble of securing this private moment for us, might I beg a favour? Would you mind asking Sergeant Kombothekra to address you as DC Waterhouse instead of Simon? I've asked him several times, but he persists in his use of first names. The other day he told me he'd prefer it if I called him Sam.' Proust compressed his thin lips. 'I said, "When two people are as close as you and I are, *Sam*, they invariably have pet names for one another. My pet name for you is Sergeant Kombothekra." '

'You're wrong about Aidan Seed,' Simon told him. 'I know no crime's been committed yet, but Sergeant Zailer and I both think something's going to happen. That's why we need to take statements now. There are protection issues here—we can't ignore our concerns. You read Gibbs' notes: he said Mary Trelease looked scared when he first mentioned Seed. Sergeant Zailer was left in no doubt that Ruth Bussey was terrified of something, she wouldn't say what.'

'Yet she didn't follow it up,' said Proust impatiently.

'Bussey left her coat behind. Sergeant Zailer found an article about herself in the pocket. It was from the local rag, dated 2006. It was about her . . . when she . . .'

'Say it in plain English: Sergeant Zailer's catastrophic error of yesteryear. Not to be confused with her more recent catastrophic error: agreeing to marry you, Waterhouse. Go on.'

'Bussey had an article about it in her pocket. Once Sergeant Zailer saw that, and put it together with Bussey's unlikely story that was full of gaps . . . well, she thought the whole thing was some sort of ploy.' Simon knew this aspect of things would do nothing for his cause.

'What?' Proust frowned so hard, his forehead looked like an accordion.

'She's embarrassed about it now, sir, but she still gets really upset and paranoid at any mention of all that. She thought Ruth Bussey was some kind of investigative journalist, undercover—you know those programmes where they target someone they think ought to be sacked, and set traps for them? She thought she might end up on *Panorama* . . .'

'No crime has been committed *yet*,' Proust repeated slowly. 'What's that film?'

'Pardon, sir?'

'You know—it's got that man in it. The scientologist with all the wives. What's his name?'

'I don't know, sir.' Simon didn't watch films, couldn't sit still long enough.

'Age, Waterhouse—it's a terrible thing. The man's job, as I recall, was to foresee and prevent crimes that hadn't yet taken place. The film was set in the future. Why do you think they didn't opt for a contemporary setting?'

Simon swallowed a groan. *Can't we skip this?*

'Could it be because there's no technology, at present, for investigating crimes that have not yet been committed? Whereas if you set your film in the future, you can pretend all the necessary gubbins is in place. Your hero can watch handy trailers of forth-coming slayings . . .'

'I take your point, sir.'

'Good.'

'Why wouldn't Mary Trelease let Gibbs inside her house?' Simon was getting desperate. 'Why did she keep him on the doorstep and bring her ID outside? And even with me—she let me in, but she wasn't happy about it. When I asked to see the front bedroom, the one where Seed said he'd killed her and left her body, she made it obvious she didn't want me in there. What's she got to hide?'

'She let you in, didn't she, however reluctantly? You found a large number of paintings in the front bedroom and not much else.'

'Yes, but . . .'

'Most people would rather not have the big boots of plod trampling all over their houses, especially over their irreplace-able works of art. No mystery there.'

One last stand, thought Simon. He took a deep breath. 'Why did it take Ruth Bussey more than two months to come to us with her story, when Seed first told her he'd killed Mary Tre-lease on the thirteenth of December last year? Why did she have that article with her about Charl . . . about Sergeant Zailer? Why did she and Seed come forward entirely of their own accord, separately but on the same day, offering informa-tion while at the same time blatantly withholding information? And why don't their accounts match? Bussey reckons Seed told her this killing happened years ago, but Seed gave Gibbs the impression that if he went to 15 Megson Crescent, he'd find a fresh body.'

'Recently deceased, not fresh,' Proust amended. 'Don't apply the same terminology to a corpse as you would to a fruit salad.'

'You know what I mean, sir. You read what Trelease said to Gibbs: "Why do you keep asking me if I'm sure nobody's hurt me? Who? Aidan Seed, this man you keep asking about? If

you're looking for a victim, you're looking in the wrong place."
That suggests there's a right place to look for Seed's victims.'

'Think about it, Waterhouse.' Proust sounded almost kindly.
'For Ms Trelease to assume Seed has hurt somebody somewhere
is only natural. There's a detective on her doorstep showing a
keen interest in him, asking if she knows him and wanting to
check she's in one piece.'

'Maybe she knows of another victim of Seed's, somebody else
he's attacked or killed, even if he hasn't touched *her*.' Simon
wiped the back of his neck with his hand. He was sweating.
'What about the question Seed asked me: "The woman you met
at 15 Megson Crescent—did you tell her what I'm saying I
did?" Did you read that bit?'

'I read all the bits. Top left to bottom right. I know how to
read.'

'According to Seed, Mary Trelease is dead—he killed her.
What does he care what I told or didn't tell a supposedly dead
woman? Sir, if you met him . . . He's like a man possessed. He
was super-rational, as if by using logic he could persuade me.
Kept saying, "If I start with the one thing I know beyond all
doubt, which is that I killed Mary Trelease, then I infer that
what you're telling me about her being alive and unharmed
can't be true." Read it!' Simon picked up papers from Proust's
desk and dropped them again, looking for the notes he'd
brought in with him. He couldn't find them. He knew Seed's
words by heart, anyway.

' "The only other explanation is that I killed someone who
later came back to life, and who's the woman you met. Since I
don't believe in the supernatural, I can't believe in that as a
possibility." Does any of that sound normal or natural to
you?' Simon demanded. 'Someone's going to get hurt, sir, if
they haven't already. I've got a really bad feeling about it.'

The Snowman sighed. 'All right, Waterhouse. You set out to
wear me down and you've succeeded. Take statements from the
whole motley bunch if it makes you happy.'

Was Simon dreaming? Could it be that easy? Proust made a series of huffing noises and straightened the piles of paper on his desk. Watching him reconsider his position on an issue, however small, was like watching a super-tanker gearing up to change course.

'Thank you, sir.'

'Nancy Beddoes comes first, though.' There was always going to be a catch. 'Dull though it is, we have to give priority to the crimes we know exist.' The inspector looked up. 'Which means Aidan Seed et al. will have to wait until you've completed your grand tour of the UK and all two hundred and seventy-six statements are in.'

'But, sir . . .'

'But sir nothing. Do you own a road atlas?' Proust reached into the pocket of the jacket that was draped over his chair and pulled out a ten-pound note. 'Buy one.' He threw the money at Simon. 'It's about time you learned that some maps go over the page.'

Ruth Bussey's front door stood wide open. The black VW Passat—the one she'd made her escape in on Friday—wasn't there, but there was a green Daewoo parked on a grass verge outside the lodge house, so someone was in. Aidan Seed?

Charlie moved out of the way as two jogging women appeared, chatting as they ran between the bollards at the park gates and up the path, past the lodge. With Ruth's coat draped over her arm, Charlie walked towards the house. She'd been hoping to have another chat with Ruth, but perhaps it was better this way, since Charlie was also curious to meet Aidan, see what sort of man confesses to a murder that neither he nor anyone else has committed.

She'd got as far as the small porch when a tall, thin man wearing a yellow fluorescent jacket over a grey suit darted out of the house, nearly banging into her. He had a wispy beard, glasses with large lenses. Charlie thought he looked exactly as a goat would, if animals were people. There was a flare of recognition in his eyes when he saw her. 'Oh,' he said.

'You know who I am?' Stupid question. Who in Spilling didn't know? It was a small town and Charlie was its most famous fuck-up.

'I know that coat,' he said, looking down at it to avoid meeting Charlie's eye. 'Ruth picked a bad time to lose it with the boiler packing in. It breaks down every three months on average, and Muggins here has to spend a day twiddling my thumbs, waiting for the engineers. Never be a landlord, that'd be my advice to you.'

'You're not Aidan, then,' said Charlie.

The goat extended his hand. 'Malcolm Fenton, Area Manager for Parks and Landscapes. I'll take that off you if you like.'

Charlie hesitated. If she gave the coat to Fenton, she'd lose her opportunity to talk to Ruth again. Mainly she wanted to ask about the newspaper article. What was Ruth's interest in her? She was about to tell Fenton she'd catch Ruth at work when she saw that she'd lost his attention. 'On time for once,' he said, looking over her shoulder. 'Excuse me.' Charlie turned and watched him trot down the porch steps. Beyond the park gates, prevented from entering by the two black bollards, was a white van with the words 'Winchelsea Combi Boilers' painted in blue on its side.

Fenton pulled a large bunch of keys out of his pocket, unlocked something at the top of one of the bollards and lowered it into the ground. Behind the van's greasy windscreen, one of the men from Winchelsea Combi Boilers chewed gum with a ferocity that made Charlie wonder if it wasn't gum at all but an organ torn from its rightful owner's body.

She glanced at the lodge's open door, started to edge towards it. 'Sorry,' Fenton shouted after her. 'I'd rather you didn't go in. I know you're a policewoman, but all the same.' He looked apologetic. Policewoman—did people still say that? 'If you leave the coat with me, I'll see Ruth gets it.'

'The door's wide open,' Charlie pointed out. 'The boiler re-pairmen are going in, presumably.'

'They practically live here,' said Fenton irritably. 'I don't mean to be ungracious, but Ruth's a private person. I know for a fact she wouldn't want me to let a stranger into her home.' He sighed. 'This is a little awkward. I mean, clearly Ruth's made herself known to you if you've got her coat, but . . .' He looked away quickly, annoyed with himself for saying too much. 'She didn't tell me she was going to make contact with you, or to expect you, so I'm afraid I can't let you in.'

Fenton's choice of words made Charlie feel uneasy. Had Ruth confided in him about Aidan's bizarre confession? No, it didn't fit. *Made herself known to you.* That implied Ruth was someone the police might either want or need to know about, that there was a pre-existing connection of some sort between them. Char-lie couldn't understand it.

'Do you know a Mary Trelease?' she asked.

No adverse reaction to the name. Fenton considered it, then shook his head.

'Is that CCTV?' Charlie was looking at the lodge's roof. She'd spotted another camera on the other side of the porch, above a ground-floor window. Was that why there were leaves clinging to the house's every surface, for camouflage? 'When were the cameras put in?'

'Why do you want to know that?' asked Fenton.

Charlie substituted a smile for an answer.

'The park had an infestation of teenage thugs a while back. Ruth suggested installing CCTV. The council thought it was a good idea.' His tone was defensive.

'When you say Ruth's a private person . . .?' Charlie began.

'I don't like the slant of your questions. Ruth's a perfectly or-dinary woman and an excellent tenant. She takes her responsi-bilities seriously, that's all. Hers is a service tenancy.' Fenton sighed, as if he'd been tricked into saying more than he wanted to. 'The lodge tenant, in exchange for a much-reduced rent, is supposed to be of assistance in the park when necessary, particularly in emergencies and out of hours. If someone falls down and breaks their leg on the path, Ruth would be expected to get involved—she's got a list of emergency numbers, but she'd be the first point of contact.'

'Most of the private people I know wouldn't live in a public park,' said Charlie, guessing that Fenton had been surprised by Ruth's suggestion of installing surveillance cameras, or else why the guarded reaction? Had it been a suggestion or a request, a plea? What was it about his model tenant that Fenton was withholding out of loyalty?

His resistance was like bellows to a fire. Charlie was tempted to run up the steps and into Blantyre Lodge after the men from Winchelsea Combi Boilers. How much of Ruth Bussey's home would she be able to see before Fenton dragged her out? Mad people's houses had a distinctive look about them; you knew instantly. She sighed. That way lay an official complaint, which was all she needed. She slipped the article from the *Rawndesley and Spilling Telegraph* out of the coat's pocket and put it in her bag.

'Put that back,' Fenton snapped. Oh, he knew Charlie's history all right, and she knew his type. He wouldn't have dared take that tone with the police under normal circumstances. Only with an officer he knew had been disgraced and nearly fired.

She'd changed her mind about giving him the coat. 'I don't feel comfortable about leaving this with a stranger,' she said. 'Ask Ruth to make contact with me again if she wants it back.'

After Blantyre Park, Charlie told herself she was going straight to work to get on with the chore that had been hanging over her for the past fortnight: drafting Counsellor Vesey's survey and accompanying letter. She told herself again and again, but no matter how many times she repeated the instruction, her brain defied her, and she found herself driving out to the Winstanley estate. She'd had enough of hearing second-hand reports; she wanted to meet the still-alive Mary Trelease, see if she was frightened, as Gibbs had claimed, or if there was anything about her that might frighten someone else.

Like Aidan Seed. Charlie frowned at the idea. It would be a strange reaction to fear, pretending you'd killed somebody. *Unless you can't bear the thought that they exist. So you pretend they don't any more, and you cast yourself in the role of killer because it makes you feel brave instead of like their victim . . .* Charlie smirked at her silly theory. It was impossible to speculate, that was what made this different from every other situation she'd dealt with since joining the police. Different, and harder to stop thinking about. Usually she could come up with some sort of hypothesis to use as a starting point, however wrong it turned out to be. Not now. She could think of literally nothing that would explain the behaviour of Ruth Bussey and Aidan Seed—even a rampant shared insanity didn't seem to fit the bill. It made her feel stupid, which she hated.

At the cul-de-sac end of Megson Crescent, three young boys with shaved heads were doing wheelies on their bikes. When Charlie got out of her car and they saw her uniform, they disappeared so fast that she couldn't help thinking of the scene in the film *E.T.*, where the kids pedal so hard they take off into the sky.

She locked her car. Loud, aggressive music was coming from one of the houses at the far end of the road, near where the boys had been. She supposed she'd better try and track them down to whichever house they'd holed up in, encourage them to make their way to school. Not that their teachers would thank her for it.

As she walked along the cul-de-sac, she counted off the odd numbers. Five and seven each had a boarded-up window. In a first-floor window at number nine, she saw parts of small faces before the curtains were yanked shut. She knew that if she rang the doorbell, she'd get no answer.

Higher priority than the boys was getting that music turned down. As she got closer to the house it was coming from, she felt the pavement shake under her feet. She couldn't believe it when she saw the number on the door: fifteen. The thumping noise was coming from Mary Trelease's house. Ruth Bussey had said Mary Trelease was around forty, so what was she doing listening to . . .? Charlie dismissed the ridiculous thought, embarrassed by it. What were forty-year-olds supposed to listen to? James Galway, with the volume turned down extra-low so as not to wake the cat?

She'll never hear the doorbell, thought Charlie, pressing it anyway. She stood back and stared at the house. Like the others on the street, it was an ugly red-brick semi with an entirely flat façade, no bay windows to give it character. Weeds grew between the broken flagstones that led to the front door. By the side of the house, next to a drain, was a scalloped lead pot with a small dead tree in it. Charlie touched one of the branches. It crumbled between her finger and thumb.

She stepped back out on to the road and looked up at the top windows. None of the curtains were open. All were as thin as handkerchiefs, she noticed, and they'd been hung badly, so they didn't fall straight. Some had holes in them where the fabric had decayed, been torn or burned. This was far from being the sort of house Charlie would have expected an artist to live in. She struggled to bring to mind the few facts she knew about art or artists. Vincent Van Gogh had been dirt poor. Olivia had made Charlie watch a docu-drama about him once. Admittedly, he probably wouldn't have given a toss about the state of his curtains.

'They can't have called you already. I've only been gone five minutes.' An angry, skinny woman with deeply ingrained wrinkles around her eyes, nose and mouth appeared beside Charlie. It looked almost as if someone had scored down the middle of her face with a Stanley knife, so pronounced were the lines. She had a caramel-coloured birthmark, the one Aidan Seed had described to Simon, and was wearing a black duffle-coat, black trousers, white trainers and a purple woolly hat that looked as if it had a lot of hair stuffed into it. Her ears, Charlie noticed, were tiny, the lobes almost non-existent—again, as Aidan had described. In her gloved hands the woman—Mary Trelease—held a packet of Marlboro reds, a red plastic lighter and what looked like a small green box.

'They?' Charlie asked. On first appearance, there was nothing sinister about Trelease. She dressed like someone who didn't give a damn what she looked like. Charlie had been through similar phases.

'The neighbours. I'll turn it down, all right? Give me a chance.' She sprinted off round the side of the house. Charlie followed her. It was hard to avoid hearing the song that was blasting out, the word 'survivor' being repeated again and again. It was a more stringent and hysterical than usual variation on the theme of he-done-me-wrong-but-I'm-still-strong. It was the sort of song Charlie would write if she could write songs, full of posturing and bravado.

After a few seconds the music stopped, though its imprint still pulsed in Charlie's brain. She took the open kitchen door as an invitation, and was about to go inside when Mary startled her by jumping down from the doorstep on to the narrow path that adjoined the house. 'There,' she said. 'Satisfied?' She eyed Charlie contemptuously, shifting her negligible weight from one trainered foot to the other, still holding the cigarettes, lighter and green container, which Charlie now saw was a box of Twinings Peppermint tea.

'Are you Mary Trelease?'

'Yes.'

'What was the song?'

'Pardon?'

'The song you've just turned off. What's it called?' Some people were willing to answer harmless questions; others weren't. Charlie wanted to know which category Mary Trelease belonged to before she asked her about Aidan Seed and Ruth Bussey.

'Is this some kind of joke? Look, if the petty arseholes at number twelve have—'

'I'm not here about the music,' said Charlie. 'Though while we're on the subject, that volume's unacceptable at any time of day. Why leave it on so loud if you're going out?'

Mary opened her packet of cigarettes, put one in her mouth and lit it. She didn't offer one to Charlie. 'If you're not here about the music, I can guess what you are here about.'

Her voice was at odds with her surroundings. Charlie hadn't been able to hear it properly for as long as the music had been playing. What was someone who spoke like a member of the royal family doing on the Winstanley estate? Why hadn't Simon mentioned her accent? 'My name's Sergeant Zailer, Charlie Zailer. I'm part of the community policing team for this area.'

'Zailer? The same Sergeant Zailer who was all over the news a couple of years back?' Mary's brown eyes were wide, avid.

Charlie nodded, struggling to contain her discomfort. Most people weren't quite so open about it. Most people shuffled and looked away, as Malcolm Fenton had, and their awkwardness made her forget, for a second, her own pain and humiliation. I should have resigned two years ago, she thought. All her allies, the people who had told her she'd done nothing wrong and advised her to brazen it out, had done her a disservice. For two years, Charlie had felt as if she'd been in hiding in public; if there was a trickier professional situation to be in, she couldn't imagine what it might be.

'Community policing,' said Mary, smiling vaguely. 'Does that mean they demoted you?'

'I transferred. By choice.'

'It was just after I moved to Spilling when it was in the papers,' said Mary. 'Made me wonder what sort of area I'd moved to, but I don't think there have been any policing scandals since, have there?' She smiled. 'You're a one-off.' Seeing Charlie flustered and at a loss, she added, 'Don't worry, it makes no odds to me. You'll have had your reasons, no doubt.'

'No doubt,' said Charlie brusquely, 'and obviously I'm not here to talk about that.'

'Well, you've picked the wrong house if your visit's community-related. You won't find much of a community round here. And, such as it is, I'm not part of it. I'm an outsider who drinks funny tea.' Mary waved the green Twinings box at Charlie. 'You should have seen their faces in the corner shop when I asked them to stock it. Anyone would have thought I was proposing to drink babies' blood.' She raised her cigarette to her thin lips. Her index and middle fingers were stained a dark yellow, almost brown.

'No, it's you I want,' Charlie told her.

'Then I know why.' The response was smooth and instantaneous. 'You're here to ask me about a man I don't know. A man called Aidan Seed. DC Christopher Gibbs came on Friday for the same reason, and DC Simon Waterhouse on Saturday. Unlike you, they didn't pull bits off my tree.'

'I didn't . . . The tree's dead,' said Charlie.

'Taking its pulse, were you? If dried flowers can be beautiful, why can't dried trees? I like my garden. I like my dead tree, and its pot. Look at this.' She led Charlie over to the wall that separated her house from the one next to it. There was something protruding from one of the cracks that looked like a green rose, but with petals that were oddly rubbery, almost cactus-like, pink-edged. 'Isn't it lovely?' said Mary. 'It's called a sempervivum. It's not there by accident or neglect. Someone planted it so that it would grow out of the wall, but you could easily mistake it for a weed. I'm sure you did.'

'Can I come in for a few minutes?' Charlie asked, feeling as if she'd lost any potential advantage she might have had. She wished she was in her office, 'helping' Counsellor Geoff Vesey to draft his letter and questionnaire—writing them for him, in other words. Vesey was Chair of the Culver Valley Police Authority, an organisation that monitored, among other things, public confidence in the police. Charlie's confidence in him was zero; the man couldn't even come up with a list of questions on his own.

'You can come in, but only because I'm not working,' said Mary. 'If I were busy, I'd ask you to leave. I'm a painter.' Her eyes narrowed. 'But you know that already. I'm sure you know all about me.' In spite of what she'd said, she was still blocking the entrance to the house with her narrow body.

'You didn't let Chris Gibbs in,' said Charlie. 'You nearly didn't let Simon Waterhouse in.'

'Because I was working on a painting, one I stayed up all night to finish. As soon as I've got rid of you, I'll be going to bed. Anyway, that's why the song was on so loud, if you care: I was celebrating. Do you have a favourite song?'

It was ridiculous not to want to answer. ' "Trespass" by Limited Sympathy.'

'The song that was on before—that's mine.'

Charlie wasn't going to ask again what it was. *If you care.* She didn't.

' "Survivor" by Destiny's Child,' said Mary in a brittle voice, like a pupil forced to hand over a treasured forbidden item to her teacher. As she spoke, the lines on her face rearranged themselves, criss-crossing around her mouth. Charlie had heard that excessively thin people aged more severely than plumper ones, but even so . . . 'I could tell you what I love about it, but I don't suppose you're interested. I suppose you're one of those people who only puts on a CD if you've got guests for dinner, with the volume down so low that nobody can hear it.'

'I don't do that, actually,' said Charlie. 'I don't rupture my neighbours' eardrums, either.'

'I told you: I was celebrating. Finishing a piece of work you're happy with—it's such a buzz. Like being able to fly. I wanted to reward myself, so I put on my favourite song and went round the corner to buy some smokes and peppermint tea. I put the volume up high so that I'd hear the song while I was in the shop.' Mary smiled vaguely, a faraway look in her eyes, as if she was thinking back to something that had happened years ago.

Charlie's skin prickled with apprehension. She thought of Ruth Bussey saying, 'I'm frightened something's going to happen.' 'Could I see the painting?' she asked. 'The one you've just finished?'

'No.' A reflex response. Anger. 'Why? You're not interested in my work. The other two weren't. You just want to check I'm who I say I am.' Mary dropped her cigarette on the path, didn't bother to extinguish it. It lay there, burning. 'You'd better come in,' she said. 'I'll go and dig out my passport and driver's licence again. This time I won't bother putting them back in the drawer, since one of you's certain to turn up tomorrow.'

Charlie followed her into a tiny brown kitchen that contained a free-standing electric cooker with a grime-encrusted top, a stained metal sink and a row of cabinets with uncloseable doors that hung askew. Mottled brown linoleum covered the floor, studded with cigarette burns. *No one has touched this place for at least thirty years*, thought Charlie, and then: *it looks even worse than my house, and that's saying something*. 'I don't want to see any ID,' she said. 'My colleagues are satisfied that you're who you say you are, and that's good enough for me.'

Mary undid the buttons of her duffle-coat and let it slide off her arms. When it hit the floor, she kicked it to one side. It lay in a heap by the kitchen door. 'It doubles as a draught excluder,' she told Charlie. Her refined voice sounded so out of place in the drab, cramped room that Charlie wondered if she was a Trustafarian—playing at slumming it, rubbing shoulders with bona fide poor people in an attempt to make her art more authentic, knowing she could escape to Daddy's mansion in Berkshire whenever it suited her.

Mary pulled off her hat, releasing a huge silver-black frizz that tumbled down her back. 'Aidan Seed's a picture-framer,' said Charlie matter-of-factly. 'Did Chris Gibbs or Simon Waterhouse tell you that?'

'Yes. I see the connection: I'm a painter, he's a framer. Doesn't mean I know him.'

'You haven't heard the name? Perhaps from other artists, even if you don't know him personally? I'd have thought, with Spilling being the size it is . . .'

'I don't know any artists,' said Mary. 'Don't think that because I'm a painter I'm in any way part of the art world. I hate all that nonsense. You join some group and next thing you know you're on a committee, organising quizzes and raffles. That's what the local art scene would be like in a town like this, and as for the London scene—all that Charles Saatchi garbage has got nothing to do with art. It's marketing—it markets its own brand of marketing and nothing else. It's about creating appetites, artificially—there's no real hunger in it. There's nothing real about it.'

'Do you know Ruth Bussey?' Charlie asked.

Mary's surprise was unmistakeable. 'Yes. Well . . .' She frowned. 'I don't exactly know her. I've met her twice. I'm hoping to persuade her to sit for me. Why?'

'How did you meet her?'

'Why's Ruth of interest to the police?'

'If you could answer my—'

'This is someone who's been inside my home.' Mary's voice was shrill. Frightened, thought Charlie. 'Why are you asking about her? Has she got some connection to this Aidan Seed person?'

'How about we do a swap?' Charlie suggested. 'You show me some of your work, I answer your question. I *am* interested, although I know sod-all about art, except that all the best stuff seems to be by dead people.'

Mary's face went rigid. She stared at Charlie. 'Are you playing games with me?'

'No.' *Of all the pissing stupid things to say.* All over her body, Charlie's skin felt cold. 'I meant, you know, Picasso, Rembrandt . . . I meant that nowadays art seems to mean slices of dead cow and balls of elephant dung.'

'I'm not dead,' said Mary very carefully, as if she wanted Charlie to pay attention.

Charlie thought that people who believed in ghosts deserved to have their brains confiscated indefinitely. She couldn't understand why it should freak her out so much to be standing in the kitchen of a shabby ex-council house listening to a straight-faced woman insist that she wasn't dead.

'I'm alive and my work is excellent,' said Mary less vociferously. 'Sorry to jump down your throat, but it's depressing to hear what Joe Public thinks: that anyone with talent is famous already, basically. And dead, of course—all geniuses are dead. If they died young and tragically and in poverty, then all the better.'

Charlie exhaled slowly. Simon hadn't told Mary what Aidan Seed had said about her. Neither, he'd told Charlie, had Gibbs. *What did it mean? What did any of it mean?*

'Do you think you need to suffer—I mean suffer deeply—in order to be a true artist?' Mary asked, screwing up her eyes, pushing her wild hair behind her ears with both hands. Was it scorn in her voice, or something else?

'I wouldn't say the one follows from the other,' said Charlie. 'You could suffer the torments of the damned and still not be able to draw or paint for toffee.'

Mary seemed to like that answer. 'True,' she said. 'Nothing great is so easily reducible. I asked DC Waterhouse the same question. He said he didn't know.'

Another thing Simon hadn't mentioned. He'd certainly have had an opinion, thought Charlie. Clearly he hadn't wanted to share it with this peculiar woman.

'I've changed my my mind,' said Mary. 'I will show you my work. I want you to see it. There's one condition, though. We agree now that nothing I'm going to show you is for sale. Even if you see a picture you think would be perfect for—'

'You don't need to worry about that,' Charlie told her. 'I haven't got the money to buy original art. How much do you normally sell your paintings for? Does it vary depending on size, or . . .?'

'I don't.' Mary's face turned blank. *As if she'd been expecting trouble and now it had arrived.* 'I never sell my work. Ever.'

'But . . . so . . .?'

'You mean why. That's what you want to ask me: why? If that's what you want to ask, ask.'

'I was actually thinking more . . . are all your pictures here, then? In this house?'

There was a long pause before Mary said, 'Pretty much.'

'Wow. How long have you been painting?'

'I started in 2000.'

'Professionally, you mean? What about as a child?'

'No,' said Mary. 'I never painted or drew as a child. Apart from when I had to, at school.'

Of course not professionally; painters who sold none of their work couldn't be called professional. I should be asking different questions, thought Charlie. I should be asking about Aidan Seed and Ruth Bussey, and then I should be going to work. Why aren't I?

She knew the answer, but it was a few seconds before she was willing to admit it to herself: because now she too was . . . scared would have been putting it too strongly, but something about 15 Megson Crescent and its occupant unsettled her. Perhaps it was nothing more than a bad atmosphere in the house, the result of years of neglect. Whatever it was, Charlie couldn't allow herself to give in to the urge to get the hell out as quickly as possible.

'I said you could see my paintings, not grill me about them,' said Mary. 'If you're not careful I'll change my mind. I don't normally show my work to anybody.'

'Why me, then?'

Mary nodded. 'It's a good question.' She smiled, as if she knew the answer but wasn't about to divulge it. 'Come on. Most of the pictures are upstairs.'

Charlie followed her into a narrow hall which was as unattractive as the kitchen. The carpet had rotted away from the walls on both sides, and was patterned with red and brown swirls, apart from near the front door where it was black. The wallpaper had half peeled off the walls. It was dark beige with a few lighter streaks and patches; it might have been magnolia at one time. A small, low radiator had lost most of its dirty-grey chipped paint. Charlie stopped to look at the painting above it of a fat man, a woman and a boy of about fourteen or fifteen sitting round a small table. Only the boy was fully dressed; the other two were in dressing-gowns. The woman was small and slender with sharp, close-set features. She was shielding her eyes with her hands and looking down. Her posture suggested a headache. No, a hangover—there were empty bottles all over the table. A morning-after-a-heavy-night scene, Charlie guessed.

At the foot of the stairs was another picture of the same man and woman, this time without the boy. The woman was combing her hair in front of a mirror, wearing a strappy white nightie. Behind her, the fat man lay on a bed reading a tabloid newspaper.

Charlie was impressed. The paintings were too seedy to be conventionally appealing, but they had life in them, and seemed to create more energy in the hall than the shadeless bulb Mary had turned on as she passed. The colours were extraordinary—vivid without being in any way buoyant or heartening. The effect was one of grim cheerlessness exposed in the glare of a searchlight. 'Are these yours?' Charlie asked, guessing they must be.

Mary was halfway up the stairs. She made a noise that was hard to interpret. 'I didn't steal them, if that's what you're asking.'

'No, I meant . . .'

'No. They're not mine.'

So she hadn't misunderstood. She'd been playing for time.

At the top of the stairs there was another picture, and a further two on the landing: the woman and the boy sitting at op-

posite ends of a lumpy yellow sofa with a torn cover, not looking at each other; the man standing next to a closed door, his
hand raised to knock, his mouth open. The third painting featured two different people: a young man and woman, both dark
with heavy eyebrows and square foreheads, both overweight,
playing cards at the same table that was in the picture downstairs.

Mary pushed open one of the three doors on the landing,
stood back and gestured for Charlie to go in ahead of her. *The
front bedroom.* Aidan Seed had told Simon he'd killed Mary
in here, left her body in the centre of the bed. Charlie's throat
felt tight as she walked in. I'm being ridiculous, she told herself. Would Mary be opening the door if there were a corpse
behind it?

The room was full of pictures, so full that after a few steps
Charlie had to stop. Many of them were obscured from view,
either by other paintings, or because they were turned the wrong
way. Charlie tried to take in as much as she could. There was a
picture of a large stone building with a square tower, a lot of
head-and-shoulders portraits, mainly of women, all of whom
looked weary, defeated by life. Leaning against one wall were
four or five big pinky-brown abstracts that looked like close-ups
of scarred human flesh, with lots of intersecting lines and funny
ridges. Like the paintings downstairs and on the landing, none
of these was conventionally beautiful, but their power was un-
deniable. Charlie found herself needing to stare at them.

Like the paintings downstairs . . . Something else was unde-
niable, and yet Mary had denied it. 'If you painted all these, then
you painted the others as well,' said Charlie, gesturing towards
the door. 'Even I can tell they're all by the same artist.'

Mary looked put out. After a few seconds she said, 'I painted
them, yes. All of them.'

Charlie would have felt pedantic asking her why, in that case,
she'd pretended she hadn't. Was she embarrassed to have her own
pictures up on the walls? She didn't seem the sort of person who

would give a toss about seeming vain. In this room, all the paintings were framed; the ones Charlie had seen on the walls had been hung unframed. Somehow, it seemed the wrong way round.

'Who are they all?' Charlie asked.

'The people in the pictures? Neighbours, mostly, or people who used to live round here. The Winstanley estate collection.' Mary's smile was like a sneer, directed at herself. She nodded at the portraits stacked against the opposite wall. 'I couldn't tell you most of those people's names now—I paid them, they sat for me, that was it.'

Charlie looked again at the faces, to see if she recognised anyone she'd ever arrested.

'You're wondering why I'd choose to paint strangers who mean nothing to me,' said Mary, though Charlie hadn't been. 'Painting people you care about is like offering yourself an emotional breakdown. I avoid it if I can, though it's not always possible. Sometimes a compulsion takes hold and you have to suffer the consequences.'

Charlie saw the tension in her posture as she spoke, the way she hunched herself together so that her body became more compact.

'If you had to paint a portrait, who would you choose? Your fiancé?' Mary was looking at Charlie's hand. 'I saw the ring.'

'I really don't know.' Charlie felt her skin heat up. No way could she paint Simon; it would be too intimate, too close. He'd never let her. He'd ended up staying the night on Saturday, after the party; he and Charlie had slept side by side, but they hadn't kissed or touched. The hug he'd given her downstairs—that had been it in terms of physical contact. Still, Charlie was pleased. She'd never been able to persuade him to stay the night before. It was progress.

'Definitely not your fiancé,' said Mary. 'So either you don't care enough about him to bother, in which case I'd call off the engagement, or you know what I'm talking about: like offering yourself a breakdown.'

'You said pretty much all your pictures were here,' Charlie changed the subject. 'Where are the rest, if you never sell your work?'

'Ruth Bussey's got one. I gave it to her as a present.' A smile played around Mary's lips. 'Remember the sempervivum I showed you outside?'

Charlie didn't. Then she realised Mary was talking about the rubbery green rose sticking out of the wall.

'Ruth told me it was called that. I didn't know. I don't know any plant names. My experience of gardening is limited. I completely ruined a garden once and decided to leave it at that. After I gave Ruth the painting—I hadn't given anybody a present in a long time and it felt strange—but I thought to myself, she's given me a present too. That name: sempervivum. Live for ever, live always—that's what it means.'

'You aren't in the habit of giving presents?' Charlie asked gently. There was a story here, and she found herself wanting to know what it was. Where was the garden Mary had mentioned? Where did she live before Megson Crescent?

'No presents,' said Mary. 'I'm not giving you a picture for free, and I won't sell you one. I only gave Ruth one as a form of apology.'

'For what?'

'I lost her her job. It's a long story, one I'm not going to tell you. It doesn't show either of us in a good light.'

'You mean her job at the Spilling Gallery?'

'What does it matter?' Mary asked warily.

A woman with a lot of boundaries, thought Charlie. *Too many for life to be easy for her.* 'I just wondered. That's where Ruth worked before she worked for Aidan Seed.'

Charlie had never seen a person's face shake before, but Mary's did. It was as if she'd suffered an internal electric shock. 'Ruth . . . Ruth works for Aidan Seed?' She tucked her hair behind her ear, repeating the action, three, four times.

'They also live together,' said Charlie. 'As a couple.'

All the colour drained from Mary's face. 'That's not true. Ruth lives alone. In the lodge house at Blantyre Park. Why are you lying?'

'I'm not. I don't understand. Why does it matter? You say you don't know Aidan.'

'My picture. I gave Ruth my picture.' She bit her lip. 'Where are my cigarettes? I need a cigarette.' She made no attempt to look for them. Her eyes were blank, moving to and fro, not settling on anything for long. 'What's Aidan Seed done? I need to know. Why are the police after him?'

Not knowing if it would prove to be the key that unlocked everything or a disastrous error, Charlie said, 'As far as we know, Aidan's harmed nobody. But *he's* telling us different. He's saying he hurt someone, badly, and he says that person was you.'

Mary's chin jutted out. Charlie guessed she had resolved to show no more emotion after her brief lapse. Another shock, then.

Charlie took a step towards her. 'Mary, believe me, I know how odd this sounds. Aidan Seed came to us voluntarily, wanting to confess to a crime. He described you—your appearance, where you live, your work . . .'

Mary wrapped her arms around herself, hugged herself tightly.

In for a penny, thought Charlie. 'He seems to have got hold of the idea that he killed you,' she said.

'Not me.' Mary let her head fall back, then straightened up, her eyes locking on Charlie's. 'Not me.'

5

Monday 3 March 2008

I'm cutting glass when I hear footsteps on the path outside. I look up, see a man's face through the window. I don't recognise him. Aidan stops what he's doing. His foot is on the pedal of the mitre machine, but he doesn't push it down. Normally he stops work only when he has to, when a customer is standing in front of him, and to pretend not to have noticed for a second longer would be too rude even for Aidan to get away with. A lot of the people we frame for dislike him, but they don't go elsewhere. When I first started here, he told me, 'You can be friendly to clients if you want to, but friendliness takes time. Your job, our job, is to protect the art people bring in. Remember that. Think of a picture as being in danger until it's properly framed. Protection is at the heart of picture-framing. That's why we do it—it's not for decoration.'

The wooden door scrapes along the ground as it's pushed open. 'Hello?' a deep voice calls out.

I'm about to answer when I see another face at the window and my breath turns solid in my lungs. Charlie Zailer. What's she doing here? Are she and the man together?

'You must be Ruth Bussey. DC Simon Waterhouse, Culver Valley CID.' He opens a small wallet and shows me his police identification. He's a heavy, rough-faced man with big hands and too-short trousers that don't quite reach the tops of his shoes.

Sergeant Zailer smiles at me. She says nothing about my coat and I don't ask. She hasn't brought it with her. When she tells Aidan her name, I will him not to look at me, not to let his surprise show. 'Okay if we have a chat?' she says.

'I've got work to do.' Aidan doesn't sound surprised, only sullen.

'It won't take long.'

'I talked to him on Saturday.' Aidan jerks his head in Waterhouse's direction. 'I've got nothing to add to what I said then.'

'Have a guess where I spent most of this morning?' Charlie Zailer's tone is soothing and teasing at the same time.

'No, thanks.'

'Fifteen Megson Crescent.'

This is followed by a long silence. DC Waterhouse and I look at one another, wondering if one of us will have to break it; at least, that's what I'm wondering.

'Fifteen Megson Crescent is where Mary Trelease lives. That's who I spent the morning with: Mary Trelease.'

Aidan gives her a cold look. 'How can a dead woman live anywhere?' he says. 'I killed her.'

Sergeant Zailer nods. 'Simon—that's DC Waterhouse—he told me you've convinced yourself of that. I can assure you, you're wrong. I met Mary Trelease, spoke to her, saw her breathing and moving around.'

Aidan pulls the underpinner towards him, takes two mitred frame edges and puts them in the machine. *Back to work.*

'Do you think I'm lying?'

I can't stand the stifling tension in the air. 'Aidan, answer her!'

'If you hop in the back of my car, I'll take you to her house so that you can see for yourself that she's fine.'

'No.'

'How did you meet Mary?' Sergeant Zailer's voice is gently insistent. 'You didn't tell Simon the full story, did you? Will you tell it to me?'

'No.'

'Mary says she's never met you. Which, if she's telling the truth, means you've never met her.'

He looks up, angry to have his attention taken away from his underpinning. 'If I killed her, I must have met her. It's simple logic.' How can he be angry? How does he expect the police to react?

'Okay,' says Sergeant Zailer. 'So tell me about meeting Mary.'

Silence. I stare at him, silently urging him to answer, knowing he won't. My last hope is disintegrating and there's nothing I can do. Nobody can help if Aidan won't talk, not even the police.

'Aidan? How many times did you and Mary meet before you killed her?'

'He hasn't killed anybody,' I say, starting to cry.

Sergeant Zailer turns her attention to me. 'Did he tell you he strangled Mary when she was naked? That he left her body in the middle of the bed, in the—'

'Shut up,' Aidan snaps.

A violent, sick feeling tears through me, making me gasp. *Strangled. Naked.*

'I don't think he told her,' says Waterhouse. 'Something I don't understand: you *did* tell Ruth that you killed Mary Trelease years ago. And you told me I'd find the body in the bed if I went to 15 Megson Crescent. Did you really think a dead body might lie undiscovered in a house for years?'

Aidan measures a length of nylon hanging cord and cuts it, as if no one has spoken. He isn't ignoring Waterhouse—it's more than that. He's pretending to be alone in the workshop, wishing us all away. 'Say something, Aidan!'

'Why don't you, if he won't?' Charlie Zailer asks me. 'You lied to me. You said you didn't know Mary Trelease, but she knows you. She told me she lost you your job, then felt guilty about it and gave you a painting. That true?'

I nod, forcing myself not to look at Aidan. I have no way of knowing how much of the story Mary told her.

'So you first met Mary when?'

'Last June.'

'June. So when Aidan told you in December that he'd killed her years ago, you'd in fact met her six months previously. Presumably you told him he was mistaken. Ruth? Did you tell him that?'

'I . . .'

'She told me,' says Aidan. 'I told her she was wrong, same as I told DC Gibbs and DC Waterhouse.'

'Mary Trelease is an artist,' Waterhouse takes over, and I release the breath I've been holding. He isn't interested in the Spilling Gallery, my run-in with Mary. No one can force me to talk about it if I don't want to. 'Your work must bring you into contact with lots of artists. What do you think of them?'

'Some are all right.'

'The ones who aren't—what's wrong with them?'

Aidan sighs. 'They treat me like a skivvy.' He raises his hands. 'Manual work. It can't be a skilled profession if you get your hands dirty, that's what some of them think. You meet them in a restaurant in town and they stare at you blankly—they don't recognise you clean. When you say hello to them and they make the connection, you can see the shock on their faces: a common labourer in a posh restaurant—who'd have believed it? Then you get the ones who paint the same picture over and over again and think they've got a unique style, rather than only one idea, and the ones who only paint in their favourite colours, the same ones they buy all their clothes and carpet their living rooms in.'

'You *really* don't like artists,' says Sergeant Zailer.

'Let's have one thing clear: I didn't kill Mary Trelease because of anything to do with her being an artist. I didn't know she was one until Ruth told me.'

'Where's the painting she gave you?' Waterhouse asks me. 'Can we see it?'

Pressure builds in my head. 'I haven't got it any more.'

'How come?'

'I . . .' I look at Aidan, but he turns away, lines up two more lengths of glued moulding. Why should I lie to protect him when he won't tell me what I'm protecting him from? 'I gave the picture to Aidan,' I tell Waterhouse. 'I haven't seen it since.'

Aidan shoves the underpinner away. 'Mary Trelease is dead,' he says through gritted teeth. 'Dead people don't paint pictures. Ruth brought home a picture by somebody—it was ugly, so I took it to a charity shop.' He's lying.

Charlie Zailer takes a step forward. 'The front bedroom at 15 Megson Crescent is full of Mary's paintings. So full I could hardly get in. You say you didn't know she was an artist. Weren't the paintings there when you were, when you killed her?'

'He didn't kill her!'

I'm surprised when he answers. 'No. No paintings, nowhere in the house.'

I catch the look that passes between Sergeant Zailer and DC Waterhouse. They're about to give up.

'I have to go out,' Aidan says.

'Where?' I ask, at the same time as DC Waterhouse is saying, 'Do you believe in ghosts, Aidan?'

'No. I believe in the material world: facts and science. I don't believe dead women come back to life,' he says quietly.

'Then, in your opinion, who is the woman that Sergeant Zailer, DC Gibbs and I have all met at 15 Megson Crescent? If you're certain you killed Mary Trelease, then the woman who looks like her and owns her home and paints her paintings, who has her passport, driving licence and other documents—she must be a ghost, surely—a very well-equipped one at that.'

'I told you: I don't believe in ghosts.' Aidan walks over to the small basin in the corner and turns both taps on hard. The workshop's plumbing is ancient; there's as much noise as there is water. 'The next time you come looking for me, be ready to charge me, or I'll have nothing to say.' He washes and dries his hands.

'You didn't answer Ruth's question,' says Waterhouse. 'You

volunteer that you killed someone years ago, but you won't tell her where you're going this afternoon.'

'Get out.'

'I think we've overstayed our welcome, Simon,' says Charlie Zailer.

'You did that when you crossed the threshold,' Aidan tells her. She gives him a contemptuous look on her way out.

Waterhouse lingers. 'You came to us, remember? Or does your memory wipe out things that have happened as well as inventing things that haven't?'

He's gone. They're both gone. Aidan slams the door, leans his head against it. Once he's breathing steadily again, he says, 'You said you went to the police. You didn't tell me you went to Charlotte Zailer.'

I haven't got the energy to pretend it was a coincidence that she turned up. Let him think what he wants.

'She's not your friend, Ruth. She might mean something to you, but you're nothing to her.'

'Where's the picture? *Abberton*—what have you done with it? Tell me what's going on.'

'Do you believe what Waterhouse said? That my memory's inventing things that haven't happened?' He starts to come towards me. 'If it hasn't happened, it's not a memory. Do you think it's possible to see the future?'

'No. What do you mean?'

'A clear image—like a photo, or a film—of something that hasn't happened yet but is going to happen.'

'No! Stop it! You're scaring me.'

'Me strangling that bitch Trelease—putting my hands round her throat and squeezing . . .'

'Don't.' I back away from him. He looks determined and, at the same time, terribly afraid. *Like a man walking into a fire.*

'They say she's alive. You say she's alive. Maybe you're all right. If you're right, then what I'm seeing in my head can't be the past. What if I haven't killed her, but I'm going to?'

'Aidan, don't do this,' I beg, putting my arms round him. He's rigid, like stone. 'What you're saying's not possible.'

'*Abberton*,' he mutters. 'It's part of a series. She hasn't done them all yet—maybe only that one, the first. But she'll do more. I can tell you how many there are going to be: nine. I can tell you what their names will be.' He pushes me out of the way, pulls the lid off a blue marker pen and starts to write on the side of a cardboard poster tube. He reads aloud as he writes, like someone in a trance. 'Abberton, Blandford, Darville, Elstow, Goundry, Heathcote, Margerison, Rodwell, Winduss.'

I stare at him, wondering who he is, who he's turning into. *He's sane.* When I told Charlie Zailer that, I believed it. 'Aidan, you're making no sense,' I say shakily.

He grips my arm. 'Go back to Megson Crescent,' he whispers, his face close to mine. 'If it's the future, it can change. It *has* to change. Tell her not to do the other paintings—make her stop. Tell her to get out of Spilling and go somewhere I won't find her . . .'

'Stop it!' I scream. 'Let go of me! It's not true. It's not possible to see the future! Why won't you tell me the truth?'

'Why won't you tell *me* the truth? What happened at Hansard's gallery that made you leave? What happened between you and her? You've never told me, not really. You want to know what I've done with *Abberton*? You want to know where I'm going when I walk out of here now? Tell me the story!'

'There's nothing to tell!' I sob. *No questions; we agreed.* Does he remember how we used to be, how easily we understood each other?

He pushes me away as if he can't stand to touch me any more, and heads for the door, grabbing his jacket on the way out. Alone in the workshop, I lock the door and turn off all the lights. I huddle in the corner by the electric heater and whisper to myself, 'There's nothing to tell,' as if by saying it I can make it true.

* * *

I first noticed the Spilling Gallery because of a painting that was in the window. I'd only lived in the Culver Valley for eleven days at that point, though I regarded it as my home in the sense that I had no plans to go elsewhere. On the day I'd left Lincoln, I'd opened my road atlas at the page that showed a picture of the whole of Britain, closed my eyes and brought my index finger down on a random spot that turned out to be Combingham, a soulless town twelve miles west of Spilling, all precinct centres and roundabouts. I drove there and hated it on sight, so I got back in the car and drove away, with no idea where I was going.

I didn't go back the way I came; I took random turns, drove random distances before turning again. All I had with me apart from my grubby VW Passat was one hold-all containing a toothbrush and other necessary items; everything else I owned was in storage, and I was prepared never to see any of it again.

I took a left, then a right, then drove straight on for a mile or so. Eventually, when it dawned on me that I would have, at some point, to stop, I set myself a limit: I would drive in any direction that took my fancy, and wherever I found myself after thirty minutes was where I would stay. As long as it wasn't Lincoln or Combingham it would be all right.

I ended up on Spilling High Street, parked on a double yellow line only metres from Saul Hansard's gallery and framing shop, though I didn't notice it then. I don't know if there were different pictures in the window, or whether my picture was there and I wasn't paying attention, but as I walked up and down the road looking at my new home town, the Spilling Gallery didn't register with me at all. At that point I hadn't thought about paintings or art for more than about twenty seconds in total in my entire life, and most of those twenty seconds had been forced on me by the radio or the television, usually prompting me to change channels.

I noticed a wool shop called Country Yarns, lots of expensive boutiques selling clothes—separate ones for men, women and children. Those selling 'ladies' wear' mostly had long, elegant names that sounded as if they belonged to princesses. I made a point of not looking at the tiny maternity-wear shop with its pistachio-green-painted front, knowing it would never be relevant to me. It was unlikely I'd ever be able to have a baby; I didn't deserve one, in any case. There were three or four pubs that couldn't have looked more traditionally English if they'd tried, each with a more elaborately worded sign than the last, advertising the landlords as 'purveyors of fine quality fayre'. An independent bookshop caught my eye, and I decided I'd pay it a visit as soon as I'd got some accommodation sorted out; I didn't know anyone in Spilling and planned to avoid all forms of socialising, so I would be doing a lot of reading, and the four books I'd packed in my black hold-all wouldn't last me long.

In so far as anything could please me, I was pleased to see a market square with a church at one end, and, at the other, a music shop selling sheet music and instruments, a cheese shop and a gift shop called 'Surprises and Secrets'. The church was a beautiful building and, as long as I didn't have to set foot inside it, I was prepared to live near it and admire its contribution to the landscape. Even so, I couldn't help wondering how many of the people who attended its services did so by choice.

I walked into the first pub I came to, the Brown Cow, because there was a board outside it advertising rooms to let. The landlord seemed happy to rent one to me. He asked me how many nights I wanted it for. I opened my mouth, then found I had no answer ready. I didn't have a plan. 'Two weeks?' I suggested tentatively, prepared to be rebuffed.

His eyes lit up. 'Grand,' he said. 'And if you want to stay longer, you'll be more than welcome.'

Tears pricked my eyes and I had to look away. He was being too nice to me. Not knowing me, he wasn't aware that I deserved none of his kindness. Maybe I'll stay here until all my money runs out, I thought, and then go and jump in a river. All the books I'd read over the past four years—since Him and Her—had failed to convince me that this wouldn't be in many ways the best course of action. I'd made a decent profit from the sale of my house in Lincoln; it would take me a year, maybe two, to give it all away to the storage company in Lincoln and the landlord of the Brown Cow. It would be an interesting experiment, I thought: see how much I wanted to survive. If I ran out of money and wanted to live, I would be forced to do something about it. Or else I could not live. Five or six years after the event, no one would be able to say I hadn't let a decent interval elapse. I'd have had more than half a decade, by then, to reflect on what I'd done.

My first eleven days in Spilling were unremarkable. I slept a lot, went out for little walks round town. Every day I went to the independent bookshop, 'Word on the Street'. Never, I thought after my first visit, has a shop had a less appropriate name. Far from being hip and contemporary, Word on the Street—or Word, as everyone in Spilling seemed to call it— looked exactly like my idea of the perfect second-hand bookshop, except with new instead of used stock: low ceilings; creaking floors; several storeys, each a completely different shape from the others; not-quite-straight passageways leading from children's books to poetry, from the fiction wall to military history.

Within a week I'd bought Word's entire 'Mind, Body and Spirit' section, and the manager had promised to replenish his supplies. I nearly bought a book called *Shame*, the memoir of a woman who had escaped the arranged marriage her parents had tried to force upon her. I took it off the shelf, then happened to glance up and see a label that said 'Biography' at the top of the free-standing bookcase. The word made me think of my father, and I had to put the book back, even though I wanted to read it.

On my eleventh morning as a Spilling resident, I went into the cheese shop, Spilling Cheeses—at least half of the local shops were called Spilling this or that—and its owner, instead of asking if she could help me, launched into a monologue. 'I've seen you wandering up and down the high street,' she said. 'You do a lot of walking, don't you? You look at all the shops, but more often that not you don't go in. I've been wondering when you'd come in here.'

This was nearly enough to drive me out, and it certainly put me off buying any cheese, but I didn't want to appear rude. People who have made no serious mistakes in their lives might not understand this, but once you've done something wrong and suffered as a result, good behaviour takes on the utmost importance. I'd resolved never to behave badly again, in my eyes or in the world's. I knew there were people who were never condemned by anybody, not for a single word or deed: uncontroversial people, ordinary people. That was the sort of person I needed to be.

'If you like a good walk, you're crazy to march up and down the pavement, with all the car fumes and the noise,' said Spilling Cheeses' owner. 'There's lovely countryside less than five minutes away by car—nice and peaceful. Middle of nowhere, really. You won't meet another soul. I can direct you if you want.'

I smiled, told her 'No, thank you,' and left in a hurry, my heart pounding. I didn't want to be in the middle of nowhere, or even near it. I wanted other souls, plenty of them. I didn't want to speak to them or strike up friendships, but I wanted them to be there in case one day I needed them. Maybe I've chosen the wrong place, I thought. Maybe I should go to Birmingham or Manchester or London. I walked quickly up the street, careful not to look back at the cheese shop. Then I started to feel dizzy, as if I was going to fall. I stopped and leaned my head against the nearest window, hoping the glass would be cold.

It was. I pressed my burning forehead against it and imagined the coolness moving in waves from outside my head to inside. After a few seconds I felt stronger, and peeled myself off the window, embarrassed, hoping no one had seen me. There was an opaque patch on the glass in front of me where my breath had misted it, and behind that, a painting. The frame was black, but the picture itself was long and red. At first I thought red was the only colour, but then I saw small, uneven gold lines behind the red blotches. Standing back, I saw that they weren't blotches at all, but textured circles and ovals, almost like over-sized fingerprints. Each one was a slightly different shade and shape—some were more orange, some seemed to have a blue undertone.

There were dozens of colours in the picture, not one. When I looked carefully, I saw that every colour was in it. And, depending on how far away from it I stood, the intriguing shapes' relationships to one another changed. From close up, a smeared-looking orange sphere appeared to leap forward, but when I stood back, some of the longer, oval-shaped forms seemed more prominent.

I felt something move inside me, pushing away the layers of fear, guilt, shame and anger that had piled up in my heart and stifled all my memories of past happiness and, along with them, any hope of future happiness, since if you can't remember ever having felt a certain way then you can't believe you ever did or will again. It wasn't only that the painting was beautiful, or that when I looked at it, I felt that a bit of that beauty belonged to me; I felt as if someone was trying to communicate with me. It was a connection, a positive connection with another person, the artist—someone entirely non-threatening because I had never met them, nor was I likely to.

I had to have that picture. I pushed open the door to the Spilling Gallery and told the man I found inside—Saul Hansard—that I wanted the painting in the window and I would pay any price for it. 'Really?' He chuckled. 'What if I said seventy-five thousand pounds?'

'I haven't got seventy-five thousand pounds. How much is it?'

'You're in luck, then. It's two hundred and fifty pounds.'

I grinned. *In luck*. It felt true, for the first time in four years. 'Who painted it? What is it? Do you know anything about it?'

'Artist by the name of Jane Fielder. She lives in Yorkshire. It's the only one of hers I've got, or I'd be trying to flog you some more. *Something Wicked*, this one's called.' He was taking it out of the window as he spoke. 'See the faint gold writing behind the red thumbprints?'

'Thumbprints,' I murmured. So I'd been right, almost.

'Well, not really, but that's what they're supposed to represent. The gold writing goes all the way down, see? Two lines, repeated: 'By the pricking of my thumbs/Something wicked this way comes." Agatha Christie, via William Shakespeare.' Saul Hansard smiled at me and introduced himself. I didn't mind telling him my name because he was so obviously harmless. He was short, in his mid-sixties, I guessed, with flyaway sandy hair, bifocal glasses and trousers that were held up by red braces. I didn't know then that he wore the braces every day. He was thin and had one of those straight-up-and-down bodies, almost like a boy's—like a ten-year-old, tall for his age.

I took *Something Wicked* back to my room at the Brown Cow and leaned it against the wall. Looking at it became my main daily activity. I also, from then on, went to the Spilling Gallery every day. At first Saul kept explaining to me apologetically that he wasn't going to get new work in for a while. I didn't care. I was happy to look at the paintings he had on the walls, however many times I'd seen them before and even though I'd decided I didn't want to buy them. It wasn't that I didn't like them. Most of them were good, I thought, but they didn't make me feel the way *Something Wicked* did.

When I found out Saul framed as well as sold pictures, I started to spend afternoons with him in his workshop at the back of the gallery because it was a way of seeing more art. He was always behind with his workload, and while he got on with float-mounting and bevelling to a constant soundtrack of Classic FM, I would sift through piles of pictures waiting to be framed, looking for something that might mean as much to me as *Something Wicked* did.

After about a month, Saul said to me, 'Forgive me if I'm being nosey, Ruth, but . . . you evidently don't have a job.'

I told him I didn't. Looking at art was my job as far as I was concerned, and I didn't care if no one paid me for it.

'You wouldn't by any chance like to work here, would you?' he said. 'I'm sure I'm losing customers all the time, with it being just me—people come in and they can't find anyone because I'm here in the back, and so they turn tail and leave. I've been thinking that what I could really do with is a friendly face to welcome—'

'Yes,' I interrupted him. 'I'd love to.'

Saul beamed. 'What a stroke of luck,' he said. He uses the word luck a lot; it was one of the things I liked about him. 'You're here anyway, so you might as well be paid for it. And you can be the first to see any new work that comes in.'

My life changed very quickly after that. I knew I couldn't stay at the Brown Cow; I would need somewhere bigger, somewhere that could accommodate all the art I was going to buy. I rented Blantyre Lodge, got my things out of storage, raided Word on the Street's art section and read as much as I could about famous artists and their work.

I took occasional days off to go to Silsford, where there was another gallery that sold contemporary art, and found the second picture I fell in love with there: *Tree of Life* by an artist called Lynda Thomas. It was a stylised image of a tree with black branches that twisted upwards like thick curls of hair. If you fixed your eye on it and moved around the room, you saw little metallic glimmers of red, gold and silver peeping out from between the leaves. The background was midnight blue, and the tree, though dark, shone against it, full of a hidden mysterious force, but nothing dangerous, nothing threatening. The painting wasn't sentimental, though it might easily have been were the artist less talented.

I said all of this to Saul, not in the least embarrassed. I had known nothing about art for most of my life, but my sudden passion for it had given me confidence. I knew I was right because I felt it; I didn't care about critics or experts, and whether they'd agree with me.

Gradually, I built up a collection. I branched out from paintings to sculptures. I relaxed my rule a bit and allowed myself to buy work that I didn't love quite as much as *Something Wicked* and *Tree of Life*. In an art collection, I decided, one didn't necessarily need or want to respond to every piece with the same intensity. Besides, I discovered, some pictures grew on you. I told Saul about my change of policy, explaining that, as well as soulmates, a person needs friends and acquaintances. He agreed. 'Have you got any friends, Ruth?' he asked me, looking concerned. In general he avoided asking me personal questions; I could hardly begrudge him this one.

'I've got you,' I said, eyes fixed on the art magazine I was reading.

'Yes, but . . . apart from me. Have you got anyone else that you . . . see?'

'I see you,' I replied determinedly, starting to feel uneasy. 'Why? You're not planning on ditching me, are you? Closing the gallery and running off somewhere without telling me?'

'Good Lord, no,' said Saul. 'With any luck, I'll be around for a long time.' It struck me that this was an odd way for him to put it. I looked up to catch his expression, but his face gave nothing away. I'd been working for him for two years by that point. Was he worried about what would happen to me after he died? Surely not. I didn't know exactly how old he was, but he was certainly on the right side of seventy. I didn't like to think about Saul dying, so I changed the subject back to art. It was the only thing I was interested in talking about, and Saul seemed happy to indulge me.

As it turned out, I was the one who deserted him, though it was the last thing I wanted to do; he was the only companion I had and I'd grown to love him.

On 18 June 2007—several dates are etched for ever on my brain, and this is one of them—I was sitting behind the counter, reading an art book called *Still Life with a Bridle* by Zbigniew Herbert, when a woman walked into the gallery. I recognised her, having seen her once or twice before, but didn't know her name. She belonged to the category of Saul's regulars that he and I called 'the Rudies'—the people who, if they found me in the gallery, would ignore me and walk straight through to the back to find Saul.

I tried to smile, as I always did when a Rudie walked in, but got no response. The woman, dressed in a tasselled gypsy skirt and white trainers, and with a mass of curly silver-threaded black hair, was carrying a picture under her arm. I saw only the back of it as she strode past me without saying hello.

I shook my head at her rudeness and turned back to my book. A few seconds later she was back, the painting still under her arm. 'Where is he?' she demanded. 'I've got a picture I want him to frame—today, ideally.'

'Isn't he there?'

'Not unless he's invisible.'

'Um . . . I don't know. He must have nipped out.'

'Did you *see* him go out?' she asked impatiently.

'No, but—'

'How long's he likely to be?'

'Not long.' I smiled. 'He's probably popped out the back and across to the post office. Can I help you at all?'

She looked down at me as if I were a piece of rubbish, contaminating her space. 'You haven't so far,' she said. 'I'll wait five minutes. If Saul's not back by then I'll have to leave. I'm not wasting my whole day hanging round here—I've got work to do.' She leaned the canvas board she'd been carrying against my desk and started to circle the gallery, looking at the pictures Saul and I had hung a few days earlier. 'Lame,' she said loudly about the first one she came to. Then she marched quickly past the others, offering a one-word comment on each of them: 'Dismal. Lame. Pretentious. Vacuous. Hideous. I see nothing's changed around here.'

The picture she'd brought in was tall, and she'd propped it up against the part of the desk I was sitting behind—perhaps deliberately to annoy me by obscuring my view of the room. On the back of the board someone had scrawled, in capital letters, the word 'ABBERTON'. I wondered if it was her surname.

Her outright condemnation of every painting she saw made me curious to see the one she wanted Saul to frame. Whether she'd painted it or someone else had, she clearly deemed it worth spending money on. No one frames art they don't value. I stood up and walked round the desk to look at the picture. She must have sensed me move because she whirled round, the bottom of her tasselled skirt whooshing out in a circle. It had a hole in it, I noticed. Her face was a mask of suspicion. 'What are you doing?' she said. Did she imagine I was glued to my chair? Why shouldn't I move freely around the gallery, as she was? I worked there, after all.

When I looked at the painting, I had the same feeling I'd had when I first saw *Something Wicked*, except stronger. It was like instant hypnosis, a magnetic attraction. I wasn't sure what I was looking at. The background—painted in dark greens, browns, purples and greys so that you could only just make it out, so that it looked as if it was in the shadows—was a residential street with houses all along it, a loop at one end, the shape of which had been massively exaggerated; it looked almost like a noose, with the rest of the road being the rope. The street was a cul-de-sac: Megson Crescent, though I didn't know that at the time.

The rude woman must have noticed my reaction because she said, 'You don't need to tell me it's good. I know it's good.'

I was too startled by the picture's power to say anything. At its centre, standing in the scene, was the outline of a person. I couldn't tell if it was supposed to be a man or a woman. Apart from its shape, there was nothing human about the figure; inside the thin black line that separated it from the rest of the picture was a mass of what looked like hard feathers, scraps of material—gauze, perhaps—some white, some with colour painted on. A churned-up angel: that's what it made me think of. It should have been grotesque, but it was the most beautiful thing I'd ever seen. 'Did you do it?' I asked.

She told me she did.

'It's amazing.'

Flattery usually worked, even with the rudest of the Rudies, but it didn't on her. Every few seconds she frowned at the door, as if willing Saul to walk through it. I held out my hand. 'I'm Ruth Bussey,' I said. 'I don't think we've ever been properly introduced, even though I've seen you before.'

'We haven't,' she agreed.

'Is your name Abberton? I noticed—'

'No. Abberton is the person in the picture.' She didn't tell me her name. When I kept looking at her, she raised her eyebrows as if to say, 'Do you want to make something of it?'

I turned back to the painting. 'Is it . . .?'

'No. It's not for sale.'

'Oh.' I was horribly disappointed, and couldn't think what to do. I could hardly challenge her—it was her painting, after all—but I knew I had to have it, had to be able to take it home with me.

'I'm going,' said the woman. 'Tell Saul he needs a new business plan, one that knows the difference between being open and being closed.' I was about to ask her name when she moved to pick up the canvas board, and I realised she was going to take it away.

I nearly cried out. 'Wait,' I said. 'Even if it's not for sale, can you . . . could you tell me something about it? What made you paint it? Who's Abberton?'

She let out a long sigh. 'He's nobody, all right? Absolutely nobody at all.'

He. So Abberton was a man. 'Do you ever make prints from your originals?' I asked 'Sometimes artists . . .'

'Not me,' she said quickly. 'You cannot buy this picture, Ruth Bussey.' Her skin looked like paper that someone had screwed up, then flattened out to find all the creases still there. I didn't like the way she'd said my name, particularly since she hadn't told me hers. 'Get over it. Buy another picture.'

I thought she'd given me a glimmer of hope. 'Have you got others I could look at, ones that are for sale?'

Her lower jaw shot out and I saw a row of white, slightly uneven teeth. 'I don't mean buy one from *me*,' she raised her voice. I should have stopped pushing it at that point, but it made no sense to me. She can't be upset because I think she's brilliant, I thought. I must be asking the wrong questions, putting it in the wrong way. No artist gets angry when you express an interest in buying their work—it simply doesn't happen, I reassured myself. If I could only make this woman understand that I was serious, that I wasn't just some airhead receptionist . . .

She had seized the picture and marched off into the back again. I decided to have one last try. I walked through to Saul's framing room, and gasped when I saw what she was doing. Another artist's work was spread out on the table, and she was leaning on it, leaning on a watercolour landscape that someone had probably taken weeks if not months to paint, writing a note for Saul. She was using a biro, pressing it down angrily as if that would help her make her point more emphatically. 'Don't lean on that,' I said, shocked.

She stopped writing. 'Excuse me?'

'That's someone else's picture!'

'It's someone else's *appalling* picture. And now it has my rather apposite words superimposed upon it, which makes it a hundred times more interesting.'

She'd done it deliberately. I read her words, the ones she planned to leave for Saul to find. Most of them were obscenities. If he didn't take one look at that note and decide never to frame anything for this awful woman again, there was something wrong with him. I looked at the bottom of the scrap of paper for a signature, but there wasn't one—I'd interrupted her before she'd had a chance to sign her letter.

I decided I didn't want to buy *Abberton* after all. It would have spoiled it for me, knowing the person who had painted it thought nothing of vandalising another artist's work.

I felt more upset than I could justify to myself. The picture I loved, even though I'd only seen it for the first time five minutes ago, had been ruined for me. More than that: it was as if *art* had been ruined, the thing that had started to cure the ache in my soul. Now it felt tainted. 'Why do you want to destroy other people's work?' I asked, unable to stop myself. 'Can't you bear the idea of anyone having talent apart from you?'

I turned round and walked back to the gallery area, shaking. A few seconds later my hair was yanked back, as if my ponytail had caught on something. I cried out in pain. It was her. She spun me round and pushed me against a wall, knocking me into a picture. It crashed to the floor and the glass broke, falling in pieces around my feet. She's going to wreck the gallery, I thought—all our paintings, and it would be my fault. *It's always my fault.* What would I tell Saul?

One of her hands was flat against my chest, the other behind her back. That was when I started to get frightened. What was she holding? She'd been in Saul's workshop, where there were knives. *Saws.* 'Please,' I said. 'Please, don't hurt me.'

'Who are you?' she demanded. 'What do you want from me?'

'Nothing. I just . . . I'm sorry. Don't hurt me. Let me go!' A storm began to rage in my mind. *The same words again, the ones I'd said over and over to Her when she yanked the tape off my mouth: don't hurt me, please, let me go.* I was no longer aware of the woman with the grey-black hair, or the gallery. The present dissolved into the past; there could never be anything but Him and Her; that one attack would last for ever, in one guise or another.

The wild-haired woman's hand emerged from behind her back. I saw a canister: paint. *Red.* My body felt formless, as if it was breaking up. She held her weapon close to my face and sprayed. I screamed. It went in my mouth and eyes, and when I closed them, she carried on spraying. I felt a heavy wetness all over my face and neck, stinging, hardening. I tried to move, but I couldn't.

'What on earth . . .?' Saul's voice.

I heard a splash, then something rolling, a metallic sound. I tried to open my eyes, saw thin red ropes in front of them where my lashes had been glued together. Her hand released me. I mumbled, 'Sorry. Sorry.' Saul and the woman were shouting over one another, saying things I didn't want to hear. I had to get to the door. I had to get out of there. I didn't pick up my handbag or my jacket. I was free to move, so I ran.

I didn't stop running until I got home. I didn't have my keys with me—they were in my bag—so I sat on the grass outside Blantyre Lodge in the rain, shaking, for what felt like hours. I could have sat in the porch but I wanted to get soaked, to wash everything away. At some point Saul appeared. He'd brought my things. He tried to talk to me, but I wouldn't let him. I put my hands over my ears, hysterical, my face still covered in red paint that made my skin feel tight, like a mask. The downpour hadn't shifted it. The paint that framers use to spray mouldings is thick, greasy; it doesn't wash off easily. People hurrying out of the park, on their way to shelter from the sudden bad weather, stared at me, then turned away quickly. One little boy pointed and laughed, before his mother stopped him. I didn't care. No one could get me here—the crazy artist couldn't, Him and Her couldn't. Not in the middle of a public park.

Eventually Saul went away. I haven't spoken to him since, though for weeks after that awful day he left me regular phone messages. He said he understood that I didn't want to go back to the gallery, and why I didn't want to speak to him or talk about what had happened, but he needed to phone me from time to time, he explained, even if I never answered. He wanted me to know that he hadn't forgotten about me, that he still cared.

The last message he left, early last August, was different. I heard that his voice had changed; he didn't sound sad any more—he sounded determined. He gave me Aidan's name and address, told me Aidan needed someone to work for him. 'My loss will be his gain,' he said. 'And yours, I hope. Please, Ruth. Do this for my sake as well as yours. I don't know what's happened to you in the past—I'm not a fool, I know something must have. Maybe I should have asked . . . Anyway. I won't let you ruin the rest of your life. Go and see Aidan. He'll look after you.'

I remember I laughed at this, sitting in the dark in my house, smoking yet another cigarette. Look after me, with so many people intent on doing me harm? Him and Her, the crazy artist with the silver-black hair whose name I didn't know, with her can of red paint . . . Everyone knew I wasn't worth looking after, because I was too pathetic and helpless to look after myself. Aidan Seed, I was certain, would be no exception.

6

3/3/08

Simon was on the phone to Sam Kombothekra when he saw Aidan Seed's car turn the corner from Demesne Avenue on to the Rawndesley Road. Seed was driving it, and he seemed to be alone. 'Gotta go,' Simon said curtly, tossing his mobile on to the passenger seat. He hadn't been sure if Seed would make his trip on foot or in the dusty black Volvo estate that had been parked at a forty-five degree angle to the side of the workshop.

'You're not planning to wait, are you?' Charlie had said. 'He's going nowhere. He lied to get rid of us.'

'We'll see,' said Simon. 'I don't think so.'

'*You'll* see,' she'd corrected him. 'I've got to get back to my enthralling questionnaire. Give me a ring if something happens.'

Simon was pleased Seed had opted to drive wherever he was going. It was easier to follow a person in a car. Behind the wheel, encased in his own private space, Seed would be less likely to look at anything but the road ahead.

As he followed the Volvo along the Rawndesley Road, Simon thought about the lies he'd told Kombothekra, and felt something he didn't often feel: proud of himself. His story had been a medley of all the things the sergeant wanted to hear: two hundred and seventy-six addresses divided into handy regional groups, a travel schedule, a brand new road atlas courtesy of the Snowman. Not a word of it true. Simon had thrown Proust's tenner in the bin—perhaps his job along with it, but at the moment he didn't care.

Seed drove at fifty miles an hour along the High Street, where the limit was thirty. It wasn't long before Simon was having to do eighty on the dual carriageway to keep up with him. Why was he in such a hurry? Was his trip—news of which had evidently come as a surprise to Ruth Bussey—connected to Simon and Charlie having dropped in unexpectedly? Wherever he was going, it wasn't Megson Crescent; that was in the opposite direction. Rawndesley, perhaps.

In the absence of Proust, and the need to defend his gut feelings, Simon was scornful of what the voice in his head was telling him. Where did it come from, this conviction that if he didn't act quickly something terrible would happen? The sense that Seed, Bussey and Mary Trelease were teetering on the edge of something horrendous, something only he could stop? Arrogant wanker, Charlie would have called him.

At the Ruffers Well roundabout, Seed didn't go straight over and on towards Rawndesley as Simon had expected him to. He took a right. Simon allowed a car to get in between them, then followed. Could Seed be heading for the A1? North or south? North, he guessed.

South, it turned out. So much for gut feelings. As he followed Seed past exit after exit, it started to seem more and more likely to him that Seed was on his way to London. 'Shit,' Simon muttered under his breath. He was a good driver in every other town, city, village—in every other part of the country—apart from the capital. London was different; other drivers played by strange rules, if any. Simon had been involved in two car crashes since he'd passed his test at the age of seventeen; both had been in central London. Both times he'd been in pursuit of a suspect and both times he'd pranged his car and lost them. Something about London made him lose his cool. Not today, he told himself. He wouldn't lose Aidan Seed.

Less than an hour and a half later, he was seeing signs that said, 'Highgate Wood' and 'West End'. It was five o'clock and starting to get dark. *Great.* Central London at rush hour. From a traffic point of view, it couldn't have been worse. So resigned was Simon to his fate that he didn't notice when Seed took a left turn ahead of him. He sped on past, then had to turn round. Seed had gone down a side street off Muswell Hill Road—something beginning with an 'R'. Simon drove back past the entrance to Highgate Wood. Ruskington Road—that must have been it. He turned right. He'd got halfway down the road when he saw Seed walking towards him. He prepared to be seen—for the inevitable confrontation—but Seed didn't notice him. He had his head down. Once he'd passed Simon's car, Simon pulled in and watched Seed in his rear-view mirror. At the bottom of the street, Seed turned left.

Why had he chosen Ruskington Road? Simon wondered. Olivia, Charlie's sister, used to live round here. She moved after her downstairs neighbour—and, by extension, the house they shared—appeared on a tacky daytime property programme. Simon could see Seed's car parked a few metres ahead on the other side of the road, in front of number 23, a white-painted four-storey terrace that was divided into flats. Simon saw a light glowing behind the curtains in the basement window and another in the highest dormer window.

Did Seed know someone who lived in one of the flats? Or nearby?

Simon got out of his car, locked it and ran towards Muswell Hill Road. He was afraid he'd be too late, but when he turned the corner, he saw Seed's broad-shouldered outline walking down the hill some distance ahead. Simon ran to catch him up. It didn't take long, and Simon didn't allow himself to get too close. As Seed passed each lamppost, the shoulder-patches of his black jacket shone under the artificial light. Simon patted his pockets. He'd forgotten his phone, left it on the passenger seat. *Damn.* Charlie would try and call him within the next half hour, he reckoned. He'd started to be able to anticipate when she was going to ring. He liked that: knowing what she was going to do.

Seed veered off the main road and down a footpath, also

downhill. He wasn't the only one. Most of the twenty-odd people between him and Simon went in that direction as well. It turned out to be a shortcut to Highgate tube station.

Seed went to stand at the back of the ticket queue. Simon ducked behind a van that was selling coffee, milkshakes and fruit juices. Once Seed had passed through the barrier, Simon flashed his badge at the fluorescent-jacketed woman standing behind the gate and said, 'CID. Quickly.' She let him through, eyes wide. Probably worried about bombs on the tube, Simon thought, but he didn't have time to stop and reassure her.

There was only the Northern line, direction north or south. It had to be south, Simon thought, otherwise Seed would have driven all the way to his eventual destination. It was presumably as easy to park in High Barnet or Finchley as it was in the Highgate/Muswell Hill area. Simon couldn't see Seed any more, so he had to hope he'd guessed right. Instead of going to stand on the southbound platform, he hung back, waiting for a train to come. When he heard one pulling in, he moved forward and walked briskly up the platform.

He spotted Seed in a huddle of people by one of the sets of doors. He knew the risk he was taking: Seed could turn round and see him at any moment, but so what? There was no law against going to London. Seed didn't have to tell Simon what he was doing there and vice versa.

Each time the train stopped, Simon leaned out to see who got off. Seed didn't alight at Archway, Tufnell Park or Kentish Town, as far as Simon could tell, though the mass of moving bodies was such that he couldn't be sure. Camden Town: no. Mornington Crescent: no. Leicester Square, Simon guessed. People who came into London for the evening usually headed to the West End. What did Proust think, that Simon was some kind of bumpkin who started to hyperventilate if he went any further than the 'Welcome to Spilling' sign outside the Queen's Hall? *Fucking wanker.*

Simon had to move fast when he stuck his head out at Euston and saw Seed walking along the platform, following the 'Way Out' signs. He jumped off the train and went after him. Euston, he thought. What was at Euston? He swore at himself, impatient with guessing and being wrong.

He followed Seed up the escalator to Euston station proper. The place was heaving. In the middle of the concourse, an un-moving crowd of hundreds stood and stared up at the boards overhead. Around this still mass, another several hundred bodies swirled—those who already knew where to find their trains, those dashing in and out of shops. Simon kept his eyes fixed on the shiny shoulder patches of Seed's jacket and made sure to stay out of his line of sight.

Seed went into WHSmith and bought something. From his vantage point, Simon saw that it was a newspaper, but not which one. Where next? Across the station concourse. Seed walked fast, like a man who knew exactly where he was going. He wasn't ambling, drifting in and out of shops aimlessly like some of the people Simon could see. He had a purpose. *He's done this before.* But done what? Simon wasn't sure.

He watched as Seed went into the station's food court and approached one of the counters. After a brief exchange with a woman wearing a red uniform and a red cap, Seed went to the till to pay—for nothing, apparently—then sat down at a small table that was unoccupied, his back towards Simon. He opened his newspaper. Simon moved closer and saw that it was the *Independent*. About five minutes later, the woman in the red uniform brought a plate of food to Seed's table.

Simon wished he'd remembered to pick up his phone. He could have phoned Charlie. And said what? That Aidan Seed had come to Euston station for his tea? She'd have pissed herself laughing.

Seed had to be going on somewhere. No one came all the way from Spilling to London to have their dinner in a train station food court. Yeah, Charlie would say, just like no one con-fesses to murdering women who aren't dead.

Simon was freezing, having left his coat in the car, and getting hungrier by the second. He groaned when Seed got up to buy more food. Two doughnuts and a coffee. *Greedy bastard.* Seed sat down again. He seemed in no hurry at all.

Finally, at twenty-five past six, he stood and stretched. He left the food court without picking up his newspaper and made for the station exit. Simon followed him out on to the Euston Road, to a crossing. He hung back, but there was no need. There were so many people pushing along the pavement in both directions that Seed would have had a job spotting him even if he'd been looking.

Simon crossed the road and kept his eye on the shiny black shoulder patches ahead. A woman coming in the opposite direction banged his arm with hers. Simon mumbled, 'Sorry,' but the woman said nothing, though their collision had been her fault. He couldn't believe how rude some people were. Aware that his mind had drifted, he pushed the thought away.

The black jacket was gone. How could Seed have disappeared so quickly? The pavement was busy but not that busy. It wasn't possible that Simon had lost him in the split second he'd spent thinking about that sodding woman.

Two people walking ahead, a man and a woman, turned right and went round the side of a wide building with large windows symmetrically spaced across its façade. Simon looked because it was the only other option. If Seed wasn't ahead, behind or across the road . . .

There he was, going in through a side door at the top of a concrete ramp. He stopped when he saw the man and woman approach, said hello to them, but it wasn't the sort of greeting that would pass between friends, Simon thought. They knew each other, but not well.

Once they'd gone inside, Simon approached the door and saw that it had been wedged open. He peered into a wide, empty foyer containing a reception desk with a cash till at one end. Beyond the foyer was a corridor leading to another door.

Closed. There was a poster on it that Simon couldn't read, and a table to the left, covered with leaflets, books and pastel-coloured pamphlets.

Three elderly men with long, straggly hair and matted beards passed him on their way in, leaving in their wake a smell of stale sweat infused with alcohol. Homeless, Simon guessed. Once they'd gone into the room, he moved. The poster on the door at the far end of the corridor was headed 'Quaker Quest'. Immediately, Simon thought of his two miserable experiences of Laser Quest in the early 1990s—birthday parties he'd been unable to avoid, friends from university who strove to be wacky. He pictured the three ageing tramps he'd just seen running around a darkened room, brandishing glowing swords.

'A spiritual path for our time,' the poster said. 'Monday evenings, Friends House, Euston, 6.30 p.m. All welcome.' At the bottom there was a website address: www.quakerquest. org. Simon picked up a leaflet from the table, a mini-version of the poster, but with more text. 'Are you looking for a spiritual path that is simple, radical, contemporary? The Quaker experience could speak to you. We offer a series of six informal open evenings, exploring such issues as equality, peace, God, spiritual practice and faith in action. We will share our individual and common insights through presentations, discussions, questions and an experience of Quaker worship.'

Simon skimmed the titles of the books: *A Light That Is Shining*, *The Amazing Fact of Quaker Worship*, *God Is Silence*. He glanced at the closed door. It sounded as if there were twenty, perhaps thirty people chatting inside. Every so often, Simon caught a whiff of egg. Were there sandwiches? Was that why the three homeless men were there—free food?

Simon picked up a pamphlet called *Advices and Queries: the Yearly Meeting of the Religious Society of Friends (Quakers) in Britain*. The booklet contained paragraphs of spiritual wisdom, numbered one to forty-two. Beneath the forty-second, there was a quote from someone called George Fox, dated 1656, about

being a good example to others and walking cheerfully with
God. Simon flicked through the pages, reading some of the
shorter passages. Number eleven made him angry: 'Be honest
with yourself. What unpalatable truths might you be evading?
When you recognise your shortcomings, do not let that discour-
age you. In worship together we can find the assurance of God's
love and the strength to go on with renewed courage.'

When you recognise your shortcomings, do not let that dis-
courage you? Not a word about addressing those shortcomings,
trying to stamp them out or replace them with more noble character traits. For the first time in his adult life, Simon felt nostal-
gic for the Catholicism of his youth.

He stood motionless in the corridor and listened as the clash
of voices subsided and a woman started to speak. The predictable welcome, the timetable for the evening—Simon could hear
most of it clearly enough. He frowned when he heard her mention Frank Zappa, assumed he'd misheard. No, there was the
name again: she was asking if everyone had heard of Frank
Zappa. *Bizarre.* No one said they hadn't, as far as Simon could
make out, but the woman told them who he was nonetheless.
'Mr Zappa is reported to have once said, "If you want God, go
direct",' she told her audience. A few people laughed.

A man's voice took over, saying, 'We Friends agree with Mr
Zappa. God doesn't need the help of a man in a silk suit asking
you for money. Quakerism is an experience-based faith—we
only trust what we've experienced ourselves. Quakers have an
unmediated relationship with God—in other words, we go direct. There's no holy book, no churches or clergymen, no official
creed, and we don't always use the same words. We define our
experience of this immense "something other" in different ways.
"The Divine" is one, "God" is another, "the light" . . .'

'You can go in, you know.' Simon turned, found a security
guard standing behind him, an elderly man with a concave
chest. 'People turn up late all the time.'

'I'm all right out here.'

'Suit yourself. They won't bite.' The man started to walk away.

'Is there anything else going on here tonight?' Simon called after him. 'In the building, I mean.'

'No. Just Quaker Quest.'

Simon thanked him. No doubt, then: Aidan Seed was inside that room—a man who'd looked Simon in the eye and sworn he believed only in the material world, facts and science.

Checking the security guard wasn't watching him, Simon turned the door handle, opened the door a fraction. Now there was a gap between it and the frame that was wide enough to see through. He saw chairs in semi-circular rows, people's backs— some straight, some hunched. There was Seed, in the middle of the front row. Simon couldn't see his face.

Beyond the chairs, the top half of the woman who had mentioned Frank Zappa was visible. She was talking now about something called 'giving ministry'. She was young, younger than Simon, with a pretty, doll-like face, which surprised him. He frowned. Had he been expecting everyone at Quaker Quest to be pig-ugly? Her hair was dark brown and glossy, centre-parted and tied back from her face. Like Olive Oyl from the *Popeye* cartoons, only more attractive. She wore a blue sweatshirt and a rectangular blue plastic badge on a string round her neck, with a large white 'Q' on it.

The other speaker, the man, wore the same uniform. He was bald, overweight and sweaty. When the woman stopped talking, he took over, defining what worship meant to him. 'It's in every sense the spring, the ground,' he said. 'It's what sends me out into the world.' Having delivered his lines, he stood back, smiling.

'When all the still centres of all the people present meet in the middle, we call that a "gathered meeting",' said Olive Oyl. 'When a meeting gathers, that's our opportunity to get to know one another in the things that are eternal. Actually ...' She paused and giggled, as if she'd just remembered a rude joke.

Simon imagined the sort of comments Colin Sellers would be making if he were here. *I'd like to meet you in the middle, darling.* Etcetera.

'To go back to the subject of ministry for a second, I had a funny experience that I'll share with you, even though it's a bit embarrassing,' said the woman. 'Sometimes, in the silence and the stillness, you start to get what seem like little messages. Some are for you to share with the meeting, others are for you alone. Over time, you learn to distinguish one kind from the other. Sometimes you get a message that seems to be teasing you.'

The tittering that followed this remark had a knowingness about it; evidently there were people in the room who knew all about receiving teasing messages from—what had the sweaty bloke called it? The Immense Something Other. *Wankers,* thought Simon before he could help it. He resolved to be more accepting and tolerant, the minute he'd got the hell away from Friends House.

'One day when I went to meeting, I was feeling a bit hot and bothered. I'd had a silly row with my boyfriend that morning,' Olive Oyl continued. 'I'd caught him rinsing some cutlery and putting it back in the drawer, still wet. When he told me there was no point drying it, that it would dry on its own in the drawer, I went ballistic. Anyway, at meeting later that morning, I started to hear this voice in my head. It kept saying, "Cutlery is not eternal."' She laughed, and her audience laughed with her. 'I knew that message wasn't to be shared—it was a private joke, just for me. And I was so grateful for that. It's no accident that gratefulness and "great fullness" sound the same.'

The radiant expression on her face made Simon want to gag, as did her contrived avoidance of the word 'gratitude'. He'd have liked to tell her what he thought she was greatly full of. Applause broke out. Simon had seen and heard enough. He was about to stand back when he saw Aidan Seed turn in his chair. He wasn't clapping with the rest of them. He was the only person Simon could see who wasn't.

Seed looked sickened. Even from a distance, in profile, through a crack between a door and its frame, his disgust was unmistakeable. 'You're not one of them,' Simon muttered under his breath. 'You're never going to be one of them. So what are you doing here?' He wasn't expecting an answer, neither from Seed, who couldn't hear him, nor from a supreme being eager to communicate with him confidentially, so he wasn't surprised when he didn't get one.

He went outside, hailed the first free cab he saw and told the driver to take him back to Muswell Hill. To Ruskington Road.

Charlie watched as the door to Seed Art Services opened with a slow creak. A few seconds later, Ruth Bussey burst out of the dark interior as if someone had shoved her from behind. She was wearing flip-flops on her feet. No socks or tights tonight either, Charlie noticed, and still limping. Charlie wondered again why anyone who hadn't sprained their ankle would pretend they had.

She hurried over, wanting to catch Ruth before she got to her car, not caring if it was obvious that she was coming from the trees by the river, where she had no reason to be unless she'd been spying on the workshop. 'Ruth!'

Ruth turned with a cry, then fell back against her Passat, pressing her hand against her chest.

'I've been knocking and knocking,' Charlie told her. 'Since five thirty. But you know that, don't you? You were in there all the time. Sitting in the pitch black with the door locked.'

'I was thinking,' said Ruth. Her voice lost itself in the biting wind that blew strands of hair in her face. 'Trying to decide what to do.'

'And did you?'

'Yes.' From her puffy eyelids and the chapped skin between her nose and upper lip, it was clear that crying had played a significant part in the decision-making process. 'I wasn't completely honest with you before, and it got me nowhere. I thought you'd laugh me out of the police station if I told you the full story.'

'Where's Aidan?' Charlie asked curtly. What did the silly cow expect—a card saying, 'Congratulations, you've stopped lying'?

'I don't know. I don't know when he'll be back. I don't know much, but I'm willing to tell you what I do know, if you'll help me. You've got to.' Ruth grabbed Charlie's arm. 'He said he was going to kill her.'

'What?' A remark like that couldn't be ignored, even if it came from the least trustworthy person on the planet, which Ruth Bussey might very well be, Charlie thought. 'Who said he was going to kill who?'

'Aidan. Mary. He called her "that bitch". He's not in Manchester—I rang Jeanette at the City Art Gallery. He wasn't there last weekend . . .'

'Slow down. You're not making sense.'

Ruth shivered convulsively in her crumpled white shirt. Charlie had her coat in the boot of her Audi. 'Leave your car,' she said. 'I'll drive you home and we can talk there.' She would get inside that bloody lodge house one way or another. She'd been irritated all day by the thought of Malcolm Goat-man Fenton trying to keep her out.

'A man's been following me,' said Ruth, as they walked down Demesne Avenue to Charlie's car. 'No, that's wrong. Not following—he doesn't stalk me when I go out or anything, but he walks past my house. With a black Labrador.' Having started to talk, she seemed unable to stop—the words flowed out, devoid of tone, as if all she wanted was to get it over with. 'I first noticed him last June. He was there every day for a while. Then he disappeared, for months. I thought he'd stopped but . . . he came back on Sunday, yesterday. I can show you— I've got him on tape. I saw him this morning too. Aidan says he's just walking his dog in the park. He gets impatient when I mention it, calls me paranoid, but he's never seen him, the way he looks at the house.'

Charlie had stopped. In order not to miss anything, she'd had to hang back. Ruth was barely moving and had stopped shivering. She no longer seemed aware of the cold. 'Has he ever threatened you? Approached you, or the house?'

'No.'

'Isn't it normal for people walking in the park to look at your house? It's an unusual building. I've looked at it in the past and wondered who lived there.'

'You sound like Aidan. He says everyone who walks in or out through the gates looks at the lodge on their way past. He's right—nearly all of them do. But this man looks in a different way.'

Aidan Seed, the voice of reason, thought Charlie. Apart from the small matter of his belief that he murdered a living woman.

'He wears a red woolly hat, the man, with a bobble on the top. Even in summer. That's not normal.'

'I'm not sure normal exists,' said Charlie. *Certainly not in your vicinity*, she might have added.

Ruth stared into the distance, eyes wide. 'He wears it because it looks stupid, comical. No one who wears a hat like that could be dangerous—that's what he wants me to think.'

'Ruth, how cold is it today? And you're wearing flip-flops, no socks or tights, nothing. There you go: proof that a person can be inappropriately dressed and not stalking anyone!' Charlie wasn't angry, as she must have sounded, but a certain amount of force was necessary to stamp out irrationality. Was Ruth insane? Was Aidan Seed? If only the answer in both cases was 'yes', that would explain everything.

Apart from Mary Trelease's behaviour. 'Not me,' she'd said, when Charlie had told her about Aidan's claim that he'd killed her. Naturally, Charlie had asked her if she was implying Aidan had murdered someone else. Mary had denied it—'I simply meant that I'm patently not dead'—but Charlie hadn't felt good about it at all. The look on Mary's face . . .

This man looks in a different way.

Charlie would have been lying if she'd told Ruth that a look in isolation could never be sufficient grounds for suspicion, though she doubted the man with the red bobble hat was anything to worry about.

'I never wear socks,' said Ruth. 'My parents used to make me wear them every day, and a vest. They were obsessed with stopping heat escaping from their bodies. Our house was like a furnace, heating and gas fires on all year round.' Her teeth started to chatter.

Charlie had to press the key-fob four times before her car's lights flashed twice: unlocked. The battery was losing its power. She'd been meaning to buy a spare and put it in the glove compartment, but hadn't got round to it. She opened the boot and handed Ruth her coat. 'Maybe your man's parents wouldn't let him wear woolly hats, even in hailstorms,' she said. Ruth didn't smile.

Once they were in the car and driving, Charlie said, 'Are you going to tell me why you had that piece about me from the paper in your coat pocket?'

'You went through my pockets. I thought you would.' Ruth seemed to shrink in her seat. 'I'm sorry about . . . what happened to you. It must have been awful for you. You looked devastated in the photograph.'

'We're not going to talk about me,' said Charlie firmly.

'That's why I waited for you on Friday. I was in such a state, I couldn't have spoken to anyone else. After what you'd been through, I thought you'd be understanding.'

'Sorry if I disappointed you.' Charlie thought about the sequence of events: the article was printed in 2006, as were several hundred others, in every newspaper in the country, each gleefully raking over the minute details of the incident that, at the time, to Charlie, had felt like the end of her life. Aidan Seed told Ruth he'd killed Mary Trelease in December 2007. Did Ruth expect Charlie to believe she'd cut the piece out of the *Rawndesley and Spilling Telegraph* more than a year before she had any cause to go to the police, and kept it just in case, at some point in the future, she had need of a sensitive police officer? Charlie couldn't ask, not without letting Ruth see how upset she was. She felt an urgent need to turn the conversation away from herself, even if that meant not knowing. She said gruffly, 'I'm understanding about things I understand. Sorry to be the bearer of "challenging feedback", as we say in the police service these days, but your and Aidan's behaviour so far has made zero sense. It might even be into minus figures, on the Richter scale of unintelligibility.'

Ruth twisted her hands in her lap. She said nothing. They drove through the town centre. Elaborate Easter egg displays crowded shop windows along the High Street.

'Has the story changed?' Charlie asked. 'What did you mean before—Aidan said he was going to kill Mary Trelease? I thought his angle was that he'd killed her already?'

'It wasn't a threat,' said Ruth. 'He asked if I thought it was possible to see the future. When I told him I was sure it wasn't, he said it was the only explanation—everyone's telling him Mary's still alive, but his memory of killing her's so vivid. If it's not a memory, it must be a . . .'

'A premonition?' said Charlie wearily. 'You're not going to like this suggestion, but could Aidan be talking all this spooky crap to scare you? To drive you away? Premonitions, murders that never happened . . .'

'I don't know. I don't think so. I'm not sure he could fake the fear I saw. He was scared of what he might do. He told me to go to Mary's house and persuade her to run away, somewhere he wouldn't find her.' Charlie felt Ruth's eyes on her. Waiting, hoping, for an explanation Charlie was unable to provide. *Unless Ruth, not Aidan, was the one faking the fear.* 'At least it means he can't be there with her.'

'Sorry?'

'I used to think you were right. Every time Aidan stayed away overnight, I wondered if he was with her, if the two of them were plotting to drive me mad, or something. I knew where she lived. I could have gone round, but I never did. I was too scared of finding Aidan there. He wouldn't tell me to go to her house, would he, if that's where he was going?'

Charlie closed her eyes, then opened them, remembering she was driving. How hard would it be to get some uniforms camped outside 15 Megson Crescent? Even if she succeeded, that level of protection would need to be justified on an hour-by-hour basis. Charlie reckoned she'd be granted a day, maximum. She wasn't sure it was worth the hassle. What if Aidan Seed chose the next day to make good his promise, prediction, whatever?

Beside her, Ruth was crying. 'I'm still scared,' she said. 'Scared something's going to happen but I don't know what. It's nothing concrete—it's not that I'm scared Aidan really has killed someone, or that he will, or that he'll go to prison. I could live with those things.'

'You're telling me what you're not scared of,' Charlie pointed out. 'What would be helpful is if I knew what you *are* scared of.'

Ruth picked at the skin around her fingernails. 'Something so bad I'm not capable of imagining it. Not death. There are plenty of worse things.'

Charlie thought 'plenty' was an overstatement.

'All I know is, there's a danger and it's . . . it's closing in.'

'Listen to me, Ruth. Don't go to Mary's. Is there anywhere you could go that's . . .?'

'Aidan told me something else, when he was talking about having visions of things that hadn't happened yet. The picture Mary gave me, the one he said he gave to a charity shop—it's called *Abberton*. That's its title. Aidan said it was the first in a series. There were going to be nine, he said, but Mary hadn't done them yet. He told me the names of the others: Blandford, Darville, Elstow, Goundry, Heathcote, Margerison, Rodwell, Winduss. He said it to prove to me that he was seeing the future.'

Charlie had no idea how to respond to this. Hearing Ruth say the names like that—an alphabetical list—had made her feel uneasy. Eight titles of paintings yet to be painted? What could it mean? It complicated things, took them beyond the level of a simple threat: *Tell her I'm going to kill her.*

'The man you're engaged to,' said Ruth. 'Do you love him unconditionally? Would you forgive him no matter what he did?'

Charlie felt hounded. Why was everybody so keen to interrogate her about Simon today? First Mary, now Ruth.

'I love Aidan so much, you've got no idea. If that love died, I'd have nothing. But that doesn't mean it's unconditional.' Ruth turned to Charlie, breathing hard in her face. 'When he told me he'd killed Mary, I . . . I didn't react well.'

'Who would?' said Charlie. Unconditional? Yes. Forgive him? Not a chance, not for any misdemeanour, however small. 'Loving someone doesn't have to mean letting them off the hook,' she said, pleased with her compromise position.

'Yes, it does,' Ruth said vehemently. 'It does, and I don't think I can do it. I'm scared of the truth, but without it I'll only torment myself imagining the worst. What if I find out something so terrible it kills my love for Aidan? If that happens, I'll know for sure that I'm not worth anything, that there's not enough love in me to forgive or heal anyone. It'll all be over—everything.'

Charlie almost smiled. If she hung around with this woman for much longer, she might start to think of herself as an irrepressible optimist by comparison.

Ruth closed her eyes, rubbed the back of her neck. 'You asked me,' she said in a voice that was barely audible. 'That's it. That's what I'm frightened of.'

Blantyre Lodge's lounge wasn't small, but it looked it, overloaded as it was. While Ruth made tea in the kitchen, Charlie started to make an inventory. She wondered how big Ruth's house in Lincoln had been, if it had housed all this comfortably: books, lamps, mirrors, candles, gardening magazines, six small Persian rugs, more exotic-looking plants than you'd expect to find in a botanical garden's greenhouse. There was also an ironing board, stepladders, a clothes-drying rack. A small sofa had three throws draped over it and eight embroidered cushions piled on its seat. One was gold and had an image of two green shoes sewn on to it, with a cloth representation of a pink ankle protruding from each one. How peculiar, thought Charlie—the effort that must have gone into the embroidery, and the end result looked as if someone's legs had been chopped off at the ankles.

Stuffed between a second sofa and the window was an old-fashioned dark wood desk with a computer on it, and, incongruously, a picnic bench of the sort one normally found in pub gardens, half unpainted wood and half dark green. For good measure, a bulky winged armchair had been crammed into the room as well. One whole wall was covered with wooden shelves that acted as a sort of display cabinet for pottery, carved stone figures, several different Russian doll sets, strange wooden blobs, heads of deer and lions and eagles made out of thin wire, some silver and some gold, an assortment of colourful plastic shapes, all of which were almost recognisable—as square, circle, triangle—but became more abstract at one end, as if they'd lost the will to be proper shapes and preferred not really being anything. There wasn't a centimetre of space to spare, should Ruth Bussey decide she urgently needed to buy another metal model of a rabbit's head. It was as if someone who had previously owned an eight-bedroom pile had downsized radically, without culling any of their possessions.

There were at least thirty paintings on the walls. Most of them were small, but one or two were huge, and ought, Charlie thought, to have been hanging over a marble fireplace in a ballroom. The largest picture was striking in its unpleasantness as well as its size. It had a rectangular gold-effect frame with four smaller rectangles protruding from it—one in each corner—and depicted a woman with long, dark hair wearing a white dress and a serene expression on her face. At the centre of the dress, there was a hole from which a distorted, grimacing face stared out, open-mouthed.

Charlie shuddered, turning her attention to a less disturbing picture of a large bull with a square body standing in front of a pink stone bell tower. Ruth came in carrying two cups of tea. Charlie would have preferred a double vodka. 'That's a ribbon-and-reed frame,' said Ruth, seeing Charlie looking at the bull. 'See the pattern on it? Aidan told me it's based on the Roman symbol for government: reeds bound together by a ribbon. Individually weak but together strong. He said it was like him and me.'

'Did Aidan buy you all these pictures?' Charlie asked.

'No. I bought them myself. Aidan framed them, though. Re-framed them, in some cases. He thinks most paintings aren't framed as they should be.' Ruth perched on the edge of one of the sofas.

Charlie didn't want to sit. Ruth's intensity was making her edgy, as was the thought that at some point she must ask again about the article. She sensed Ruth would tell her if pushed, and she dreaded the answer. The more she worried at it in her mind, the less likely it seemed that there was an entirely innocent, harmless reason why Ruth had had that article in her coat pocket. 'Tell me about losing your job at the Spilling Gallery.'

'Didn't Mary tell you?'

'Not really. She implied it was her fault.'

Ruth shook her head. 'It was mine,' she said unhappily. 'If I'd . . .' She stopped. 'Do you ever wish you'd done almost everything differently?'

To someone else, Charlie might have said yes without missing a beat, but Ruth already had too much information about her. 'Tell me the story,' she said brusquely. 'If you want my help, you'd better tell me everything you kept to yourself on Friday.'

Ruth lowered her eyes. For a second, Charlie thought she was going to refuse. Then she said, 'Mary came in one day. To the gallery. I didn't know her name at the time, and I didn't find out that day. I didn't find out until much later.'

'Okay.' It was a start.

'She had a painting with her, one of her own, which she wanted Saul, my boss, to frame. It had 'Abberton' written on the back of it in capital letters. There was a . . . a sort of person in it, the shape of a person with no face. It was impossible to tell the sex. It was just an outline: a head, two arms . . .'

'I'm familiar with the human anatomy,' said Charlie. Obviously no penis protruding from the canvas, then, she thought.

'I asked who Abberton was, and Mary refused to tell me. She . . . she got angry. I wanted to buy the picture and she didn't want to sell it, and when I asked . . .' Ruth put her mug down and covered her mouth with her hands. After a few seconds she said, 'Sorry. When I asked if I could maybe buy another of her pictures, a different one, she said no.'

'When was this?' asked Charlie.

'June last year. She attacked me, physically. I stormed out of the gallery and never went back. Then I changed jobs and—'

'Hang on. You've seen Mary since, right? You've been to her house. Have you asked her again who Abberton is?' What was the connection between the name Abberton and the eight other names Aidan had given Ruth? Nine people known to Aidan and Mary?

'No.' Ruth was trembling.

'Why not? You're on better terms now, presumably. She told me she was trying to persuade you to model for her.'

'It's none of my business. If you call a painting after a person and then depict them only as an outline, what does that mean?' Charlie had the impression Ruth had asked herself this question many times. 'Surely it has to mean there's something painful or problematic associated with them in your mind, something you'd rather not remember.'

'I didn't see any outlines of people when I was looking at her pictures this morning,' Charlie told her. 'I saw people with faces and features.'

'You mean up on the wall? The ones of the family?'

'Mary's family?'

'No,' said Ruth. 'A family who used to live on her estate, I think.'

Charlie wondered why Mary had chosen to paint them so many times. She'd mentioned a compulsion to paint people she cared about. *Like offering yourself an emotional breakdown.*

'They're brilliant, aren't they?' said Ruth. 'Did you see the one of the boy writing in pen on the wall?'

'No. Where was that one?'

Ruth frowned as if she was trying to remember. 'In one of the downstairs rooms.'

Charlie had only seen the kitchen and the hall before going upstairs. 'What was he writing? On the wall?'

' "Joy Division". I don't know what it means.'

' "Love Will Tear Us Apart",' said Charlie automatically.

'What?' Ruth sounded startled. 'Why did you say that?'

'It's the title of Joy Division's most famous song. Don't ask me to sing it to you.'

Ruth said nothing. There was a trapped look on her face.

'Joy Division are a band,' Charlie told her, trying not to sound scornful. 'You haven't heard of them?'

'I didn't listen to pop music as a teenager. My school friends all watched *Top of the Pops*, but it was banned in our house, effectively.'

'What do you mean "effectively"?'

Ruth sighed. 'My parents never actually told me I couldn't do anything. Their particular brand of mind-control was far too subtle for that. Somehow I just knew I had to pretend not to want to do the things they'd disapprove of.' She looked up at Charlie. 'Were your parents strict?'

'I thought so at the time. They tried to stop me from pursuing my hobbies: smoking fags, getting hammered, taking boys I hardly knew up to my bedroom.'

Charlie didn't want to talk about her teenage years, but there was an avid look in Ruth's eyes. 'Fights aplenty. My sister was the good one—didn't drink, didn't smoke, didn't screw around. Never challenged the regime, thereby making it look fair, and shafting me in the process. Her greatest triumph was to defy medical science and single-handedly defeat ovarian cancer. I can't even give up smoking.'

Ruth was nodding. Keep your fucking mouth shut, Charlie ordered herself. She felt an urgent need to take back some of the poison she'd released. 'It's horrible having to admit your parents were probably right,' she said. 'Without Mum and Dad's interventions, I'd have been mainlining cheap cider and hosting orgies every night of the week, especially school nights.'

'There were no rows in my house,' said Ruth. 'There was only ever one opinion. I never heard my mother and father disagree about anything.'

'Well . . .' Charlie cast about for something to say, feeling uncomfortable, wondering how they'd ended up here. She and Ruth weren't friends, swapping confidences. What would Ruth expect in exchange for her unhappy childhood stories? No, that was the wrong way to look at it. What might Ruth offer in return, if Charlie showed herself willing to act as a sounding board? There were still a lot of questions she wanted to ask; it would help if Ruth was favourably disposed. 'Whenever I catch a bit of those *Supernanny*-style programmes, that's what they seem to advise,' she said. 'Parents need to back each other up, not undermine one another.'

'That's so wrong,' Ruth said vehemently. 'If a child never sees its parents disagree, how's it supposed to learn that it's okay to have your own mind? I grew up thinking that if I ever said, "I disagree with you", the sky would fall down. My parents only ever read the Bible or biographies—ideally of Christian martyrs—so I had to pretend I did too. I hid my real books where they'd never find them. I used to be sick with envy when I heard my friends scream at their parents that they hated them, when I heard their mums and dads scream back, "As long as you're under my roof, you'll live by my rules." At least my friends could be honest about what they *wanted* to do.'

Christians, thought Charlie: pure evil. The Romans had the right idea throwing them to the lions. What a pity she'd omitted that line from her engagement party speech. She'd barely skimmed the surface of controversial; Simon had massively overreacted.

'I lied to you on Friday because I needed to,' said Ruth. She picked up her tea and took a sip. 'I don't disapprove of lying. I don't think there's anything wrong with it if there's an unreasonable constraint in your life stopping you being the person you want to be.'

'How's your relationship with your parents now?' Charlie asked.

'I don't see them, not any more. We haven't spoken since I left Lincoln. After years of being too scared to do it, I finally broke their heart. No,' she corrected herself, 'that's not what I did. I put myself out of harm's way, that's all. It's up to them if they choose to allow their heart to break.'

Charlie noted the singular, used twice in rapid succession: heart, not hearts.

Ruth said, 'Some people choose never to see themselves in the mirrors you hold up for them. That's their choice. I assume it's what my parents have chosen. I've got a PO box address—it was in the letter I sent them when I moved to Spilling. They've never used it.'

'They live in Lincoln?' Charlie asked. No wonder Ruth had got the hell out.

'Nearby. Gainsborough.'

'You gave up a lot when you moved. I Googled Green Haven Gardens this afternoon. Sounds like you had a thriving business.'

Ruth's body jerked, as if she'd been shot. Charlie wasn't surprised. She knew all about feeling invaded, finding out that someone was more interested in you than they ought to be. *Interested enough to carry your story in their coat pocket.* She pushed the thought away. 'Organic and chemical-free before it was fashionable,' she said. 'And you won three BALI awards.'

'I won the main BALI award three years running,' Ruth corrected her, her eyes full of suspicion.

'I was only skim-reading,' said Charlie. 'I had two seconds between meetings. I might have missed some of the finer points.'

'Why are you interested in Green Haven? That part of my life's over.'

'Why did you give it up?'

'I didn't want to do it any more.'

Charlie nodded. It was an answer and, at the same time, no answer. She hoped Ruth wasn't regretting how much of herself she'd already given away.

'Let me show you the tape,' said Ruth, standing up. Charlie didn't know what she meant at first. Then she remembered: the man in the red bobble hat. She rolled her eyes behind Ruth's back, lacking the heart to point out that her watching footage of a man walking past a house and looking at it would achieve nothing. She followed Ruth out into the hall and saw what she'd missed on the way in. Above the front door with its unusual leaf-patterned glass panel was a shelf with a TV on it, a video player, and a row of cassettes numbered one to thirty-one. One for every day of the month?

While Ruth reached up to put a tape in the machine, Charlie surveyed the hall. Apart from the door to the lounge, there were three others: kitchen, bathroom and bedroom, presumably. Only one was ajar, and through it Charlie caught a glimpse of shiny maroon fabric and a pink cushion. That had to be the bedroom. Checking first that Ruth was still busy with the machine and the remote control, Charlie pushed the door gently to open it further.

Yes, this was Ruth's bedroom, Ruth and Aidan's, though the only evidence of a man's presence was a bulky watch with a leather strap lying on the floor. The rest was over-the-top feminine: ornate perfume bottles lined up on the window-sill, a pink voile scarf draped across the bed, silk curtains, also pink, white lacy underwear strewn everywhere, a pink heart-shaped hot-water bottle. Even the paperbacks with creased spines in lop-sided piles looked girly, with titles like *Hungry Women* and *Public Smiles, Private Tears*.

Ruth was busy rewinding a tape. 'Sorry,' she said. 'The remote's bust. I have to keep my finger pressed down on it to make it work. It takes ages.'

'No problem,' said Charlie. She leaned into the bedroom to get a look at what was behind the door, and nearly cried out in shock, lurching back out into the hall. She'd seen it only for a split second, but it was enough. *What the fuck . . .?* Her mind reeled. It was absurd, the sort of thing you might have an anxiety dream about—too extreme and too ludicrous to happen in real life. But this was real; Charlie knew what she'd seen.

Nearly a whole wall in Ruth's bedroom was covered with newspaper cuttings about her, Charlie.

She pulled the door to, her heart juddering, the full range of headlines pulsing in her brain, phrases that had haunted her for two years, that she struggled every day not to think about: colourfully worded assaults on her character, selected by hacks for their shock value or alliterative appeal.

Headlines that Ruth had collected and stuck up on the wall beside her bed. *Why?* More recent articles too, Charlie could swear—though she had no intention of looking again to check—about her return to work, the forum she'd set up to tackle business crime in the area. No, she hadn't imagined it. As well as the many photographs of her crying at the press conference in 2006, there had been one or two of her in uniform, after her transfer out of CID, wearing her polished I'm-so-proud-of-what-I've-done-for-the-community smile. She felt sick.

'Here we go,' said Ruth.

Charlie knew she didn't have long to compose herself if concealment was her preferred option, and all her instincts were screaming at her to conceal, withdraw, hide herself away. To demand an on-the-spot explanation from Ruth would constitute exposure on a level that, in her state of shock, she couldn't even contemplate. No, she must avoid a confrontation at all costs, or something disastrous would happen: she'd end up attacking Ruth physically, or become hysterical. *Later. Deal with it later.*

She blinked furiously to banish the tears that had sprung up out of nowhere, and tried to focus on the white bookshelves on the opposite wall that sagged slightly in the middle and made the hallway half as wide as it would otherwise have been. Ruth was evidently a collector of self-help books as well as the self-appointed archivist of Charlie's disgrace. In a better mood, Charlie would have found these titles amusing: *What if Everything Goes Right?*, *The Power of Now*, *What You Think of Me Is None of My Business*.

She didn't know what she thought. All she knew was that her insides had liquefied, she felt as if she might throw up and she wanted desperately to leave this house.

'I asked my landlord to install CCTV when I first noticed the man hanging around,' said Ruth. 'He thought I was making a fuss about nothing, but in the end he agreed. Some rowdy lads had colonised the park at night, and I managed to persuade Malcolm that we could kill two birds with one stone. By the time the cameras were in, the man had stopped walking past. I didn't get him on tape until yesterday.'

Charlie wondered if Ruth had videotapes of her from two years ago, old news reports, the press conference she'd given, the extended interview she'd agreed to at the insistence of the press office, when public opinion was still violently against her three months after the scandal had broken.

Later. Not now. There were other things to think about, like fighting back: finding out everything she could about Ruth

Bussey and using it to devastate her sad, inadequate little life. At the moment, Charlie told herself, the advantage was hers; Ruth didn't know she knew.

She watched the grainy image on the screen change, saw a man in a woolly hat approach the park gates with a black dog. 'Has Aidan seen this?' she asked. If by some remote chance Bobble Hat was spying on Ruth, did Aidan know about it? Did he know who the man was? *Spying on someone who spied on others, who broke into their private pain and . . .*

'No,' said Ruth. 'Only Malcolm's seen it, apart from me, and now you. Aidan and I haven't spoken properly for months.' She looked bereft. 'I thought if Malcolm knew what the man looked like, he could look out for him. He's often here when I'm not—bit of a guardian angel, really. He keeps an eye on things for me. There, look, you can see the man's face.'

Malcolm. He must have seen the display wall in the bedroom. No wonder he'd reacted oddly when Charlie had turned up in person. *Clearly Ruth's made herself known to you . . . She didn't tell me she was going to make contact.* Did Malcolm Fenton know why Ruth was obsessed with Charlie? Did Aidan Seed? He had to, surely, if he shared Ruth's bed. What possible reason could there be? How many other people had seen the wall? Had the men from Winchelsea Combi Boilers seen it? Had they also recognised Charlie this morning?

Her eyes were fixed on the screen, but she wasn't really looking. Ruth's voice cut through her thoughts and she realised she'd missed most of the show. 'Look, you can see his face clearly now. See the way he's looking at the window?'

No. It couldn't be.

It was. Bobble hat or no bobble hat, it was him. With a black Labrador, for Christ's sake? Now Charlie knew two things Ruth didn't know she knew.

'He's probably just a nosey bastard,' she said. If Ruth noticed that her tone or manner had changed, she showed no sign of it. Charlie couldn't remember the last time she'd trusted anyone less than she trusted this strange woman who was staring at her wide-eyed, apparently waiting for help of some sort. 'Why did you seek Mary out?' she asked abruptly.

'Pardon?' Ruth paused the tape.

'You said she attacked you. You left the gallery and never went back. Sounds pretty upsetting. Yet subsequently you went to her house. Why?' *I'm going to stick my fingers into every hole in your story, bitch, and I'm going to pull and pull until the whole thing snaps and I get to watch you fall apart.*

'For the painting,' said Ruth. 'For Aidan. Aidan wanted it. But that was later, much later.'

'All right, so what happened next? After the incident with Mary in the gallery last June, and you leaving your job? That was six months before Aidan told you he'd killed her, right?'

'I can't tell you everything you want to know.' Charlie heard panic in Ruth's voice. 'I can tell you everything *I* know, everything that happened, but not why, or what it means.'

'I'll settle for anything that isn't a lie.'

'No more lies,' Ruth promised. 'What happened next was that Aidan and I went to an art fair in London.'

7

Monday 3 March 2008

The *Access 2* Art fair at Alexandra Palace in London was the first one I'd ever been to. I didn't know such things existed until Aidan told me. One of the artists he frames for was going to have a stall there, and sent Aidan two free tickets. Aidan tore open the envelope at work one day—it must have been October or November last year. It's strange, that's the one detail I don't remember. Everything else about the art fair is fixed in my mind as clearly as if someone had filmed what happened from start to finish and implanted the footage in my brain.

I saw Aidan grinning down at something. 'What?' I asked.

He passed me the envelope. I opened it, pulled out two stiff rectangular cards and a folded leaflet.

'*Access 2* Art? What's that?'

He waited for me to read the leaflet, knowing all the relevant information was there. He and I have never been good at answering questions.

'It says here hundreds of artists will be exhibiting,' I said.

'Have you ever been in a maze?'

'You mean like the one at Hampton Court?'

'That'll do,' said Aidan. 'Picture Hampton Court maze, except bigger. Instead of hedges, picture endless rows of stalls selling paintings, prints, sculptures, so many that you start to worry about finding your way out once you've gone in. You start to walk a little bit faster, unsure if you've walked down that aisle ten times already or never before. You look at so many pictures that you lose the ability to see them. You start to feel as if you've eaten a bucket-load of sweets, or the visual equivalent. It gets to the point where you don't think you could stand to see another painting as long as you live . . .'

'I'd never feel like that,' I told him.

'. . . but you've got no choice. Every corner you turn, there's more of the same: hundreds of artists and galleries flogging their wares.'

'Stop it!' He was teasing me deliberately. 'You'd better be telling the truth.' There was a light, fluttery feeling in my stomach. What Aidan had described was my idea of heaven. I was already fantasising about finding something special. I hadn't felt strongly about anything I'd seen for several months—not since *Abberton*, which I tried very hard not to think about—but I was used to seeing only nine or ten paintings at a time, twenty at most; no more than a small gallery's walls could accommodate.

'I've got to go to this,' I said, clutching the tickets as if someone might take them away from me.

'It starts on Thursday the thirteenth of December,' said Aidan. 'All you have to do is square it with your boss for you to have the day off. Oh, that's me.' He pretended to think about it. 'You can have the day off.'

'I won't need to. It says here it's all weekend. We could go on the Sunday.' Aidan and I sometimes worked Saturdays if we were busy, which we usually were.

'No. Take the Thursday off,' he said. 'If you're going to an art fair you need to be there when it opens.'

'The pictures can't all sell before we get there,' I protested. 'The stuff I like best never sells, anyway. Apart from to me.'

'That's not why,' said Aidan. 'You've got to see the pictures before any of them are sold, or as few as possible. Once red dots start to appear, you look at the work in a different way: the successes and the failures. The popular ones and the rejects.'

'Let's go for the whole thing,' I suggested, bobbing up and down on the balls of my feet, too excited to keep still. 'Thursday to Sunday. If we've got a full four days, we'll be able to see everything. I won't have to choose too quickly, or panic that I've missed anything.'

Aidan's face had lost its happy glow. 'You're right,' he said. 'It might take that long to do it justice, but . . . Ruth, I can't go. I can't close up here, not even for a day. Too many people are relying on me for exhibition deadlines.'

'Oh,' I said, and heard my own disappointment thudding dully through the air, like a clumsily thrown ball. I couldn't imagine going without him. We'd hardly been apart since the day we'd first met in August. 'Can't you . . .?'

'Oh, sack it,' he said, changing his mind so quickly that I didn't understand what he was saying at first. 'They can wait. They can all wait.'

'You mean . . . you'll come?'

'I'll come, but only for Thursday and Friday. I'll go home Friday evening. Saturday and Sunday I'll stay up all night if I have to and make up the time I've lost.'

I smiled. 'So they won't have to wait after all.' Aidan pretends to have contempt for our artist customers, but I think secretly he admires them. Maybe he even envies them a little. How could he feel no affinity with artists, when his approach to his work is so creative? If he's framing something for me, he doesn't use ready-made mouldings. He starts from scratch. The same for himself: all the frames on the walls in his room behind the workshop are hand-made—the ones with nothing inside them. 'They're my only works of art,' he once said. 'Frame-makers used to be perceived as artists, and frames as works of art, before they were mass-produced. At one time, it was normal for a picture frame to cost more than the picture inside it.'

'I'll come back with you on Friday and help,' I said. 'Two days will be fine.'

'We need to start training now, like marathon runners,' said Aidan. 'That's the only way we'll be able to get round the whole show. Don't wear high heels or we'll never make it.'

I laughed. Aidan gave me the look, the one that made my heart twist. I knew he wanted to grab me and kiss me but didn't dare. I didn't either. We spent a lot of time looking at each other in those days, as if we were both trapped behind glass. 'I love you so much,' he said. I said it back to him. It was what we did instead of touching. To us it seemed normal. I knew that most couples kissed or held hands before declaring love for one another, but I didn't care. Aidan and I were all that mattered. We were perfect, just right. It was other people who were conducting their relationships the wrong way round.

Aidan turned back to his gold-leafing. 'Shall we stay in a hotel in London?' he asked, his voice giving nothing away. I knew what he was asking me. I said yes.

Every day after that, I thought about the art fair. Aidan and I talked about it endlessly. We'd looked on the website at the list of artists who were going to be exhibiting. Some Aidan had already heard of; quite a few had been his customers at one time or another. One or two still were. He wanted to show me some of the individual artists' websites, but I didn't want to look at them. I wanted to see everything for the first time on 13 December, the opening day. As the date approached, I started to worry about how I would feel when I didn't have any of it to look forward to any more—*Access 2 Art*, our night in the hotel. I couldn't bear to think that the two things I was awaiting so avidly would soon be in the past.

On the Thursday morning, we got up at 4 a.m., packed our overnight things in my black hold-all, drove to Rawndesley and caught the six o'clock train to London in order to be there in good time for the fair's opening. We ate cooked breakfasts in a bar at King's Cross station that was full of groups of loud men gulping down pints of lager and burping. 'I can't believe they can do that first thing in the morning,' I said to Aidan, which prompted him to order a bottle of champagne.

'There's drinking and then there's drinking,' he said. 'This is the first time we've been away together—we should celebrate.'

'And it's the art fair,' I reminded him.

His smile vanished.

'Aidan?' I asked. 'What's wrong?'

'Nothing. Nothing,' he repeated. It sounded more convincing the second time he said it. 'If you want to spend two days looking at art then so do I. I hate the thought that I'm getting behind with work, that's all.'

'We'll work late Saturday and Sunday,' I promised. 'We'll catch up. There isn't that much to do.' I wanted to erase the troubled expression from his face. 'You've got to train yourself to be your own best friend,' I said. I'd been reading a book called *Be Your Own Life Coach*, and this was one of its recommendations. 'Would you tell your best friend to spend every waking second working, or would you think he deserved to relax and treat himself occasionally?'

This made Aidan smile. 'I'd tell him to start reading proper books instead of the personal growth crap he seems to be addicted to,' he teased me. 'There's better ways to help yourself than sitting around all day examining your own psyche, and working hard's one of them—that's what I'd say to him.' I elbowed him in the ribs. I didn't mind him teasing me. I loved the fact that we could disagree and it didn't matter.

We got to Alexandra Palace ten minutes before the art fair opened. We were the only people there, waiting. 'Like fanatics,' Aidan said. I told him I was proud to be one. We were tipsy, sleepy, heavy and full from the bacon, eggs and black pudding we'd eaten, but I knew I'd shake off my physical lethargy as soon as the doors opened—I'd be off like a racehorse.

In the large foyer, two women sat behind a table, selling tickets and programmes. I was about to dart through the double doors into the main hall, but Aidan pulled me back. 'Wait,' he said. 'I want to show you something.' He bought a programme, turned to the back and spread it open so that I could see it. 'This is the only way you can appreciate the scale of what we're about to walk into,' he said. On the inside of the back cover, there was a map of the fair, a double-page spread that folded out. The stalls were depicted as small white squares, with black numbers inside them. There were four hundred and sixty-eight in total, filling two large interconnecting halls. On the floor plan's reverse side was a list of all the numbers with a name next to each one—the artist or gallery whose stall it was. 'Aidan!' I said, clutching his arm. 'Jane Fielder's here—stall 171.' I couldn't believe I'd missed her name when Aidan and I had looked at the list of exhibitors.

'Who?'

'You know—*Something Wicked*. The red thumbprints, the first painting I ever bought.'

'Your favourite artist.' He pretended to be worried. 'There won't be much left for sale on her stall once you've done your worst. I'd better hire a lorry, and get myself an early morning job cleaning offices.'

'Do you think she'll be here herself?'

'Sometimes they are and sometimes they aren't. Right, where do you want to start?'

'Jane Fielder,' I said without hesitation. At first we followed the plan, but stall 171 was on the far side of the second hall, and I found it impossible to walk down the aisles without looking. I got sidetracked, then sidetracked again. Most of the stalls, if they belonged to individuals rather than galleries, were manned by the artists themselves and they all seemed eager to talk to me, happy to answer my questions about their work. By lunchtime we were still nowhere near stall 171, and I was losing track of the list I'd been keeping in my head of possibles: the pictures I thought I might be interested in buying but needed to see again. 'I need to write down the numbers of the stalls I want to come back to,' I told Aidan. 'Can we find the entrance we came in at and start again, retrace our steps?'

Aidan laughed. 'I told you it was a maze. We can do whatever you want, but . . .'

'What?'

'Why don't we just have a wander? There'll be plenty of time for writing lists tomorrow.' Seeing my impatience with this attitude, he said, 'I know you've seen a lot of stuff you want to look at again, and met some people you like, but I don't think you've seen it yet.'

'Seen what?'

'It. The picture you'd do anything to get your hands on, the one you'd pay double the price for in order to be able to take it home.'

We spent the rest of the day browsing, talking to artists. Or rather, I talked. Aidan hung back, listening, happy to leave me to it. Between stall-stops, he warned me against being too effusive. 'You're getting the artists' hopes up,' he said.

'But I like their work,' I told him. 'Why shouldn't I be enthusiastic? Surely they're happy to be praised, even by people who don't end up buying their pictures.'

Aidan shook his head. 'Praise minus sales equals lies. That's the equation in these people's heads. Until you put your money where your mouth is, they won't believe you however much you say you love their stuff.'

After lunch—a quick sandwich in the foyer café—I came to a stall that had me mesmerised. The artist was a woman called Gloria Stetbay, who looked scarily elegant. I didn't get a chance to talk to her; she was surrounded by a tight circle of people who didn't seem keen to make room for one more. Stetbay's work was mostly abstract, and made me realise that many of the other abstracts I'd seen were far from being the real thing. Stetbay's pictures looked like multi-coloured sand dunes, ruched and textured; I could have been looking at the skins of strange, glowing planets. She did things with colour and surfaces that made everything I'd seen up to that point look anaemic.

Aidan waved a flyer in front of my face. 'You're in good company,' he said. 'She's got work in Charles Saatchi's private collection.' I didn't give a monkey's about Charles Saatchi. 'Is this it?' Aidan asked. 'Have we found it?'

'I can't. The cheapest one's two thousand pounds and it isn't my favourite. I won't tell you how much that is.'

'I'll buy you whatever you want,' he said, surprised I didn't know this without having to be told. 'Which is your favourite?'

'No. It's too much.'

'Nothing's too much if it's for you,' he said solemnly. We were still standing inside Gloria Stetbay's stall. Two American women next to us were talking about another art fair they'd been to that was much better attended on the first day. 'London isn't what it used to be,' one said. 'Even *Frieze* is starting to look like it's trying too hard. And what is it with razor blades? Suddenly everyone's covering their canvases with razor blades—is that supposed to be edgy?'

'I didn't know what it was like to have good feelings in me until I met you,' Aidan said, not caring who heard. 'I love the way you love art. I love the way you want to buy it, and keep buying it, not because of any bullshit about investment or profit or status but as a kind of good luck charm. You love it and you want it close to you, to ward off harm. It's like magic for you, isn't it?'

I nodded. I'd never expressed it in that way to myself, but he was right.

'That's what you are for me,' he said. 'I was planning to wait until later to ask you, but I can't. Will you marry me?' I didn't do what women are supposed to do, didn't remain cool and elegant as I told him I'd think about it. I screamed and waved my arms in the air like an idiot. 'Is that a yes?' he asked, as if there could be any doubt. There was none—not in my mind, at any rate. Aidan looked worried, though. 'Sure you don't want to wait until tomorrow before saying yes?' he asked. I knew what he meant: we'd come to London to have sex for the first time, among other things. This wasn't the first clue I'd had that he was nervous about it.

'Sure,' I said. 'Nothing could change my mind.'

'Don't say that,' he told me, looking even more anxious.

He bought me the Gloria Stetbay piece I loved instead of an engagement ring. We never did get to Jane Fielder's stall; instead, we wandered happily and aimlessly, arguing about the art we saw—what had substance and what was empty. When I remember that day—which I do, often—it appears in my mind separately from what happened next, as if one world closed down at some point on Thursday 13 December, and a new one opened up, a horrible, frightening one that I wanted no part of.

I know the exact moment it happened: ten thirty at night. Aidan and I had been out for dinner at an Indian restaurant called Zamzana. We'd taken the Gloria Stetbay with us, leaned it against the wall so that we could admire it while we ate. Afterwards we went back to our hotel, the Drummond. At reception, Aidan stood back, left it to me to hand over a credit card so that an imprint could be taken, to sign the receptionist's form in two different places. I was acutely aware of his presence behind me, of him listening intently to every word I said, every nuance of my voice, even though all I was talking about was wake-up calls and morning newspapers: 'No thanks. Yes please, the *Independent*.' Once we had our room key, I turned away from the desk to face him. He looked serious. Prepared. 'Shall we have a drink before going up?' I said. 'I'm sure the bar's still open.'

He shook his head, and I felt like a coward. We'd put this off for too long, that was the problem. Now too much hinged on it being a success.

In silence, we walked to the lift, took it up four floors. Thank goodness no one was in there with us; I don't think I could have stood that. When the doors slid open with a ping, I decided to lead the way, following the arrows on the oval-shaped brass signs. I wanted Aidan to see that I was as bold as he was. I was doing fine until I had to unlock our room with one of those stupid keycards. The tiny square light kept flashing red, and I got flustered. After my third try failed, my fingers were so slippery I couldn't even get the card out of the slot. Aidan took over. For him, the light flashed green. We were in.

We stood beside the double bed, looking at each other. 'So. What now?' I said.

Aidan shrugged. 'I suppose we should touch or something.' I ought to have found it absurd—perhaps laughter would have shattered the tension—but this was the first direct reference either of us had made to the four months of agonised, yearning celibacy that we'd endured. Aidan's words were enough to pierce the invisible barrier between us. I ran to him and threw myself, hard, at his chest. It was a few seconds—a terrifying chasm that seemed to grow wider and wider—before I felt his arms close around me and I dared to breathe again. We kissed. For more than an hour we did nothing but kiss, standing beside the double bed, with the black hold-all containing our overnight things lying by our feet.

Eventually our lips were throbbing, raw, and we had to stop. 'How are you feeling?' I asked Aidan.

'Good,' he said. 'Better. You?'

'Still scared.' Inspired by his bluntness, I thought I'd try the direct approach too. 'I'm not sure how we get from here to ... the next stage.'

'Neither am I,' he said.

'How do other couples do it?' I was thinking: how did I used to do it, with other people? Seventeen others, before Aidan. At one time it had seemed easy. The first time Aidan took me out for dinner, we'd talked about our previous relationships. He told me there had been nothing serious for him, only 'a lot of futile one-night stands—non-starters, each and every one'.

'There are no other couples like us,' he said now. 'We've both known what we've got in common from day one, haven't we? I saw it in your eyes, when I found you on my doorstep last summer. You saw it in my eyes too.'

I nodded mutely. His new-found frankness was making me feel uncomfortable.

'We've both been to Hell and managed to claw our way out. I've spent most of my life wanting nothing but to bury what I've been through—you seemed to need to do the same.'

'Aidan, I can't . . .'

'We haven't asked questions. We haven't pushed it. I reckon we've respected each other's privacy a bit too much.'

His words turned me back into a coward and I didn't care. 'Don't ask me,' I whispered. 'I can't.'

'It's not going to work,' he said. I heard despair in his voice, as if something had torn inside him. It frightened me. 'We can't make it work, not like this, not if we're both determined to hide everything that matters.'

'We love each other.' My voice shook. 'That's what matters most, and we haven't hidden that.'

'You know what I mean. I know you're scared. I'm not exactly feeling calm about it myself, but I think we need to tell each other.' Aidan cleared his throat. 'I'm willing if you are.'

It'll be easy from now on. That's what he said, once I'd agreed. Once I'd said I was willing. If he meant the sex, he was right. It felt natural from the start, has ever since: passionate, intense, binding. It has become our refuge, the safe, dark place we escape to when the glaring brightness of everything that's wrong between us shines in our eyes until we feel we're going blind. Ironic that the one thing we lacked has become the only thing that sustains us.

In that hotel room, Aidan told me he'd killed someone years ago, a woman. As soon as he said her name, Mary Trelease, I felt a coldness clutch at my heart, a sense of something being off balance, in the wrong compartment.

Straight away, I knew I'd heard the name before, though I was certain Aidan couldn't have mentioned it to me until now. There was no way he'd have casually dropped the name of a woman he'd killed into one of our previous conversations. Could I be imagining it? I wondered. Briefly, I considered telepathy as a possibility. If Aidan had killed a woman called Mary

Trelease, as he claimed, her name would be imprinted on his consciousness for ever; could it have passed from his mind into mine, without being spoken aloud? I dismissed the idea within seconds. Was Mary Trelease famous? Was that why I'd heard her name before? Not knowing was the worst thing, the inexplicability of it. I *couldn't* know the name, and yet I did. I sat motionless on the bed, bathed in dread. I wanted to ask Aidan who Mary Trelease was, but we'd agreed not to ask questions, and all the ones that occurred to me sounded frivolous and flippant when I rehearsed them silently.

Aidan was in a terrible state after he told me. I couldn't look at him, but I could hear him. It sounded as if he was disintegrating, and all I could do was sit there with my hands clenched in my lap, staring at the floor. Aidan and extreme violence, life-threatening violence, did not go together. No, I thought. *No.* I pictured Him and Her, allowed myself to think of their names for the first time in years, and something flared in my mind as it never had before, making them real; it was as if I was in the hotel room with them instead of Aidan. The three seemed to merge, so that I couldn't distinguish between them, and for a fleeting moment I hated them all equally.

Aidan kept saying my name—'Ruth? Ruth? Say something! Tell me you love me, Ruth, please!'—but I couldn't answer. He reached out to touch me and I flicked his hand away. I sat like a prim statue on the edge of the bed, doing and saying nothing, though I wanted to scream and hit him and call him a murderer. Eventually he stopped trying to get a response from me, and deafening silence engulfed us. I'd rejected him when he most needed love from me, and we both knew it.

That's my biggest regret. Whatever Aidan has done or not done, I hate to think of how badly I let him down that night.

But of course, he hasn't done anything. I'm not the only one convinced of this; the police agree with me.

I don't know how long that awful silence lasted. All I know is, after a while, the horror-haze that had filled my head cleared.

I remembered who Aidan was: the man I knew and loved. If he'd killed someone, it couldn't have been murder. There had to be an acceptable explanation. I got up, put my arms round him, told him it didn't matter—whatever he'd done, I still loved him. I would always love him. I hated myself for saying those words—'it doesn't matter'—about a woman's life; I only said it to compensate for what I saw as my own treachery. How could I have felt hatred for him? How could I have *believed* him? Aidan wasn't evil. I couldn't imagine ever being able to think of him as a killer. He's got it wrong, I thought. Even before I knew it wasn't true, I didn't believe it.

We made love for hours and hours, delaying the moment when words would once again become necessary. The morning sky was already breaking up the darkness by the time we finally fell asleep early the next morning. I woke up to the sound of Aidan saying my name. I opened my eyes. He wasn't smiling. 'It's midday,' he said. 'We've missed half the day.' His eyes were dull and hard. I'd never seen him look so out of reach before, and it scared me.

I said nothing as we got dressed. Aidan made it clear with his body language that he didn't want to talk. He phoned reception and asked for a taxi to be ordered. I heard him say, 'Straight away' and 'Alexandra Palace'.

'We're going back to the art fair?' I said.

'That's why we came.'

'We don't have to go back,' I told him. It was the last thing I wanted to do. I wanted us to be alone, not in a hall full of people and noise. 'We could go home. Let's go home.'

'We're going to Alexandra Palace,' he said tonelessly, as if a machine were speaking from inside him.

I knew then that something was badly wrong. I wanted to ask him what was the matter, but it would have sounded ridiculous. The night before, he'd confessed to a killing. That would be traumatic for anyone; today he had to live with the consequences. We both did. I wanted to ask who else knew about what he'd done. I'd only known him four months. He might have been in prison before I met him. Mainly I wanted to apologise for the way I'd frozen and shut him out when he'd first told me, but I was so afraid he wouldn't forgive me that I didn't dare.

When a receptionist phoned the room to say that our taxi was outside, I asked Aidan about the Gloria Stetbay picture—did he think it would be safe in the room? 'No idea,' he said, as if he couldn't have cared less. He pretended not to notice that I started crying.

We arrived at the art fair and went through the motions, walking up and down the aisles. I looked at paintings without seeing them. Aidan didn't even look. He kept his eyes straight ahead, glazed, and marched up and down as if he'd set himself a goal of a certain number of footsteps and was counting them off one by one.

Eventually I grabbed his arm and said, 'I can't stand this any more. Why are we like this? Why aren't we talking?'

I saw him grit his teeth, as if he couldn't bear my touch. Less than twelve hours ago we'd been having passionate sex. It made no sense. 'I've already said too much,' Aidan muttered, not looking at me. 'I shouldn't have told you. I'm sorry.'

'Of course you should have told me.' I made a mistake then. I said, 'Was it an accident? Was it self-defence?'

He let out a harsh, contemptuous laugh. 'Which would you prefer? Accident or self-defence?'

'I . . . I didn't mean . . .'

'What if it was neither? What if I murdered someone in cold blood, a defenceless woman?'

I felt my face twist in pain. *Defenceless.* 'You didn't. You can't have,' I said faintly.

'People change, Ruth. People become different people during the course of their lives. If you loved the person I am now, you'd forgive anything I'd done in the past, no matter how bad. I'd forgive you anything, anything at all. There's no crime so terrible that I wouldn't instantly forgive you for it. Obviously the feeling isn't mutual.'

He was breathing hard and fast in my face, waiting for my response. I said nothing. He kept using words that paralysed me like shots from a stun-gun, words that had been repeated end-lessly in court seven years ago: *a defenceless woman. Parcel tape over my mouth . . .*

By the time I recovered and realised I had said nothing, that I'd failed to respond, Aidan was walking away. 'Wait!' I shouted after him, but he'd turned a corner. I ran as fast as I could, try-ing to keep my eyes fixed on the point at which he'd disap-peared from view, but by then I was hysterical, shaking, babbling nonsense to myself, convinced I'd driven him away for ever. There were too many corners, too many intersections be-tween one row of stalls and another. Every junction looked the same as all the others. I looked down one aisle, then a second, then a third, but saw no sign of Aidan. In desperation, I asked some of the artists who were sitting in little white cubicles deco-rated with their own work. 'Have you seen my boyfriend? He might have come down here a minute ago. He's tall, wearing a black jacket with shiny patches on the shoulders.' Nobody had seen him.

I ran and ran, up and down the aisles in both halls. Aidan wouldn't have left without me. He couldn't have. He would never abandon me like that. Completely by accident, I found myself at Jane Fielder's stall, number 171. I didn't ask the woman standing next to it if she was Jane Fielder, or tell her how much I liked her painting that I'd bought from the Spilling Gallery—finding Aidan was the only thing in my head. *Any-thing*, I thought. *I'd forgive him anything.* 'Have you seen a man with dark hair, tall, wearing a black jacket with shiny patches here?' I tapped my shoulders. The woman shook her head.

'I saw him,' a voice called out from across the aisle. 'He walked past a minute ago. Like a sort of donkey jacket, is it?'

I turned, saw a young woman. Hair dyed yellow, with black

roots showing, a red patterned scarf wrapped round her head. Skinny legs, cerise fishnet tights over black sheer ones, heavy black boots to halfway up her calves. She was minding the stall opposite, sitting beside a large free-standing sign that said, 'TiqTaq Gallery, London'.

I ran over to her, nearly colliding with her chair and knocking her to the ground. I managed to stop myself just in time. 'Which way did he—?' I broke off as something caught my eye. I blinked, breathed. *No. No.* I backed away. This was some sort of hideous practical joke; it had to be.

'Which way did he go?' the young woman asked on my behalf, seeing I was having trouble getting the question out. 'That way—towards the exit there. Are you okay?'

I wasn't. I had to get away, but felt too weak to move. I leaned against the partition that separated Jane Fielder's stall from the one beside it, and stared at the TiqTaq Gallery's space from across the aisle, rubbing my forehead with my left hand, pressing my fingers hard against my skin.

'Careful, you're leaning on a picture,' said a voice behind me. I couldn't speak, or shift my weight elsewhere. I couldn't do anything except stare past the woman with the dyed blonde hair at the painting in a green-stained wood frame that was hanging behind her. It stood out from all the others. It would have even if I'd never seen it before; it was in a different league from everything else TiqTaq had to offer.

Abberton. Framed, signed, dated 2007. I forced myself to close my eyes, then open them and look again, to make sure it was real. I walked towards the picture, seeing nothing else; it might have been the only thing in an otherwise empty room. Now I understood why the name of the woman Aidan said he'd killed had sounded familiar, even though she'd never introduced herself to me. I'd done plenty of paperwork for Saul; I'd probably sent her a bill or a receipt, or seen her name on one of the 'Work Pending' lists Saul used to pin up everywhere.

That same name was painted in neat black letters in the bottom right-hand corner of the painting in front of me: Mary Trelease.

It took me about four seconds to realise that if Mary Trelease had painted *Abberton* in 2007, Aidan could not have killed her years ago. He'd made a mistake. I felt myself swell with relief. Of course he wasn't a killer. I'd known that all along. All I needed now was to find him so that he could see the picture for himself, but the woman from the TiqTaq Gallery had said she'd seen him heading for an exit. What if he was in a taxi on his way to King's Cross?

I was unwilling to move from TiqTaq's stall. I knew I couldn't let *Abberton* out of my sight. It was my evidence— indisputable proof that Aidan hadn't done what he thought he'd done. It occurred to me that there might be more than one Mary Trelease, but I quickly dismissed the idea. Even if there were dozens or hundreds of women with that name, the artist who had assaulted me in Saul's gallery had to be the one Aidan thought he'd killed. She was a painter; he framed pictures. They both lived in Spilling. It couldn't be a coincidence. Perhaps they'd had a fight. She might have attacked him—a hypothesis that seemed entirely consistent with what I knew of her character—and he'd defended himself . . . My mind raced ahead, going through the possibilities, but I couldn't focus on anything for long. Shock was still slamming through me and I couldn't think coherently.

'I need to buy a painting,' I said to the woman with the dyed hair. 'That one there.'

She shrugged. If I wanted to forget about the man I'd been looking for and boost her profits instead, that was all right by her. 'Great,' she said, though her tone and manner conveyed little enthusiasm. She hadn't looked to see which picture I'd pointed at. 'Let me dig out the relevant forms.' Languidly, like someone with all the time in the world, she bent to open a desk drawer.

'Can you put the "Sold" sticker on first?' I asked, trying not to sound as impatient as I felt. 'I don't want anyone else to see it and think it's still for sale.'

She laughed. 'You might not have noticed, but people aren't exactly queuing up. I've barely had anyone glance in my direction since yesterday morning.' Pulling the lid off a pen with her teeth, she said, 'Right, I'll fill in my bits, then I'll hand it over to you to do yours. You know you pay the total upfront? It's a fair, so there's no deposit system.'

I nodded.

'We take cash, cheques, all major credit cards. Which picture is it you want?'

'*Abberton*,' I said. It was a lie. I didn't want it; it was the last thing I wanted. Neither did Mary Trelease want me to have it. She had made that clear enough. I couldn't put a picture on my wall knowing the artist didn't want it there. As soon as I'd found Aidan and shown him *Abberton*, I would give it away— to Malcolm, I decided. He often made admiring remarks about my art collection.

Please let Aidan still be in London, I thought. I didn't want to have to take *Abberton* back to Spilling. The idea of having it in my home was unthinkable. Already I felt oppressed by it in a funny sort of way, even though I hadn't touched it yet and didn't own it. I had always known it was an object that possessed a certain power—that was what had drawn me to it in the first place—but now that its maker had traumatised and humiliated me, the force of the picture seemed wholly negative. It was ridiculous, I knew, but I was afraid of it.

'*Abberton*,' the woman repeated slowly, writing it on her form. 'Artist's name?'

'Mary Trelease.' I was surprised to have to tell her. Saul Hansard wouldn't have needed to ask. How could she represent her artists properly if she wasn't familiar with the titles of their work? Everything about her demeanour suggested indifference. I wondered how much commission TiqTaq took. Aidan had told me most galleries take fifty per cent, even the ones that make no effort to promote an artist's work.

'Mary Trelease?' The woman looked up at me, seeming suddenly nervous. For a moment, I was terrified she was about to tell me something I knew to be impossible. *You must be mistaken. Mary Trelease died years ago. She was murdered.*

The young woman walked over to *Abberton* and tapped its surface with the biro she was holding. 'This is the picture you want?' The disbelief and annoyance in her voice let me know that I was making life difficult for her.

'Yes.' I took my credit card out of my wallet to show her I wasn't going to back down, waited for her to say I couldn't have *Abberton*—Mary Trelease had told her to sell the painting to anybody but me. But I hadn't told this woman my name; how could she know who I was?

'Sorry, my mistake,' she said, a rueful smile appearing on her face. 'It's already sold.'

'What? But . . . it can't be. There's no red dot on the label.' I noticed for the first time that there was also no price, nothing written beneath the title and Mary Trelease's name. All the other pictures on TiqTaq's stall had prices apart from one or two that were labelled 'NFS'—not for sale—and their labels were printed. Why was *Abberton*'s handwritten? Had it been added at the last minute?

'I told you—I made a mistake. Someone bought this picture yesterday.' The smile was still there but it was straining to stay in place. 'I meant to put a "Sold" sticker on, but I never got round to it. I was rushed off my feet.'

'You told me it had been quiet since you got here,' I blurted out. 'I don't believe the picture's sold. Why won't you sell it to me?' I had to be allowed to take *Abberton* away with me. I had to. Aidan needed to see it; it would make everything all right between us again, as if his confession last night and his anger today had never happened.

The young woman screwed her eyes up, the better to inspect

me: this crazy specimen that had put itself in front of her. 'Do you think I don't want to make money? I'd gladly sell it to you if it was for sale.'

A combination of confusion and desperation had emboldened me, and I spoke to a complete stranger as I never would have dared to if there had been less at stake. 'Show me the sales form,' I said. 'Show me your copy, the yellow copy.' I indicated the form she'd been filling in for me. All the artists and galleries at the fair had the same ones, with three layers: white, yellow and green. Aidan and I had watched Gloria Stetbay's assistant fill one in yesterday and keep the yellow copy for herself.

'This is ridiculous.' Dyed-hair woman tried to laugh, but it wasn't convincing.

I walked towards her. She moved to stand in front of *Abberton*, as if she feared I might snatch it off the wall. 'You represent Mary Trelease, is that right? If her painting's up on your stall, that means you must represent her.' Aidan had taught me the basics about how the art world worked. 'If this picture is sold, I'd like to buy something else by her. Does she have other work that's available?'

'I wouldn't know that sort of thing. You'd have to pop into our gallery on Charlotte Street and—'

'Is someone there now, one of your colleagues?' I wasn't going to let it drop. She was lying to me, and I would force her to admit it. 'You could ring and ask them. Tell them you're with someone who's keen to buy any painting you've got by Mary Trelease, as long as it's signed, dated and recent.'

'There's no one there who'd . . . Look, I'm not . . .' She was getting flustered. She spread both her hands and lowered them slowly in a calming gesture. 'To be honest, I don't think we've got any other stuff by her, okay?'

'Do you represent her or don't you?'

'I'm not going to discuss details of the gallery's relationship with a particular artist . . .'

'An artist who refuses to sell any of her work,' I snapped. 'I'm right, aren't I? Mary Trelease sells her paintings to nobody. Why not?' I was certain my hunch was correct. Mary often used to bring in pictures for Saul to frame, ignoring me as she walked past me time after time, yet he never put her work up in the gallery. Saul always exhibited paintings by the artists he framed for; he used to tell me all the time that it was the best way to advertise his own work as well as theirs. So why not Mary's?

'I don't know what you're talking about,' said the woman. 'All I know is, we've sold one picture for her. This one.' She jabbed her thumb at *Abberton*. 'There's nothing I can do about it. I can't un-sell it. I'd be happy to sell you any of the other stuff you can see here. Everything else is available.'

I shook my head. 'If *Abberton*'s sold then whoever bought it will be back here to collect it, won't they? Did they say when?' An art fair wasn't like a gallery exhibition, Aidan had told me the day before. You didn't have to wait until it finished to collect your purchases—you could pick them up any time before the end of the last day.

I got no answer, so I kept pushing. '*Are* they coming to collect it? Or did they pay extra to have it delivered to their home? Can you check that for me, on the yellow form?'

'No, I can't. Even if I knew, I couldn't . . . Look, I really don't see how I can help you any more. I hope I'm not going to have to call security.'

This shocked me, the idea that someone could feel threatened by me. 'I'll go,' I said. 'Just . . . could you do me one favour?'

She eyed me suspiciously, waiting for the worst.

'Could you make sure the picture stays where it is until I come back? I don't care about buying it—I don't want it. But I need to show it to my boyfriend and . . . I don't know where he is.'

'The tall bloke in the donkey jacket you were looking for?'

I nodded.

She sighed, and seemed to soften. 'I'll do my best,' she said, 'but if the buyer comes to pick it up, there's not an awful lot I can do.'

I left without saying thank you or goodbye. I'd wasted enough time already. She was right. Assuming *Abberton* really was sold and she wasn't lying, the person who had bought it could arrive to collect it at any moment. I ran outside and stuck out my arm to stop a taxi, then realised there weren't any, only several people who looked as if they were waiting. One glanced at his watch, sighed and walked off down the road.

'Come *on*,' I breathed through gritted teeth. A taxi had to come. I had to get back to the hotel—that's where Aidan would be. He'd have gone back there to check out, to pick up our bag and the Gloria Stetbay. A taxi appeared, and a woman in a grey trouser suit with a mobile phone pressed to her ear moved forward to greet it. She opened the back door. I ran at her with my wallet already open and offered her twenty pounds if she'd let me take it instead. It was an emergency, I told her. She looked unconvinced, but took the money and stepped back, relinquishing the cab.

At the Drummond, I told the driver to wait outside for me. I didn't have the patience to wait for the lift, so I ran up four flights of stairs to room 436. I banged on the door and called Aidan's name. 'Please be here,' I whispered. 'Please.'

The door opened, but not very far. I heard footsteps walking away. I pushed the door fully open, banging it against the wall. Aidan stood in the centre of the room with his back to me. Short of leaving me stranded outside in the corridor, he couldn't have been less welcoming. I didn't care; I knew this bad patch would end as soon as he'd heard what I had to say. 'Mary Trelease,' I panted.

He swung round.

'What does she look like?'

'I don't know. That depends how long it takes a body to decay. You'd need to ask a pathologist.'

'Skinny, masses of black curly hair that's starting to go grey, cut-glass accent, bad skin—lined, like a much older woman's. Pale brown mole beneath her lower lip that's shaped like . . . like a double-ended spanner, sort of. Or how you'd draw a dog's bone in a cartoon . . .'

Aidan roared and flew across the room at me, clamping his hands around my arms. I screamed, frightened by the strength of his reaction. 'What are you saying?' he demanded. 'Where did you get that description from?'

'I've met her. Aidan, you've got to listen to me. You haven't killed her. She isn't dead. She's an artist, isn't she? Remember the woman I told you about, the one I had a run-in with at Saul's gallery? It was her! The picture she brought in, the one I wanted to buy—I've just seen it at the art fair, on a stall belonging to a gallery. TiqTaq, they're called. The painting's called *Abberton*. It's of a sort of person, but with no face . . .'

Aidan released me, staggered back across the room as if propelled by a physical force. 'No,' he said. Flecks of white had appeared at the corners of his mouth. He wiped them away with his hand. He'd started to sweat. 'Shut up. Shut up. You're lying. What are you trying to do?'

'You got it wrong!' I told him triumphantly. 'You didn't kill her, years ago or at any other time. She's not dead. The picture I saw, *Abberton*, it's dated 2007. It wasn't framed when I met her six months ago, but since then she's had it framed. She's alive, Aidan.' I didn't need to ask if the woman I'd described was the right one; his face was white with terror.

'I killed Mary Trelease,' he said. 'But maybe you've known that all along. Maybe that's why you turned up at the workshop asking for a job, and why you're telling me this now.' Fury blazed in his eyes. 'Who are you really, Ruth Zinta Bussey?' His sarcasm shook my heart. 'What was the plan?' He walked towards me slowly. 'Make me fall in love with you and then wipe me out? Drive me insane? Is that going to be the extent of my punishment, or is there more to come? Are you going to go to the police?'

'I don't know what you're talking about!' I sobbed. 'There's no plan. I love you! I'm not trying to punish you, I'm trying to make you see that you've done nothing wrong. Come back to Alexandra Palace with me and I'll show you the picture, *Abberton*. I've got a taxi waiting outside.'

He looked at me, through me. '*Abberton*,' he said in a hollow voice. 'You're telling me I'll find a picture called *Abberton*, by Mary Trelease at the *Access 2* Art fair?'

'Yes! Dated 2007. But you've got to come now—the woman on the stall told me it was sold. I think she was lying, but I'm not sure, and if someone comes to collect it . . .'

Aidan picked up his wallet and the black hold-all, and pushed past me into the corridor. He left the Gloria Stetbay picture—my engagement ring substitute—leaning against the wall. Watching him slam the door on it, I knew the answer to the question I was too scared to ask. Our engagement was off. Aidan wouldn't mention it again.

By the time I got to the taxi, he was sitting in it as if he'd been there for hours, shoulders hunched, his face a grim mask. 'Get in,' he said. I didn't understand. He was acting as if he was forcing me to go with him, when I was the one who had suggested it. 'Alexandra Palace,' he told the driver. 'As fast as you can.'

'Talk to me, Aidan, please,' I begged him. 'What happened between you and Mary Trelease? Why did you think you'd killed her? Why do you think I'm trying to drive you mad? Why would I?' I'd been so certain that the nightmare would be over as soon as I told him about *Abberton*, but it wasn't; I couldn't bear the disappointment. I buried my face in my hands and started to weep.

'Don't cry,' said Aidan. 'It won't help.'

'Please, tell me what's going on!'

'I shouldn't have told you anything. I should never have mentioned her name to you.'

'Why don't you trust me? I don't care what you've done—I love you. I should have said that last night, as soon as you told me, but I was confused. I knew it wasn't right—I knew you could never kill anyone!'

'Keep your voice down.'

'That's why I clammed up, not because what you'd told me changed how I felt about you but because I didn't believe it could be true. And the name Mary Trelease—I knew I'd heard it before, but I couldn't remember where. I must have seen it when I worked for Saul, on a bill or something.' I stopped, out of breath.

Aidan didn't look at me, but he took hold of my hand and squeezed it. He was staring out of the window, thinking hard, concentrating on something I couldn't see or share, something from his past. Almost whispering, I asked, 'Did you and Mary Trelease have some kind of . . . physical fight?' I pictured Aidan pushing her, her falling, knocking her head against something. Aidan panicking, fleeing the scene, assuming he'd killed her . . .

'Shhh,' he said, drawing out the sound as he exhaled slowly. As if I was a child, still young enough to accept comfort without substance. I knew then that there was no point asking him anything else.

We arrived at Alexandra Palace and I paid the driver. 'Do you remember the stall number?' Aidan asked me.

'It's opposite Jane Fielder's stall, number . . . number . . .' The churning in my head had dulled my memory.

'One seven one,' he said.

I followed him as he pushed past people milling in the aisles, browsing idly as Aidan and I had the day before. It seemed like a lifetime ago. 'There it is,' I blurted out when I saw Tiq Taq's sign from a distance. I looked at my watch: three o'clock. I'd left to go back to the hotel at half past one. My throat tightened. Blood pounded in my ears.

The woman with the dyed blonde hair had gone. In her place was an older woman with a pre-Raphaelite hairstyle—a long plait coiled into a conical bun at the nape of her neck. She was wearing a white linen suit, a clingy red scoop-necked T-shirt and brown sandals with coloured beads on them. Her face, hands and feet were tanned. As we approached, Aidan said, 'There's nothing there that's anything like what you described.' He turned away in disgust.

Mary's painting had gone. A picture of exactly the same size hung in its place, of an ugly naked woman standing next to a chicken. She had straggly hair and limbs as thick as a rugby centre forward's. I hated her, whoever she was. She had no business being there, where *Abberton* ought to have been. I thought, I knew this would happen. *I knew it.* All the way to Alexandra Palace in the taxi, I'd had a feeling not of hope but of dread: I was convinced *Abberton* would be gone, though I'd tried to deny it to myself. I'd read about negative expectations leading to negative outcomes, and now I blamed myself for the picture having vanished. 'Whoever bought it must have picked it up,' I said to Aidan. 'It was here, I swear it.' I grabbed his arm, tried to make him look at me, but he pushed me away.

'Excuse me?' I said to the woman with the coiled plait, loud enough so that Aidan could hear me from the other side of the aisle. 'I was here at lunchtime. I spoke to your colleague, the one with blonde hair.'

'Ciara,' said the woman, smiling. 'She's gone, I'm afraid. I'm Jan Garner. TiqTaq's my gallery. Can I help you?'

'You had a picture called *Abberton*. By an artist called Mary Trelease. It was there.' I pointed to the naked woman and the chicken.

Jan Garner shook her head. 'No,' she said. 'We didn't and it wasn't. You must be mistaken.'

I couldn't speak. Well trained though I was in fearing the worst, I hadn't foreseen this. Why was this stylish, polite, sophisticated-looking woman telling me a blatant lie? She must have known I knew she was lying.

'It was here at half past one this afternoon,' I insisted. 'The girl—Ciara—said it was sold, someone had bought it yesterday. Whoever bought it must have come to collect it.'

'I've always hated telling people they're wrong, but I'm afraid you are.' Jan Garner pulled a sheet of paper out of a file.

'Look, here's the list of everything we brought with us from the gallery: title and artist's name.'

There was no *Abberton* on the list. No Mary Trelease.

'But . . . it was here!' I turned to look at Aidan, who had moved further away. I could see from the set of his back and shoulders that he was listening to every word while pretending to look at another gallery's stall.

Jan Garner shook her head. 'Sorry,' she said. 'When I took over from Ciara, she said we hadn't sold anything so far. Which means the same pictures are up now as were up yesterday morning—nothing's changed. Are you . . .?'

I didn't hear the rest of what she said. Aidan had started to walk away, and I ran to catch him up. I was terrified of losing him again. 'Wait!' I shouted after him. 'She's lying! I swear on my life! Come back with me and I'll prove it to you. We can ask the people on the stalls opposite. They must have seen *Abberton*.'

'Shut up.' He took my arm and dragged me out of the hall into the foyer. 'I need you to tell me everything. Everything, Ruth—every detail.'

'I've already told you . . .'

'Tell me again. This *Abberton* picture—what is it, what's it of? What did the other woman say to you—Ciara? What happened at Hansard's gallery between you and the woman you think was Mary Trelease? What exactly was said?'

'I don't remember, not word for word—it was six months ago.'

'I don't care how long ago it was!' Aidan bellowed. People nearby turned to watch. He lowered his voice. 'I need to know. Start talking.'

So I did. I described the picture: the street scene background in greens, purples and browns, the outline of a human form filled with a kind of stuffing: stuck-on scraps of hard, gauze-like material, some painted, like curled-up jewels. Aidan let out little gasps through clenched teeth as he listened to my description, as if every word I uttered caused him terrible pain, but each time I stopped, worried about the effect I was having on him, he demanded I carry on.

I went over my conversation with Ciara. Aidan wanted to hear about every look that had passed across her face, every movement she made, the inflections in her voice. Then I told him as much as I could bear to about what had happened at Saul's gallery. I didn't mention the red paint.

That I didn't understand no longer mattered to me. Aidan didn't either; I could see that clearly, from the way the frown-lines on his forehead deepened as he listened to what I had to say. When he's worked it all out, he'll tell me, I thought. At least now he seemed to believe me. I comforted myself with the knowledge that Mary Trelease was alive.

Aidan said nothing in the taxi on the way to King's Cross. Neither of us mentioned the Gloria Stetbay painting. Four thousand pounds, and it would probably be found by a maid and thrown in the bin. I should have gone back for it—I can see that now; it was criminal not to—but at the time I didn't feel entitled to go back and claim it as my own, not once Aidan had decided to leave it in the hotel.

On the train, forty minutes into the journey, he finally spoke. 'When we get back, we'll go to mine to pick up a few things and then we'll go to yours,' he said. 'I'm moving in with you. I'm not letting you out of my sight from now on.' He said it as if he was passing sentence, suggesting something that would be unwelcome to me—a punishment—instead of what I'd wanted to happen since the day I met him.

'Good.' I searched his face for an indication of his meaning. Was he worried about me and wanting to stay close to protect me? Did he think Mary Trelease was a danger to us? Or was it a lack of trust that made him feel he had to watch my every move?

Did he regret not having killed Mary, now that he knew he hadn't?

I had no way of answering any of these questions. 'I'd love it if you moved in,' I said.

But my punishment wasn't over yet. Aidan said, 'I'll need that proof you promised me. If the painting you're talking about really exists, if you didn't make it up, find it. Find it and bring it to me.'

8

4/3/08

Simon knew something was wrong as soon as he walked into Proust's office. Wronger than usual: sub-zero already, and he hadn't opened his mouth yet. A man he didn't recognise stood behind the inspector, leaning against the wall, holding a manila folder. Neither he nor Proust said anything. Both seemed to be waiting for Simon to take the initiative, which he could hardly do, having no idea why he'd been summoned. He thought he'd wait it out.

Unless the Snowman had ditched one of the many tenets he often boasted had served him well for fifty-odd years—which struck Simon as unlikely—then it had to be the other man who smelled as if he'd fallen into a bath full of aftershave. Proust disapproved of scented males. Simon guessed he wouldn't make an exception for one who reeked of seaweed mixed with acid.

The man wore a toffee-coloured suit with a white shirt and a green tie that was silk or some other shiny material. He looked to be in his late thirties, and had the eyes of a jaded Las Vegas croupier, out of place in his pink, unblemished face. Human Resources? The Snowman didn't introduce him. 'Where were you yesterday afternoon and evening?' he asked Simon.

No way he can know. 'I went up to Newcastle, made a start on the Beddoes—'

'I'll ask you again: where were you?'

The croupier looked nearly as angry as Proust. Simon tensed. Was this trouble of a different order of magnitude? It was hard to tell; around the Snowman, he always had the impression that his marching orders were imminent. Was he about to make the biggest mistake of his career? Had he already made it? 'I followed Aidan Seed to London, sir.'

The inspector nodded. 'Carry on.'

'Sergeant Zailer and I spoke to Seed and Ruth Bussey yesterday afternoon, sir. The exchange left us both feeling even more concerned . . .'

'Skip the justifications. I want your movements, from when you got into your car to follow Seed until you arrived home.'

Wishing he knew who the croupier was and why he was there, Simon did as instructed. When he got to the part about following Seed to Friends House, the Snowman and his anonymous guest exchanged a look. When he told them he'd eavesdropped on the Quaker Quest meeting, the croupier asked him to report exactly what he'd heard. He had a Cockney accent. Simon waited for Proust to say, 'I'll ask the questions,' and was disconcerted when he didn't.

He told the two men everything he remembered: Olive Oyl, the fat, sweaty bald man, Frank Zappa, the Immense Something Other, the quote about cutlery not being eternal. 'How many of the people in that room do you think you could describe with any degree of accuracy?' asked the croupier.

'The two speakers, no problem,' Simon told him. *Was he job?* 'There were three tramps there too. I think they went for the free grub. I could probably describe them, though not as precisely.'

'You left Friends House before the meeting ended?' said Proust.

'Yeah.'

'What time was that?'

'I don't know—eight-ish.'

'And you went where?'

'Back to Ruskington Road, where I'd left my car.'

'Was Mr Seed's car still there, outside number 23?'

'Yeah.'

'Did you drive straight home?'

'No, sir. I approached the house—number 23—and looked in through the ground-floor windows, and the window of the basement flat.'

'What did you see?'

'Nothing much. Empty rooms.'

'Empty of people, or entirely empty?'

'No, they had furniture and stuff in them.'

'I trust you'll be able to give DC Dunning a thorough description of each room you peered into, complete with all the *stuff* you saw.'

DC Dunning. From London? 'Yes, sir. I'll do my best.'

The croupier moved forward, opened the file he was holding and placed a blown-up colour photograph on the table: the front of 23 Ruskington Road. With a biro, he pointed at the bay window on the right. 'Did you look through this window?'

'Yes.'

'What did you see?'

'A dining table and chairs. The table had a glass top. A sideboard against one wall.' Although it was only last night, Simon found it hard to be certain. He'd taken a quick look and decided there was nothing of any interest: no bookshelves stuffed with books about Quakerism, nor anything else to link the house to Seed. 'Maybe a rug and . . . a tall plant in a pot? Yeah, I think a plant.'

Dunning and Proust exchanged another look. 'Anything else?' Dunning asked.

'No. Not that I can remember.'

'What about on the walls?'

'What do you mean?'

'Was there anything up on the walls?'

Simon struggled to bring to mind an image of the room. 'I don't know. I didn't notice.'

'Pictures? Photographs?'

'It was darker inside than out. If there were pictures, I didn't see . . .' He stopped. Now would be a bad time to get something wrong. *Think.* 'There must have been something on the walls,' he said eventually.

'Why must there?' asked Proust.

'Like I said, I didn't notice. I'd more likely have noticed if the walls were bare than if they weren't. People usually put something up, don't they? Put it this way: nothing about the room struck me as odd. It looked . . . lived in. Normal.'

'Did you see anything leaning against a wall?' asked Dunning.

Simon hadn't a clue what he was talking about. 'No,' he said. 'Like what?'

'You say the room looked lived in?'

'That's right.'

'So nothing you saw suggested to you that people might recently have moved in?'

'No. Such as?'

'Packing crates, maybe pictures leaning against the wall, waiting to be put up? Picture hooks, a hammer? Cardboard boxes with "dining room" written on them?'

'No. Nothing like that.'

Dunning retrieved the photograph, replaced it in his file. 'What next?' Proust asked.

The bad feeling Simon had about all this intensified with each question. 'I went to get a kebab from a takeaway I'd passed on the way in—don't ask me where or what it was called. Junction of Ruskington Road and Muswell Hill Road, turn right, keep going for about four hundred yards or so. I got my kebab, then I drove back to Ruskington Road, sat in my car and ate it, waiting for Seed to come back.'

'In effect, you staked out Mr Seed's car, and 23 Ruskington Road,' said Proust.

'Yes.'

'Did Mr Seed return?'

'Yes, sir. At about half past nine. He and the woman I'd seen at the meeting, the speaker with the tied-back brown hair, they walked up the road together towards the house—number 23.'

'Were they speaking as they walked?' asked Dunning.

'She was.'

'Did you hear any of what she said?'

'No.'

'Her tone? Could you gauge her mood?'

'Good,' said Simon without hesitation. 'She was prattling on, like people do when they're happy or excited. They stopped by Seed's car and he opened the boot, took something out . . .'

'What?' Dunning pounced.

'I couldn't see—there was a van in the way. Whatever it was, he carried it into number 23. The woman unlocked the door and opened it for him, and they both went in. A light went on in that window, the one you were asking about. I moved my car, drew level with the house to try and see in, but I had to move after a few seconds—there were cars coming up behind me. There's traffic parked along both sides of Ruskington Road, so overtaking's impossible. All I saw before I had to move was the woman drawing the curtains, still talking, and Seed standing behind her.' Simon looked at Dunning. 'After that, I called it a night, drove back home.' He cleared his throat, realising he'd inadvertently lied. 'Actually, I . . . I drove to Sergeant Zailer's house.'

'Does the name Len Smith mean anything to you?' asked Dunning.

'No.' Simon had had enough. This man was a detective, like him. Cooperation ought to work both ways. 'What's going on? Did something happen at the house after I left?'

Dunning produced another photograph from his file and thrust it in front of Simon's face. 'Have you seen this person before?'

Simon found himself staring at a heavily made-up woman with short hair that seemed to sweep back from her face in waves. It was a completely different look, but he recognised her all the same. 'Yeah. It's her, the speaker from Quaker Quest.' *Olive Oyl.*

'The woman you saw enter 23 Ruskington Road in the company of Aidan Seed?' Dunning clarified.

Simon nodded.

'Her name's Gemma Crowther. She was killed last night,' said Dunning. From his tone, he might have been filling Simon in on the football results. 'Shot. In her dining room, some time before midnight—that's when her partner, Stephen Elton, came home and found her. He'd been at Quaker Quest too, but he stayed to clear up after the meeting.'

'The fat bald guy?' Simon asked.

'No.' Dunning dropped Olive Oyl's picture on Proust's desk and pulled out one of a young man—perhaps as young as early twenties, or else the photo was an old one—with prominent cheekbones and shoulder-length dark blond hair. All he needed was some of his girlfriend's make-up and he could have been the front man of a glam rock band. 'Did you see him?'

'No.'

'You're sure?'

'Positive.'

Dunning continued to hold the photograph aloft as he said, 'So you saw Gemma Crowther alive and well at half past nine . . .'

'Seed killed her,' said Simon. As he was saying it, it occurred to him that he ought to wait, oughtn't to give Dunning the impression that he was someone who leaped to conclusions in advance of having all the facts. *Too late.* 'Have you got him?'

'You're not hearing me, DC Waterhouse. As things stand, I've got you, by your own account, as the last person to see Gemma alive.'

'You mean apart from Aidan Seed?'

Dunning carried on as if he hadn't spoken. 'I've got two witnesses telling me you were behaving suspiciously near her home—looking through windows, hanging around in your car, watching the house. They made a note of your car registration, thought you were a would-be burglar, picking your moment to break in.'

'I've explained what I was doing there.'

'I've got no one's word but yours that Aidan Seed was at Quaker Quest or at 23 Ruskington Road yesterday, and I know you think nothing of lying. I just heard you lie to your guvnor when he asked where you were yesterday. I've also heard you've got a history of, among other things, violent outbursts and obsessive behaviour. You've been a detective for longer than I have— you put all that together and tell me what you come up with.'

Simon had trained himself, over the years, to see keeping his temper in check as a feat of strength. Dunning was trying to get a rise out of him; he needed to pour the full force of his anger into resisting. These days he knew how to turn himself into a rock—impermeable. It didn't feel like weakness any more, not hammering people to the ground with his fists when they pissed him off.

'I don't understand why you'd care enough to tail Aidan Seed to London instead of making your and everyone else's life easier by following through on the action you'd been assigned,' said Dunning. 'That's something you'll have to explain to me. A man who's committed no crime . . .'

'Hasn't he? If Gemma Crowther's dead at midnight and I saw Seed with her at half past nine . . .?'

'There were thirty-seven people at the meeting at Friends House,' said Dunning. 'Unless they're all lying, not one of them knows the name Aidan Seed. According to them, and to Stephen Elton, Gemma's partner, she left the meeting with a Len Smith, a social worker from Maida Vale who'd become a good friend of hers.'

'Does the physical description match Seed's?' Simon asked. 'A social worker from Maida Vale? I take it you've had no luck finding him.'

'I'm told Smith has been attending regularly for several weeks.'

'There is no Len Smith! It was Seed—he's your killer. I saw him go into that house with her. Unless one of your witnesses saw him drive away while she was still alive . . .'

'Neither of them saw *you* drive away when you say you did,' Dunning announced with a smug smile—his first. 'Shortly after half past nine.'

'I didn't leave then or they weren't looking then?' said Simon angrily. 'There's a difference. Ask your witnesses if they saw Seed's car outside the house. Get a photo of Seed and show it to the Quaker lot—they'll tell you he's the man they know as Len Smith.'

Dunning gave him a look he'd used himself many times, on scrotes who wouldn't talk.

'You're not serious?' said Simon. 'Me? I'm on your side of the fence. I lock up the killers.' Proust sat hunched over his desk like a stone effigy, saying nothing.

'I'm part of a team of twelve,' said Dunning matter-of-factly. 'In my team, we stick to our tasking briefs. Different detectives are handling different aspects of the investigation into Gemma Crowther's death, and guess what? I got you, babe. Which means you and I are going on a little trip to the Big Smoke, and you're going to elaborate on the story I've just heard from your DI about you and Sergeant Charlotte Zailer—who's also your fiancée, I believe?'

Simon hated the way he said it as if it were somehow questionable, as if his and Charlie's engagement meant neither of them could be trusted. *Babe?* Had Dunning called him that, or had he imagined it?

'. . . your and Sergeant Zailer's fixation on Aidan Seed, his girlfriend Ruth Bussey and a woman called Mary Trelease.'

'All people you should be speaking to,' Simon told him. 'Are you?'

'You're going to make me understand why you care so much

about all these people, and let's hope the story makes more sense than it did the first time I heard it. At the moment, the way I see it, I've got one in the bag: someone in the right place at the right time, behaving irrationally and suspiciously—that someone being you.' Not giving Simon a chance to respond, Dunning asked, 'Where's Sergeant Zailer?'

'Off work. Sick.'

'You mean at home?'

'Far as I know.'

'Was she in London with you yesterday evening?'

'No.'

'Where was she?'

'At Ruth Bussey's house.' Simon sighed. 'Look, we don't have to have a problem here. I'll tell you what I know, and I'll tell you what I don't know but strongly suspect. Same goes for Charlie—Sergeant Zailer. You want to put your murder case to bed, the best way to do that quickly and efficiently is to let us help you.'

Proust stood up, leaning his hands on his knees as he rose. Simon had almost forgotten he was there. 'If I'm about to lose DC Waterhouse, I need to find out where we're up to on various things so that I can sort out handover. Can you give us a moment, DC Dunning?'

'Handover?' Simon echoed. How long did Proust think he'd be gone?

'Fine.' Dunning headed for the door. 'I'll be waiting outside.'

Once they were alone, Proust said, 'DC Dunning has tried several times to reach Sergeant Zailer at home, with no success. If you know where she is, I'd strongly advise you to share that information with him.' The inspector sounded distant. Tired. For once, Simon wouldn't have minded a spurt of his customary garrulous sarcasm. No point apologising for yesterday; he wasn't sorry. The only mistake he'd made was to leave London when he did; he might have saved Gemma Crowther's life if he'd stayed another hour.

He knew what he'd tell Dunning about Charlie: fuck all. She was in a state, and wanted as few people as possible to know. Proust, at least, wasn't asking to be told; only that Simon should reveal all to Dunning. *Handover*. 'Sir, much as I'd like to be shot of Nancy Beddoes, there's no need to reassign anything of mine—chances are I'll be back later today.'

'There is no chance, DC Waterhouse, that you will return to this building later today, or tomorrow, or the day after.'

Simon regretted his attempt to lighten the atmosphere. 'Dunning's trying it on, sir. He'll change his tune. He knows I'm telling the truth and he knows I can help him.'

'I had no choice but to try to explain your interest in Aidan Seed,' said Proust. 'Just so that we're clear. Soon as I heard you'd been in London, I knew it had to be related to Seed. I presented the facts as fairly as I could, and I told Dunning you've got good instincts and a good track record. I couldn't pretend you hadn't had your ups and downs over the years, but I made sure to put them in context. I don't believe I could have done any more.'

'Sir, for . . .' Simon felt his control slipping. 'You're talking as if we're never going to see each other again. We both know Seed's going to be charged with Gemma Crowther's murder . . .'

'Do we?' The inspector turned away from Simon and faced the 2008 planner that was Blu-tacked to the wall behind his desk.

'Forget Dunning for a second, sir. You agree with me, don't you? Seed killed Gemma Crowther—he must have. Think of what we know for certain: Ruth Bussey said she was scared something bad was going to happen. Last night, she told Charlie Seed had been away a lot, lying about where he was. Turns out he's been pretending to be a Quaker, to get close to Crowther. *Knowing* he was going to kill her. He told me he believed only in the material world, facts and science—so what's he doing at a Quaker rally? Dunning asked me if I could gauge Gemma Crowther's mood, but he didn't ask me about Seed. While she was chatting away merrily, he had a face like a thundercloud.'

Like a man who knew he was about to kill somebody, as soon as the curtains were drawn. Simon kept the thought to himself, knowing how it would be received. 'Ruth Bussey also told Charlie he'd changed his story: not that he'd killed Mary Trelease, but that he was seeing the future, a future in which he was *going* to kill her.'

'DC Waterhouse . . .'

'Sir, we've got to treat that as a threat, and act on it. Tell me that's going to happen, whether I'm here or not. We can't leave this to Dunning. Do you trust him, after what you've just heard? I don't. Mary Trelease is ours, not his. Dunning doesn't care if Seed's on his way round to Megson Crescent with a shooter while he's wasting time leafing through my Reg 9s—it's not his patch, is it?'

'Enough,' said Proust quietly.

Simon was determined to stir him up. 'Ruth Bussey told Charlie last night that a man's been hanging round outside her house, showing an unhealthy interest. Charlie thought she was probably imagining it, until Bussey showed her the CCTV footage.'

'CCTV?' It was difficult to read a person's back, but Simon had the impression from the sudden tensing of the shoulders that Proust regretted asking, allowing himself to be drawn in.

'Bussey lives in the lodge house at the entrance to Blantyre Park. Apparently she was so concerned about this man that she asked her landlord to install surveillance cameras. Anyway, soon as Charlie got a look at his face, she recognised him. His name's Kerry Gatti. He works for First Call.' Simon knew Proust would have heard of the firm, and waited for him to ask in what capacity Gatti was employed there, or to comment on the cruelty of giving a boy a girl's name. *Nothing.* 'He's a private investigator, sir,' Simon told him.

No response.

'Did you hear what Dunning said about Gemma Crowther's partner? He got back at midnight. The meeting must have finished at nine, or thereabouts. How long does it take to clear up a hall? Is the boyfriend a suspect? An associate of Seed's, perhaps? What's Dunning told you that he hasn't told me?' Simon picked up the empty mug on Proust's desk, made as if to launch it at the back of his head. He replaced it with a bang; even that got no reaction. 'Len Smith's got to be Seed, right?'

'Call DC Dunning back in,' said Proust. 'You can discuss your concerns with him, from Crowther's boyfriend's alibi to your bafflement over the inconsistency of Aidan Seed's metaphysical position.' Finally, he turned round. The surface of his skin was webbed with colour; his face looked like a blood-blister waiting to burst. 'Even if I wanted to, I couldn't answer your questions about this case. Because of your apparent involvement in it. This is what you set in motion when you deliberately deceived me and Sergeant Kombothekra and charged down to London to meet the Light Brigade. This: the situation we find ourselves in. I'm sorry if it's not to your taste.'

Simon was pleased to get a response. 'Mary Trelease said "Not me", when Charlie told her Seed had confessed to killing her. She said it twice—"Not me". Charlie thought she was trying to suggest Seed had killed someone else.'

Proust's eyes moved to the glass that separated his cubicle from the CID room. Dunning, watching from the other side, saw him looking and started to inch towards the door. The Snowman raised a hand to stop him. 'What was Ms Trelease's response?' he asked. 'I assume Sergeant Zailer asked her if that was what she'd intended to imply.'

'She denied it, sir. But she would, wouldn't she? If she'd fully made up her mind to talk, she'd talk. If she was scared, though, maybe she'd only risk a hint—the sort that can easily be explained away if you lose your nerve.'

'Where's Sergeant Zailer today? She's not ill in bed, is she?'

Simon's answer was too slow in coming, as slow as the change in the Snowman's demeanour was instant. The eyes glazed and froze, the face slackened. So this is how it feels to be cut loose, thought Simon, as Proust gestured for Dunning to come back in and take out the rubbish.

Dominic Lund chuckled. 'You're on a hiding to nothing,' he told Charlie, his mouth full of spaghetti bolognese. A line of oily orange sauce snaked down his chin. 'If a case could be made, I'd happily take your money and make it, even if we were guaranteed to lose. I like cases like that. Usually win them too. This, though? You know it's a joke, right?' He delivered his expert opinion without once looking at Charlie, then laughed again, as if to illustrate his point. She'd noticed that he preferred not to look at people directly; he'd dictated his food order to his open menu, not to the waiter standing beside him with a notepad.

Lund was an intellectual property lawyer, a partner at Ellingham Sandler's London office. He was tall, dark, heavily built, fat around the middle, and looked to be in his mid-forties. Olivia had recommended him. 'I doubt there's anything you can do about it,' she'd said on the phone last night, 'but Dominic Lund's the person to ask. That man works miracles. He's *the* person to have on your side.' Charlie had deliberately blanked out the first part, heard only that here was someone who might be able to help her. A miracle-worker. He'd been fourth on a list of the most influential names in UK law, according to Liv. The editor of a newspaper she regularly freelanced for had been awarded a huge sum in compensation after a rival daily printed a photograph of her leaving a substance abuse treatment clinic. Both the victory and the hugeness of the sum had been down to Lund, apparently.

Now Charlie wished she'd thought to ask her sister for the first three names on the list. Liv had said nothing about Lund being callous, entirely lacking in social graces and, as a result, impossible to talk to. On the phone this morning, his PA had told Charlie he would see her today but not in his office—for lunch, at Signor Grilli, an Italian restaurant on Goodge Street. In response to Charlie's mystified silence, the assistant had said,

'It's where he meets people. He likes it there,' as if she'd assumed Charlie might know this already.

Lund had arrived late, patting his pockets and muttering that he'd forgotten his wallet. He could go back to the office for it, he said, but then he and Charlie would lose their 'window'. Charlie told him it didn't matter, she'd pay. Always worth splashing out on a miracle, she'd thought to herself. Lund had tossed a perfunctory thank you in her direction without looking up. Now she was wondering if it was a ruse. Did everyone who consulted him have to buy him lunch? And why this loud, hectic little restaurant in particular? Lund seemed hardly to notice what he was shovelling into his mouth. His BlackBerry was the main recipient of his attention. It lay on the table in front of him; every time it bleeped, he grabbed it with both hands and spent a couple of minutes panting and huffing over it as if it were an addictive pocket computer game that he couldn't bear to put away, one that offered bonus points to anyone who gave it his all.

Charlie's pizza lay untouched on the table in front of her. She wanted to ask Lund to repeat back to her everything she'd told him, to check he'd listened properly before deciding her problem wasn't worth his time or effort. 'I'm talking about a display,' she said. 'It's not tucked away in a cupboard somewhere—it's blatant. She's got them up on a wall for anyone who walks into that room to see: a complete . . . information resource about the worst, most traumatic event of *my* life, *my* past, and that's only the bit I saw. Who knows what else she's . . . collected? The wall might be just a fraction of it. Last Friday she was waiting for me when I arrived at work . . .'

Lund's BlackBerry beeped. He grabbed it and slumped down in his chair for a session of enthusiastic finger- and thumb-jabbing, throughout which he breathed heavily, muttered occasionally and ignored Charlie. When he'd finished, he looked up briefly and said, 'She waited for you at work for a valid reason, right?'

'I don't know about that. She told me a bullshit story about her boyfriend saying he'd murdered a woman who's not even dead. And she refused to tell me why she wanted to talk to me in particular. When I asked her yesterday why she'd had an article about me in her coat pocket, she didn't give me a proper answer.'

'Miss Zailer . . .'

'It's Sergeant,' Charlie corrected him angrily.

'If I were you I'd relax.' Lund wound some more strands of spaghetti round his spoon, the long fringe of his dark hair dipping into the sauce in his bowl. Then he sucked up the pasta, making a noise like a vacuum cleaner, spattering the tablecloth and his shirt with sauce. He raised his voice and said something in Italian to nobody in particular—into the air, or so it seemed. Then, as if nothing unusual had happened, he switched back to English. 'It's her bedroom wall, she's got a steady boyfriend—how many people are likely to see it? Her, him, a few close friends maybe.'

'I don't care if no one sees it,' Charlie snapped. 'She's got no right to have it. Has she? Are you telling me a complete stranger-stalker-weirdo can amass information about my life and turn it into an . . . an exhibit for her own amusement, and there's no way of making her stop?'

'You've not been listening to me if you need to ask.'

'I want her to destroy it, everything she's got on me, or hand it over to me so that I can destroy it!' Charlie was aware that she was almost shouting.

'Your wishing something doesn't make it legally enforceable,' said Lund. His tone suggested nothing could matter to him less. 'There's nothing here for me to work with. Zero. First, there's no exhibiting involved. If she was going round sticking this stuff up on billboards all over town, it'd be a different matter, but her home's her private property. Any information she's got about you was in the public domain—in newspapers, which she bought, presumably. She didn't steal them from your house, did she? Haven't you got any old newspapers or magazines lying around at home? *Vogue, Elle, The English Home?*'

'No.' Charlie spat the word at him. Did she look like she had nothing better to do than read about handbags and cushions? 'Keeping a few newspapers and magazines isn't the same thing as obsessively gathering cuttings about one person. I don't keep anything that constitutes an invasion of someone else's privacy, no.'

Lund had disappeared beneath the table. He was rooting around in his briefcase. When he surfaced, he was holding a crumpled copy of the *Daily Telegraph*. He put it down on top of Charlie's untouched pizza. As he pointed to a small article at the bottom of the page, orange oil began to seep through the paper. 'David Miliband,' he said. 'Our Foreign Secretary. Not for too long, hopefully. If I want to cut out these three paragraphs about him and glue them to my shaving mirror, that's my choice, a choice I'm perfectly entitled to make. Do you think the boy Miliband could stop me? I've said this twice already, but I'll say it again: the invasion of privacy argument doesn't stand up. If this woman was broadcasting your private diary to the world, or going through your knicker drawer to find this stuff, the situation would be different. It'd be different if she was using the information she's collected for a purpose that's deterimental to your well-being, but she isn't.'

'She's fucking stalking me!' Charlie pushed Lund's newspaper off her plate, towards him. 'You don't think that's detrimental? Her bedroom wall's part of it—it's all part of the same thing, and I need it to stop! She waited for me outside my nick, she wouldn't explain . . .'

'From what you said, you didn't try very hard to get an explanation out of her.' Lund rotated his lower jaw to mask a yawn. It made a clicking sound. 'I'd have demanded to know what she was about and refused to take no for an answer. You didn't even tell her you'd seen the bedroom wall—why not?'

'Because I was shit scared, all right?' Charlie hissed. The

truth was embarrassing, but since she was never going to see Dominic Lund again, she decided it didn't matter. So what if the fourth most influential person in UK law thought she was a pathetic, gutless wimp? 'Even you can't deny this woman's unnaturally obsessed with me. At the moment she's restraining herself—she thinks I don't know, so she can afford to take her time. If I'd told her what I'd seen, she might have pulled out a knife and sliced me up—how did I know what she'd do? She's not normal. I needed to get away and think it through.'

Charlie sniffed hard, wiping away her tears quickly so she wouldn't need to admit to herself she was crying. Two tears didn't count as crying. 'I was desperate to get the hell away from her, but I didn't, not immediately. I sat in her house for another two hours, listening to an elaborate story about an art fair. I kidded myself I was staying to try and figure her out, but it wasn't that. It was fear. This woman's had me in her sights for God knows how long, she's toyed with me, manipulated me—me and maybe several other people. I've no way of knowing how much of this dead-woman-who-isn't-dead act is genuine—it could easily be a trap of some kind. And last night she wanted to tell me a story, and you know what? I listened like a good girl, hoping that if I did what she wanted, if I could convince her I was her friend and her ally, then maybe she'd change her mind about whatever God-awful thing she's planning to do to me.'

Lund looked unsurprised but amused by Charlie's outburst. 'Miss Zailer—Sergeant, rather. You're in retreat from reality. From what you've said, there's no reason to think this lady's stalking you or that she wants to harm you. Yours was clearly a name she knew, so when she had a problem she wanted to take to the police, she thought of you. That's not stalking. As for not explaining why she had the article on her person when she came to see you—so what? It's not against the law to withhold an explanation, or to cut things out of newspapers and stick them on the wall. If everyone in the UK decided to fill their houses with column inches about you, there'd be damn all you could do about it.'

'Okay.' Charlie forced herself to breathe slowly and steadily. 'Realistic. I can be realistic.'

Lund raised his eyebrows, making no secret of his doubt. His BlackBerry bleeped again, sucking his attention towards it like a mind-magnet. In an instant, Charlie had become invisible. Even more invisible. By the time Lund had finished prodding his machine, she'd composed herself. 'What if we were sneaky about it?' she said. 'Couldn't you send the woman a letter, scaring the shit out of her? I'd be willing to pay over the odds.'

At this, Lund looked up and grinned. 'I'm not a thug-for-hire. What's your sister told you about me?'

'I'm not asking you to give her a kicking.' Charlie tried not to sound as if she was begging. 'What about threatening her with a court case unless she takes the whole lot down and destroys it? Even if there's no legal action we can take, she won't know that. She's a picture-framer, not a lawyer. She'll be scared—anyone would.'

Lund shrugged, wiping his face with his napkin. His entire face, not only the area around his mouth. Now his cheek as well as his chin was smeared with orange grease. 'And when she consults a lawyer and he tells her it's a joke? That's my reputation stuffed, isn't it? Either I'm unethical or completely tonto. And if your woman's got anything about her, she'll take it to the press. I would.'

'Please. There must be something you can do. I can't bear it, knowing it's there. I keep seeing it in my mind, wondering who's seeing it in real life, reading all those things about me. Can't you understand that? Are you telling me that's not a violation of my privacy?'

'The law doesn't care how you feel,' said Lund. 'Legally, you're trying to violate *her* privacy. I'd go to the papers if I were her, for sure. "I was harassed by psychopath's ex-girlfriend, says picture-framer." More headlines for her to stick up in her gallery, more infamy for you.'

'Fuck you.'

'What?' Lund frowned. 'Oh, come on. Let's not pussyfoot around.' He leaned back in his chair and stared up at the ceiling.

Charlie dug her fingernails into her palms as hard as she could. *Focus on the physical pain.* 'I didn't know he was a psychopath. I was another of that evil fucker's *victims.*' Seeing Lund's expression, she said, 'Not in *that* way. I just mean . . . it wasn't my fault. The inquiry found in my favour, even if the shitty tabloids didn't.'

'I know all that,' said Lund, yawning openly. 'I'm telling you what the press would say, if this woman was canny enough to approach them.'

Charlie stood up, pushing back her chair. 'Forget it,' she said. 'Invoice me for the hour you've spent ripping my self-esteem to shreds. You can pay for your own lunch.'

He waved away the suggestion. 'They know me well enough here,' he said. What the fuck was that supposed to mean? 'Don't take it out on me—I'm trying to help you. The best thing you can do is forget the whole thing: the psychopath, the gutter hacks, the woman—all of it. Why let it bother you? You should put it behind you.'

Charlie couldn't breathe. He'd refused all her appeals for real help, and now he was trying to fob her off with hackneyed snippets of homespun wisdom. She wanted to kill him.

Lund smirked as if he'd remembered a filthy joke. 'Olivia tells me you're getting married.'

Charlie moved the words around in her brain. Liv hadn't mentioned knowing Lund personally. 'Have you seen my sister recently?'

'Last week. Simon, isn't it? Your fiancé? Also a cop.'

'How well do you and Liv know each other?' *Vogue, Elle, The English Home* . . . The magazines Lund had suggested to Charlie were all ones Olivia subscribed to. *No. Please, no.*

'How well does anyone know anyone? Liv can't believe your parents haven't tried to talk you out of marrying him,' said Lund amiably. 'Says she's tried, but you won't listen to her.'

Charlie's insides had turned to lead. She opened her mouth to speak, but found she couldn't. Every last word had declared itself unavailable.

'My impression is that you don't really listen to anyone,' Lund added, his eyes drifting to the screen of his BlackBerry. Were there messages on it from Olivia?

Charlie pulled her handbag off the back of her chair and marched out of the restaurant. Outside, walking fast in no particular direction, she realised she'd broken the strap. She heard a stifled cry that must have come from her. Where to go, what to do next? Not Olivia's flat. She'd kill her sister if she saw her now. Better to calm down first. Charlie pulled her phone out of her bag, made sure it was still switched off. She ached to ring Simon, but knew that if she spoke to him in her present state, they'd end up having a row. Simon, like Dominic Lund, didn't understand why she hadn't simply tackled Ruth openly about the newspaper cuttings. He thought the bedroom wall thing was odd, but didn't understand why it had upset Charlie to the extent that it had. *He thinks I'm overreacting.*

A street sign caught her eye as she tried and failed to light a cigarette in the cold wind: 'Charlotte Street'. How many Charlotte Streets could there be in London? Charlie answered her own question: more than one, easily. Still, it was possible. This seemed the right sort of area, and she could see what looked like a gallery further down the road.

She dropped her unlit cigarette and lighter back into her bag and broke into a run. A few seconds later, the possibility became a reality. There was the name, in orange and brown letters on the glass: TiqTaq. This was the gallery Ruth Bussey had mentioned last night. Charlie took a deep breath and went in.

* * *

Did a paper cut-out count as art? Charlie couldn't ask the tanned middle-aged woman in the patchwork jacket who sat behind a battered wooden table at the back of the gallery. She was on the phone, trying to make an appointment to get her legs waxed, sounding upbeat at first, saying, 'I completely understand,' and then increasingly impatient when it started to become apparent that even next week was fully booked. Charlie wondered if she was the older woman Ruth Bussey had met at the art fair: Jan something or other. TiqTaq's owner.

If she was, presumably all work exhibited was approved by her. She evidently saw some merit in the framed lines of paper dolls holding hands that were up on the walls. Each had been cut out of different coloured paper and was a different size; each carried a price tag of between two and five thousand pounds. I could have done these, Charlie thought. A few big sheets of paper, a pair of scissors . . . *What a scam.*

'Can I help you?' The woman was off the phone. 'Shall I talk you through the exhibition? I'm Jan Garner. TiqTaq's my gallery.'

So Ruth Bussey had told the truth about that, at least. In fact, Charlie had believed every word of her story. Even feeling the way she did about Ruth at the moment, she could tell when a person stopped lying; the relief was unmistakeable. Simon disagreed; they'd argued about it last night, at some ungodly hour. 'Anyone who's lied once is untrustworthy always,' he'd said. 'Clever liars admit to old lies to distract you, so that you don't spot the ones they're in the middle of.'

Charlie shook Jan Garner's extended hand. 'Charlie Zailer,' she said. 'I'm hoping you can help me with something else, actually—nothing to do with the exhibition.'

'Happy to if I can,' said Jan. 'Fancy a cup of tea?'

Could this work as a matey chat? Charlie wondered. Useful if it could, since she had no official reason to be here. 'Yes. Thanks.'

'Earl Grey, Lady Grey, lapsang, green with mint, green with jasmine, lemon and ginger . . .'

'Earl Grey'd be lovely,' said Charlie. The long list of fancy teas made her think of Olivia, who drank things like fennel and nettle, and would no doubt drink weeds stewed in dirty bathwater if it had the right label on it. Charlie pushed the thought of her sister away.

While Jan made the drinks, she pulled an information sheet out of a plastic rack near the door and read about the paper dolls exhibition. It was called 'Under Skin'. The dolls weren't cut out of coloured paper, as Charlie had assumed, but out of pages from road atlases which were then stuck together and 'encased in watercolours' so that each row looked like a continous, uncut piece of paper. How long must it have taken, Charlie wondered, and what was the point of it, apart from to show that appearances could deceive? *Big deal.* Did anyone need something so obvious pointing out to them?

Jan appeared from the back of the gallery with two tall china mugs. 'Right, fire away,' she said, handing Charlie her drink.

'Are you familiar with the work of an artist called Mary Trelease?'

The smile on Jan's face instantly became strained. 'Not in touch any more,' she said.

'I just wondered . . . I've seen some of Mary's paintings and—'

'You've seen Mary's work? Where?'

'At her house.'

Jan laughed. 'She let you in and showed you her pictures? So I'm guessing you're her closest friend, if not her only friend.'

'No, no, nothing like that.' Charlie smiled and took refuge in her cup of tea. 'I hardly know her. I've met her once, that's it. I went to see her about something else.'

'Doesn't sound like the Mary Trelease I know, letting a stranger see her paintings. She hates anyone to see her work. She won't sell it, won't exhibit, won't promote herself in any way.'

'How do you know her?' Charlie asked.

'Why do you want to know, if you don't mind my asking? What did you say your name was again?'

Charlie decided she'd better be frank. She told Jan her name, and that she was with the Culver Valley Police. 'I'm sorry,' she said. 'I'm so used to firing off questions. I forget that when I'm out of uniform, I need to persuade people to answer me instead of ordering them to.'

'Mary lives in the Culver Valley,' said Jan, her eyes sharp. 'Is your interest in her professional or personal?'

Charlie sipped her tea, and considered carefully before answering. 'Today's a day off for me,' she admitted. 'I suppose I'd have to say personal, though I first heard Mary's name when someone—' She broke off. 'I'm afraid that, because there is a police angle to this—or, rather, because there might be—I can't tell you too much.'

'You said you went to see Mary about something else . . .' Jan stopped, seeing Charlie's expression. 'That's part of what you can't tell me, right?'

''Fraid so. Look, as I say, I'm here as an interested visitor, not as a cop. There's really no reason why you should tell me anything.'

'I'm happy to tell you what little I know about Mary.' Jan seemed reassured. 'You're definitely not her best friend?'

Charlie smiled. 'If you're holding back some vitriol, there's no need. It's no skin off my nose whether you love her or hate her. I'm just interested to find out as much as I can.'

Jan nodded. 'I'd never heard of her until one day in October last year, when she turned up here unannounced, no appointment, nothing. You've met her, right? So you know how striking she looks—that hair, the ultra-posh voice. Like a mad queen who's lost her kingdom. I was a little intimidated by her.'

You and me both, thought Charlie.

'She'd brought a picture with her, one she wanted framed. She told me she lived in Spilling and that she'd fallen out with her old gallery, the one that used to frame all her work . . .'

'Did she say what about?'

'No. I didn't ask.'

'Sorry. Go on.'

'She informed me, rather regally, that I was going to frame the painting for her, even told me how much I should charge her—same as the old gallery would have. I'd have laughed if she hadn't been so obviously serious. She told me that, from now on, I would be framing her pictures. At that point I had to interrupt and tell her I didn't do framing—I'm not a picture-framer. It took a lot of guts, let me tell you. She'd been in here less than five minutes and already I was terrified of being a disappointment to her.'

Charlie smiled. She was used to dealing with people who released the occasional jerky, incoherent sentence if she was lucky. Jan Garner was a welcome contrast.

'It was hard to tell her without sounding patronising that in London, galleries that sell contemporary art don't do framing, whatever happens in Spilling. The artists I represent deliver their pictures already framed.'

'How did she take it when you told her?' Charlie asked.

'Oh, badly. Mary took everything badly. I offered to recommend framers, but she wouldn't let me. I asked her why she'd come to London. I mean, I know it's a relatively short train journey, but still . . . wouldn't it have been more convenient for her to find a picture-framer in Spilling? There must be others apart from the gallery she'd fallen out with.'

Apart from Saul Hansard, there was only one that Charlie knew of: Aidan Seed. 'What did she say?'

'That it had to be me. Beyond that, she wouldn't elaborate. To this day, I don't know why she chose me rather than anyone else, or how she first heard of me. I asked her again later, once we'd established a working relationship and knew each other better, but she still wouldn't say.' Jan caught Charlie's puzzled look and said, 'Oh, sorry. I should have said: yes, I did end up framing pictures for Mary. Having them framed for her, rather, by a friend of mine. Mary Trelease is a woman who makes sure she gets what she wants.'

'But you'd told her you didn't do framing,' said Charlie. 'How did she persuade you?'

'She didn't. Her picture did. *Abberton*.' Jan's eyes lost their focus and she sighed. 'It was brilliant. Something really special.'

Charlie glanced at the nearest of the paper-doll pictures. 'In a different league from those,' said Jan, reading her mind. 'Mary's paintings—that first one I saw and every one I saw subsequently—they were *alive*. They were beautiful and ugly at the same time, full of passion.'

'So you agreed because you liked her work,' Charlie summarised. *Abberton*: another thing Ruth Bussey had told the truth about.

'Not at first,' said Jan. 'At first I tried to persuade her to let me represent her. That was when she told me she'd never sold a single picture and never would. It was also when I got to hear her rules: I wasn't allowed to show her work to anyone, or mention her name to anyone—oh, it was crazy! I didn't understand the woman at all, but I quickly saw that if I wanted to maintain any connection with her, I'd have to take her on her terms, which meant doing her framing. I hoped that in time she'd come round to the idea of exhibiting her paintings, but she never did. Not while I knew her, anyway. I don't know what she's doing now. You'll know more about that than I do.' Jan eyed Charlie tentatively.

Charlie didn't see that it would do any harm. 'She's the same. Fiercely private about her work. And you have no idea why she's like that?'

'I could hazard a guess,' said Jan. 'Fear of failure? Fear of commercial considerations coming into play, and how that might change things? If you forbid the sale of something, you have no opportunity to see whether people want to buy it or not. If you don't let people see your work, they can't hate it. Mary used to say it was a matter of principle, that you can't and shouldn't put a price on art, but I never believed that line. I think she was scared, and I can't say I blame her. The art scene chews people up and spits them out. It's merciless.'

Charlie couldn't help smiling. 'We're talking about people buying pictures, right? Or not buying them? Nothing life-threatening?'

'You can laugh, but I could tell you some horror stories. There was a young artist recently whose entire degree show sold to a world-famous collector. Usually if that happens, you're made—you can write your own ticket—but in this case it didn't work. There was a huge backlash against the idea that one collector could up the value of an artist's work just like that. Both the collector and the artist became the target of some of the most vicious word-of-mouth I've ever heard. The irony is, the artist's a talented guy. His work's great.'

'Then why the viciousness?' Charlie asked.

'Bad timing, that's all. It had happened too often—the Charles Saatchi effect, we call it. All it takes is for a few artists to build their careers on it and become world-famous, and suddenly everyone's suspicious and ready to make sure no more slip through the net.'

Charlie downed the rest of her tea and tried to look more sympathetic than she felt. If Charles Saatchi threw a few million in her direction, she wouldn't care how many people slagged her off afterwards. She'd buy diamond-studded earplugs and go and lie on a beach in the Caribbean where the whining of jealous bastards wouldn't reach her.

Jan's eyes were wide and bright as she plucked another sorry tale from her repertoire. 'I represented an artist once, years ago, who was out-of-this-world fantastic: talented, ambitious, absolutely guaranteed to succeed.'

'Better than Mary Trelease?' Charlie couldn't resist asking.

Jan chewed her lip as she thought about it. 'Different. No, not better. It'd be hard to say anyone was *better* than Mary. Mary's a genius.'

'And this other artist wasn't?'

'No, I think he was—in a very different way from Mary, much more muted. He had his first show with me. He wasn't expecting much from it and neither was I—these things tend to build slowly if they build at all. I did my best to get publicity, but it's never easy for a first show. The private view was reasonably well attended, nothing out of the ordinary. Only three of the pictures sold. But somehow, even though the first night had been nothing special, word got around. Quality will out, that's what I always say. Within three days, all the pictures in the exhibition were sold—every last one, all to people who were eager to buy more as soon as more were available.'

Jan put her hand to her throat, which had turned pink. 'It was the most exciting moment of my career, that's for sure,' she said. 'I had to beat the collectors off with a stick. And that's collectors plural—not just one man buying the whole lot to publicise himself as much as anything else.' Jan let out a heavy sigh. 'I hate to think about it now.'

'What went wrong?' Charlie asked.

'I rang the artist to tell him all the work was sold and the buyers were begging for more. He was thrilled, as you can imagine. Completely beyond his wildest dreams. Then I waited. And waited. I heard nothing from him. I called him—he didn't return my calls. It took me a while to realise he was avoiding me. In a paranoid moment, I even wondered if he'd decided to dump me, buoyed up as he was by his success. Why should he pay commission to a gallery when he could keep all the money for himself? But it wasn't that at all. When I finally tracked him down, he told me he'd stopped painting.'

'What?' Charlie hadn't been expecting that.

'He said he couldn't do it any more. Every time he picked up a paintbrush, he froze. I tried to persuade him to get help, but he didn't want to. All he wanted was to leave it behind. I couldn't force him.'

'Stupid idiot,' Charlie said, before she could stop herself.

'With approval come expectation and pressure.' Jan looked sad. 'Perhaps Mary's approach is the sensible one. It's still a tragedy, though—all those amazing paintings and no one's seeing them, no one but her. She does the most wonderful portraits. Did you see any of those?'

'A few,' said Charlie. 'Her neighbours.'

'Hardly.' Jan laughed. 'Mary's not interested in anyone who's had it easy. She said to me once, "I only want to paint people who have really suffered." She painted disadvantaged, deprived people. There was a particular estate, I can't remember its name . . .'

'The Winstanley estate?'

'That's the one.'

'Her neighbours,' Charlie said again. 'Mary lives on the Winstanley estate, on a semi-derelict cul-de-sac that you wouldn't want to walk down on your own at night or even during the day. She lives side by side with . . .' Charlie had been about to say, 'the dregs of the dregs,' but she stopped herself. She had a hunch Jan's view of the underclass was somewhat rosier than her own.

'But Mary's . . .' Jan looked flustered. 'She's . . . I always assumed she'd live somewhere . . . you know. I mean, what's a Villiers girl doing living on a run-down estate?'

'Villiers?' Charlie had vaguely heard of it.

'It's a girls' boarding school in Surrey. I've only heard of it because I happened to grow up in the next village,' said Jan, a hint of apology in her voice. 'Mary went to school with diamond heiresses and the daughters of film stars. Seriously.'

'Her family are rich?' Charlie pictured 15 Megson Crescent, its peeling wallpaper and blackened carpets.

Jan laughed. 'They must be if they sent her to Villiers. She told me the fees were around fifteen grand a year when she went, and that was years ago. A lot of her friends were called "The Hon" this or that. Mary said most of them were thick, but then she never seemed to rate anyone's intellect very highly.'

'Did you ever see any of her other pictures, apart from the ones she brought in for you to frame? When I was at her house I saw some unframed ones she'd put up on the walls—of a family who used to live on the estate, I think.'

Jan looked puzzled. 'Mary was obsessive about framing her work. She didn't regard a picture as finished until it was framed. She used to hassle me mercilessly, wanting everything framed straight away. It was almost as if . . .'

'What?'

'I don't know. As if she didn't think they were safe until they were behind glass, or something. Or as if she didn't think they counted, somehow. Are you sure the unframed pictures you saw were hers?'

'Positive.'

'How odd.' Jan rubbed her collarbone, thinking. 'I'm not saying you're wrong—Mary's style's unmistakeable—but I can't understand it. It's just not Mary to leave her work unframed.' She peered into her empty mug. 'Another tea?'

'No, thanks,' said Charlie. 'I'd best be off in a minute.' She didn't know how to ask about the *Access 2* Art fair without sounding as if she was trying to catch Jan out: *I know someone who says you lied.* 'I take it you no longer frame for Mary,' she said eventually. 'What went wrong?'

'Two things, and they happened in quick succession. Mary painted something I hated—something I objected to, actually— and I couldn't pretend to feel otherwise about it. She took exception. I still framed it for her, but that wasn't good enough. She was used to me raving about the brilliance of everything she did—the last thing she expected was disapproval, but I honestly couldn't help it.'

'How come?'

'The picture was of a young woman who was . . . well, dead.' Jan sounded apologetic. 'I can't remember her name, though I knew it at the time—it was the painting's title. Not a neighbour this time—someone Mary had been at school with. Another Villiers girl. A writer. She only wrote one novel, though, before she hanged herself, tragically young. Not that there's an age when suicide isn't tragic. I wish I could remember her name.'

'Maybe Mary was close to her,' Charlie suggested, remembering what Mary had said about painting people you cared about. *Like offering yourself an emotional breakdown.*

'Yes,' said Jan. 'She told me they were inseparable, that this woman had meant everything to her and nothing to me. As if that gave her every right, and I ought to shut up if I knew what was good for me.' Noticing that Charlie looked puzzled, she added, 'Sorry, I should have explained. Mary painted her dead, with the noose round her neck.' She shuddered. 'The full suicide scene, in all its vivid, gory, undignified detail. The picture was utterly grotesque. I can't imagine I'd be more shocked if I saw a real dead body. I mean, the poor woman . . . oh, her name's on the tip of my tongue, what is it? It'll come to me.' Jan looked angry. 'I know she's dead and it can't hurt her, but still, her family . . . Even if Mary never shows the painting to anyone, even if all she does is stick it in the loft . . .'

Charlie's thoughts drifted back to the forbidden zone: Ruth Bussey and the wall of newspaper cuttings. Jan would have understood why Charlie wanted it destroyed, even if Dominic Lund didn't. The thought that it was there, that it existed, was unbearable, no matter who saw or didn't see it. Charlie felt a deep coldness in the pit of her stomach.

'. . . forced my true opinion out of me, then savaged me for it,' Jan was saying. 'She kept going on about murder, as if I'd accused her of it.'

'Murder? I thought you said the woman killed herself?'

'"Anyone would think I murdered her," "I'm an artist, not a murderer—I didn't kill her, I only painted her." That sort of thing. Yes, she did kill herself—when Mary started talking about murder, I got confused, so I asked again, to check.'

'What did Mary say?'

'She said, "She chose to die," as if that choice gave Mary the right to paint the poor woman disfigured by death.' Jan shrugged. 'I disagreed. Choosing to die and choosing to have a portrait painted of your corpse are two very different things. Don't you think?'

She chose to die. That didn't necessarily mean the same thing as 'She killed herself.' It could mean 'She chose to behave in a way that compelled me to kill her.' In her former life as a detective, Charlie had heard countless versions of that justification. Always from murderers.

'Mary wasn't about to pardon what she saw as my betrayal,' said Jan, 'particularly where this picture was concerned. It was one that really mattered to her, I could tell. After that, things were stilted between us at best, and then the art fair debacle killed our relationship stone dead.'

'What happened?'

'The picture Mary brought in the first time she came— *Abberton.* That was another one that was desperately important to her—she had favourites, Mary. Most artists do, come to think of it. The essential paintings and the dispensable ones. I'd had *Abberton* framed but Mary didn't like the frame I'd chosen. She brought it back in a few weeks later, said she wanted the wood stained green, so I had it stained green. What Mary wants, Mary gets. The picture was here, waiting to be collected—she said she'd pick it up as soon as she'd finished what she was working on. She hates to be interrupted if she's got a painting on the go.'

Jan's expression darkened and when she spoke again, her words were clipped. 'My then assistant, Ciara, took it upon herself to slip *Abberton* into a pile of stuff we were taking to an art fair, even though I'd expressly told her it wasn't to be exhibited. She ignored me—she told me later she hadn't heard me say it, but I knew she was lying. I think she decided—rightly—that it was the best thing we had and would attract people to our stand if we displayed it prominently.'

Charlie could tell from her tone that this still bothered Jan. She hadn't yet put it behind her, as that wank-head Lund would doubtless have advised.

'I should never have trusted Ciara to set up alone. She didn't think very far ahead, because pretty soon a woman was demanding to buy *Abberton* and she dug herself in deeper by pretending it was sold. Apparently the woman started to behave oddly, seemed not to believe her. She insisted that if she couldn't buy this picture then she wanted to buy another one by the same artist. I think Ciara got genuinely scared then—she thought the woman might be a spy, sent by Mary to catch us out.'

'Unlikely,' said Charlie.

'You didn't see this woman,' said Jan. 'She seemed a little bit unhinged. The first I knew of any of this was when I turned up at lunchtime to take over from Ciara. There was no sign of Mary's picture; by that point it had been hidden, and I had no idea it had ever been at the fair. As far as I knew it was in my workroom, waiting to be picked up by Mary.'

'The woman came back?' Charlie tried to sound as if she didn't already know.

'Yes, with a man in tow, but again, that was weird. It was as if he was pretending not to be with her, standing with his back to us, listening to our conversation. I didn't realise he *was* with her, didn't even notice him until he started walking away and she ran after him. She'd been shouting at me about how a picture by Mary Trelease had been on our stand that morning, and saying Ciara had lied to her about it. Course, I didn't know what she was talking about. I told her she was mistaken. It didn't take me long to work it out—I found *Abberton* hidden under a pile of prints under the table a few seconds later, but by that point the strange woman had gone.'

'How did Mary find out?' Charlie asked, guessing she must have.

Jan's face crumpled in distress at the memory. 'I told her. I had to. I didn't believe the woman at the art fair was a spy, or anything so absurd, but it wasn't beyond the bounds of possibility that she knew Mary and would tell her. I thought I ought to do the decent thing and 'fess up.'

'I assume it didn't go down well.'

'Mary slammed the phone down on me. The next day she came like a deaf-mute to collect the painting—wouldn't look at me, wouldn't speak to me. I haven't heard from her since. She wouldn't take my calls and didn't answer my letters. Eventually I gave up.'

'And Ciara?' Charlie was curious.

'She left the week after the art fair,' said Jan tersely.

Charlie read a sacking between the lines. 'I don't suppose you've got any photos of any of the pictures you framed for Mary?' Charlie was growing more curious about *Abberton* the more she heard about it. She wanted to see what the fuss was about.

'I did have,' Jan lowered her voice, as if afraid to admit it. 'It was one of the first things Mary made me promise—that I would never take a photograph of any of her paintings. When I promised, I intended to keep my word, but . . . once I'd framed *Abberton*, once I thought about Mary coming to take it away, I took a few photos. Not to show anyone, just to keep as a souvenir of something that had made such an impact on me, made me think about my work in a different way.

'After the Ciara fiasco, after Mary slammed the phone down on me, I deleted the photographs of *Abberton* from my digital camera and my computer. I thought it was only fair—I shouldn't have had them in the first place. I'd abused Mary's trust. It was clear we weren't going to have the relationship I'd hoped we would have.'

When Jan turned to face Charlie, her forehead was creased with anguish. 'So, no,' she said. 'I have no photos of *Abberton*, nor anything else of Mary's, and every day I ask myself if I made the right decision. It'll sound ridiculous when I say this—no doubt I've led an extremely sheltered life—but pressing that delete button's one of the hardest things I've ever had to do.'

9

Tuesday 4 March 2008

It's four o'clock, and I'm finally ready.

I've spent the day going through every file and piece of paper at Seed Art Services. I started at six in the morning; I locked the door, pushed both bolts across and sat in the hall with the lights off, using a torch I'd brought from home, so that the workshop would appear empty to passers-by. There were a few knocks at the door, people calling my name and Aidan's, but I hardly heard them.

Aidan keeps meticulous records, and once I was satisfied I had a full list, I phoned each of his business contacts and asked them if Aidan was with them, or had been yesterday evening and overnight. They all said no.

Aidan has two friends that I know of. One, Jim Mair, lives in Nottingham. Aidan told me he works for the Citizens Advice Bureau. The other is David Booth, Aidan's best friend from school, whom I've met several times. He works at a brewery in Rawndesley. I believed him when he told me he hadn't seen Aidan since a bit before Christmas last year.

It took me a while to track down Jim Mair. When I did, he sounded puzzled that I should even have thought to try him. He hadn't seen Aidan for nearly ten years, he said.

Aidan's parents are both dead, and he drifted out of touch with his stepfather a long time ago. He has a brother and a sister, seven and nine years older than him respectively, with whom he exchanges Christmas cards every year, though he speaks to neither of them. I found their details in his address book and rang both to ask if Aidan was with them. Both said no and sounded alarmed by the suggestion that he might be.

I am not disheartened. I knew I would find him in none of these places, with none of these people, and always expected that I would have to take the next step.

For the second time, I am about to set off to 15 Megson Crescent. I'm not scared any more, neither of Mary nor of finding Aidan there. It will be almost comforting to have my worst fears confirmed, as I know they will be. A conspiracy: the hardest thing of all to forgive; conspirators who don't care if you forgive them because they don't care about you and never did.

Because there's only one way that any of this makes sense: if Aidan and Mary are working together to drive me out of my mind.

I lock the workshop. As I pull my car keys out of my pocket, a scrap of paper falls to the ground: Charlie Zailer's mobile phone number. I asked her for it last night; she looked as if she was going to say no at first. I pick it up, feeling guilty for ignoring her advice: *Don't go to Mary's house.*

I drive along the Silsford road, under the overhanging trees that lean in on both sides to meet in the middle—a tunnel of lush foliage. Where I am now it's beautiful, but soon the trees will thin out, the road surface will deteriorate, and I'll see grimy squat houses that make my lodge house look enormous. A little further on I'll pass the primary school that's made of grey-green concrete and looks like a prison block, and Bob's Bargain Centre on the corner of the street that leads to the Winstanley estate.

Last time, I drove so slowly I must have looked like a kerb-crawler—anything to put it off. Today I slam my foot down on the gas. I want to get it over with.

Her house hasn't changed. Aidan's car isn't parked outside, or anywhere else on Megson Crescent. I bang on the door. 'Open up!'

Mary looks worse than I remember. That scored crêpe skin, the horrible woolly hair, like a knitted doll whose maker had a few balls to spare and got carried away. I want to wrench the ugly, coarse spirals out of her scalp one by one. 'Ruth,' she says, clutching the door with both hands, clinging to it as she pulls it back to let me in. 'You came back.' She's surprised. Was she counting on my being scared for ever?

'Where is he?' I ask.

'He?'

I barge past her, pushing open doors. There's no one in any of the downstairs rooms. Only me and Mary in the hall. And the people in the paintings on the walls, the small woman with doughy skin and pointed features all bunched up in the middle of her face. In one of the pictures she's looking in a mirror and her reflection is staring straight at me. She looks mean, as if she wants to accuse me of something.

'Ruth?' Mary touches my arm. 'What's wrong? Who are you looking for?'

'Aidan. Where is he?' I start to climb the stairs.

'Aidan Seed? The man the police keep asking me about?' Mary follows me. 'I don't know him.'

'You're lying! He was here last night. He was here last weekend.'

'Calm down.' She comes towards me on the landing, tries to take hold of me.

'Get away from me!'

'All right. Don't worry, I won't touch you. Can we sit down and talk about this? I don't understand what's happened or what you're accusing me of, but I promise you, Aidan's not here.'

I turn away from her and give the door behind me a hard shove, smacking it against a wall. The bathroom. Tiny. No Aidan. Above the lavatory there's an airing cupboard. I start to pull out towels, sheets, pillowcases. Soon it's empty.

Nothing.

'Where is he?' I say again.

'He's not here, Ruth. Let's go downstairs and talk. I was hoping you might have brought me something.' She mimes writing.

My eyes move to the next door, the one she's blocking with her body. 'Get out of the way. He's in there, isn't he? With all the paintings.'

Her smile dips, pulls into a tight line. 'Your Aidan Seed isn't here. I can see you're not going to believe me until you've checked for yourself. Go ahead, be my guest. I'll be downstairs, when you're ready to talk.'

Once she's gone, I start to search the rooms. In her bedroom, I empty drawers and a wardrobe, not bothering to put anything back. I look under the bed, behind the mould-spotted curtains. Aidan isn't there. Nor are his clothes or any of his possessions.

A voice in my head whispers: *What if you're wrong?*

The second door won't open all the way. The room is too full of Mary's pictures. Carefully, I manoeuvre myself in. There's a pounding sound coming from downstairs: music. I hear the word 'survivor' shouted once, twice. The smell of smoke drifts up to me. I know she's in the kitchen with a cigarette in her hand, waiting for me to admit defeat.

If a person wanted to hide in this house, this is the place they'd pick. One by one, I drag the canvases through to the other room, Mary's bedroom. She must be able to hear what I'm doing, but she doesn't try to stop me. Before long, the room is full. Canvases are piled up on the bed, leaning against it on every side. I've used up every inch of space, yet the front bedroom is still far from empty. I'll have to start putting things in the bathroom.

My arms ache, but I can't allow myself to give up, even though I know by now that I won't find Aidan here.

I stop when I see a word I recognise. It's been written in black marker pen on the back of an unframed picture: BLANDFORD.

Abberton, Blandford, Darville, Elstow, Goundry . . .

Hardly daring to touch it, I force myself to turn the canvas round. A chill spreads through me. It's unfinished, but Mary has done enough work on it to make it instantly familiar. An outline of a person—again, one that could be male or female. Head and shoulders only this time, and nothing inside the black line, not yet. Behind the figure, part of the background has been painted in: a bedroom. This one, the one I'm standing in—Mary's picture room. The curtains and wallpaper are the same, though there are no piles of pictures in the painted version. Instead, there's a double bed with a chair next to it. On the chair, there's a glass ashtray with a hand holding a cigarette over it, the ash waiting to drop.

. . . *Heathcote, Margerison, Rodwell, Winduss.*

Aidan was right. *Abberton* was the first of a series. *Blandford*, though incomplete, is the second. I heave things out of the way, looking for other similar pictures, perhaps one that Mary's only just started, but I find nothing. So far she's got no further than the second of nine.

My breaths come too quickly, making me feel dizzy. I tell myself there's nothing to be afraid of: a mystery is only a mystery until you know the answer. I'll ask Mary—I'll make her tell me. There must be a reason why Aidan knew all the names. *Who are they, these nine people?*

I'm about to leave the room when I notice an iron handle next to the edge of a painting of a large stone building with a pointed roof and a square tower on one side. Without the windows, it might be a dark rocket, waiting for lift-off.

I move the painting to one side and see a small wooden door with a sloping top set into the wall. I pull it open, find myself staring into a little cupboard, nowhere near big enough to hide a man of Aidan's size. I'm about to close the door when I spot something on the floor. A framed picture, face-down, with a printed label on the back.

I pull it out and nearly laugh with relief when I see that the name on the back isn't Darville. It's a woman's name: Martha

Wyers. I'm on the point of shoving the picture back in the cupboard when something stops me.

I turn it over, then drop it a second later, as if it's burned my
skin. It falls at my feet, picture-side up and I stare, horrified. A
noise escapes from my lips. I feel as if I've lost all control over
my life, as if I've been set down at the centre of somebody else's
carefully orchestrated nightmare, and am being pushed further
in, a little bit at a time.

I'm looking at a painting of a woman with a rope knotted
round her neck. It's the most horrible thing I've ever seen. It isn't
a dead body, only the image of one, but it makes no difference.
Mary is too good a painter. I am in the presence of Martha
Wyers, whoever she is. *Was.*

I can see everything: the texture of the rope, the frayed parts.
How it has cut into her flesh. The bulging eyes, the purple-grey
hollows beneath them, the thick protruding tongue, livid bruises
on the skin around her mouth, a white, crusty ridge along her
lower lip . . .

I smell smoke. Closer than before. *Mary.*

'I see you've found Martha,' she says.

The hardest thing I've ever had to do was get through the court
case, with Her staring at me as if she wanted to lunge across the
court and gouge out my eyes, and Him determinedly looking
down at his lap so that he wouldn't see my face. Forcing myself
to go to Mary Trelease's house for the first time was the second
hardest.

It's possible to do anything, however difficult, if you can't
imagine how your life will go on otherwise. Aidan had said to
me, 'Bring me the picture,' so I had no choice. After London, he
would barely speak to me, apart from telling me constantly that
he loved me, with a shadow behind his eyes, and I started to
suspect he was using sex as a way of avoiding conversation. The
comfort it offered soon ceased to have an effect, and I saw that
we couldn't go on as we were. Every time I pleaded with him to

open up to me, he repeated what he'd said at Alexandra Palace: 'Bring me the picture. Bring me *Abberton*.'

I thought that if I could only put the painting in front of him, with Mary Trelease's name and the date on it, he would see that he hadn't killed Mary, whatever else might have passed between them. I didn't care if I never knew what that was; all I wanted was to be happy again, for Aidan to be happy. He'd moved into the lodge, as promised, as soon as we got back to Spilling after the art fair, and I was trying hard not to think of it as him making good his threat. I longed for him to trust me as he had before London, knowing it was down to me to make that happen.

On 2 January, after a desolate Christmas, I steeled myself and phoned Saul Hansard. 'Ruth,' he said, sounding thrilled to hear from me. I felt guilty for having cut him out of my life, but knew I would again as soon as I'd got the information I needed from him. The sound of his voice made my skin prickle with shame.

'Mary Trelease,' I said. 'I need her address.'

I should have known this would worry him, but I was having trouble thinking beyond my own needs and fears, mine and Aidan's. 'Why?' Saul asked gently. 'Whatever you're thinking of doing, I'm not sure it's a good idea.'

'I'm not going to cause any trouble,' I said. 'I want to talk to her, that's all.'

Saul said he'd told Mary, seconds after I'd fled the gallery, that he wouldn't be framing for her any more. He'd told me this before, in one of the many messages he'd left on my voicemail since that day in June, but it seemed important to him to say it again. 'I know,' I said. 'Thank you.'

'She's a scary woman, Ruth. I don't need to tell you that.'

A panicky sensation started to flicker inside me. Our conversation was dragging me back to the past, the last place I wanted to go. 'I won't tell Mary I got the address from you,' I said. 'Please, Saul. It's important.'

He agreed in the end, as I had known he would. Then he

couldn't find it, and told me he would have to dig it out later. When he phoned back that evening, Aidan was there, watching me from across the room as I wrote it down.

'Well?' he said.

I could have explained that I'd contacted Saul and asked for Mary's address, but I didn't. We'd got into the habit of saying the bare minimum. Fewer words seemed to mean less pain. 'Fifteen Megson Crescent,' I said. 'Spilling.'

Aidan's face stiffened into a mask of shock. 'The same house,' he murmured. Something had blown open inside his head; some new horror had seized him. He stormed out of the room. I heard him crying in the hall as if he'd collapsed there, unable to get any further, and pressed my hands over my ears, feeling utterly helpless, thinking: the same as what—the house where he killed Mary?

Dead people didn't move house . . . Was 15 Megson Crescent where Mary had lived when Aidan knew her? *Where he had killed her?* But she wasn't dead. No matter how I tried to think about it, from whichever direction I approached it, nothing made sense.

The next day, I didn't need to tell Aidan why I wasn't going to work with him. I looked up the route in my A–Z and set off to the Winstanley estate. Impossible as it is to see the future, sometimes you can feel its presence ahead of you, dark and cloying, waiting to swallow you up. My face started to itch as I drove, the skin to feel tight as it had when Mary had sprayed me with red paint. I twisted the rear-view mirror towards me to check there was nothing there, although rationally I knew that my face would look perfectly ordinary. Red paint couldn't reappear once it was washed off; it could hardly seep up through my pores and spill out after so many months.

I stood in Mary's untended front yard, my whole body a screaming knot of tension, and knocked on the door. When she opened it and saw me, she let out a loud breath and looked at me with some emotion on her face that I couldn't identify. 'Ruth

Bussey,' she said slowly. 'Come to inspect my hovel and feel superior.'

I didn't know what she was talking about. The idea of my feeling superior to anybody was so laughable that I couldn't think of anything to say in response.

'Saul Hansard as good as threw me out on the street after our spat at the gallery. It must be nice to have a gallant hero to protect you.'

Strange equations filled my mind: sarcasm equals aggression equals attack. I clenched my hands into fists, turned, ran. 'Wait, don't go,' Mary called after me. I collided with a wall, too frightened to think about which way I was going, and felt something sharp spike my skin through my shirt. I looked down. There was a small red dot on the cotton.

'I'll get you a plaster to put on it,' said Mary. 'There are some in the bathroom cabinet, if they haven't crumbled to dust by now. They've been there since I moved in. So's that killer weed.' She beckoned me towards her.

I couldn't believe she was inviting me inside. To mask my confusion, I muttered, 'It's not a weed.'

'Pardon?'

'Nothing.'

Mary walked over to where I was standing and stroked the plant that had pricked me. 'You know what this is?'

I nodded, not looking at her. I'd seen hundreds. Never one sharp enough to pierce skin, though, until now. I was trembling, unable to keep still.

'Tell me.'

It seemed easier than talking about what I was doing at her house. 'It's called a sempervivum. It's been planted there, to grow out of the wall.' I felt idiotic, after injuring myself so clumsily, and expected her to burst out laughing.

'In that case, I'd better not yank it out,' she said grudgingly. 'Come on, if you're coming.' She took it for granted that I would follow her. I did, round the back of the house and into her kitchen, which was horrible and falling apart. 'You're shocked by the state of the place,' she said.

'No.'

'I've done nothing to it since I moved in.' She said something then about the charm of a found object, but I wasn't fully listening. How was I going to get *Abberton*? Why hadn't I foreseen how impossible it would be? I considered telling the truth, then rejected the idea. *My boyfriend thinks he killed you years ago— would you mind giving me the picture you refused to sell me last June, so that I can prove to him that you're alive?*

Mary told me to wait in the kitchen while she went to fetch a plaster. I didn't need one—my wound was a pinprick, almost non-existent—but I didn't want to risk antagonising her. As soon as she was out of sight, I felt trapped in the room, even though the door was open. Frantically, I itemised objects I could see to calm myself: kettle, microwave, a tea towel with 'Villiers' printed on it beside a picture of what looked like a big stone castle, four boxes of Twinings Peppermint tea, stacked one on top of the other . . .

I couldn't concentrate or keep still. I went out into the hall, which was small, narrow and smelled of a mixture of noxious substances: smoke, gas, grease. There was another open door to my left, through which I could see, above a gas fire with bent bars and ropes of dust clinging to it like grey tinsel that had lost its shine, a painting of a boy with a pen in his hand. He had written the words 'Joy Division' on the wall and was standing back to survey his work. His face wasn't visible, only the back of his head. Instantly, I recognised the picture as Mary's handi-work. Something about the boy's posture made it look as if he might turn round any second and catch me spying on him. I found the painting disconcerting; it made me want to lower my eyes. How did she do that? How could she take a brush and some paints and produce something as extraordinary as this?

Mary leaped down the stairs, landing beside me, making me cry out in alarm. 'Here we go. Sorry, didn't mean to startle you.'

She was holding a plaster in her hand. I couldn't understand why she wasn't still angry with me, why she cared that I was bleeding.

I put out my hand to take the plaster, but Mary was already ripping the paper tabs off it. Once they were gone, she put the plaster between her teeth and pulled up my shirt. I hadn't been expecting it, and I recoiled. My back hit the wall. It was too late. She'd seen the scar, the thick pink line that divides my stomach in half. She must have seen my bra, too, having pulled my shirt up higher than she needed to.

She wasn't interested in that, though. I could see where her eyes had landed, on my damaged skin. After the operation, I'd heard a nurse who thought I was asleep say, 'Better hope she never puts on any weight. That stomach ever gets fat, it'll look like an arse.' A male nurse had laughed and called her a catty bitch.

Mary was fascinated by my scar. She stared unashamedly. I itched to yank my shirt ends out of her hand and cover myself, but I was afraid to give my own wishes precedence over hers. She wanted to look, and I knew what happened when I displeased her.

She licked her finger, wiped a spot of blood from my skin and rubbed the plaster on, her knuckle moving back and forth across the material. She's insane, I thought as she smiled at me. It occurred to me that this so-called help might be a subtle form of attack. If her aim was to humiliate me, she'd succeeded again.

'What do you think of it?' she asked, nodding at the Joy Division picture through the open door. 'Do you like it?'

'Yes.'

She looked puzzled. 'What, that's it? I thought you loved my work. So much that you couldn't wait to get your hands on it.'

'It's . . . it's good. They're all good.' Two more of her paintings were up in the hall, one of a man, a woman and a boy sitting round a table, the other of the same man and woman, her looking in a mirror, him behind her, lying on the bed. Her face was visible only in the glass, reflected; her gaze seemed to taunt me, and I turned away. Against the drab wallpaper, Mary's paintings stood out, vibrant and mesmerising, like diamonds shining out from a bed of sludge. The sight jarred; these pictures looked wrong here, violently out of kilter, yet without them the house would have had nothing. I had a powerful sense—one of the strangest feelings I've ever had—that 15 Megson Crescent needed Mary's paintings.

'I know—you wouldn't want them on your wall,' she said, mistaking my awe for distaste. 'A pretty scabby family, all things considered, but that's life on the Winstanley estate. You're brave to risk a visit. That lot don't live here any more, but there are more of the same, and even worse.'

'I'm not brave,' I told her. Couldn't she see I was petrified? Was she mocking me?

'I'm glad you're here,' she said. 'I owe you an apology for what happened last June. I didn't mean to frighten you.'

Talk about something else. Please, change the subject. I'd clamped my mouth shut and my jaw was starting to ache.

'*I* was frightened. Selfishly, I didn't think . . .' She left the sentence unfinished. 'It still bothers you, doesn't it? What happened at the gallery.'

How dared she expect confirmation from me? Rage began to blister inside me, but I tried to nod as if I felt fine. My natural reaction to anger: bury it before it's used against me. Deny it an outlet. It was practically the first thing I learned as a child in my parents' house: I wasn't entitled to my natural responses, especially the more 'un-Christian' ones. I was allowed to manifest only those states of mind that would please my mother and father, make them proud of me. Anger, particularly anger directed at them, didn't qualify.

'Why *does* it still bother you?' Mary waited for an answer I had no intention of giving her. 'Do you blame yourself, is that it? Why do we do that? Human beings, I mean. Why do we take each mishap that strikes us, and twist it until it loses its randomness and becomes a big black arrow pointing at us, proving our worthlessness?'

Her words, so unexpected, went all the way through me. I knew I wouldn't forget them for a long time.

'When I lost it with you, it reminded you of something else, didn't it? You've been attacked before. I'm right, aren't I? Your reaction that day was pretty extreme—I can't believe that was all down to me. Don't tell me if you don't want to.'

I stood rooted to the spot, my eyes fixed on the smear of blood on my shirt.

'The way I behaved that day had nothing to do with you, what you said or did,' said Mary. 'No attack is ever really an attack on the victim. It's the perpetrator attacking an aspect of himself that he loathes. He or she.'

Try telling that to the victim, I thought.

'I don't sell my work. I never do. I don't even like people seeing it, unless they're people I trust, and I trust nobody. I'm a coward. You were a strange woman demanding to buy my painting—I felt threatened. Exposed.' She lit a cigarette.

'Why?' I asked. My turn to wait for an answer.

Mary didn't seem bothered by the long silence. It was a while before she said, 'Is there anything in your life that's . . . in your past, I mean, anything that's too painful to talk about?'

How could she know? I told myself she couldn't.

'I think there is.' She pointed to my stomach. 'The scar. The story that goes with it. It's all right, I'm not asking you to tell me.'

The moment for denial came and went. I'd as good as admitted she was right.

'Has it ever occurred to you to write it down? Your story, I mean. I saw a therapist for years. I stopped when I realised there was no fixing the broken bits. That's okay—I can live with it, if you can call my half-life in this shit-hole living. Because that's what it's like, isn't it? I know you *know*, Ruth. When your world falls apart and everything's ruined, you lose part of yourself. Not all, inconveniently. One half, the best half, dies. The other half lives.'

I tried hard to hide the effect her words were having on me.

'This therapist—she said I wouldn't be able to move on for as long as I was determined to apportion blame. She told me to write it like a story in the third person, describe how all the characters felt, not only me. It's a way of showing that everyone involved has a point of view, or some such crap.' Mary stubbed her cigarette out on the wall. Immediately, she lit another. 'I didn't do it. Didn't want to see anything from anyone else's point of view. You know?'

I watched the pain rampaging across her face as she spoke, and wondered if my face sometimes looked like that.

Mary laughed quietly. 'I digress,' she said. 'That's what happens when you don't talk to a soul from one week to the next. Can I paint you?'

'No,' I said, hating the idea, not sure if she was serious.

'Why not? Your face is perfect—like a fairy's or an angel's. Not that I've seen either.' A cunning look came into her eyes. 'I won't forget what you look like. You can't stop me painting you if I want to.'

'Please don't.'

'Some people get no say in the matter.' She gestured at the pictures on the walls.

'I don't want to be painted,' I told her. 'If I did, you'd be the person I'd choose to paint me.' I was pleased with this answer: firm but generous. She couldn't fault me.

'Why's that, then?' she asked.

'Of all the artists whose work I've seen, you're the best.'

She rattled off a list of names in a bored voice. 'Rembrandt, Picasso, Klimt, Kandinsky, Hockney, Hirst—better than all of them?'

'I've never seen their work,' I said. 'Only pictures of it.'

Some emotion—triumph?—flared in Mary's eyes. When she next spoke, her voice was hoarse. 'Ruth,' she said. I looked up in time to see her mouthing my name several more times, soundlessly. 'Wait.' She stood up.

I was waiting already, to see what she would say next. She'd said my name for the sake of saying it, it seemed, not as the precursor to anything. She went upstairs again. When she came down she was holding *Abberton*. My heart started to race when I saw it. In my mind, all this time, it had represented that terrible day at Saul's gallery; I tried not to think about it, but when I did it made me feel disorientated, out of control. Now that I had faced Mary, now that she'd apologised to me, it was different. Something had shifted.

'If you still want it, it's yours,' said Mary. 'Gratis.'

'What? But . . .'

'I didn't trust you before. I do now.' She looked embarrassed, tried to smile. 'Anyone who knows they haven't seen a painting unless they've seen the original is all right in my book. You'd be amazed how many people put a poster of Botticelli's *The Birth of Venus* on their wall and imagine they've got Botticelli's *The Birth of Venus* on their wall.'

I felt terrible, as if I was cheating her somehow. I'd come here to get *Abberton* for Aidan, not for myself. His proof: Mary's name and the date at the bottom. She knew nothing of my ulterior motive. I tried to persuade myself I was doing nothing wrong, imagined opening my mouth and saying Aidan's name to see how she would react. *Impossible.*

I didn't want her to know his name, or that he was my boyfriend. I wanted her to know nothing about us. I despised myself, knowing that no matter what Mary said or did, I would never trust her.

She held up her hands and made a frame shape in front of my face with her fingers and thumbs. 'What's your story, Ruth Bussey? Before I paint a person, I need to know their story. What happened to you? How did you get that scar?' This time she didn't say that I didn't have to tell her if I didn't want to, so I said it to myself. 'You think it makes you strong, suffering in silence, bearing the burden alone? So what if it does? What's the advantage of being strong? Do you know what happens to strong people? I do. Weak people attack them. Why do you think I went for you in the gallery that day?'

I stiffened. How long before I could escape?

'You seemed so strong, and I felt so weak. Weak people always attack strong people—it's safer. It's weak people who are dangerous, who lash out uncontrollably and hurt you back. Strong people can walk away—no repercussions, you see, if you attack a strong person. Want to know how I ended up so weak?'

'No, I . . . no.' I picked up *Abberton*, afraid she'd change her mind and take it back. 'I've got to go.'

Mary grabbed my hand. 'Tell me your story and I'll tell you mine.'

I tried not to panic, said again that I needed to leave. I'd opened the front door and was almost out, with *Abberton* under my arm. 'You'll tell me one day,' she said as she released her grip.

I ran to my car, gulping in fresh air as if I'd been trapped underwater. I didn't look back at the house. I knew I would see Mary in the doorway, watching, waiting. As I drove away, uncertain as I was about everything else, I became convinced of one thing: Aidan's insane belief centred around a woman who was every bit as insane as the things he'd said about her.

I didn't know what that meant, but it had to mean something.

10

4/3/08

'It isn't a *relationship*,' Olivia said indignantly. 'I'm not sure you've noticed, but I don't have those. That suits you fine, doesn't it? Me having no one, being on tap whenever you want me.'

'Don't twist this! I don't want you to be lonely, or . . .'

'Terrified of telling any man I fall for that I lost my womb and ovaries to cancer and can't have children?'

'You always fucking do this! You throw the c-word at me for the sympathy vote and expect me to back down!' Charlie wished her sister would stand up to argue. Olivia sat curled on the sofa in her tiny, designer-fabric-swathed Fulham flat, still in her cream satin pyjamas and dressing-gown though it was getting on for early evening. She wasn't fond of physical exertion. Apart from sex with Dominic Lund, as it turned out.

Charlie felt like a bully shouting down at her. She also knew she had no plans to stop shouting any time soon. 'How do you think I felt? After I've poured my heart out to him, begged him for help, and had to sit there like an idiot with him telling me what a loser I am. *Enjoying* trashing my confidence, revelling in his wisdom and my helplessness. Do you know what he called me? A psychopath's ex-girlfriend. Quite a gentleman you've got there. When I told him to fuck off, he dropped his bombshell: "By the way, not only am I not going to lift a finger for you, but I'm fucking your sister and we're both laughing at you behind your back." It didn't occur to you that I might have appreciated having that information in advance?'

'Your self-absorption knows no bounds,' said Olivia, her face pink with outrage. 'I'll throw another c-word at you in a minute. Will you listen to yourself?'

Charlie was in no state to listen. 'Why didn't you tell me?'

'I don't see what the problem is. You needed legal advice, I recommended Dommie. It wasn't as if—'

'*Dommie?* This is a bad dream,' Charlie muttered. 'I'll wake up in a minute.'

'I didn't tell you because you've got a long history of thinking every decision I make is—'

'Is he the best you can do? A semi-autistic cheapskate who can't even look at people when he speaks to them and forgets his wallet on purpose when he goes out to lunch, who plays with his BlackBerry compulsively the way teenage boys play with their dicks, who looks like a buzzard . . .'

'A *buzzard?*'

'He looks like a big bird of prey—don't tell me you hadn't noticed! Acts like one too.'

'All right!' Olivia held up her hands. 'Yes, he's the best I can do. Is that what you want me to say? Somehow he's managed to upset you, so you decided to come here and upset me, and you've succeeded. Job done. Happy now?'

'Go on,' Charlie taunted her. 'Use that word you threatened me with.'

'It's only a casual thing, Char. It hasn't been going on for very long. I wanted to—'

'How long's not very long?'

'I don't know, about six months.'

'Six *months*! I told you Simon and I were engaged three fucking seconds after I knew myself! Since when you've been prancing around sanctimoniously, exuding disapproval, loudly dooming us to failure at every opportunity . . .'

'Prance? I don't prance.'

'All I'm doing's trying to be happy for a change. You keep saying you've said your piece and from now on you'll keep your mouth shut, but it never works, does it? You can't restrain your-self from pointing out that Simon's weird and frigid and socially inept, and he's never said he loves me . . .' Charlie had to pause as a tide of rage swept through her, pushing all coherent thought aside.

In its wake, she found her voice again. 'Socially inept,' she re-peated quietly. 'And all the time, you're bedding *Dominic Lund*? Coward—that's another word that begins with "c". Fucking hypocrite—that begins with "f". You sneak around in secret to protect yourself, at the same time as showering me with con-demnation. All those times you've laid into Simon . . .'

'I've got nothing against Simon! I like him. All right, I think you're mad to—'

'And I think you're mad. *Insane.* Off your trolley!'

'Dominic's got a brilliant mind. He's a brilliant—'

'Please, call him Dommie if that's your special name for him. Don't let me stop you.' Charlie was starting to enjoy herself. Sometimes the only way to get rid of your own pain was to cause someone else's. 'Now you know how it feels when some-one rips the man you love to shreds,' she said.

'I'm not sure if I love him. It's a complicated . . .'

'You know what else he said to me? That I never listen to anyone. This is a man who's met me all of once.'

'Perceptive of him,' said Olivia.

'He was quoting you!'

'He's got an amazing memory. He's cleverer than Simon.'

'Oh, grow up!'

'I didn't mean it like that. I only meant . . . you of all people should understand the appeal of a clever man.'

The part of Charlie that was capable of feeling normal hu-man emotions had shut down. At moments like this, she usually tried to make things worse because that was something she knew she could do and do well. 'Let's make a pact, okay? You don't come to my wedding and I won't come to yours. As for Mum and Dad, they can choose. One or the other, whichever of us they think has made the least shit choice of partner. They'll pick you, of course, because you put in the hours pandering to them and I don't. Come to think of it, I can't see Dad missing a day's golf to come to either of our weddings.'

'Say it to his face if you've got a problem! You'd never dare, would you? You try to turn me against them hoping I'll start trouble with them so that, if and when I do, you can stand back and look all innocent—*you're* the coward, not me! And I don't pander to them, I consider their feelings—it's not the same thing.' Olivia wiped her eyes with one hand and sighed. With the flat of her other hand, she slammed shut the lid of the laptop that was sitting beside her on the sofa. 'I guess that's my working day over,' she said, each syllable dripping with sacrifice.

'Work? You mean writing airhead shit for the bits of the papers that everyone chucks in the bin? Still in your pyjamas at nearly six o'clock—you call that work?'

Olivia didn't stand up, but she swung her legs round and straightened her back. 'I'm a journalist,' she said in a jagged voice. 'I write about *books*. Books are not airhead shit. My work is worth as much as yours.'

Like hell it is.

'Once or twice, it's true, I've written articles about fashion or shopping, and you've stored that up to use against me in your campaign to prove that everything I do is a load of frivolous crap.' Olivia wiped her eyes.

'Diversionary tactics,' Charlie said flatly. 'Don't think I don't know them when I see them. I see them a lot.' She'd always thought Liv was proud to be frivolous, believed frivolity to be a good worth striving for.

'You know what? I don't even mind you thinking that my life's work is a huge waste of time. Maybe if I did what you did, I'd feel the same about anyone who didn't have to deal with dead bodies and psychopaths every day. I'm sure I would.'

'I'm not in CID any more, not that anyone seems to notice.'

Charlie sighed. 'These days all I see is questionnaires and evaluation forms.'

'What I object to is that you don't even bother to pretend!' Liv was determined to have her say. 'You *constantly* put forward this view of the world in which you're essential and I'm completely worthless and useless, and you expect me to . . . to *subscribe* to it!'

'Oh, please. When do I put forward—?'

'All the time! With your every word and action, with every face you pull. Did you know I'm writing a book?'

'Yeah, yeah. Neither am I.'

'I *am*!'

'You used to say that all the time when we were teenagers. You never wrote more than a paragraph.'

'Okay, fine, that's true!' Finally, Olivia stood up. 'What Dom said's also true. How come it's okay for you to be as blunt as you like but not for anyone else? He told you there was no case to make and you're blaming him because it wasn't what you wanted to hear.'

' "No case to make," ' Charlie sneered. 'I see you're fluent in legal bullshit-speak.'

'Dom called you a pyschopath's ex-girlfriend because that's what you are! You always will be. Fucking deal with it. Doesn't mean it's *all* you are. He didn't say it to be vicious, and he wasn't revelling in your powerlessness or rubbing anything in— that's bollocks. He's just . . . unusually straightforward. You don't know him like I do.'

'No, I'd need to open my legs a bit wider to achieve that, wouldn't I?' Charlie wasn't ready to be mature and sensible about anything. Not yet. That she could see she would eventually have to be infuriated her, created the need to do more damage.

'Shouldn't be too hard for you,' Liv retaliated. 'Think back to before you got engaged to Simon. You had your legs spread so wide most of the time, I'm surprised you managed to walk. You were the human equivalent of a T-junction.'

Charlie tried not to show her shock. Could Liv have thought that up on the spot, or had she formulated the insult long ago and been waiting ever since for the perfect opportunity to deliver it? Had she shared it with Lund? Had they laughed about it together?

'Any bloke who fancied it could have taken a run at you from a distance and got a hole in one,' Liv added for good measure.

'Golf slang,' said Charlie. 'Mum and Dad would be so proud. *Dommie* told me you've been trying to turn them against Simon and me.'

'That's rubbish. He can't have said that—it's not true and he doesn't lie.'

'Saint Dommie!'

'He might have said I'm surprised they haven't expressed concern about your marriage plans. I *am* surprised.'

'And I had to hear that, and more, from someone I'd gone to for *help*, a lawyer who, as far as I knew, had no other connection to my life! If I'd known you and he were an item, do you think I'd have let him . . .?' The question hung in the air, incomplete.

'Let him what?'

See my desperation. Charlie couldn't say it. She'd told Olivia about Ruth Bussey's bedroom wall, but she'd taken care to present herself as far less bothered than she was. She'd made flippant jokes—'Crazy bitch. Do you think she fancies me or something?'—to hide the depth of her distress, and thrown in the Ruth-Aidan-Mary Trelease story as a distraction, to direct the focus away from herself. Now that she'd demeaned herself in front of Dominic Lund, he was in a position to tell Liv exactly how wretched and messed up Charlie was, if he hadn't already, and there was nothing she could do about it.

'Why *are* you so upset about this Ruth Bussey woman, Char? I don't get it. Okay, it's weird, I agree, but she's probably harmless.'

'Covering an entire wall with articles about someone and pictures of them is stalker behaviour,' Charlie recited in a monotone. 'Stalkers can flip and they can attack. Sometimes they kill. Don't fucking tell me this woman's harmless—you know nothing.'

'You're right,' Liv snapped. 'She's probably waiting outside with a Kalashnikov pointed at the front door.' Seeing Charlie's murderous expression, she shrugged and said, 'See? Whatever I say, it's the wrong thing. I'm sick of being your punch-bag. This isn't about me—it isn't about Dominic. It's *Simon* you're angry with, Simon who's making you miserable . . .'

'Here we go again!'

'You're jealous because I'm getting laid and you, despite being engaged, aren't!'

Charlie's vision narrowed to a slit. A shimmering red tunnel opened in front of her and she allowed it to suck her in. She lunged for Olivia's computer, held it over her head and threw it at the wall. The crash it made when it hit was painful to listen to—the sound of irrevocable damage. Charlie closed her eyes, remembering too late the other reason she'd come to Olivia's. 'Shit,' she whispered. 'I needed that computer. Can you try to boot it up for me while I get a drink? What have you got that's strong and alcoholic?'

'I haven't backed up my work,' said Olivia shakily. 'That's three days' worth of—'

'I'm sorry,' Charlie interrupted her martyr speech. 'You're a saint, Dominic Lund is a saint and I'm a sack of shit, okay? And I mean that from the bottom of my heart.' She headed to the kitchen in search of vodka, calling over her shoulder, 'Just get that fucking machine to work.'

There was no vodka. Absinthe would have to do. Charlie poured the pale green liquid into a tumbler and took two big gulps, hoping it would work fast. Not fast enough. She downed the rest of the glass, then poured another. She took her phone out of her pocket and switched it on. Five missed calls from callers who'd withheld their numbers. Unusual. There was one message, from Simon. 'Where the fuck are you? Ring me as soon as you get this.' Charlie listened to it again, trepidation making her stomach churn. Something was wrong. He knew where she was; she'd told him she was going to London to see Lund.

She rang him, got his voicemail, left a message saying she was worried, that she was at her sister's now and he should ring her as soon as he got the chance. Then she glugged more absinthe, jabbed '118118' with her thumb and got the number for Villiers girls' boarding school in Wrecclesham, Surrey. Might as well ring now, put off facing Liv for a few more minutes.

The voice that answered the phone sounded as if it belonged to a woman who had been put on earth to do nothing but answer telephones with perfect politeness. Though all it said was, 'Villiers, good afternoon,' it conveyed a sense of delight in anticipation of being able to help anyone with anything, and made Charlie feel less awkward about posing her question.

'This is going to sound strange,' she began.

'That's perfectly all right. I can do strange. Frequently have to,' said the woman. A secretary, Charlie assumed. 'You should hear some of the calls we get.'

'I'm after the name of an ex-pupil of yours who went on to become a writer. Does anyone spring to mind who fits that description?'

'A fair few,' said the woman proudly. 'You should come and look at our boasting gallery some time.'

'Can you give me some names?' Charlie reached for the pad of A4 paper and pen that Olivia kept near the phone; though, irritatingly, not so near that you didn't have to lean to reach it and risk pulling the phone's base off the shelf. As the woman name-dropped women writers, Charlie made a list. She'd heard of only one of the six the secretary mentioned, and put a cross beside her name. She hadn't committed suicide; Charlie had seen her on *Question Time* last week.

How to ask if any of them were dead without sounding crass, or making the secretary clam up? 'Are . . . as far as you know, are all these women still writing?'

A gasp of alarm came from behind Charlie, followed by the sound of the absinthe bottle and her glass being pulled along the worktop, away from her. She turned to find Olivia glaring at her, miming surprise at how little was left in the bottle. She waved the list of women writers in front of her sister's face.

'I'm sorry, I'm not sure I can help you there. We try to keep up with our old girls' careers as best we can, but there are so many of them. Let me think . . .'

'I'll put it another way,' said Charlie. 'Do you know if any of these women definitely aren't still writing?'

Olivia snatched the pen from her hand. Next to each name she wrote something, rolling her eyes as if Charlie ought to have known: 'Still writing poetry about muddy puddles that no one buys.' 'Depends what you mean by "still writing". She puts her name to about four books a year, but they're all "co-written", i.e. written by unknown skivvies.' 'Yes—she's good—I tried to lend you one of hers but you vetoed it because it was set abroad and in the past.'

'May I ask what your interest is?' A note of caution had infused the impeccable voice, enough to convince Charlie that she and the woman on the other end of the phone were thinking, at that moment, of the same person: the woman Mary Trelease had painted dead. Charlie closed her eyes. The absinthe was starting to make its presence felt; her veins were buzzing.

'It's sort of personal,' she said. 'I can promise you that anything you tell me will go no further.' Recklessly, she added, 'I think you know which of these women I'm asking about, don't you?'

'I don't think I'm going to be able to help you.' Shrill and defensive. *Was it something I said?*

Beside the name of the woman Charlie had seen on *Question Time* recently, Liv had written, 'Ideas above her station—thinks writing formulaic thrillers qualifies her to interfere in politics.'

Every name on the list had one of Liv's mini-essays beside it apart from one: Martha Wyers. Charlie pointed to it. Liv shrugged, then, in case that wasn't clear enough, drew a big question mark next to it.

'Martha Wyers,' said Charlie. 'She's not writing any more, is she?'

'I cannot help you,' the woman repeated firmly. 'If you care about Martha or this school at all, please don't pursue it. There's been enough suffering already without journalists digging for dirt and causing even more.'

'I'm not a journalist. Really, I'm not going to—'

'I should never have given you her name.' The words were breathy and indistinct, as if she'd pressed her mouth too close to the mouthpiece. She hung up.

'Any luck with the computer?' Charlie asked Liv.

'You're slurring your words. Of course not. That's nine hundred quid you owe me, plus a two-thousand-word article about why endings are as important as beginnings in fiction.'

'Instalments do you? Tiny ones? Where's the nearest internet café?' Charlie was already heading for the front door.

'Right here,' said Olivia drily. 'I've set up my other laptop. You can use that. One condition: would you mind not hurling it at the wall?'

'You've got two laptops?'

'It's handy—you never know when one's going to be smashed up by a vandal.'

'I've said I'm sorry . . .'

'Sarcastically, yes. I don't suppose it'll matter to you, but I bought the second laptop to write my book, and that's all I've ever used it for. I didn't want it to be used for anything else.'

Charlie stopped at the entrance to the lounge. 'I can go to an internet café,' she said. 'Make up your mind. Do you want to help me or not? Only in exchange for praise, presumably.'

'Use it. I've set it up,' said Liv wearily. 'What's going on, Char? Any chance you're going to tell me?'

Charlie clicked on the Internet Explorer icon. When the Google screen appeared, she typed 'Martha Wyers, Villiers, suicide' into the search box. Nothing came up that looked right. The first page of results yielded a selection of science journal articles by a Dr Martha Wyers of Yale University. 'Don't give me this shit,' Charlie moaned at the computer.

'Are you sure it's not the same person?' Liv asked, peering over her shoulder.

'I doubt it.'

'Check,' Liv advised.

'Thanks for that tip. Of course I'm going to check,' said the part of Charlie that, in the presence of her sister, was permanently frozen at the age of fourteen.

Google was bursting at the seams with Dr Wyers' details and achievements. It didn't take long to find a CV. 'Born in 1947 in Buffalo. Never lived in the UK, never attended Villiers school . . .'

'It's not her,' said Liv.

'No.'

Charlie tried 'Martha Wyers, British writer, suicide' and 'Martha Wyers, British writer, Villiers, murder' with no success. Yale's Dr Wyers wasn't letting anyone else get a look-in.

'You can find out, can't you?' she asked Liv. 'Martha Wyers was a writer, you know everything there is to know about books . . .'

'Was Martha Wyers killed by a stalker?'

'What?' Seeing her sister trying so hard, looking so helpful and enthusiastic and making completely the wrong connection made Charlie want to hit her. She ought to ring Simon again. Why had he sounded so riled? He was the one she needed to talk to. Would he pursue the Martha Wyers angle?

He'd tell you you're crazy, that's what he'd do. Aidan Seed says he killed Mary Trelease. Mary Trelease painted Martha Wyers, who killed herself. No reason to think Martha Wyers was murdered by Seed or anyone else. Except that Jan Garner had talked about murder, Mary mentioning murder in connection with the dead woman writer. 'No, Martha Wyers wasn't murdered by a stalker,' Charlie told Liv impatiently. 'Not as far as I know, anyway.'

'You don't know if she was murdered or if she killed herself, so why don't you search for Martha Wyers, writer—keep it simple?'

It wasn't a bad suggestion, except that Charlie was unwilling to let her sister see her following instructions and infer from that that she'd made a good point. As luck would have it, Liv's phone started to ring and she went to the kitchen to answer it.

Charlie typed 'Martha Wyers, writer' into the search box and was about to press 'enter' when Olivia reappeared, red in the face, agitated. 'That was Simon.'

Automatically, Charlie stood up, holding out her hand for the phone. Why hadn't he rung her on her mobile? When she saw the expression on Liv's face, her arm fell to her side.

'What?' she whispered.

'I'm sorry, Char,' said her sister. 'It's bad news.'

Dear Mary   4 March 2008

This is something I never thought I'd do. Like you, I saw a therapist for a while, and like you I found that it didn't achieve much. Unlike your therapist, mine recommended letter-writing, but I suppose it amounts to the same thing. You want my story—this is it.

In my old life, I was a garden designer—before I moved to Spilling I had nothing to do with art or artists. I had a thriving business and won awards for my work. In 1999 I won the principal BALI (British Association of Landscaping Industries) award for the third time in three consecutive years. There was a six-page feature about me in *Good Housekeeping* magazine, with pictures of my gardens that had won prizes, and interviews with the people I'd designed them for. As a result of this publicity, my services were in demand. I had a sudden influx of new clients and a waiting list three years long. Some people got impatient and decided to go elsewhere. Others were happy to wait their turn. Only one woman fell into neither of the above categories.

She phoned me and left a message, saying she needed to speak to me urgently. When I rang her back, she told me she was sick, and asked if there was any way I could fit her in sooner. She didn't specify what was wrong with her, but said she didn't know how long she had left to enjoy her garden, and as things stood there was, she said, 'little about it to enjoy'. I considered telling her I had made prior commitments to other people and didn't want to let them down, but decided in the end that, in such an unusual case, it was better to be flexible. None of my other clients or prospective clients was terminally ill.

She was a primary school teacher, in her early thirties, married with no children, and lived in a village close to the Leicestershire–Lincolnshire border, on Woodmansterne

Lane, a narrow road with detached fake stone cottages, modern but trying to look old, hidden behind hedges as solid as concrete walls and thick-trunked trees that seemed to stand guard on both sides. I thought as soon as I heard the street name that it was unusual and a little bit sinister. It made me think of a stern woodman, whatever one of those was. My reaction was too mild to be called a premonition—the most I can say is that I felt something I didn't normally feel when I noted down clients' addresses.

Woodmansterne Lane was the perfect place to live if you wanted privacy, she told me the first time I went to the house. She was obsessed with privacy, mentioned it constantly, whenever we met. On the wall by the front door there was an oval-shaped plaque with the words 'Cherub Cottage' painted on it. The name was her invention. For our first meeting, she wore a smart grey suit— the sort no primary school teacher needs to wear to work—with sheer black tights and enormous dog's-head slippers that made her look utterly ridiculous.

I can still picture those dogs' faces, as vividly as if they were in front of me. Each one had a red cloth tongue dangling diagonally from its mouth.

On my first visit to Cherub Cottage, I also met her partner. He was a pharmacist who said very little, but when she spoke, which she did ceaselessly, I could see him trying to gauge my reaction to her. He was better looking, better dressed and younger than she was. When I first met him he was twenty-six. He seemed to have no quirks of his own, though he tolerated hers without complaint. As I saw more of her, I realised how much he had to put up with: she would not allow any food to cross her threshold that didn't come from Marks & Spencer; she forced him to redecorate their house from top to bottom every year, and new curtains and carpets every three years; she sent a tedious, self-aggrandising round robin letter to everyone they knew at Christmas, full of exclamation marks. Reading the one she sent me, I could hardly believe it wasn't a parody. Some of her household appliances had names. The microwave was called 'Ding', the doorbell 'Dong'.

During that first discussion the three of us had, I kept trying to include her partner and find out what he wanted Cherub Cottage's garden to be, but whenever I succeeded in coaxing an opinion out of him, she automatically said, 'No,' and corrected him. From what I managed to glean from him, in between her negations, it seemed he was happy with things pretty much as they were. The front and back gardens they'd inherited from the previous owners of Cherub Cottage (or number 8, as it had been in those days) couldn't have been more traditional: lush green lawns surrounded by flower beds on all sides. He said he wouldn't mind if I filled the gaps in the beds, that he thought they ought to be fuller—that was the only adjective he could think of to describe what he wanted—but when I started to talk about a riotous, voluptuous planting plan, he nodded eagerly. 'A cottage ought to have a ramshackle garden,' he said, before she leaped in with one of her 'no's.

'I don't want it messy,' she said. 'Any flowers, I want them colour-coordinated and in rows, not sticking out all over the place. Can you pick up a pink and purple theme? Pink roses, and purple slate in the beds instead of dirt? I saw that in a magazine.' She always said 'dirt' when she meant 'earth'.

I was used to working with clients who valued my opinion, who looked to me for guidance, and I would have felt like a criminal if I'd taken her money in exchange for making her garden uglier. As tactfully as I could, I explained that I didn't think purple slate would work. 'That's more suitable for very contemporary-looking houses,' I said. 'I know your house isn't old, but it's a country cottage first and foremost. I'm not sure we want to depart too much from the traditional—'

'It's not about what you want, it's about what I want!' she said, putting me in my place. 'It's *my* inheritance from my Auntie Eileen that's paying for it, so it's my opinion that counts.' Even knowing she was ill, it was difficult to feel sorry for her. I suggested to her that perhaps she ought to look for another garden designer; I took pride in my work, and could see already that the garden she was going to force me to create for her was one that would embarrass me. There would be no BALI award for Cherub Cottage's new garden, that was for sure, not if I gave her what she wanted: something pretentious and out of keeping with its surroundings.

'I chose you because you won that prize,' she said. Then, pointedly, 'I haven't got *time* to find another designer. I don't want to get stuck in a sourcing loop.'

This last phrase baffled me at first, until I realised it had to be some sort of business-speak for being unable to find something. I caught her boyfriend's eye and saw the trace of a smirk on his face, as much of one as he was confident of being able to get away with.

'What about bark?' he said, looking at me. 'I heard someone on telly say bark's a good alternative to slate. For beds. Just as neat, but less showy.' I think that's the longest speech I ever heard him make in all the time I knew him.

I nodded. 'Bark might work,' I said, though I still favoured traditional earth flower beds. But I found myself wanting to say yes to him, if only because she never did. I wanted to compensate.

'Purple slate,' she said flatly, as if neither he nor I had spoken. 'And one of those plastic borders round the lawns, so we don't have to keep trimming the edges. And at the back, I want a gravel crossroads—I've got a picture of one that I cut out of a magazine, I'll show you—with a fountain or something in the middle. Maybe a statue. Something eastern to pick up a multicultural theme.'

The picture turned out to be of the Prince of Wales' garden at Highgrove, which was more than big enough for the 'gravel crossroads' she described not to look ridiculous. If I gave her what she claimed to want, four tiny green squares would be all that was left of her lawn at the back. It would look absurd.

I was about to tell her this when I saw him shake his head as if to say there was no point. I should have left then and never gone back, and not only because of what happened later. It was clear she would be a nightmare client. I reminded myself that she was ill, and that I was there for his sake as well as hers. I sensed that he wanted me around. I have no idea, now, whether he did or not, whether he was indifferent to me and I blindly chose to believe otherwise, but at the time I thought he was silently pleading with me not to leave him alone to deal with her and her ludicrous unfulfilled wishes.

I suppose I was drawn to him because I knew how it felt to be unable to speak freely in your own home. He reminded me of how I used to be before I left home. My parents are evangelical Christian control freaks, expert emotional blackmailers, and I spent my childhood and adolescence pretending I was who they wanted me to be, stifling the person I really was because all my life I'd had this never-quite-articulated but very real threat hanging over my head: go against them on anything, however minor, and I'd do unimaginable damage to us all.

There's no doubt that, on that day at Cherub Cottage, he and I entered into a conspiracy: us against her. Yes, we would give her what she wanted, but we both knew it would be awful, and, more importantly, we knew we were the clever ones and she was the dimwit. Not only did we know it but we enjoyed the knowledge. Despite what happened subsequently, I know I didn't imagine it: he was as conscious of our secret, shared superiority as I was.

I agreed to redesign their gardens, and gave them my questionnaire to fill in. I gave it to all my clients, not caring if it seemed unnecessarily formal when mostly they had already described to me exactly what they wanted. Time and time again I found that being made to answer the questions helped people to form a clearer idea of what they were looking for, and it certainly made life easier for me.

She handed the questionnaire to him, didn't even look at it. I arranged another appointment with them in a few days' time, telling them I'd take measurements then. As the day approached, I found I was looking forward to seeing him again. When I arrived at the house, she wasn't there. He was alone, apologetic and far more awkward than he had been last time. It was as if, without her there to keep us both in check, he was afraid to talk to me. When I asked where she was, he shrugged. 'You can still measure,' he said. He didn't give me back the questionnaire, but instead handed me a few crumpled sheets of paper I didn't recognise, covered in large sloping handwriting that leaned to the left.

I was surprised to see he had transcribed all my questions, as well as writing down his answers to them. 'Why didn't you write on the form I gave you?' I asked him. He shrugged. His answers—and it was clear they were his, not hers—were short. In response to the question, 'Who will use the garden?' he had written, 'Us'. To 'What will they use it for?' he had replied, 'Sitting'. I nearly laughed when I saw his one-word answer to my longest, most expansive question: 'Do you want to develop your garden all in one go or gradually year by year? How "instant" do you need your garden to be? How long are you prepared to wait for it to mature?' Underneath his handwritten reproduction of my words, he had added just one of his own: 'Quick'.

I measured up, as instructed, and when I came back inside he was waiting for me with a drink, a glass of red wine. He'd poured one for himself, too. I didn't have the heart to tell him I had to drive home, and thought it odd that he'd assumed without bothering to ask that I would want wine.

He led me into a lounge I hadn't seen before. It had a horrible artificial look of 'best' about it. The carpet was mustard-yellow and the walls were gleaming white, as were the three leather sofas arranged in square-bracket formation in front of an obscenely large television set that seemed to devour all the space and energy in the room. Beside one of the sofas was a cube of a coffee table with mirrored surfaces, and beside another her dog slippers with their wretched red tongues, neatly aligned. Almost as big as the TV screen were three framed photographs, the lounge walls' only decoration. 'Not my doing,' he said, seeing me staring at the pictures. I tried to disguise my distaste but I probably didn't do a very good job. All three pictures were of him and her, barefoot, looking idyllically happy together against a background of unblemished white. Each had been blown up so that it covered most of a wall. In one, it looked as if the photographer had asked them to run towards the camera from a distance and then fall over: they were both laughing, their limbs entangled. In another her expression was solemn, her head coyly tilted, and his face was in profile, his lips on her cheek—a supposedly profound private moment, captured for ever, to be enlarged and stuck on the lounge wall to show off to guests: *look how happy we are.*

I was so busy staring at the photographs that I didn't notice him approach me from the side, and when he tried to kiss me I sprang away from him, spilling some of my wine on the carpet. He ran to get stain remover. I recognised that run. It was me, thirteen years earlier, hearing my parents' car an hour before I'd expected to, racing to my bedroom to hide the book I'd been reading: *Riders* by Jilly Cooper. I made it. By the time my father walked into the living room, I was back in my chair with *Thomas Cranmer: A Life* propped up in front of my face, my heart a bouncing boulder in my chest.

The stain remover did the job. Within seconds the drops of red were gone, but he kept spraying white foam on the carpet. He must have used nearly a whole can. I wasn't close enough to him to hear it, but I knew what his heartbeat was doing.

He took his wine glass and mine through to the kitchen—a safe place, lino instead of carpet. His eyes were suddenly wary; perhaps he'd finally taken in what his state of high alert hadn't allowed him to register sooner: he'd tried to kiss me and I'd rejected him.

'Why do you stay with her?' I asked. I knew it was an inappropriate question, but the atmosphere was so strained by that point that normal protocol no longer seemed to apply.

'The pictures aren't too bad,' he said, as if they were all that had made me ask.

'Is it because she's ill?'

'Ill?'

Something cold clutched at my throat. 'She told me she was dying.'

He nodded. 'She does that sometimes.'

That decided me. 'I can't work for you,' I said. 'For *her*.' I wanted him to try to kiss me again.

'You can't pull out now. She wants you.'

'I don't care . . .' I started to say.

'*I* want you. I want to show you something.'

In a sort of trance, I followed him out of the room and upstairs, thinking that I would look at whatever it was and then leave. He took me into a box room with a skylight that wouldn't have been big enough to fit a bed in. In the middle of the carpet there was a red and blue-painted model of a train with three carriages. Next to this was a chair and, around it, piles of what looked like superhero comics: *Spiderman, The Incredible Hulk.* Lined up against one wall were several pairs of Chelsea boots, black and brown.

A ghetto blaster stood on the windowsill, surrounded by towers of CD cases. 'This room's my den,' he said. 'That's mine.' He pointed to a picture on the wall. It was long and rectangular, the size and shape of a full-length mirror, and made me think of Soviet propaganda, though the words on it were French—'*Etat*' at the top and '*Exactitude*' at the bottom—printed in chunky masculine letters over the red, black and grey image of an enormous train emerging at speed from a tunnel.

'It's nice,' I said, not sure how I was meant to respond. But when I said that, he smiled, and I was glad I'd lied. I thought the picture was awful—harsh, almost fascistic.

I did leave shortly afterwards, as I'd promised myself I would, but he and I both knew I would work on their garden as agreed. When I went back to the kitchen to retrieve my handbag, I noticed my questionnaire—the typed version I'd given them at our first meeting—under a pile of house and garden magazines. I could see it had been written on, that the handwriting was small and rounded, not large and left-leaning. He saw that I'd spotted it, and stuffed his hands in his pockets as I pulled it out and started to read. It wasn't hard to work out what had happened: he'd been understandably appalled by her answers, so he'd copied the questions out again in order to be able to present me with a less offensive document. His thoughtfulness touched me. I think that was the moment I fell for him, when I saw what she'd written and realised how much effort he'd put into sparing my feelings.

To the question 'How long will you be living in the house? Should I plan for five, ten, twenty years?', she had answered, 'I'm not psychic.' Underneath 'Do you need privacy? Any particular part of the garden?' she had written, 'We've got privacy. No part of our garden is overlooked. Surely this sort of generic questionnaire is bad for your business? Why don't you tailor your questions to individual clients' needs?'

In person she'd been rude, but this was worse. These were words she'd had a chance to think about, ones she'd committed to paper. She had saved her most cutting response for last. The final question was about the pH and texture of the soil, any micro-climates there might be in the garden, frost pockets, shelter, prevailing winds. Many of my clients didn't have a clue about this sort of thing and wrote 'Not sure' or 'Don't know', but I still felt the question was worth including, because sometimes people knew more than you expected them to, and it could be a big help to have this kind of information upfront.

Beneath my last question, she had written, 'Get a life!'

'Sorry,' he said. 'She doesn't mean it.'

'Is she always like this?' I asked. Not at all inappropriate, I felt, under the circumstances.

'You will come back, won't you?'

'I'm not sure,' I said.

'Please. I . . . I promise, I won't touch you again.' He blushed.

I thought about his 'den', the ghetto she'd confined him to in a house that was otherwise hers, and about my bedroom as a child, the tapestry slogans on the walls, stitched by my mother: 'Jesus is the silent listener to every conversation', 'Seven days without prayer makes one weak'. I suppose I was looking for someone whose pain matched mine. I was doing the same thing years later when I met Aidan, when I had even more pain to find a match for.

Against my better judgement, I kept them on as clients. The next few times I went to Cherub Cottage, she was there, and he was as he had been the first time I'd met him—full of confident knowing smiles at her expense. I tried not to meet his eyes but it was hard. I couldn't believe he was the same man who, in her absence, had behaved like a gauche schoolboy. I'd started to have sexual fantasies about him by then, ones that involved far more than sex. In my idealised version of our story, fate had given me a clear mission: I was the only person who could save him from her. If I let him down, he'd never escape her clutches or the confines of his petty, constrained life with her.

Over the next few weeks, I worked on designs for their garden. She'd said at our first meeting that she wanted 'something eastern', which turned out to mean a large granite Buddha on a plinth that she'd seen in a catalogue. I didn't try to talk her out of it. If she wanted the centre-piece of her small Lincolnshire garden to be a fat stone man sitting on a pillar, that was her choice.

Work started in March 2000 and took a month. I got landscapers in to help me, which at first she protested about. 'I thought you were going to do it all yourself,' she said, and I had to remind her that I'd told her I did only the design and the planting. I never challenged her about her lie, and she didn't refer again to her made-up terminal illness.

Whenever I had a moment alone with him, I badgered him about leaving her. I told him I'd wanted to respond when he'd tried to kiss me, but I couldn't, because he wasn't available. Sometimes he said he understood, other times he lunged at me, saying, 'Come here,' and trying to grab me, but I wouldn't let him touch me. I told him if he stayed with her he'd be a prisoner for the rest of his life, whereas if he left her he could have me. He couldn't leave her, he said, which only made me more determined. I was convinced no one besides me would ever be able to liberate him; I had to try harder. I started wearing revealing clothes to work, making sure he caught glimpses of my cleavage, wearing short skirts and bending over when he was standing behind me so that he could see my underwear. I wanted him to know what he was missing.

By this point, I was too involved to see the difference between love and an unhealthy obsession. It was a battle between good and evil as far as I was concerned: I was good and she was evil, and I had to win if I wanted to save him. I played dirty without giving it a second thought, trying to bribe him, bringing money into it. I told him how much I earned—more than a primary school teacher—and that financially he'd be better off with me than with her, all the while congratulating myself on my virtue for refusing to have sex with him. Guessing that she either couldn't have children or didn't want them in case they disturbed her perfect white living room, I told him I wanted to have his children. That didn't make him leave her but it made him cry. 'I can't,' he kept saying. 'I just can't.'

The garden was finished one day while they were both at work. It looked dreadful, but it was exactly what she'd ordered: regimented pink flowers, purple slate, gravel crossroads, eastern deity. They owed me twenty-three thousand pounds, give or take some small change. She got back from work first, saw it and burst into tears. 'I hate it,' she said. 'It's disgusting.'

That I had not been expecting. When I asked her what the problem was, she said, 'I don't know. It doesn't look like I imagined it would. I hope you don't think I'm paying for this!' She started weeping, got back into her car and drove away. I had no choice but to wait for him. When I told him what had happened, he raised his eyebrows, as if at a minor inconvenience, and said, 'She'll come round. Don't worry, you'll get your money.'

'Damn right I will,' I said. 'You signed the contract.'

'What will I do when you've gone?' he said. He took me in his arms and clamped his lips on mine.

I pulled away and said, 'We need to talk. Properly.' Finally, I thought, he's realised he needs to leave her.

He was the blushing boy again. I hadn't mentioned my religious upbringing to him so far; now I was going to use it to my advantage. I'd suffered eighteen years of it, so the least it could do was help me now, I thought. I told him I was a Christian, that I was gagging to go to bed with him, but I couldn't persuade myself it was all right to go to bed with someone who had a partner. I wittered on about marriage being sacrosanct, adultery an unforgivable sin, all the things I'd heard my parents say. He wasn't married to her, but they lived together as man and wife—I told him that from my point of view it amounted to the same thing.

I didn't mean a word of it. I was using sex, or rather the promise of sex, as leverage to make him leave her for me.

'Are you saying you want to marry me?' he asked, looking as if the idea was hurting him, scorching his brain. I hadn't been, but only because it hadn't occurred to me. I read the truth in his eyes and I knew I was right: he'd proposed to her, perhaps several times, and she'd said no.

'Yes,' I said. 'I want to marry you.'

He gritted his teeth, grabbed his hair with his hands and closed his eyes. 'I *can't* leave her,' he said.

I went home, defeated. Three days later a cheque arrived for the money they owed me. Two weeks after that he rang me. I said, 'Hello?' and heard only silence, but I knew it was him. I said his name—a common, popular name, one that gives me a jolt of shock every time I hear it, even all these years later.

He asked me to come round. 'Now,' he said. 'Please.'

'Have you left her? Are you going to leave her?' I asked.

He said yes.

I didn't believe him, but I got into my car and drove to Cherub Cottage because I wanted it to be true. He was alone when I arrived. He gave me a glass of red wine. It tasted funny but I drank it anyway. He told me she had gone, that she wouldn't be back, and tried to persuade me to go upstairs with him. I refused. Her possessions were still all over the house—her dog slippers, her magazines, her diary. I knew he was lying to me. 'Give me a cuddle, then,' he said. It seemed like a harmless request, and my desire to touch him after not having seen him for a fortnight was stronger than ever before. We lay down on one of the white sofas in the lounge. I didn't care, as I fell asleep with his arms around me, that he hadn't told me the truth. I could well understand why he wanted to pretend, and I assumed he knew she wouldn't be back any time soon. Perhaps she'd gone to stay with a friend, I thought. I kidded myself that he might still leave her, that he'd obviously found he couldn't go on without me, since he'd summoned me so urgently.

I didn't resist the sleepy feeling when it came. If I thought about it at all, I probably put it down to the wine, or to feeling happy and relaxed with him. I didn't find out until later that he'd drugged me—crushed four two-milligramme Clonazepam pills and put them in my wine.

When I woke up, or came round, I was tied to the stone plinth in the back garden. My arms were tied against my sides so that I couldn't move them, and there was something in my mouth, which had been taped shut with the thing inside it. I know now that it was a pink bath sponge. A lot of the detail I only found out later from the police, or in court.

I couldn't scream or move, or understand what had happened to me or why, which was the worst thing of all. At first I was alone in the garden, alone with my terror. Then she came out of the house. She laughed when she saw me, and told me she'd take the gag out of my mouth if I promised not to scream or cry out. I nodded, because I'd been crying and my nose was starting to block up—I was afraid I'd suffocate.

She took the sponge out of my mouth. 'You've been fucking my partner, and thinking you could get away with it,' she said.

I told her it wasn't true.

'Yes, you have. Don't lie.'

I swore to her that I hadn't, begged her to untie me.

'You told him to leave me, didn't you?'

That I couldn't deny. She stuffed the sponge back in my mouth, taped it shut again and went back into the house.

The next time she came outside, it was almost dark. She reached down and picked up a handful of gravel from one of the new paths. She threw a small pebble at me from a distance of about a metre, and it hit my cheek. It hurt more than I'd have thought a tiny stone could. 'In some parts of the world, they stone you to death for fucking another woman's man,' she said. That was when it got worse. I couldn't speak to defend myself. She kept throwing the stones, some from further away, some from right in front of my face—at my head, my chest, my arms and legs. It went on for hours. After a while, the pain became unbearable.

She brought a table and chair out into the garden, then a bottle of wine, a corkscrew and a glass. All night she drank wine—two more bottles after the first one—and threw stones at me, stones I'd ordered for her. I'd brought samples in two sizes for her to look at, and she'd chosen the smaller ones, thank goodness. If they'd been any larger I'd have died—that's what I was told later. She didn't throw them constantly. Sometimes she stopped and sat down, drank, lectured me. She said I was lucky I lived in England and not lots of other places, because this was nothing compared to what would happen to me in some countries.

The next morning it got worse. She took the sponge out of my mouth and pushed in a handful of gravel. She told me to eat it. I spat it out but she forced more in and tried to push it down my throat. In the end I swallowed and she did it again, kept doing it. She preferred making me eat the stones to throwing them at me, once she'd tried it.

After that, my memories are blurred. I started to pass out and come round, so that I was never sure how long I'd been there, whether this night was the same night or a new one. I found out later that I spent seventy-two hours tied to the stone plinth. At one point she ripped the tape off my mouth and I vomited blood all over her. That made her angry, and she slapped me across the face.

After a while my chest and stomach filled with a burning pain that seemed to radiate through to my back. I felt unbearably thirsty. Sometimes when she took the tape off, I asked for a drink, and she laughed at me. I expected to die of thirst if I didn't suffocate. I began to vomit clear liquid—it seeped out around the tape. She sneered, 'You say you're thirsty, but you're puking water. Swallow it instead and you won't be thirsty any more.'

I lost my grip on my mind, became incoherent, and when she let me speak, it didn't make sense. I was aware of what she was saying, but couldn't think straight. Everything seemed remote apart from the pain. Waves of it started to pour through me: powerful, uncontrollable spasms in my stomach, which were worse even than the thirst. Then I started to pass the stones I'd eaten. I couldn't help it. That was the worst agony of all.

Later, the doctors told me the names of all the injuries I'd suffered. My throat and oesophagus were badly cut, which had caused something called mediastinitis. I needed surgery to sew up the cuts, an endoscopy to inject the lacerations that couldn't be sewn with adrenalin. I had rectal fissures, a perforated bowel, peritonitis, a paralytic ileus. These are words most people will never hear, but I heard them endlessly in the hospital and in court. They went round and round in my head, what she'd done to me. I had to have a laparotomy, which was what caused the scar.

I was in hospital for three weeks. It's easier to race ahead to that part, to after I was free and in the hands of people who were trying as hard to help me as she had to harm me. The strange thing was that she must have decided, at a certain point, to let me go. She could have killed me—all she needed to do was leave me where I was—but instead she called the police, in tears, and told them to come to the house. They played the recording in court. She said, 'Come quickly, there's a woman in trouble, I think she's dying.' The police had found her hysterical, drunk, claiming not to know how a half-dead person had ended up tied to a stone column in her back garden.

He pleaded guilty to false imprisonment and GBH. He admitted to drugging me with Clonazepam and tying me up, but would say nothing about his reasons for doing either. Though she was the one who'd done the damage, he was still guilty of GBH by law because he was 'more than ancillary' to her attack on me. He admitted to knowing in advance what she'd planned to do, though her plan had contained only the throwing of the stones, in accordance with the punishment, under Sharia law, for adultery. Making me eat the gravel had been an improvisation on her part.

After that one moment of weakness in which she saved my life with her phone call to the police, she became herself again. She pleaded not guilty, against the advice of her legal team, claiming he had done it all and she'd had nothing to do with it, hadn't even known about it.

Once I'd recovered and was let out of hospital, all I wanted was to put it behind me insofar as that was possible. I can't remember at what point I realised that the people who were supposedly on my side were trying to force a whole new ordeal upon me, one I didn't have the stamina for: a court case, publicity. I was told I wouldn't be able to stop the papers printing my name because there had been no sexual element to the attack. I refused to talk to the press, so they presented her version of the story as fact: I had been sleeping with her boyfriend and she'd stoned me as a punishment. In court, under cross-examination, she emphasised more than once that I was an adulteress and had deserved it, even though she stuck to her story that it was he who had done the stoning, not her. The jury didn't believe her. Everyone could see she was proud of what she'd done.

I don't know what he told her. I can't see why he'd say we'd had sex when we hadn't—what good would that do him? My guess is that he told her the truth but she didn't believe him, or she believed him but chose to pretend she didn't. After all, the more grave my offence, the more justified her response. I can't prove it, obviously, but I don't think she was punishing me for sleeping with her boyfriend, whatever she said in court. She was punishing me for the terror she'd experienced when she found out I was waging a campaign to split them up. Maybe they had a fight and he told her he was leaving her for me, and in a moment of ragged, uncontrollable horror, she saw herself disintegrating without him. A person can lose everything that makes them who they are in a moment like that.

Having my name and a distorted version of the story continually in the papers condemned me to a living hell. I knew that everyone knew, or thought they did, and that I would never be able to escape the rumours. One night I heard, on a local radio station, a caller expressing the opinion that I had 'probably deserved it', that 'women should keep their hands off other women's property'. Then came the next blow: the police told me I would have to appear in court and give evidence against her. I collapsed— actually physically collapsed—when they told me. Of course I didn't want her to get away with it, but I also didn't want to be anywhere near her ever again, no matter what protection I had. I didn't want to have to sit in court and listen to PC James Escritt describe the state I was in when he found me in the garden of Cherub Cottage.

My medical records were needed to secure a conviction, and I had to authorise the hospital to make a statement about my condition when I arrived. I begged to be spared a court appearance in exchange for agreeing to the medical statement, but that wasn't possible. I was told that without me as a witness, the CPS would drop the case, because the chance of getting a guilty verdict would be less than fifty-one per cent. James Escritt, who had been my main point of contact throughout, even after CID got involved, did his best to arrange for me to deliver my testimony from behind a screen, or from another room in the building by video-link, but the judge refused. I'd had bad luck, apparently—more bad luck—in being assigned a judge who was known for his inflexibility.

I was a mess in court: shaking, dribbling, unable to move my limbs in the way I wanted to, feeling as if the various bits of my body weren't properly fitted together and might fall apart at any moment. I held up proceedings by fainting twice during cross-examination. My parents had wanted to come to court with me, but I'd managed to persuade them not to. Ever since I was a child, their presence has made me feel worse in times of trouble, not better. Fortunately, I was able to put them off without saying anything so tactless or honest. I distrusted those of my friends who claimed to want to come and give me 'moral support', suspecting them of wanting nothing more than proximity to a juicy story that they'd be able to dine out on for years.

He testified against her, endorsing my version of events. There was no need for him to stand trial, because he'd admitted his guilt. She was found guilty, and burst into tears when it was announced. 'It's not fair!' she screamed. 'Why does the system always punish the victim?' He also cried on hearing the verdict, even though he'd helped to convict her. I watched him mouth, 'I'm sorry'—at her, not at me.

That was the last time I saw them. I didn't go to hear sentencing, but I was informed of their sentences: seven years for him, ten for her, because she'd pleaded not guilty. Via the family liaison officer who had been assigned to me, I made it clear that I didn't want the CPS to send me any more information about either of them. It sickened me to think that one day a letter might arrive saying one or other of them had been released early for good behaviour. I didn't want to know.

I stuck it out in Lincoln for another three years after the trial, feeling as if I was in prison too. Everyone I met either asked prying questions or appeared mortified to have to speak to me. No one wanted me to design a garden for them; even if they had, I'd have found it impossible, unthinkable. Still, it didn't occur to me to move and start a new life, not until one day in 2004.

I had gone to my parents' house for dinner, and, for once, decided to risk a little honesty when they asked me how I was feeling. 'Bad,' I said. 'I don't think I'll ever feel anything but bad again.'

They started to talk about prayer, as I had known they would, about asking Jesus for help. And then my mother said, 'He would forgive you, you know. We forgave you straight away, the minute we heard what had happened. Jesus is loving and merciful—'

I interrupted her and asked, 'Forgave me for what?', because I knew what they meant. They could only mean one thing. It hadn't occurred to me until that moment that my parents didn't believe my story. They believed her lies, the newspapers' lies, the late-night radio phone-in lies; they thought I'd been having sex with him. After all the lying and pretending I'd done over the years for their sake, they didn't believe me against the woman who had nearly killed me.

'I don't believe in God,' I told them. 'But if he exists, I hope he doesn't forgive you. I hope he lights a match under both your souls.' All those years of trying so hard not to upset them—I suddenly found I was aching to devastate their sad little fantasy world, to say things that would torture them, that they'd never be able to forget. I didn't hold back. I inflicted as much pain as I could using only words, then walked out of their house, leaving them ravaged and howling.

I moved to Spilling shortly afterwards. Things were better in Spilling. No one seemed to know anything about me—I could say my name without getting the looks I was so sick of getting in Lincoln. I sent my parents a PO box address, but they've never used it. I ought to feel terrible about this, probably, but I don't. I feel free. I found a house in Blantyre Park, the opposite of an enclosed, private garden. There was nowhere where I could be tied up

and tortured. How sick to think that was what first attracted me to the place. But life is sick. It was sick when it
sent you, Mary, into the gallery where I'd been working
happily with Saul to ruin things for me all over again. It
was sick when I went to see Charlie Zailer at the police
station and a stone got into my shoe and cut my foot so
badly I could hardly walk. I couldn't take it out, couldn't
bear to see or touch a stone that had been pressed against
my skin. I can't even say the word 'stone'. I'm surprised I
can write it.

I went to see Charlie Zailer last Friday. Did she tell you
that? I know she's been here and spoken to you about Aidan. I went to her because Aidan told me he'd killed you
and I was frightened and didn't know what to do. He believes he strangled you, or says he does. He told the police
that you were naked when it happened, in a double bed in
the front bedroom of your house. It wasn't long after he
made his 'confession' that I discovered who you were: the
woman who had attacked me at Saul's gallery. Why would
my boyfriend say he had murdered someone who was still
alive? I know you know something about this, Mary. You
must do. I don't care how bad the truth is. All I want is to
understand.

Ruth

11

Tuesday 4 March 2008

'Your turn,' I say to Mary when she looks up from my letter. 'You promised. A fair exchange, you said. Where's Aidan?'

'Aidan Seed,' she says softly. 'The man you're so sure I know.'

'Did he kill Martha Wyers? Did you? Both of you together?' The painting is still imprinted on my mind. I don't think I'll ever forget it. No one would paint someone dead like that, in such lurid detail, unless they relished the death in some way, wanted to savour it. The picture had an atmosphere of triumph about it; I don't think I can have imagined that. I want to see it again, but I'm scared to go charging upstairs like I did before, scared that Mary wouldn't be here when I came back down. I'm not letting her out of my sight, not until she's answered my questions.

'Martha killed Martha,' she says, lighting a cigarette. 'She hanged herself. I suppose you think I'm sick, painting her like that.'

I don't acknowledge the question. She's getting nothing from me until she gives me something back.

'People deal with grief in different ways.' Her voice hardens, as if it angers her to find herself caught up in justifications. 'When you lose everything that matters to you, you want something to show for it.'

'You loved Martha.'

'Very much. At the same time, nowhere near enough.'

'You think you could have saved her?'

'Could and should.'

'What happened?' I ask, leaning forward in my chair. I don't know what time it is, but it's late. Dark outside. Mary hasn't closed the curtains. Every now and then she looks out at the lamplit street beyond the window, her sharp eyes scouring the night. *For Aidan?*

'This man,' she says, waving my letter at me. 'Was there anyone before him? Men, boys? Girls?' She smiles.

How many more questions will she make me answer before she answers mine? 'At first I only dated good Christian boys,' I say. 'The sons of my parents' friends.'

'I'm surprised they let you date anyone,' says Mary.

'Only once I was sixteen, and only trips to public places like the cinema. When I left home and they couldn't keep tabs on me as easily, I went for anybody who was nothing like the people I'd known through church. The further removed from that world, the better. I went for the sort of men who would have reduced the church boys to quivering wrecks.'

'That sounds dangerous.'

'Not really. I didn't respect or care about any of them. I just wanted to prove I could sleep around and the world wouldn't fall apart. And it didn't. The first man I really felt anything for was . . . Him.'

'What about Aidan Seed?'

'What about him?'

'You love him.'

'Yes.'

Mary smiles at my hesitation. 'A man who tells you he's killed someone who you *know* is alive: me. A man who fucks with your brain so badly that it drives you half insane.'

I hate this.

'Don't you see the pattern?'

'You're not a shrink,' I tell her. *She hates Aidan. Hates him more than anything.* With this insight, the conspiracy I've constructed in my mind—Mary and Aidan against me—starts to dissolve. At first I'm relieved—I can forgive him anything but that, anything at all, I know I can—but the respite doesn't last long. Not good enough, I think to myself. Not the same as being able to forgive him anything, not unconditional.

'I could be a shrink,' says Mary. 'I don't believe I'd need any training whatsoever. All I'd need is experience, which I've got, and a brain, which I've got.'

'We made a deal. I've told you everything.'

'No, you haven't.'

How does she know? My mind fills with all the things I've kept back: the *Access 2* Art fair, Aidan's prediction about the nine paintings, his insistence that I bring *Abberton* to him as proof. *Proof that he didn't murder Mary.* Why would anyone who knew they'd strangled someone demand to see proof that they hadn't? Sometimes, because my understanding nothing has become normal, I forget how little sense it all makes. Then I remember again and am as shocked as if I were realising it for the first time.

'We made a deal,' I say again.

Mary lets air out through clenched teeth, a hiss of disgust. 'You're here because you want the truth about Aidan. You think I must be able to explain it to you. You don't care how bad it is—you want to know.'

'That's right.'

'You've still got a choice. You could leave this house, forget him, forget about Martha. Forget me. The safe option.'

'I don't want to be safe. I want to know.'

'I don't know Aidan Seed,' says Mary, looking past me into the distance.

No. Not possible.

'I used to, though. I knew him a long time ago.'

'I haven't seen Aidan since the day Martha died. The tenth of April, 2000.' Mary puts my letter down on the table and bends over it, pushing her bushy hair out of her eyes. 'When were your seventy-two hours?'

I don't need to ask what she means. To me, that number will only ever mean one thing. 'Later.' I force myself to give her one more piece of information, of my life. 'It started on April the twenty-second.'

'Close enough,' she says. Then her face goes blank. 'Aidan was there when Martha jumped.'

I hardly dare to breathe.

'He also didn't stop her.'

'You were there too?'

'Three's a crowd,' she says in a sing-song voice. 'I don't think Aidan wanted Martha dead. I'm the one he wants dead. Maybe he did. If he did, he'd have stopped wanting it when she jumped. Too late. You freeze, I suppose. It happens too quickly.' Mary's hands are shaking. 'Once she'd gone down, there was no way I could get her up. I tried—' She breaks off. 'Aidan could have got her up, he could have lifted her, but he didn't try. He called an ambulance. He ran to the phone. Ran away. He saw I was struggling, but he didn't help me.' She breathes hard, locked into the terrible memory. 'He froze. When you can't stand the situation you're in, you tell yourself it's not real—it's an illusion. I told myself the same thing.'

'Why didn't he tell me any of this?' I blurt out.

'Did you tell him about Cherub Cottage?'

'No.'

'Why not?'

I shake my head. 'I couldn't.' *Couldn't tell anyone. Until I had to.*

'Maybe he wanted you to carry on loving him,' says Mary. 'How could you, once you knew he'd stood by and let someone die?'

'He told me he'd killed you. Why did he say that?'

She rubs her thumb along her lips and back again. 'He wants me dead. He's going to kill me, or try to. It's a threat.'

'No! Aidan's not a killer.'

She laughs. 'Don't kid yourself.'

'It makes no sense. If he wanted to threaten you, why not do it to your face?'

'He's clever. I'd have called the police, wouldn't I? I assume it's an offence to threaten someone's life.'

'I don't know.' I can't think straight, can't process any of this.

'Of course it is. It must be. There'd have been reprisals for him, and he doesn't want that. He thinks he's suffered enough.'

'Why? Why has he suffered?'

'His childhood,' says Mary, assuming I know what she's referring to.

I feel ashamed of my ignorance. Aidan never wanted to talk about his family. I didn't push it; I was equally reluctant to talk about my parents. *Don't ask, don't tell.*

'He tried to save her later,' Mary mutters.

'Aidan tried to save Martha?'

'Once he'd rung the ambulance. He's no weakling—well, you know that. It was easy for him to get her down. The emergency services operator must have told him to do it: lift her up, or cut her down or whatever. Stop the rope from strangling her.'

I don't want to have to visualise it.

'I've thought about this a lot,' says Mary. 'A man rings up saying a woman's just hanged herself in front of him. If you were the person on the switchboard, what would you think? You'd assume he'd rushed to save her first, wouldn't you, and only rung you afterwards? Soon as you found out she was still hanging there, dying while he wastes time on the phone, you'd tell him to get back in there and save her.'

I wince.

'How do you feel about your boyfriend now? A man who only tries to save a dying woman once a disembodied official voice has told him to, who dreams up a sick, devious way to threaten my life. You know he described me in great detail, right down to my birthmark?' She points to the patch of brown skin beneath her bottom lip. 'That was him letting me know I'm his target. If he tells the police he's strangled me, murdered me, what are they going to do when they find me alive and well?'

She lights another cigarette, coughing. 'Alive, anyway. I've probably got lung cancer, the amount I smoke. The police aren't very bright. Aidan knew they'd rush back to reassure him once they'd found out his story wasn't true. Poor, deluded man, they'd think—what a shame. His determination to make them believe him sent them back here twice, three times. What if he's right? they thought. Even though we've all met this woman he claims to have murdered, we'd better check again. And then you turn up, and I hear from you as well that he says he's killed me . . .'

She stands up, wrapping her wild hair round her hand, yanking it straight. 'Evil bastard! He knew it would scare me more than a straightforward threat. How do you think it feels to have your death discussed as if it's already happened?

'Why?' I ask.

She looks at me oddly.

It's a simple question, an obvious one. 'Why would Aidan want to frighten you? Why would he want to kill you?'

'Will you let me take you somewhere?' she asks.

'No. Where?' I think of Charlie Zailer's advice: *Don't go to Mary's house.*

'Villiers.' The name on the tea towel in Mary's kitchen. I saw it last time I was here. 'My old school. There's a house in the grounds, Garstead Cottage. I use it for painting, when I'm not here. Martha used to write there. Her parents rent it from the school. We'll be safe there. Martha was a writer—did I tell you that?'

'No.'

Mary sighs, starts to rub her temples with her fingertips. 'Then you don't know how Aidan and Martha met.'

'No.' How could I? 'Why did Martha kill herself?'

'Come with me to Villiers,' she says. 'If you want the truth about me, Martha and Aidan, there's something you need to see.'

12

5/3/08

'DC Dunning's already heard everything I can tell you,' Simon said to DS Coral Milward. Dunning sat beside her, clutching his own arms as if miming a strait-jacket. He reeked of the same acid-seaweed aftershave he'd had on yesterday—his version of a chemical weapon, thought Simon; all the better for being legal.

Dunning had interviewed Simon and Charlie last night, together and separately. Each time, the room they were in was dingier. This one wasn't much bigger than a toilet cubicle, and had some kind of hard, woven substance on the floor that looked like the plaited bristles of a brush. It was decayed to a rusty colour around the edges, coarse hairs sprouting round one or two dark-rimmed holes in the middle. The room was too hot as well as ugly. They were all sweating, Simon most of all. He didn't care. Stench-wise, as in every other respect, he was proud to give as good as he got.

'You don't need us to go over it again,' he said. 'We've both told you everything we know.' He was acutely aware of the details Charlie hadn't volunteered: Mary Trelease's post-mortem portrait of a dead woman called Martha Wyers, Ruth Bussey's bedroom wall. Simon knew her silence was down to embarrassment. There was probably no connection between Martha Wyers and the murder Dunning and Milward were investigating; Charlie didn't want to look stupid, and she wanted even less to tell a pair of hostile strangers about Bussey's collection of Charlie Zailer memorabilia.

Simon felt uneasy about his role in the lie. Even an arsehole like Neil Dunning had the right to do his job unimpeded. On the other hand, if Dunning ever got round to taking the interest in Bussey and Trelease that Simon had told him countless times he ought to, he could find out for himself about Martha Wyers and Bussey's collection of cuttings, decide for himself if they were important.

Last night, all Dunning had seemed to want to talk about was Simon's 'irregular' behaviour on Monday. He persisted in using this description, even after Simon had explained that taking things too far was something he did habitually. *Funny, the situations you find yourself in.* He'd never thought he would end up in someone else's nick telling stories of his own reckless-ness to another DC, to prove that irregularity was something that had been with him for a long time and had never led to a violent death.

Simon knew Dunning didn't really fancy him for Gemma Crowther's murder, but Dunning wanted him to think he did. Coral Milward was an unknown quantity, a fat middle-aged woman with short blonde hair, three thin gold chains round her neck and gold rings with pink cameos of women's faces at their centres on three of her stubby-nailed fingers. Probably coral, Simon thought, in honour of her name. This was the first he had seen or heard of DS Milward. Unlike Dunning, she smiled a lot. She was smiling now. 'You don't ever ask witnesses to repeat their stories?' she asked in a soft west-country accent.

'I'm glad you said "witness", not "suspect".'

Another smile. 'I was being tactful. I want to show you a photograph.'

'Of Len Smith?' asked Simon.

'No.'

'Show me a photograph of Len Smith, so I can tell you that the man you know as Len Smith is Aidan Seed.'

Milward hesitated before saying, 'We have no photograph of Len Smith.'

'There is no Len Smith. Have you found Seed yet? Have you looked for him?' Simon only ever felt this alert and on form when he was under attack; might as well make the most of it. It was what his life was about: triumphing over persecution. Not hard to find low-level persecution being beamed your way if you looked hard enough.

Milward consulted her notes. 'Aidan Seed. The picture-framer.'

'The Aidan Seed who killed Gemma Crowther. The only Aidan Seed I know, the one I've been talking about until I'm hoarse.' Simon couldn't resist adding, 'If I knew of more than one Aidan Seed, I'd have mentioned it. To avoid confusion. Show me your photograph.'

'I will,' said Milward. 'You were right about Seed's car, incidentally. It's parked outside Gemma Crowther's house.'

'It'll stay there,' Simon told her. 'Seed won't be back for it.' He heard Charlie sigh. She hated it when he played prophet. 'If I had to guess, I'd say he's still in London: easiest place in the world to melt into a crowd and disappear. Plus, he'll think it more likely you'll look for him on his home turf or, at the other extreme, ports and airports, St Pancras—'

'Enough,' Milward cut him off. 'Assuming you're right and Seed's our killer, why would he have left his car at the scene? One, he'd have needed it to get away, and two, why leave evidence of his presence when he could have taken the car and we might never have known he was there?'

Simon counted them off on his fingers. 'One, he didn't need the car if he was heading into town—no one drives into central London. We *know* Seed doesn't—I saw proof of that on Monday night. Check CCTV footage between Ruskington Road and Highgate underground—he'll have gone for the tube within half an hour of killing Gemma Crowther, or jumped on a bus on Muswell Hill Road.'

'Simon,' Charlie muttered, 'you don't know that.'

'Two, I agree the car's evidence of his presence at the scene, which could mean one of two things. Either he's hoping you'll have him down as missing, possibly also dead, as likely to be another of the killer's victims as to be the killer himself . . .'

'Bit of a stretch, isn't it?' Milward frowned.

'I'm keener on the second possibility: he knew that as soon as Gemma Crowther turned up murdered, he'd be high up on the list of suspects whether you found his car or not.'

Dunning rubbed his nose. Milward looked perky again—a contented piglet.

'I'm right, aren't I?' said Simon. 'There's a link between Aidan Seed and Gemma Crowther. Which you wouldn't have found as quickly as you did if I hadn't given you Seed's name.'

Silence from the other side of the table.

'That's okay,' he said. 'You're welcome. How long are you going to wait before searching Seed's car? Or have you impounded it already?'

'Let's not waste words,' said Milward. 'You know I can't tell you anything. I'm interested to hear your thoughts, though.'

Simon had plenty. 'If there's a link between Seed and Crowther, is it one that supplies Seed with a motive for murder?'

Milward ran her tongue over her lower lip before saying carefully, 'Let's suppose, hypothetically, that it were.'

'Crowther can't have known,' said Simon. 'She knew him as Len Smith, she invited him back to her house. She didn't know about whatever it was that linked them and gave him a reason to want her dead. Her boyfriend didn't know either—only Seed knew.'

'Cloud-cuckoo-land,' said Dunning impatiently, turning the Vegas croupier eyes on Simon, eyes that had seen it all before: the worst humanity had to offer. 'Either Gemma knew Aidan Seed or she didn't. If she knew him, not much point in him changing his name to fool her. If she didn't know him, why bother?'

'You can do better than that,' said Simon. 'Or maybe you can't. It's possible to know a name but not the face that goes with it.'

'We've no reason to think Gemma knew Aidan Seed's name, and therefore no reason to suppose he would change it,' said Dunning. 'That's my point one.' He tapped his thumb in a parody of counting. 'Point two: even if Aidan Seed and Len Smith are one and the same, and that's a big if, how do you know Gemma Crowther and Stephen Elton, her boyfriend, weren't in on the secret?' The look he threw at Milward suggested he'd happily take an answer from her if Simon couldn't provide one. 'Point three: you saw Aidan Seed at Friends House on Monday night—that doesn't mean he's Len Smith. They could be two separate people—they might *both* have been there.'

'You've found a link between Seed and your victim,' Simon directed his reply to Milward. 'Seed's car was parked outside her house. Not Len Smith's. Seed was pretending to be a Quaker to get close to Crowther in order to kill her.'

'Unless you were the one he lied to,' said Dunning. 'You said when he told you he only believed in the material world, Ruth Bussey was listening.'

'Yeah. So?'

'Did you know Ruth Bussey's parents are devout evangelical Christians?'

'No.'

'Yes,' said Charlie.

'And that she doesn't speak to them or see them, hasn't for several years?'

'Yes.'

'No,' Simon said again. Making Dunning's day, no doubt.

Why the fuck hadn't Charlie told him? Probably she'd figured Ruth Bussey's family background had nothing to do with anything. There had been too much to talk about last night and this morning, not least whether the two of them had fucked up their careers beyond all repair. It wasn't much comfort that they hadn't been officially suspended. Neither of them was wanted back at work for as long as they were 'helping' DC Dunning with his inquiries; anything more official would wait until the results of those inquiries were in.

'If you had a girlfriend who'd turned her back on her religious background, mightn't you lie to her if you wanted to hang out with Quakers?' Dunning asked. 'Even more so if you were one of them, or thinking of signing up?'

'Signing up?' said Milward. 'It's not the army, Neil.'

'So you're taking an interest in Ruth Bussey,' said Simon. 'I didn't think you'd even registered the name. Do you know where she is? Far away from Seed: that's where you want her to be. He's dangerous, and he's no Quaker. He was playing a part. Phoney name, phoney faith. And why Len Smith? Is there a Len Smith in Seed's past? Have you looked?'

'No, we haven't,' said Dunning tonelessly. When he spoke, Milward looked ill at ease, and vice versa. Was it a competitive thing?

'Did anyone apart from Seed have a reason to want Crowther dead?' Simon asked.

'I can't answer that,' said Milward, tipping Simon an easily deniable nod. Had he imagined it?

'The boyfriend, Stephen Elton—why didn't he go home with Crowther after the Quaker Quest meeting? They lived together. If he stayed behind to clear up, wouldn't Crowther and Len Smith have waited for him, so that they could all go back together? Were Seed and Crowther having an affair? Did Elton find out?'

Milward folded her arms, waiting for the questions to stop.

'What was Stephen Elton doing between the end of Quaker Quest and midnight? It wouldn't take him two hours to clear away some chairs and get back to Muswell Hill at that time of night.'

'Wouldn't it?'

'You don't know where he was all that time,' said Simon. 'You like him as a suspect—it's usually domestic if it's not drug- or gang-related. So he also had a motive to kill Crowther, did he?'

'Excuse him,' Charlie said to Dunning. 'He gets carried away.'

'I'm interested in hearing all you can tell me about Seed.' Milward had started to behave as if she and Simon were alone in the room. 'You've met him. We haven't. Forget about his car being outside Gemma's house, forget about his being at Quaker Quest and using a false name—what can you tell me about him as a person? *Is* he a killer?'

'We don't know,' said Charlie. 'Simon doesn't know.' Was there a note of satisfaction in her voice? 'He told us both he'd killed a woman who's still alive. His girlfriend seems intermittently scared of him, though she's insisted several times that he wouldn't hurt her or anyone else. We've told you all this . . .'

'I believe Seed's a killer,' said Simon. 'All right, I don't *know*. But he described a murder to me in vivid detail—too vivid to be invention, I thought when I heard it. Mary Trelease is alive, though, which means Seed's also a liar, unless he's crazy. If he is a liar, he's the best kind.'

'What kind is that?' asked Milward.

'One who blends lies seamlessly with the truth and counts on you spotting the truth but not the join. He killed another woman, maybe more than one, before he killed Gemma Crowther. He might still kill Ruth Bussey and Mary Trelease, which is why you need to find them.'

'Aidan Seed the picture-framer. The two of you visited his picture-framing workshop on Monday afternoon.'

'Why do you keep saying that?' Simon asked. 'Are you suggesting he isn't a picture-framer?'

'What about this photo you wanted to show us?'

'We'll come to it,' said Milward. She turned her attention to Charlie, who'd asked the question. 'I don't understand your role in all this. You were worried about Ruth Bussey when she first came to see you, yet you didn't take a statement from her. Then you found out Aidan Seed had been in and spoken to a CID officer, DC . . .'

'Chris Gibbs,' said Simon wearily.

'That's right. Gibbs and DC Waterhouse both checked out Seed's claim, and DC Waterhouse relayed the result of those checks to Seed. End of story, and even if it wasn't, your CID were dealing with it. Why did you go to Mary Trelease's house on Monday morning when you should have gone to work?'

'I went on my way to work,' Charlie corrected her. 'I knew Ruth Bussey was frightened . . .'

'But you didn't take a statement from her,' said Milward.

'She ran away before I had a chance. I had a bad feeling about what she'd told me, and, after talking to Simon, I had a bad feeling about the whole business. I wanted to see Mary Trelease for myself and hear what she had to say.'

Milward looked down at her notes again. 'A conversation that left you with the impression that Aidan Seed had killed somebody, though obviously not Ms Trelease.'

'That's right. She said, "Not me". She clearly implied that he'd killed somebody. Look, can you at least tell us what's being done to find Ruth and Mary? Sam Kombothekra went to both their houses and Ruth Bussey's place of work this morning and there's no sign of either of them.'

'Does DI Proust know DS Kombothekra's been doing favours for you instead of the job he's supposed to be doing?' asked Milward. 'Maybe I ought to ask him.'

That shut Charlie up.

'Perhaps it's different in the provinces, but in London police officers work on the cases they've been allocated, not on whatever takes their fancy. My understanding, and correct me if I'm wrong, is that your CID is neither investigating Bussey, Seed and Trelease nor keeping them under surveillance. Mary Trelease in particular . . . Even you, DC Waterhouse, will have a hard job persuading me she's pertinent to my case.'

'You can't be that stupid, surely,' said Simon. 'Ruth Bussey and Aidan Seed share an obsession with Mary Trelease. If they're involved, she is. You can't shunt her to one side. Look for a connection between Trelease and Gemma Crowther, if you haven't already.'

'So now Mary Trelease killed Gemma Crowther?' said Dunning. 'Make your mind up.'

'You know I'm not saying that.' Simon looked at Milward. 'Does he know, or is he too dense to keep up? If a man pretends he's killed one woman, then goes and kills another, the first question I'd ask is: what's the connection between the two women?'

Nobody had ever asked Olivia Zailer to list her least favourite words, but if they had, 'logic' and 'research' might well have been among them, suggestive as they were of excessive amounts of time and effort. Yet here she was, immersed in both and even quite enjoying it. The dearth of decent telly programmes helped, as did the raspberry liqueur cocktails she'd been drinking. Olivia didn't think they were scrambling her brain too much.

There was no Wikipedia entry on Martha Wyers; the online world seemed largely unaware she'd ever lived and died. Olivia could find nothing about Wyers' suicide or murder, whichever it was. She'd phoned a few of her literary journalist friends but none of them knew anything. A couple said the name 'rang a vague bell', so noncommittally that Olivia wasn't sure she believed them; more likely they didn't want to admit to never having heard of an author who, for all they knew, had just won a prestigious award or secured the highest advance since the dawn of time for her latest book.

The Amazon website, at least, knew who Martha Wyers was. She'd published only one novel, *Ice on the Sun*, in 1998. It was unavailable, even from Amazon marketplace; out of print, and not a single used copy advertised. Must have failed quite spectacularly to make any impact at all, thought Liv. There was a short synopsis of the novel which was interesting, but not as interesting as the only customer review, dated 2 January 2000, contributed by one Senga McAllister: a four-paragraph five-star rave about the book's bleak, searing beauty.

Liv knew Senga. They'd worked together briefly before Liv went freelance. Senga was still at *The Times*, and remembered both Liv and Martha Wyers. She'd known nothing about Wyers' death but declared herself unsurprised. Her first question was, 'Did she kill herself?'

Suicide, then, thought Liv, re-reading *Ice on the Sun*'s blurb. Definitely. Bleak, searing suicide. Not murder.

Now she was waiting for Senga to email her the text of a *Times* feature she'd written years ago that included an interview with Martha Wyers. Before reading her novel, Senga had met Wyers and interviewed her. *Decided she was the sort of person who might one day take her own life.* Olivia smiled to herself, feeling quite the detective.

The new message icon flashed on her screen and she clicked on it. She started to read what Senga had sent her and saw that it was incomplete: a headline, an introductory paragraph, then space, then a chunk of text about Martha Wyers.

What if . . .? She tried to cast the idea from her mind but it wouldn't shift. Punching the air in triumph, she imagined herself proved right already. God, she was clever! Time for a celebratory cocktail while she waited for Dom to arrive. No, not yet. First the important stuff. Let no one accuse Olivia Zailer of putting an urgent need for a pink drink before a selfless crusade for the truth. She emailed Senga asking to see the whole of the feature. It was worth a try. If she turned out to be wrong, Charlie didn't need to know anything about it.

'You've had your turn in the limelight,' Milward told Simon coolly, from which he inferred that she hadn't thought to look for anything that tied Gemma Crowther to Mary Trelease. *Stupid.* She hadn't liked it when he'd called her that. Tough. 'Sergeant Zailer, did you ask DS Kombothekra to check up on Ruth Bussey and Mary Trelease?'

'Yes, I did,' said Charlie. 'If you tell DI Proust, make sure you blame me and not Sam. I didn't give him much choice. I led him to believe he'd find each of them with Aidan Seed holding a knife to her throat.'

'Your maverick methods are legendary,' Milward told her. 'I've heard they include having sex with murder suspects.'

'Then you heard wrong,' said Charlie. 'I believe you're referring to a serial rapist I dated for a while. No one ever thought he was a murderer. Anyway, we weren't serious. Just a bit of fun, you know.'

Simon tensed. Why couldn't she ever stop?

'I see,' said Milward, smiling. 'My mistake.'

'You mentioned a photograph,' said Charlie. 'Where is it? I want to see it.'

'You will.'

'What are you waiting for? Has it occurred to you that if you were straight with us instead of playing games, we might actually get somewhere?'

'What time did you leave Ruth Bussey's house on Monday evening?'

'Here we go again. Half past ten.'

'After which you drove home.' Milward was reading from notes. 'DC Waterhouse joined you at your house shortly after eleven, and the two of you spent the night there.'

'Yes.'

Milward and Dunning were bound to be wondering how Simon felt about sharing a bed—sharing a life—with the ex-lover of one of the sickest psychos in the UK prison system. He wondered himself.

'And then, on Tuesday morning, you phoned work and pretended to be ill. Why?'

'I didn't pretend. I felt ill, then I felt better.'

'Better enough to fancy a day-trip to London,' said Milward caustically.

'Yes. I thought I'd go shopping. We don't have real shops in Spilling, only mud huts selling painted masks.'

'How did you travel?'

'By train, as I said last night. My answers aren't going to change.'

'You caught the slow train—the 9.05 from Rawndesley to King's Cross?'

'And got in at 10.55. Yes.'

'What did you do in London?'

'For the third time, I looked round art galleries in the morning and went to see my sister in the afternoon. Then Simon rang me and told me about all this shit, and I came here.'

'All this shit being Gemma Crowther's murder?' Milward leaned forward. 'Are you always this flippant about the deaths of young women?'

'No. Only on Wednesdays.'

'The trouble I'm having, Sergeant Zailer, is that I haven't spoken to Ruth Bussey. You might be lying about what time you left her house. How do I know you didn't drive to London on Monday evening?'

'And kill Gemma Crowther, you mean? Why would I want to kill a woman I hadn't heard of until yesterday afternoon? Oh, and I don't kill people. Though I endlessly long to.'

'DC Waterhouse, your fiancé, was seen prowling round Gemma's house, looking in her window, only hours before she died. Let's say you *did* drive from Spilling to London on the Monday night . . .'

'Say it if you want, but I didn't.'

'You'd be unable to provide an alibi for DC Waterhouse, wouldn't you? If you weren't at home, you don't know he got back at eleven. If he didn't get back at eleven, that means he didn't set off from Muswell Hill at nine thirty. We've got a pathologist's report telling us Gemma Crowther died no earlier than ten p.m. Do you see what I'm saying?'

'Let me check: I'm lying to protect Simon, because I know he murdered Gemma Crowther. Is that it? Or I left Ruth's before ten thirty, went to London and murdered Crowther myself?'

'This is bullshit,' said Simon. 'I'll collate the CCTV footage for you if you like, since I'm exiled from my job indefinitely. I'll find you lots of black and white pictures to prove we were both where we say we were at all the right times.'

'Don't show them the one of me smoking next to the "No Smoking" sign outside Rawndesley station,' Charlie chipped in. 'They might tell.'

'Which art galleries did you go to?' Milward asked her.

'I didn't notice their names. I was just browsing. Oh—one of them might have been called TiqTaq. Apart from that, I don't remember. Sorry.'

'Tell them the truth, for God's sake,' said Simon, sick of her attitude and her games. 'She had lunch with a lawyer called Dominic Lund.'

'My sister's boyfriend,' said Charlie quickly, smiling. 'He's right. I had lunch with Dommie at Signor Grilli, an Italian on Goodge Street.'

'And you lied about it why?' said Milward.

'It's complicated. My sister's boyfriend?' Charlie gave her a meaningful look. 'I'm sure I don't need to spell it out.'

Simon stared at the sprouting carpet at his feet. What the fuck was she playing at? *Dommie?*

'So you didn't go to any art galleries?' said Milward.

'Yes, I did. After lunch.'

'Mary Trelease is a painter. Aidan Seed is a picture-framer.'

'I know.'

Milward licked her front teeth. Eventually she said, 'I don't believe you felt ill on Tuesday morning. I don't believe you had lunch with Dominic Lund at Signor Grilli, though he might be seeing your sister and you might know that's where he was yesterday lunchtime. I don't believe, frankly, that you spent all of Monday obsessing about Aidan Seed, Ruth Bussey and Mary Trelease when you should have been working, only to decide the next day that you fancied a completely unconnected day-trip to London.' Milward slapped her hands flat on the table. 'I know when two people are lying, and you two are those people.'

'Brilliant,' Simon muttered. 'Do we ever get to leave this room?'

'We ought to take a break,' Dunning said to Milward.

'The photo.' Charlie made a show of yawning.

'Oh, that. I almost forgot.' Milward pulled a large photograph out of her file and threw it down on the table.

At first Simon wasn't sure what the livid mess was that he was looking at. Then he saw, and had to count in his head and make his eyes blur over. It had been a while since he'd had to do that. He'd got used to the ordinary unpleasant sights his job afforded him, but this went way beyond. He felt Charlie stiffen beside him.

The picture was of a mouth. Open. Gemma Crowther's, Simon guessed. Post-mortem. Her top and bottom lips had been cut on both sides, pulled back and nailed to her face. Symmetrically: five nails along each lip. Most of her teeth were missing, and in their place were picture hooks, nailed in wonky lines into the gums of both her top and bottom jaw. They looked as if they had been arranged as neatly as possible, hanging down into her mouth like thin gold teeth.

Simon heard Charlie say, 'You told us she was shot.'

'She was,' said Milward. 'He did this after he killed her. Don't ask me why. Could be he—or she, if the killer's a woman— wanted to *frame*, if you'll excuse the pun, a picture-framer.'

'For God's sake!' said Charlie. 'Have you made any progress? Whoever did this is a sick fuck—you need to catch him, not waste time fucking us around.'

'Where did they come from?' asked Simon slowly. 'The picture hooks and the nails. Did he bring them with him, or . . .'

'Or?' Milward waited, eyebrows raised.

'The pictures on the walls, in Crowther's flat. Were they still up when you got to the scene?'

'What pictures, detective? You've been asked to describe the room you saw several times. You've said you can't be sure there were any pictures.'

'Tell us,' Simon snapped. 'Were the pictures still on the walls?'

'No,' said Milward, after a short pause. 'The only pictures in the flat were photographs of the happy couple in a range of sizes. In every room, they'd been taken down and leaned against walls and furniture. Leaving only holes. No nails, no hooks.'

'So, what—he shot her, then knocked her teeth out with . . . what? A hammer?'

'Why do you say that?' asked Milward.

'I'd use a hammer to hang a painting. That's what he used.' Simon nodded to himself. 'How did he cut her lips back like that? A Stanley knife? I saw one at Seed's workshop.' He paused for breath. 'He took down all the pictures, collected the hooks and nails, and hammered them into her lips and gums. Why? What was it about her mouth?'

'That's the wrong question,' said Charlie, standing up. Simon saw that the back of her shirt was dark with sweat. 'How many pictures were leaning against the walls? How many hooks and nails in Gemma Crowther's mouth? Did the numbers correspond?'

Milward looked at Dunning, whose face coloured. 'It should be in the file,' he said. She passed it to him and he started to leaf through the pages, his agitation growing more apparent as the silence dragged on.

'You don't know how many hooks she used for each picture,' said Simon.

'Have you ever hung a painting?' Charlie asked him. 'A photograph, anything framed?'

'Yeah,' he lied, feeling heat creep up his neck. He'd Blu-tacked a few posters to walls, that was it.

'You have, I assume?' Charlie said to Milward.

She nodded. 'I'm a one-hook woman. I've never hung a picture heavy enough to need two.'

'It's nothing to do with heavy,' said Dunning, shooting his

skipper a look designed to obliterate. 'If you use two hooks, the picture's more likely to stay straight, especially if it's a big one.'

'I think there's a picture missing,' said Charlie. 'I think this murder's about that—that's why the killer used picture hooks and nails to mutilate Crowther's face.'

'Why would anyone want to steal a cheesy photo of—?' Milward began.

'Not a photo,' Charlie cut her off. 'A painting. It's called *Abberton*. It's by Mary Trelease.'

'So, this is the table you sat at with *Dommie*.'

'Pure coincidence,' said Charlie with a bland grin. Her heart wasn't in it. 'Either that, or this is my table of lust, and I bring all my rides here.' They'd been dismissed by Milward three quarters of an hour ago. Charlie had hailed the first free cab that had come their way, told it to drop them on Goodge Street.

The man who had served Charlie and Lund yesterday— Signor Grilli himself? Charlie wondered—approached their table. Instead of asking if he could take their order, he said, 'Is okay, I see you're no ready.' He might as well have said, 'I can see you're too busy rowing to think about food.'

'Is it true?' Simon asked. 'Are you seeing Lund?'

'I'm not going to dignify that with a—'

'Then why say it? Is it your new hobby, making me look like a twat in front of as many people as possible?'

'*You?* Oh, they loved you. I was the despicable one.'

'You encouraged them to despise you! Boasting about something that ought to disgust you, as if you think being a rapist's girlfriend is something to be proud of.'

'Ex-girlfriend.' Charlie pretended to look at the menu. The tables around theirs had fallen silent. Even the music playing in the background sounded as if it was deliberately leaving lots of spaces between the notes. Charlie spoke clearly, for the benefit of any eavesdroppers. 'Funny—I seem to have gone from one extreme to the other. From a man who has sex with women against their will to one who won't shag one woman, not even his own fiancée, even if she begs . . .'

'If you carry on like this, I'm leaving.' Simon pushed his chair back.

'The restaurant, or our relationship?' Charlie asked. 'Just so as I understand the exact nature of the threat.'

'Do you want a smack in the face?'

'At least if you hit me, we'd be touching.' She was only half joking.

'When it suits you, you make me the enemy. Whenever you're feeling shit about something, I get the brunt of it. You knew I'd never hung a picture.'

'What? You haven't?' Charlie laughed. 'Actually, I didn't know. Bloody hell, Simon . . .'

'You knew, and you wanted to show me up, because you'd been shown up: forced to boast about the fuck-up that nearly ruined your life, and still might. You seem to want it to!'

'Stop.' Charlie gripped her menu with both hands.

'Except you weren't forced at all—it was your choice. You could have said, "Yeah, okay, I made a mistake. But I didn't know what he was when I got involved with him." Why couldn't you have said that?'

'Why don't you write me a script next time? The press office did it two years ago. They told me what to say.'

'There's no point in us talking.' Simon picked up his menu, held it between his face and Charlie's. 'Let's get something to eat while we can, before they call us back in.'

'Do you think they will?' It was almost a comfort to think about Milward and Dunning; against them, Charlie and Simon were allies.

'I would. We're better than they are.'

'I'm not hungry.' Charlie sighed.

'Then why are we here? It was your idea.'

'I thought Lund might be here. I was hoping to persuade him not to tell Milward that he and I aren't screwing each other's brains out, if she asks him. True, I'd have been wasting my time—Lund'd rather chew off his own scrotum than help me, but since I've sunk so low already today, I might as well go that bit further and beg a favour from a man who . . . looks like a buzzard.' She covered her face with her hands. Her own voice was starting to grate on her tattered nerves. It was no fun, being on the wrong side of the table in an interview room. She felt as if she still was. The table and room had changed, but the vibes of condemnation were the same.

'You should have told them the real reason you met Lund. Why didn't you?'

'What, tell them Ruth Bussey's decided to make an exhibition of me and I ran to a lawyer for help only to hear that there's fuck all I can do about it? I think I've had enough public humiliation for one lifetime, don't you?'

Simon reached across the table, grabbed her wrist. 'They're investigating a murder, one of the sickest. Some things are more important than your pride.'

'My *what*? You think I'm proud? Some detective you are.' She didn't pull her arm away. The angrier he got, the more remote from him she felt, as if his reactions had nothing to do with her.

He stood up. 'I'm going to order a pizza. Are you sure you don't want anything?'

'I'll have a taste of yours.'

'Will you fuck. I'm starved.'

She listened as he ordered two pizza funghis. He should have said 'pizzas funghi'. Simon was no linguist. She pointed out his mistake when he sat back down. 'I got "two" right,' he said. 'That was the important part.' He was feeling better, she could tell, though they'd resolved nothing. Because he'd ordered some food?

'So. You've really never hung a picture? What else don't I know about you?'

'What do you want to know?'

'Simon, we're engaged!'

'I know that.'

'Christ, this is ridiculous! All right, then: where would you live, if you could live anywhere in the world?'

'I don't know. I've never thought about it.'

'Well, think.'

'Are you serious? At the moment, all I can think about is a disfigured mouth with gold picture hooks for teeth. You think Mary Trelease killed Gemma Crowther, don't you? Because Crowther had her picture, the one she gave Ruth Bussey. So, what: Bussey gave it to Seed who gave it to Crowther?'

Charlie didn't want to talk about this, not now. She wanted to tell him that if she could choose anywhere in the world to live, she would choose Torquay. She'd always loved it. She'd had her first and only holiday romance there.

Their pizzas arrived suspiciously quickly, their temperature somewhere in the no man's land between cold and warm. Charlie didn't care, and Simon certainly wouldn't, she thought. That was one thing they had in common, though Simon was more extreme. Food was something he put in his body in order not to die. He didn't care what it tasted like as long as it filled him up. As recently as last week, he'd have taken pains to avoid eating in front of Charlie. Now he seemed fine about it, as if having a meal together was a natural thing to do. Like the four chaste nights they'd spent together so far, Charlie saw this as progress.

Once the waiter had gone, she said, 'All I know is, Trelease is protective over her work. Whether she's protective enough to kill to retrieve one of her paintings, I have no idea, but the picture-hook teeth? That's a woman's touch.'

'I disagree,' said Simon, ripping strips off his pizza like a savage and stuffing them into his mouth as if he didn't have a knife and fork in front of him.

'A man wouldn't have had the idea. It's too . . . intricate.'

'So's the way Seed's mind works. He's a craftsman. Whatever his motives, there's nothing crude or obvious about them. How can there be? A man who confesses to a non-murder. An atheist who leads a secret life as a Quaker . . .'

'Maybe he's been infiltrating all the major religions,' said Charlie. 'Maybe Monday's his Quaker day, Tuesday he's a Hindu . . .' She sighed, bored by her own joke. 'I'm going back to Spilling after lunch to talk to Kerry Gatti. I need to do something under my own steam. Want to come?'

'No.'

Charlie gave him a look. 'Tell me you're not crazy enough to try to get near Stephen Elton.' She pulled her phone out of her bag and switched it on, now that she was as sure as she could be that she and Simon had stopped fighting. 'Olivia,' she told him, listening to her sister's message. 'She wants us to go round. I asked her to find out as much as she could about Martha Wyers.'

'A name you didn't mention to our metropolitan friends,' said Simon.

'Because there's probably no link.'

'So we're not going to Olivia's?'

'We're going. She said she's got something I'll want to see. Though admittedly, based on past experience, that might turn out to be a picture of Angelina Jolie's new baby in *Hello!* In which case, I'll beat her to death with a spade.'

'After what we've just seen, I'm not in the mood for jokes like that.' Simon had finished his pizza and moved on to Charlie's.

Her phone vibrated, knocking against her plate. She picked it up. 'Liv?'

'It isn't,' said Sam Kombothekra, whose peculiar way of answering questions with 'It is' or 'I did' instead of a simple 'Yes' always made Charlie smile. 'It's Sam,' he said.

'I'd never have guessed.'

'Is Simon with you?'

'Uh-huh.'

'Strange things are happening here, Charlie. I thought you'd both want to know. But listen, if the Snowman finds out I've discussed any of it with you . . .'

'Relax, Sam. He's not tapping your phone. What strange things?'

'Have you met a DS Coral Milward?'

'This morning.'

'Seems she's Proust's new soulmate. He's just told me my team's at DC Dunning's disposal for the foreseeable future. No explanation, no details as yet.'

'So they're not as stupid as they look,' said Charlie. 'They'll want you to work the Spilling angle—Bussey, Seed and Trelease. It's good.' She looked at Simon. 'Means they're taking us seriously.'

'I told Proust it was crazy not to have Simon with us on this. Do you know what he said? "The extent of Waterhouse's involvement in Gemma Crowther's murder has yet to be determined." Can you believe that?'

Charlie repeated the quote to Simon, who shook his head in disgust. 'Ask Kombothekra what he said in response.'

Charlie tried to pass him the phone but he backed away from it. Was he angry with Sam? 'Wrap it up,' he muttered, glaring at Charlie.

'Sam, I'm going to have to—'

'He only said it for effect. He knows exactly why Simon was outside Gemma Crowther's place on Monday: he'd followed Aidan Seed, who, as we now know, was not only at the scene but had a motive the size of a . . . a . . .' Sam stopped, unable to think of anything big enough.

'Motive?' Charlie prodded Simon to make sure he was paying attention.

'No one's told you?' Sam sighed. 'I don't know why I'm surprised. Who'd want to break a case when they can score a point instead, right?'

'Sam, for fuck's sake! What's the motive?'

'Crowther and her partner Stephen Elton both served time for false imprisonment and GBH.'

'*What?*'

'Elton got parole in March 2005, Crowther in October 2006. Somebody's idea of justice.'

Charlie frowned. This didn't sound like Sam. Normally he was determined to find potential and promise in every scrote that crossed his path. 'Devout Quakers and GBH don't often go together.'

'However devout they went on to become, in April 2000 they tied a defenceless woman to a pillar in their back garden so that Gemma Crowther could spend *three days* forcing stones down her throat and launching them at her face and body—stones from a garden she'd designed for them. They didn't feed her or allow her to drink, didn't let her use the toilet, nearly suffocated her with a bath sponge and parcel tape. She was in hospital for three weeks, left scarred for life and probably infertile.'

Stones from a garden she'd designed . . . 'Sam . . . oh, my God.'

'Yeah,' he said, exhaling slowly. 'Makes it a bit harder to mourn Crowther's passing, doesn't it?'

'The defenceless woman was Ruth Bussey,' said Charlie, looking at Simon. 'She was their victim.'

13

Wednesday 5 March 2008

When I wake, my head is clear. I know where I am straight away. All the details of this room are familiar, though I saw them for the first time only last night: blue and white checked bedspread and pillowcases, beige loop carpet, the loop so coarse it makes me think of a bathmat. Small, square pine cabinets on either side of the bed, a pine dressing table with a three-sectioned mirror at one end of the room, a wooden blanket chest at the other. Yellow curtains with red and gold tasselled tie-backs. I can hear banging coming from downstairs that sounds like crockery, and a radio.

I'm in Garstead Cottage, in the grounds of Villiers school—the cottage Martha Wyers' parents rent, and allow Mary to use. *We'll be safe there*—that's what she said. I have fallen out of my life and into hers.

I pull back the bedclothes. I'm wearing the pyjamas Mary threw at me last night, too tired by that point even to speak: they're pink, with 'Minxxx' printed across the top. The soft moans of animals from outside draw me over to the window. I open the curtains and look at the view in daylight: fields full of cows, a wall separating the farmland from the school's land, the square-towered stone bulk of the main school building at the top of the steeply rising path. It's the building Mary painted, the picture I saw in her house.

Garstead Cottage nestles in a dip beside the path, a few metres beyond Villiers' main gates. It's down a level from the land around it and has an air of being hidden. Last night, Mary told me I didn't need to bother closing the curtains. 'No one ever looks in,' she said. 'Not girls and not teachers. It's like being in the middle of nowhere.'

The door opens and she walks in. 'Late breakfast,' she says. 'Actually, it can double as late lunch.' She's wearing a grey T-shirt with blue paisley pyjama bottoms and carrying a large blue cloth-bound hardback book. Horizontally, in both hands. Balanced on top is a teapot trailing a green label on a piece of string, a cup, and a sandwich overhanging the edges of a saucer that's too small for it. 'I'm hoping it's not every day someone brings you peppermint tea and a Marmite sandwich on a tray. Well, a book,' she corrects herself. In the pocket of her pyjama bottoms I can see the outline of her cigarette packet.

Something has changed. I'm not scared of her any more.

Pieces of last night start to come back to me: Mary's insistence that she couldn't tell me; she had to show me. She didn't want to talk while she drove, so we listened to the radio for a while. Then she put a CD on; the 'Survivor' song started to play. 'Martha was playing this when she hanged herself,' Mary said matter-of-factly. 'Odd choice, don't you think? If you're going to commit suicide, why play a song that's all about coping without somebody, growing wiser and smarter and stronger?'

'Maybe . . .' That was as much as I could say. I didn't feel comfortable speculating.

'Irony, do you think? I don't think so. Arrogance: that's what I think it was.'

I asked her what she meant, but she frowned and shook her head. 'Not tonight,' she said. 'Not if you want me to get us there intact.' Then she took her mobile phone out of the glove compartment, saying she had to ring Villiers. She asked for someone called Claire. I listened as she ordered her to contact the local police, to meet us and them at Garstead Cottage in two hours' time.

'Why the police?' I asked.

'It's my routine,' said Mary, turning up the volume on the stereo so that I couldn't say anything else.

As we pulled in through the school's large sculpted iron gates, the police car was ahead of us. Claire Draisey, who turned out to be Villiers' Director of Boarding, was waiting for us next to the side door of Garstead Cottage, taking shelter from the drizzle in a partially covered wooden outbuilding that was attached to the house. In it were two old bicycles, a watering can and a large cardboard cut-out of a cow in profile, a cow wearing a yellow earring. I didn't register the oddness of this until later; at the time, it seemed one of the less odd aspects of the situation.

Claire Draisey's manner was brisk, impatient. 'This has to be the last time, Mary,' she said. She was wearing a red dressing-gown and slippers, and looked exhausted. I'd warned Mary that everyone at the school might be asleep, but she'd dismissed my concern. 'They get woken up all the time,' she said. 'It's a boarding school—goes with the territory. The staff who are soft enough to need to rest don't live on site. In exchange for their beauty sleep, they're frowned upon and overlooked for promotion.'

Strangest of all was what Claire Draisey didn't say: she didn't ask Mary what or who she was worried about, why she wanted the police to check the house. The policeman who was there didn't ask either. He and Draisey had a familiar manner around one another, as though they'd done this many times before. He checked that all the doors and windows were secure. He and Mary went into the cottage together and checked for intruders. Mary asked him if he'd wait outside in his car until it was light, but Claire Draisey said, 'Don't be silly, Mary. Of course he can't.'

'This time there's been an actual threat,' Mary told her. 'It's not only myself I'm worried about.' She indicated me. It made me feel flustered. So does the breakfast and tea on a tray. I don't want to like Mary, not after what she did to me at Saul's gallery.

If she can attack me and still be a good person, what does that say about me?

What does it say about Stephen Elton and Gemma Crowther?

'I can say their names,' I tell her as she puts the sandwich into my hands. 'The people who lived at Cherub Cottage. I've called them Him and Her for years. I couldn't write their names when I wrote you the letter. But now that you know the story, I can say them. He was called Stephen Elton. She was called Gemma Crowther.'

'Was?'

'Is.'

Mary nods. 'I know.'

'What?' The air around me thins out. I feel dizzy, as if I've been deprived of oxygen.

'There's a lot I need to tell you.'

'You can't know their names. It's not possible.'

'You'd better sit down,' she says, bending to pick something up. The sandwich. I didn't realise I'd dropped it. I stay on my feet.

'After that day at Saul Hansard's gallery, when you tried to force me to sell you my painting, I was scared. You were too keen. I didn't trust you. I thought you—' She breaks off, tuts at her inability to say what needs to be said. 'I convinced myself that you meant me harm. I . . . I had to know who you were, who'd put you up to it. As far as I could see, it could only be one person.'

'Aidan?' I guess.

'Aidan.'

'But . . .'

'It won't make any sense to you, not yet. Not until I show you what he did to me.' Mary sits down on the bed, pulls her cigarettes and lighter out of her pocket. 'I told Saul I wanted to write to you and apologise. He wouldn't give me your address, but he told me your name, said I could write to you care of the gallery. I *was* sorry, or rather, I was prepared to be, if it turned out . . .'

'What?' I say.

'I had to know why you wanted that picture so much. It was unnatural, the way you latched on to it, as if you *had* to have it. Have you heard of First Call?'

'No.'

Mary lights a cigarette, inhales. 'They're a firm of private investigators in Rawndesley. Someone I used to know works there. I paid him to find out about you. Your background, everything—as much as there was to know about you, I wanted to know it.'

'The man with the red bobble hat and the dog.'

'You saw him?'

'He kept walking past my house. Looking in at the windows.'

'You were suspicious of him even with the hat and the dog?' She almost smiles. 'I'll have to tell him he's wrong. He thinks they make him look innocuous. He's a bit of a clown, but he got the job done, gave me the information I wanted. From him, I found out about your religious background, your award-winning garden design business.' She pauses, as if reluctant to state the obvious. 'And what happened to you in April 2000. Gemma Crowther and Stephen Elton, the court case.'

My skin feels as if tiny bugs are crawling over every inch of it. *A stranger watching me, reporting back to Mary . . .*

'I've hired him before, successfully. I knew he could dredge up anything of interest. First Call mainly work for insurance and credit card companies, on fraud cases, but they've got one or two people who specialise in what they call "matters that require complete discretion". He's one of them.'

She shrugs. 'What can I say? I'm sorry. He followed you for a few weeks—weeks during which, by all accounts, you hardly left the house. When he told me that, I felt terrible. It was never my intention to drive you out of your job and turn you into a recluse. There was no way I could have known what had happened to you in Lincoln.' Mary bites her lip. 'I'm sure my impassioned self-justification speech is the last thing you want to hear. Anyway . . . I had him keep an eye on you long enough to satisfy me that you had no connection, past or present, to Aidan Seed, and then I called him off.'

'I saw him on Sunday. And Monday,' I tell her.

Her expression hardens. 'When a cop turned up on Friday asking about Aidan, I panicked. I'd thought things were stable; clearly they weren't. I needed to know what had changed. And then Charlie Zailer came round on Monday morning to tell me you were Aidan's girlfriend. About fifteen minutes after she left my house, I got a call from First Call telling me the same thing.'

'I didn't know Aidan last June,' I say, aware I'm not the one in need of a defence. 'I met him later, in August. I needed a job, and Saul told me Aidan needed an assistant.'

'How perfectly ironic,' says Mary. 'It was my fault you met him. One more thing to feel bad about.'

I want to tell her that meeting Aidan's the best thing that's ever happened to me, but I can't say it and mean it, not without knowing what he's done. *Not unconditionally.*

'Did you know Aidan used to work for Saul, before he set up on his own?' Mary asks.

I shake my head.

'That's another reason I thought he had to be pulling your strings—the Saul connection. It seemed too much of a coincidence.' Anguish flares in her eyes. 'I thought you wanted the painting so that you could give it to him.'

I look away. I'm not brave enough to tell her that was exactly what happened, only later. Not in June last year, but after Christmas, when I went to Megson Crescent for that very reason: to get *Abberton* because Aidan wanted it. Needed it.

Mary sucks hard on her cigarette. 'When I told Saul I'd been thrown by how pushy you were, he said you were always like that about pictures you fell in love with. That's how you met him, right? He told me the story: you wanted a painting that was in his window and told him you'd pay any price for it, however high. I realised then that you weren't trying to work me—you really did fall in love with *Abberton*.'

'Yesterday, at your house, I found another canvas. It was unfinished, but it looked a bit like *Abberton*. There was a different name on the back: *Blandford*.'

'What about it?' Mary flicks ash on the carpet, rubs it in with her bare foot.

'Is it . . . are the two pictures part of a series?'

'Why do you want to know? Yes, part of a series,' she says quickly. 'Why?'

'A series of how many?'

She lifts her chin: a defensive stance, designed to keep me at a distance. 'I don't know yet. I'll see how far I get before I run out of steam.'

I've got no choice, not if I want to find out the truth. 'Nine,' I say. '*Abberton, Blandford, Darville, Elstow, Goundry, Heathcote, Margerison, Rodwell, Winduss*.'

Mary cries out, as if I've stuck a needle in her heart. Her body folds in on itself.

'What is it, Mary? Why do those names frighten you?'

'He told you, didn't he?'

'Told me what? Who are they?'

Her eyes glaze over. 'I don't know who they were,' she whispers. 'They never told us. Isn't that funny?'

'Were?' The word falls through my brain in slow motion. 'They're dead?'

She makes an effort to pull herself together. 'Gemma Crowther's dead,' she says.

'What?'

'Did you know she was out of prison?'

I didn't want to know. I asked not to be told. I wrote that in my letter . . .

'Ruth?'

'No. No.'

In some parts of the world, they stone you to death for fucking another woman's man.

Dead. Did Mary say that Gemma Crowther was dead?

'I didn't want to tell you like this.' Her words come out jerkily. 'When you came round yesterday, you were in such a state— I couldn't tell you then. You were ranting about Aidan hiding in my house. You wouldn't have listened. I'd spent most of the day with a detective from London. He'd just left when you arrived. Gemma Crowther was murdered, she was shot. Twice—in the head and in the heart.'

Gemma Crowther, murdered. Yes; it makes sense. People who behave as she did might well end up getting murdered. *In the head and in the heart.*

I'm trying to get a grip on what I've heard when Mary says, 'If you still think it's the truth you want, ask me who killed her.'

14

5/3/08

Olivia was looking out of her first-floor window as Simon and Charlie got out of the cab. By the time they'd paid, she was at the front door.

'I don't give a fuck about Martha Wyers,' said Simon, by way of a greeting. Then, to Charlie, 'Kerry Gatti's who we should be talking to.'

'Did you say Kerry Gatti?' Olivia asked. She got no reply. 'I don't believe this.'

'I say we go.'

'I wouldn't.' Olivia glared at him. 'There's a great big whopping connection between Martha Wyers and your case, or whoever's case it is. Are you helping the London police or are they helping you?'

'That's none of your business,' Charlie told her. She hadn't forgiven her sister for yesterday. *I'm sorry, Char. It's bad news.* Charlie had imagined Simon half dead, held hostage by a psychopath, until Olivia had abandoned the grief-stricken act and passed on his message. She hadn't forgiven Simon, come to think of it, for leaving the message with Olivia rather than telling her himself. Charlie knew why he'd done it. He'd thought she'd be angry with him for dragging her into it, or that she'd taunt him for being careless and getting caught out.

That the two of them weren't wanted back at work for as long as they were of interest to Dunning and Milward was no more than an inconvenience that would, in time, be rectified.

Charlie wasn't worried about her job, and no one at work wanted to lose Simon, not even the people who disliked him personally. Not even the Chief Super and the Chief Constable, neither of whom could stand the sight of him.

'Tell us what you think we need to know,' he said grudgingly to Olivia.

'Thank you. Well, firstly, even though I didn't manage to find anything about Martha Wyers' death, I'd bet a million pounds that she committed suicide. She wasn't murdered.'

'That's the equivalent of a less extravagant person betting a fiver,' Charlie pointed out.

'A billion, then. She published one book—a novel. I looked it up on Amazon. It's about a woman who falls passionately in love with a man she hardly knows, and it ends up wrecking her life. The blurb on Amazon even contains the word "suicidal".'

'For fuck's sake!' said Simon. 'Half the novels that have ever been written are about that. That's the plot of *Anna Karenina*. Tolstoy didn't commit suicide. Charlie, we're wasting time here.'

'Listen, will you?' Olivia snapped. 'When I told Senga McAllister at *The Times* that Martha Wyers was dead, the first thing she asked me was if she'd killed herself. In 1999, while Senga was still a jobbing arts reporter, she wrote a feature called *Future Famous Five*, a profile of five arty types that readers ought to look out for in the new millennium: stars of the future, that sort of thing.' Olivia paused to draw breath.

'Martha Wyers was the author they chose. Senga chose her personally. She hadn't read the novel at that point, but she'd read a few of her short stories and thought she was easily the most brilliant new writer she'd come across for years.'

'Brilliance requires originality,' said Simon. 'A novel about a woman with a broken heart's not original, not if it's written in 1999.'

'Does he really mean that?' Olivia asked Charlie.

'Carry on, Liv. Ignore him.'

'There are different *kinds* of broken hearts, Simon. I hope you never have to find that out.'

'What the fuck's that supposed to mean?'

'Liv,' Charlie waved her hands in front of her sister's face. 'Carry on.'

'Senga was a bit embarrassed about having picked Martha Wyers.' Olivia glanced at Simon as if she planned to deal with him later. 'Her first novel turned out to be her only one. She sank without trace.'

'That's death for you,' said Charlie. 'It tends to impede productivity.'

'Wyers never wrote anything else, and faded into obscurity soon after the feature went to press. Some of Senga's colleagues who'd picked these up-and-coming stars—the music critic, the drama critic—their choices are now famous, household names.'

'Such as?'

'Pippa Dowd was the music choice.'

'From Limited Sympathy,' Charlie told Simon. 'He hasn't heard of anyone,' she explained to Liv.

'And the actor was Doohan Champion.'

'He's a talentless streak of piss!'

'As well as a multi-millionaire, yes,' said Liv drily. 'I suppose it must be hard to predict which careers will succeed and which fail—no one can foresee the future.' Seeing the look on Simon's face, she went on quickly, 'Anyway, then Senga said something I remembered later on, when she emailed me the article and I saw that all the bits apart from the section on Martha were missing. She said, "At least I wasn't the only one who got it wrong. The art critic and the comedy buff ended up with egg on their faces, too. Their picks also sank without trace." I thought: I wonder who the art critic chose? I wondered if it was Mary Trelease.'

Simon turned on Charlie. 'What does she know about Trelease?'

'Plenty,' said Olivia. 'I know there's a woman called Ruth Bussey who's got a thing about Charlie, whose boyfriend Aidan

Seed thinks he killed an artist called Mary Trelease even though
she isn't dead.'

'You told her the *names*?'

Charlie looked away. She'd told Liv a lot more than she
normally would. They'd needed something to talk about that
wasn't the cuttings on the bedroom wall and how Charlie felt
about them. She'd had a good story and she'd used it. You can't
make a story come to life without naming the characters.

'So what if the painter in the article's Mary Trelease?' Simon
demanded. 'So what if Trelease and this Martha Wyers woman
were part of the same colour supplement feature in 1999? So
fucking what?'

'Liv's trying to help, Simon.' To her sister, Charlie said, 'A
connection between Martha Wyers and Mary Trelease doesn't
really help us. If we need one, we've got it already: they both
went to Villiers School. They were contemporaries there.'

Olivia looked angry, then puzzled. Then she laughed. 'You
both seem to be assuming that the young visual artist *The Times*
chose was Mary Trelease.'

Simon moved towards her, ready to snatch the papers she
was holding from her hand. 'Was it or wasn't it?'

'No, as a matter of fact.'

Charlie pursed her lips. 'Liv, whatever you're . . .'

'We've pissed about enough here already,' Simon called over
his shoulder, halfway to the door. 'Let's go.'

'It was Aidan Seed,' said Olivia, holding the printed-out article for Charlie to take. 'Now do you want to see this? Yes,' her
face set in a hard smile as she watched Simon's about-turn, 'I
thought you might.'

15

Wednesday 5 March 2008

'When did Gemma die?' I ask.

'The police wouldn't tell me much, but from the questions they asked, it must have been Monday night,' says Mary. 'They wanted to know my movements.' She walks over to the window, opens it, flicks ash out. The cows are still moaning in the fields, as if they're in pain.

Forty-eight hours ago, Gemma was alive.

'Why did the police speak to you?'

Mary tucks her hair behind her ears. It springs back, like dark thunderclouds enveloping her thin face. 'I didn't believe Charlotte Zailer when she told me you were Aidan's girlfriend. I thought, no. Can't be. When I had it confirmed by First Call, my heart nearly stopped. Once I'd got myself together, I drove to Aidan's workshop, waited outside in my car. A bit later, Zailer turned up with another cop I recognised—DC Waterhouse. He'd been round to see me on Saturday, also about Aidan. The two of them went inside.'

'I was there,' I tell her.

'They stayed for a while, then left, except Waterhouse didn't go far. He sat in his car and waited at the top of the road. A few minutes later, Aidan came out, got into his car and drove away. Waterhouse followed him, and I followed Waterhouse. The three of us drove to London in convoy. To Muswell Hill.' She watches me for a reaction. 'I started to have a feeling, then, that I knew where he was going, except it made no sense.'

'Where?' I ask, breathless. All those times Aidan was away, when he told me he'd been in Manchester, working for Jeanette Golenya. Lies, every time.

'I knew Stephen Elton and Gemma Crowther had been paroled. My First Call guy—he's thorough. He'd given me their new address, details of their new jobs . . .'

'What jobs?'

Mary frowns. 'Do you really want to know?'

'Yes.'

'Stephen Elton works for the Ford dealership in Kilburn. He's some kind of mechanic. Gemma Crowther works . . . *worked* for an alternative health centre in Swiss Cottage called The Healing Rooms. My friend visited her there. She gave him a hot-stone massage.' She's talking about the man with the red bobble hat and the dog. *Someone I used to know. I've hired him before*—that's what she said. Finally, those words filter through. 'Proud as punch, he was, when he told me that. Said it was a perk of the job—charged me for his treatment, cheeky sod.'

'Stone,' I repeat blankly.

Mary opens her mouth, says nothing. It hadn't occurred to her.

Gemma Crowther, a healer. 'Stephen was a chemist, a pharmacist,' I say. '*She* was a primary school teacher.'

'Yeah, well, obviously they'd have had difficulty getting similar jobs after what they'd done. And not so much difficulty getting taken on by a garage, or some quack outfit like an alternative healing centre. Some places check out prospective employees' backgrounds more diligently than others, presumably.' Mary throws her cigarette butt out of the window and rubs the small of her back with both hands.

'Their new address—it was in Muswell Hill?'

She nods. '23b Ruskington Road. That's where Aidan was going on Monday.'

'But he didn't know about . . .'

'Yes, Ruth. He knew.'

Nothing will make me believe it. Aidan, seeing Stephen and Gemma behind my back? *No.*

'When he turned on to Ruskington Road, Waterhouse overshot and carried on down the main road. By the time he'd realised his mistake and come back, Aidan had parked outside number 23. Right outside it, as if the space belonged to him. Waterhouse didn't see me—and he was too busy concentrating on Aidan, who by this point was walking back to the main road. Neither of them saw me.'

'Why?' I blurt out. 'Why would he park outside the house and then walk away?'

'I've no idea,' says Mary impatiently. 'All I know is, Waterhouse followed him.'

'Did you follow them?'

'No. On foot, it was too risky. My hair's hard to miss. Once they were gone, I went for a snoop. The bell for Gemma and Stephen's flat had their names on it. Surnames only: Crowther and Elton, like the newspapers called them.'

Dong. Their doorbell at Cherub Cottage was called Dong.

Disgust warps Mary's face. 'Underneath the names, in tiny writing and in inverted commas, was the word "Woodmansterne".'

I clear my throat. 'They lived on Woodmansterne Lane. In Lincolnshire. You mean . . .?'

'If I had to guess, I'd say they decided to call their rented flat after their old street name.'

'Yes. They'd do that. *She* would.'

'I rang the doorbell,' says Mary. 'I was bloody amazed at my own nerve. Don't ask me what I'd have said if someone had answered. I had no idea—it was an impulse thing. No one was in, though.' She fumbles for another cigarette, lights it. 'There's a bay window to the right of the front door. Through it, I saw a framed photo of the happy couple, one of the ones you described in your letter: him kissing her cheek.'

Bile rises in my throat. That picture. *Standing in Cherub*

Cottage's pristine white sitting room, Stephen trying to kiss me . . .

'I knew it was them. First Call had sent me press cuttings from the trial, photos, the works. I recognised their faces. Easy to see why you made it your mission in life to save him from captivity—that little-boy-lost look.'

'They're still together. He testified against her, she tried to pin the whole thing on him, and still they're together, with those pictures on the walls.' *As if I never happened.*

'Tacky studio photos weren't all they had up on the walls,' says Mary with venom in her voice. 'I saw something else go up.'

'What do you mean?' She made me write that letter, reliving everything I went through, when she knew. She already knew.

'I waited, on the street. In my car. I'd gone as far as London— I wasn't giving up that easily. After a while Simon Waterhouse came back.'

'Did he see you?'

Mary shakes her head. 'He was only interested in Crowther and Elton's house. He had a snoop around, then went to sit in his car. Like me. At about half nine, Gemma Crowther and Aidan Seed walked up the road together.'

I try not to flinch.

'Aidan opened the boot of his car, took something out, carried it into the house. I couldn't see what it was—I wasn't close enough, and there was a big white van parked behind Aidan's car, blocking my view.' Mary twists her hair round her hand. 'The lights went on inside. Gemma closed the curtains. That's when Waterhouse called it a night.' Her smile is full of scorn for anyone who could give up so easily.

'You didn't?' I guess.

'No. There was a small gap in the curtains, but big enough to see through.'

Gemma Crowther and Aidan in a room together.

Mary waits for me to ask. When I don't—can't—she says,

'There was a banging sound. He had a hammer in his hand. He was hanging a picture for her. Guess what picture?'

I freeze. It has to be, otherwise Mary would tell me. She wouldn't make me guess. *She blames me.*

'Yours,' I say. '*Abberton.*'

'My painting,' says Mary, unemotional. 'Yes. In the home of strangers. In the home of *those* strangers.'

'I gave it to Aidan to prove to him that he couldn't have killed you,' I try to explain. 'He kept insisting he had, no matter what I said. *Abberton* had your name on it, and the date: 2007. He told me he'd killed you years ago.'

'How did you know I'd signed and dated it?' Mary turns on me. 'I hadn't when I brought it in to Saul's place last June.'

I tell her, as coherently as I can, about the *Access 2 Art* fair.

'My God,' Mary mutters, chewing her lip until drops of blood appear. When she next takes a drag of her cigarette, it comes away red at the end, as if she's wearing lipstick.

'I gave Aidan the picture and never saw it again,' I tell her. 'He wouldn't tell me what he'd done with it. Mary, I'm sorry . . .'

'A present's a present,' she says in a brittle voice. 'I gave it to you, you gave it to him, he gave it to her.'

'What did you do? When you saw it, I mean?'

'What could I do? I got in my car and drove home. When I left, Gemma Crowther was alive and she was with Aidan Seed. That should tell you everything you need to know about your *boyfriend.*'

'Why did the police talk to you?' *Why not me?* Maybe they'd tried. I ignored everyone who came to the workshop yesterday; maybe one of those knocks was the police.

'Some nosey bastard neighbour saw me and came and asked who I was—I should have lied but I didn't think quickly enough. As it turned out, it was lucky she saw me. She watched me leave, and heard the two gunshots after I'd gone. Waterhouse had gone,

I'd gone—the only person still there with Gemma was Aidan. Even the cops should be able to work it out.'

Something hard and huge is welling up inside me. Why do I feel as if I've let Mary down? It's crazy. I owe her no loyalty. Aidan's the person I love and ought to trust. He's never intentionally hurt me, and she has.

It hits me then: I've forgiven her. If I can forgive Mary, then I can forgive Aidan, whatever he's done. And after that? Where would I stop?

'Ruth? What's the matter?'

'I'm the one,' I tell her.

'What do you mean?'

'All this time, I've had this . . . this fear. I was scared of not being able to forgive Aidan once I knew the truth—or rather, that's what I thought it was, but I was wrong. It's the exact opposite: I'm afraid I'll forgive him too easily, and not only him—everything and everybody. Aidan, you, even Stephen and Gemma. Once you start to imagine what another person's pain and terror must have felt like . . .' My throat blocks. I can't speak.

'How can you stop yourself forgiving them? Is that what you were going to say?'

I'm aware that I'm crying. It doesn't seem to matter. 'My parents used to say, "We're Christians, Ruth. Christians forgive, always," but I don't *want* to forgive anybody!'

'Why not?' Mary's voice is stern.

'Because then there'd only be me who . . . who . . .'

'You think you're unforgivable. You don't want to be the only one.'

Her understanding strikes me as a small miracle. 'I tried to brainwash Stephen against Gemma. I did everything I could to split them up, all the time thinking I was virtuous and honourable for refusing to have sex with him.' I wipe my eyes with the palms of my hands. 'I couldn't see . . . Sex is just sex. Or, when it's not, it's love. Either way, it's not toxic, like trying to control someone else's mind. All the tactics my parents used on me, I used on Stephen. I know there's no justification for what he and Gemma did to me—doesn't mean it wasn't my fault or that I didn't deserve it.'

'If you start forgiving everyone, you might get carried away and forgive your parents,' says Mary. 'Where would that leave you? They haven't forgiven you, have they, in spite of their Christians-always-forgive slogans? You sent them an address and they've never used it. Quick to give up on you, weren't they? And these are people who've devoted their whole lives to preaching mercy.'

'Not only preaching it. Practising it too. After what happened to me, when they came to see me in hospital, they told me they'd forgiven Stephen and Gemma. They said I should too. In their whole lives, I'm the only person they haven't forgiven.'

'Which makes you the only unforgivable person in the world, right? The worst person in the world.'

'Yes.' Now that Mary's said it, I feel deflated. As if something swollen inside me has been punctured. Is this what I've been so afraid of, this realisation? It's a relief now that the fear's gone and there's nothing left except flat, grey exhaustion. My eyes start to close.

Mary taps me on the shoulder. 'Wrong,' she says. 'If you want a unique selling point, how about this? You're the only person who's ever laid into them personally. You yelled at them, said some things that were pretty hard for them to take—probably no one else has ever done that. It's easy to forgive attacks when you yourself aren't the victim. "Stephen and Gemma? No problem: all they did was nearly kill our daughter. Someone shouting at us and telling us we're wrong about things? Sorry: unforgivable." Do you see what I'm trying to say?'

I think I do. If I can bring myself to forgive Stephen and Gemma, I'll be better than my parents, more Christian than they are, even though I'm not a Christian and don't believe in God. Aidan, Mary, Stephen, Gemma, Mum, Dad, me. I can maybe forgive us all.

'My point is,' says Mary, 'your parents are two great big stonking pieces of shit. Fuck them.'

I manage a weak smile. 'Tell me about Aidan and Martha,' I say.

Instantly, the gleam in Mary's eyes starts to fade, as if she's been cut off from her energy supply. 'On one condition,' she says. 'This is my story, so I get to be judge, jury and executioner. If you're tempted to exonerate anybody, do it in the privacy of your own head. I'm not as enlightened as you.'

I nod. Mary is freer than I am. She doesn't worry about balancing the blame books. She takes her unhappiness and does what she wants with it. Could I be like her from now on, or will I always feel as if there's some kind of external moral arbitrator watching every move I make, unseen and infallible?

Mary lights a cigarette. 'Martha and Aidan met at a job interview. Fellow Commoner in Creative Arts, Trinity College, Cambridge. Aidan got it, Martha didn't. She put a brave face on it, went on until everyone was sick to death of her about how she didn't get it because she wasn't common enough.' She smiles. 'We had a student teacher once who asked us how many television sets our families owned. Martha had the most: seven. The teacher was shocked. She was a bit of a luddite grow-your-own-vegetables type. She asked Martha what rooms the tellies were in, and Martha listed six: one of the lounges, the kitchen, her bedroom, her parents' bedroom, her den, the summer house. The teacher was waiting to hear about the seventh, and Martha must have realised how it would sound, so she clammed up. The teacher asked her outright. Martha turned as red as a tomato, and had to admit that it was on the jet.'

'A private jet?'

'She was the only Villiers girl at the time whose parents had one. Loads of families had helicopters, but their own jet? They've probably all got them now. Anyway, Martha's privileged background had nothing to do with her not getting the job at Trinity. Aidan was a better painter than she was a writer, and she knew it.'

The room closes in on me. 'Aidan was a painter?'

'Didn't he tell you?'

'No.'

'You never saw him painting? Never saw any of his work?'

'He didn't . . . he doesn't paint.' I am listening to a story about a stranger, trying to match the details to someone I thought I knew. 'I'd know if he did. He . . .' I shouldn't want to tell her, but I do. There's no reason not to. 'When I met him, he was living in one room behind his workshop. There were empty frames all over the walls, frames he'd made—they're still there, but there's nothing in them.'

'So he stopped,' Mary says softly, rocking back and forth. 'Good.'

'Why would he do that? Why would he frame nothing?' *Why didn't he tell me he knew about Gemma and Stephen? How did he know?*

'How many empty frames?'

'I . . . I don't know. I've never counted them.'

'More than ten?'

'Yes.'

'As many as a hundred?'

'No, nowhere near that. I don't know, maybe fifteen, twenty.'

'I know how many. Count them when you next get the chance—you'll see I'm right.'

Everyone but me knows things they can't possibly know. I don't know even the things I could so easily have known. Should have known. Was Aidan's family poor? Was he common, to use Mary's word? I try to collect together in my mind everything he's told me about his childhood: he loved animals, would have liked a cat as a pet but wasn't allowed one. He never had his own bedroom, and wanted that more than anything: privacy. His brother and sister were much older than him, as remote as strangers.

'There are eighteen,' says Mary. 'Eighteen empty frames.'

The Times, 23 December 1999

FUTURE FAMOUS FIVE

**You might not know these names yet, but you soon
will. From novelists and painters to actors, from
singers to comedians, Senga McAllister talks fame
and fortune with the young British talent heading
your way.**

Today I'm at Hoxton Street Studios to meet five
unbelievably talented people. They're doing a
photo-shoot for a double-page spread in *Vogue* as
part of its *New Talent, New Style* promotion, but
they kindly spared a few minutes each, in between
having their hair sprayed and their eyebrows
plucked, to chat to me about how it feels to scale
the dizzy heights of success.

Aidan Seed, 32, painter. Aidan is a precocious
talent. Artist in residence at London's National
Portrait Gallery, before that he spent two years
enjoying the enviable title of Fellow Commoner in
Creative Arts at Trinity College, Cambridge. Aidan
tells me this post was open to writers, artists and
composers, so it wasn't only other painters he had
to beat off in order to get it. He laughs. 'There was
no beating involved. I doubt I was the most talented
artist who applied that year—I got lucky, that's all.
Someone liked my stuff.' Self-deprecation aside, the
art world is buzzing with hype about Aidan's
immense talent. Next February he has his first one-
man show at London's prestigious TiqTaq Gallery.
Owner and art dealer Jan Garner describes him as
'astonishingly gifted'. I ask him what being a Fellow
Commoner involved. Aidan tells me, 'Trinity's got
its strongest reputation as a sciences college, and the
post I held is its way of supporting the arts.
Literally, being a patron of the arts in the old-
fashioned sense. They didn't expect me to do
anything apart from paint, and they paid me a

salary. It was a dream job.' So why 'Commoner'? 'It means I'm not a scholar,' says Aidan. 'They didn't give me the post because of any academic achievements.' He smiles. 'It doesn't mean they thought I was common, though I am.'

Aidan is proud of his working-class background. His mother, Pauline, who died when he was twelve, was a cleaner, and he grew up on a council estate in the Culver Valley. 'I didn't have a toothbrush until I was eleven,' he tells me. 'As soon as I had one, I used it to mix paint.' Pauline, a single parent, was too poor to buy him paints or canvas; he was forced to steal what materials he could from school. 'I knew stealing was wrong, but painting was a compulsion for me—I had to do it, no matter what.' His family would have discouraged any artistic interests, so Aidan stashed all his early work at his friend Jim's house. 'Jim's parents were from a different world to mine,' Aidan tells me. 'They always encouraged me to paint.' As a child and young adult, Aidan painted on any surface he could find: cardboard boxes, cigarette packets. When he left school at sixteen, he got a job in a meat-packing factory where he worked for long enough to save the money he needed to fund his art degree. 'The years at the factory were hard,' he said, 'but I'm glad I did it. I had a brilliant art teacher at college who said to me, "Aidan, if you want to be a painter, you have to have a life." I think that's really true.'

Although obviously gifted, the most extraordinary thing about Aidan is that he has never sold a painting, despite many offers from eager prospective buyers. He paints over canvases he isn't entirely satisfied with, of which there have been many throughout the years. He works slowly and laboriously, and won't part with work until he thinks it's perfect. I have the impression that he's a hard man to please when it comes to his own output. 'I'm working on a number of paintings concurrently. They're all ones that have been evolving for some time now, the only ones I've ever done that I think are truly worthwhile, fit for presentation to the public.' These pictures are the ones that will make up his show at TiqTaq in February. They're dark, brooding, atmospheric and unfashionably figurative. 'I don't give a toss about fashion,' says Aidan with unmistakeable pride. 'You can use traditional techniques and still produce modern work. I don't understand artists who want to chuck out centuries of painterly knowledge and expertise as if they never happened. My aim is to build on what's gone before, historically, not start from scratch. To me, that'd feel like arrogance.'

I ask him if the pictures at TiqTaq will be for sale, if he will finally allow people to buy his work. He laughs. 'I don't think I'll have much choice,' he says, adding on a more practical note, 'I think that's kind of the point of the exhibition. Jan [Garner] would have a word or two to say if I refused to sell anything.' Eager art collectors had better secure their places in the queue. I've got a hunch Aidan Seed is an artist people will be talking about for decades to come.

Doohan Champion, 24, actor. Doohan has the sort of chiselled beauty to make young girls swoon. He first came to the great British public's attention as Toby, the troubled teenage hero of *Wayfaring Stranger*. The critics raved about him, and he's been rising meteorically ever since. 'I no longer have to look for work,' he says. 'I can pick and choose. It's a great position to be in.' A quick glance at Doohan's early career and it's obvious fame and fortune have always been waiting in the wings. Encouraged by his mother, a dentist's receptionist, Doohan went from playing the lead roles at school in Leeds to the Eldwick Youth Theatre, widely regarded as a rival to the National, where he stayed for four years. 'It was a good way to dodge homework,' laughs

Doohan. 'But I soon came to feel passionately about acting.' His passion was rewarded—he won the Gold Medal for his year. 'I could tell I was on the right lines when more and more girls started to ask me out,' jokes Doohan. 'There was no way I was giving up!'

More than 30 agents wanted to sign him when he graduated. Doohan is sitting back and waiting for the acclaim to flood in when his film *Serpent Shine* opens next year. He plays Isaac, a young schizophrenic who is threatened with the loss of his family home after his alcoholic father dies. 'It's a moving piece, very strong indeed,' says Doohan. I ask him if the fame game is as sexy as it seems to those of us on the outside. 'You know what?' he says. 'It's even better. I'm in demand, I'm making a mint. It's bloody great.' Then he looks downcast, suddenly. 'Although I wouldn't like to get too famous. I like being able to go for a few drinks at my local without being hassled.' Sorry, Doohan—I fear this won't be possible for much longer!

Kerry Gatti, 30, comedian. The first thing Kerry tells me is that he's a bloke, not a bird, though with his large frame and deep voice, I can see that for myself. His name, he says, has embarrassed him since childhood. 'My mum thought it was a unisex name, like Hilary or Lesley—frankly, either of those would have been just as bad.' He laughs. 'Boys' names for boys, girls' names for girls, that's my manifesto.' So why's he never changed his? 'My mum'd be hurt,' he explains. Kerry has done great things since he wrote his Freudian analysis of *Blake's Seven* while studying drama at Plymouth University. One of the stars of ITV's recent hit comedy series *The Afterwife*, written by the makers of Father Ted, he has just finished touring with Steve Coogan. On the road since September, with an extended run in the West End, Kerry is surely entitled to look exhausted. 'I'm knackered after doing the show,' he admits.

'Your entire day is geared towards those two hours. It's easy to go a bit mental afterwards, but the work schedule's pretty gruelling, so I can't indulge myself too much, unfortunately!' Kerry tells me he's always loved making people laugh. 'I used to do it at school, when I should have been working. I was one of those irritating kids who never apply themselves, but the teachers can't come down too hard on them because they're funny—they make everyone laugh. Yes, even the teachers. Even the headmaster, sometimes, though he'd have been a challenge for even the most talented comedian!' On the available evidence, that most talented comedian is none other than Kerry himself. While at university, he honed his comic skills in stand-up clubs with the likes of Jack Tabiner and Joel Rayner. Signed up by his agent after a show-stopping open-mike slot at Laugh? I Nearly Died at London's South Bank Centre, Kerry secured a bit part as Nero the Nerd in the ITV sitcom *I Thought You'd Never Ask*. The show won an award, and shortly afterwards Kerry found himself touring in Australia and New Zealand with *Side-splitters*. 'There we were, paddling in the sea with cans of lager in our hands, saying to each other, "So this is our job? F***ing brilliant!"'

Born in Ladbroke Grove, at the age of eight Kerry was part of an ILEA (Inner London Education Authority) programme for gifted children. 'At the weekends I wanted to play football with my mates, but instead I had to go to workshops with Ted Hughes,' he says. 'I absolutely hated it.' Kerry's mother has never worked. His father was a security guard throughout his childhood, and is now a partner in a firm called Staplehurst Investigations. 'You mean a private eye?' I ask, impressed. 'Yeah,' Kerry laughs, 'but it's all boring financial stuff, corporate and dull. It's not like you imagine: sneaking up on illicitly bonking couples with a camera—that'd be much more fun.' Kerry's parents never had much in the way of educational opportunities themselves and were determined that their son should. 'They wanted me to go to university and study English literature, but there was no way I was doing that.' He left school at 16, only to return a year later when he realised unemployment wasn't the dream of a perfect relaxing life he'd imagined it to be. 'All right, so I caved in,' he laughs. 'I went to university—but I didn't do English effing literature, though I suppose there was quite a lot of it in my drama degree—but there was also stuff that felt practical and real, which is what I loved about it.'

So what's next for Kerry? A cameo role in the new BBC sitcom, *The Reclining Avenger*. Other than that, too many things to list, he tells me lazily. 'Everyone is going to hate me next year, because I will be everywhere.' Ask him where it's all leading and he grins. 'I'd like to play Blake in a remake of Blake's Seven. That's my number one ambition.'

Pippa Dowd, 23, singer. Limited Sympathy is the only exclusively female band ever to be signed to Loose Ship, the ultra-cool label run by Nicholas Van Der Vliet, who also signed Stonehole and Alison 'Whiplash' Steven. Pippa Dowd is Limited Sympathy's lead singer. 'Don't ask me who we're like,' she says tetchily, when I dare to open with this no doubt predictable question. 'I don't care if it's bad for marketing to say we're not like anyone else. We're not. Listen to our album if you want to know what we're like.' I already had, and plucked up the courage to tell the formidable Pippa that, in my humble opinion, Limited Sympathy's music has some things in common with The Smiths, New Order, Prefab Sprout, and other bands of that ilk. 'What ilk is that?' she asks. 'You mean good bands? Yes, I hope we belong in the category of bands who produce good music.' Already photographed for the front cover of *Dazed and Confused*, Pippa and Limited Sympathy are expected to be huge when their first single 'Unsound Mind' is released next March. Has Pippa got her eye on the number one slot? I ask, hoping it's less controversial than my last question. 'It's important to separate your performance goals from your outcome goals,' she tells me. 'The only thing you can control is your own performance—after that, what happens will happen. I want to be the best singer-songwriter in the world. I'm ambitious, and proud of it. I've always wanted to be the very best. Being the most successful too would be nice, though that's less important to me than the quality of my work.'

Pippa has slogged hard for every inch of her success. Born in Frome and raised in Bristol, she has been trying to get her foot in the door of the music industry since the age of 16, when she dropped out of school. 'Things happen in such a crazy way,' she says. 'I'd been plugging away for eight years and was starting to think about giving up, I was so sick of it. Endless student union gigs do nothing for a person's morale. I was on the point of calling it a day and doing something sensible with my life when I met the girls. By "the girls", she means the other five members of her band: Cathy Murray, Gabby Bridges, Suzie Ayres, Neha Davis and Louise Thornton. Pippa met them during a recording session at Butterfly Studios in Brixton. Gabby Bridges, who was already signed to Sony and had her foot in the door at Loose Ship, was impressed by Pippa's voice and asked her to join her fledgling band, which at the time was called Obelisk. The name Limited Sympathy was Pippa's idea. 'I thought Obelisk was stupid,' she says. 'What is it? Just some random tourist attraction in France? I didn't want to be part of a band called that, and it turned out none of the girls were keen on it. One day I was bitching to them about my parents, who have never encouraged my music career. I told them my dad said to me when I was really broke that he had limited sympathy for me, because he believed I'd

brought it on myself for choosing to pursue my
unrealistic dreams instead of becoming a dull-as-
ditchwater accountant like him. That phrase had
stuck in my mind—"limited sympathy"—because it
was so dishonest. What he really meant was that he
had no sympathy at all, so why didn't he say that?
Anyway, I suggested it as a band name and the girls
loved it.' A couple of months later, Limited
Sympathy had a three-album deal.

As well as being lead singer, Pippa, astonishingly,
manages the band. 'We had a manager originally,'
she says, 'but it didn't work out. He wasn't as
efficient as I am, and I ended up doing the bulk of
the work myself. Eventually we decided to let him
go.' Limited Sympathy's first album, out in January,
is intriguingly entitled *Why Didn't You Go When
You Knew I Wanted You To?* Pippa says she can't
tell me why it's called that—it's not the name of any
song on the album. 'It wouldn't be fair to tell you
the story,' she says. 'It's based on something that
really happened with our ex-manager.'

Though Pippa resolutely refuses to talk about where
she wants to end up—'outcome goals', as she calls
them—I put it to her that the ultimate accolade for
anyone in a band is to have one of your songs
playing as background music in *EastEnders*. 'I don't
think so,' she says dismissively. 'Not until they
upgrade to a more salubrious setting. Have you seen
the hideous wallpaper in most of those houses? I
don't want my songs associated with that.' That's
me told!

Martha Wyers, 31, author. Fiction writer Martha
Wyers has more awards and accolades to her name
than most people twice her age. She won first prize in
a children's short story competition at the age of 11,
and has been bagging prizes ever since. How many in
total? I ask her, and she looks embarrassed. 'I don't
know, maybe thirty?' she says, blushing. These

include the prestigious Kaveney Schmidt Award and the Albert Bennett short story prize. Now she's branched out into full-length fiction, and her first novel, *Ice on the Sun*, was published in hardback last year by Picador, and is now out in paperback. Editor Peter Straus describes the book as 'A stunning debut, the best novel by a young author that I've read in a long while.' 'I suppose it's a literary novel, but I hope it's readable too,' Martha says. 'I was gripped by the story while I was writing it, and I want readers to be gripped too.' She is keen to talk about the book, and admits she became 'comprehensively obsessed' with it while writing it. It's the story of 27-year-old Sidonie Kershaw, who falls insanely in love with the enigmatic Adam Sands at an interview for a job they're both after (a job Adam eventually gets). Sidonie can't get him out of her head, even though she doesn't know him from . . . well, Adam! She pursues him relentlessly, ends up frightening and repelling him, and driving herself into an abyss of despair. Sounds a bit depressing, I dare to suggest. 'The only depressing books are bad ones,' says Martha firmly. 'Look at *American Psycho*—it's uplifting because it's art, because it's so brilliantly written, powerful and memorable. There's so much pain and horror in the world—emotional, physical, you name it. It's the writers who don't tackle these issues that depress me.'

Born and brought up near Winchester, you might say that Martha was born with an entire silver dinner service in her mouth. Her father is an investment banker, and Martha describes her mother as 'an aristocrat who wouldn't ever have had to work if she hadn't wanted to', though as it happens she always has and she now runs a T'ai Chi school that she set up herself. The family home is an eighteen-bedroom Hampshire mansion. The grounds are regularly used by touring companies for open-air productions of Shakespeare and opera. Martha's mother is passionate about the arts, and always wanted her only daughter to do something creative. An ex-pupil of Villiers, the exclusive girls' boarding school in Surrey, she sent Martha there too, in keeping with family tradition. 'I love Villiers,' says Martha. 'If I ever have a daughter, that's where she'll go.' On a novelist's income? I ask. 'I'm lucky,' Martha admits. 'Money isn't a problem for me, because of my family. But it annoys me when people assume my life's always been easy because of this. Financial problems aren't the only kind. I know other writers who are always flat broke, but they're happier in themselves than I am.' Isn't she happy, then? Most people would be, with a two-book deal from one of the country's finest publishers and an ecstatically reviewed first novel already out. 'I worry compulsively about the next book—I still don't know what it's going to be about,' Martha admits. 'What if it's no good? I'm scared all I'll do is write another version of my first book except worse. I could end up being a very public failure by the time I'm thirty-five.' I ask her about her love life—does she have an Adam Sands equivalent? 'If you're asking if I've got a boyfriend, the answer's no,' she says. 'But in the past I've been through hell as a result of loving a man too much, so in that sense the novel's autobiographical. See what I mean?' She smiles. 'There are some situations where money's no use whatsoever.'

I have one last question that I'm bursting to put to all of these rising stars, partly inspired by Martha's closing words, so I round them up for a group session. I ask them what they'd do if they had to choose between professional fame, success, plaudits, fans, applause—all their wildest career dreams come true—but an unfulfilled and unhappy personal life, *or* a personal life full of love and happiness and all things good, but total lack of recognition professionally—a career down the tubes. 'That's an infantile question,' says Pippa. Aidan is shaking his head. 'You haven't asked it right,' he says. 'It's not about fame or success.' 'Speak for yourself!' Doohan quips. I ask Aidan if he'd care to rephrase my question. 'What matters to me is being able to do my work, not how well it does commercially,' he says. 'Yes, it's great if other people appreciate what I do, but all that really matters to me is being able to paint.' I ask if it matters more than personal happiness. 'Yeah,' he says. 'If I had to choose, I'd choose my work over anything else. Creative satisfaction, feeling like I'm achieving something substantial with my art—that's the most important thing, whether the world notices me doing it or not.' On the other side of the coin, though, we have Kerry, who is laughing uproariously at Aidan's response. 'What, so you'd turn down a rolling programme of bliss from dawn till dusk, even if no one took the blindest bit of notice of your paintings? Not me, mate. I'd choose a happy life over my work any day. No offence to your arts supplement, and obviously I'm pleased to be in it, but I'm only a comedian, for f***'s sake. It's not like my work's that important—I'm not some brilliant doctor finding a cure for cancer.' Doohan refuses to choose. 'I want it all, me,' he says. 'I can have it, too, according to the terms of the dilemma you've set out for us. If I'm ecstatically happy, that has to mean I'm happy about all aspects of my life, which would have to include my work. Therefore it must be going well. Right?' He's a cheeky boy, that Doohan!

Martha is the only one who seems unsure. 'Work,' she says eventually. 'That's my official answer.' She won't say any more. Obviously, I'm intrigued. I'll certainly be having a read of her novel, as well as immersing myself in the powerful and varied talents of her four fellow fame-seekers, all of whom are sure to become household names in the very near future. Remember, you heard it here first . . .

16

5/3/08

'It's a minor detail,' said DC Chris Gibbs impatiently. He and DC
Colin Sellers were inside Ruth Bussey's lodge house. Kombothekra
had told them to have a thorough look round. Neither knew what
he was looking for. 'She's either fit to split or she's not—end of
story. If she's got nice legs, nice tits, a nice arse, nice face . . .'

'I'm not saying it'd be a deal-breaker,' said Sellers.

'A hunchback, false teeth and leprosy wouldn't be a deal-
breaker for you. You'd hump anything.' Gibbs glanced towards
the open front door, outside which an unhappy Malcolm Fenton, landlord of Blantyre Lodge, was waiting not so patiently to
lock up. Under his breath, Gibbs launched into his favourite
Sellers impression: ' "All right, love, wipe yourself, your taxi's
here; it's four in the morning, love, pay for yourself . . ." '

'If you're too shy to answer the question, that's fine.' Sellers
patted him on the back. 'I understand, mate.'

'I've answered the question. I don't fucking care! Why don't
you ask Muggins?'

Fenton—or Muggins, as Sellers and Gibbs called him, on account of it being how he most often referred to himself—
appeared in the hallway. 'I've had about enough of this,' he said.
'Ruth isn't here and she's done nothing wrong. If you think I'm
going to stand here listening to your foul language while you
violate her privacy, you've—'

'Sorry, Mr Fenton,' said Sellers amiably. 'I'll make sure he
puts a fiver in the swear-box when we get back to the nick.'

'You don't give a fuck what I think,' Gibbs muttered, once Fenton had withdrawn. 'You want me to ask you. Go on, then, let's hear it. What *is* all this shit?' He picked up one of Ruth Bussey's wire animals and grimaced at it before putting it down again.

'I don't like half-measures,' said Sellers. 'Brazilian's fine, natural and wild's also good—the wilder the better. Anything in between . . .'

'What? You'd say no?'

'I'm just saying, I like the extremes. All or nothing.'

'Half-measures is fine by me, as long as she's fit,' said Gibbs. 'Anyway, a Brazilian's *not* nothing—it's a landing strip. You mean a Hollywood.'

'A *what*? You don't know what you're talking about, mate.' Gibbs shook his head.

'I've got a theory,' said Sellers. 'These half-measures women—and that's *most* women, far as I can tell—they're only thinking about themselves, how they'll look in a bikini. They're not thinking about what men are going to like. I mean, you say you're not bothered, but in an ideal world . . .' Sellers tailed off when he looked up from Ruth Bussey's desk and saw that Gibbs had left the room. He raised his voice. 'I'm going to start asking around. If it turns out most men agree with me, well, then an important point needs making loud and clear, so that women get the message.'

'Shut it and come and look at this.'

'Where are you?' Sellers went in search of Gibbs. He found him in the bedroom, and was about to make the sort of joke he was known for among his colleagues when he saw the wall. 'Fuck me stupid,' he said.

'She's obsessed with Charlie,' said Gibbs, staring at the collection of articles. When he turned round, he saw that Sellers had a smug smile plastered across his face. For a second, Gibbs thought he was about to resume his musings on the subject of female pubic hairstyling.

'She's not obsessed, she's following orders,' said Sellers. 'Look.' He went out into the hall and came back with an open book in one hand and a bookmark in the other. 'I'm glad I took my time when you and Muggins were trying to chivvy me along. Look at this.' He handed the book to Gibbs, waited while he read the relevant section.

'So? If she's reading this shit, it proves she's not right in the head. So does that.' Gibbs nodded at the wall. 'It comes from a book—so what?'

'She might not be right in the head, but she's not a danger to the sarge—that's all that matters, right? What are you doing?'

Gibbs had his phone clamped to his ear. 'Ringing Waterhouse. If some freak had pictures of my bird all over her wall, I'd want to know about it.'

'We're not supposed to be—'

'So you keep saying.' Gibbs turned on him. 'You and the Snowman. You can be his best fucking frosty friend if you want to, but I'm with Kombothekra on this one. Waterhouse has done nothing—no more than usual anyway.'

'I'm not saying he has.'

'Then where's your loyalty?'

'It's not our decision to make, is it? When the Snowman finds out you and Kombothekra have been feeding Waterhouse information behind his back, I'll still have a job.' Sellers grabbed Gibbs' phone out of his hand and held it in the air. 'You could keep yours too if you don't do anything stupid.'

'This is about Stacey, isn't it? What Charlie said about her at the party—the vibrator and all that.'

'It's got nothing to do with that.'

'Course it has. With you, it comes back to pussy every time. Remember how the Brazilian conversation started? You were speculating about the Snowman's daughter. How about I tell him that?'

Sellers slumped against the door. He knew when he was beaten.

Gibbs grinned. 'It's not a problem—I'm used to it. All you need to do is remember you've got no claim to thinking you're better than anyone else and we're sweet. Now give me back my fucking phone.'

'Where is she?' DS Coral Milward knocked her rings against the underside of the table. 'I've left her two messages. She's not got back to me.'

'She mentioned something about an art gallery,' said Simon. 'Where's DC Dunning?'

Milward's eyes dipped at the mention of his name. 'He's not looking round White Cube, that's for sure.'

'What's that?'

'Why don't you ask Sergeant Zailer? She's an art lover, apparently.'

'Dunning not into art?'

'I wouldn't know.'

'Is it the aftershave?' Simon asked.

'I'm sorry?'

'Your antipathy towards Dunning.'

Milward pulled her thick arms out from under the table and folded them. The knocking sound stopped. She was wearing a new shirt since this morning, with pearl cufflinks. 'So the rumours are true,' she said. 'I'd heard that overstepping the mark is your speciality.'

'I'm on your side, for what it's worth. You smile more. And stink less.'

'Don't fuck me about, Waterhouse. Is your fiancée's art gallery jaunt this afternoon connected to my case?'

'You'd have to ask her.'

Milward leaned forward. 'We know Aidan Seed used to be an artist. He was a bright young thing, had a successful exhibition, then jacked it in. Why? Most people don't deliberately balls up promising careers. Present company excepted.'

'I've no idea.'

'Trouble is, I don't believe you.'

Simon shrugged. 'Your problem.'

'Saul Hansard didn't know either. Him I did believe.'

'Why would Seed have confided in Hansard?'

Milward let him see that she was debating whether or not to tell him. She made him wait a few seconds for her answer. 'Seed was working as Hansard's assistant when he had his one and only exhibition in London. Also when he decided to stop painting and take up framing.'

'Seed worked for Hansard?' Simon frowned. 'Ruth Bussey worked for Hansard before she worked for Seed.'

Milward seemed to be waiting for him to continue.

'Mary Trelease used to have her work framed by Hansard.'

'Not while Seed worked there. Later. Later still, she switched to a London gallery, the same one that hosted Seed's solo exhibition in February 2000: TiqTaq, on Charlotte Street. That's where Zailer is now, am I right?'

'Think you'd have got as far as you have without our help?' Simon asked her.

'Where have I got? Two thirds of the way down a dead-end street, if you ask me.'

'Did Hansard tell you Bussey and Trelease met at his gallery, and had a row that ended in a physical attack? Seed killed Gemma Crowther as revenge for what she did to Ruth Bussey. He's going to kill Mary Trelease for the same reason. Maybe Stephen Elton too, unless Elton's guilty plea and the fact that he didn't actively participate in the attack on Bussey in Lincoln . . .'

'You know about that?' Milward smiled. 'You didn't know this morning.'

'You didn't tell me,' said Simon, trying to keep his anger down.

'So who did? See, the trouble I'm having is that you seem to know a fraction too much. If I find out you've had contact with Bussey, Seed or Trelease and not told me . . .'

'I haven't. Sounds like you haven't either. What's being done to find them?'

'You should be pleased it's not your problem,' said Milward. 'My problem is that I've got a chief suspect—'

'You mean Seed?'

'No. I don't mean Seed.'

'There was no break-in, right? Narrows your suspects down to Seed or Elton.'

'I've got a suspect and a motive,' Milward continued as if he hadn't spoken. 'Nothing in the bag yet, but I'm hopeful. Meanwhile, on the fringes of my investigation, I've got your little mess: Seed, Trelease, Bussey, Hansard.'

'The fringes?' Simon couldn't believe it. 'You're wrong. I don't know what's going on, not yet, but I know one thing: my mess, as you call it, is centre stage. You'll get nowhere unless you treat it as such.'

'You're an arrogant turd, Waterhouse.'

'So I've heard.'

Milward looked as if she'd like to take a swipe at him. 'I've got motive,' she told him again. 'Motive's where I'm strong. What have you got? Phantom stranglings, pictures disappearing from art fairs, mysterious predictions: Seed naming a series of nine paintings Mary Trelease hasn't done yet—you expect me to take all that seriously?'

'No,' Simon told her. 'I expect you to bury it because it confuses you. And it's not nine, it's eight—the paintings Mary Trelease hasn't done yet.'

Milward frowned. 'Nine,' she said, looking at her notes.

'The first, *Abberton*, she's already done.'

She slammed her file shut. 'I don't like all this ... clutter around my investigation. I *really* don't like it. How did Zailer know a picture went missing from Gemma's flat the night she was killed? How did she know it was *that* picture?'

'She didn't know. She was guessing.'

Milward let out the breath she'd been holding in several

short bursts. 'We found it in the boot of Seed's car,' she said. '*Abberton*. It's too weird for my taste, but it's got something to it—not like most of the rubbish that's peddled as art these days.'

Simon shook his head, trying to take it in. No, that couldn't be right. Seed might abandon his car—Simon had told Milward this morning why he'd do that—but not the painting, not once he'd removed it from the house after killing Crowther, knocking her teeth out with a hammer and replacing them with picture hooks. *Abberton* was crucial. It had to be. No way he'd have left it in the boot.

Think. Seed gave Crowther the picture—he must have done. Then he killed her and took it back. Why? That part had never made sense, not really. Why had Simon allowed himself to over-look it for so long?

'Stephen Elton says there's no way *Len*, aka Aidan Seed, would have killed Gemma.' Milward's voice seemed to come from a distance. 'Says the three of them were close friends. Seed slept on their sofa regularly rather than drive home late—and no, he and Gemma weren't having an affair, before you ask. Elton was adamant Gemma would never be unfaithful—saw it as being beyond the pale. As opposed to nearly torturing a woman to death,' she added tersely, 'which doesn't seem to have troubled her conscience unduly. I've seen Elton lie and I've seen him tell the truth, and he was telling the truth when he said that.'

'I never thought Crowther and Seed were having an affair,' said Simon. He'd seen the way he'd looked at her as they walked down the street together. It wasn't how a lover would have looked at her; Simon knew that for sure, despite never hav-ing been anyone's lover. *Are you a virgin, Simon?* Charlie had asked him once, years ago. He didn't give her an answer, still hadn't.

His phone rang in his pocket.

'Go ahead,' said Milward. 'If it's Zailer . . .'

'It isn't.' Simon was relieved to see Chris Gibbs' name on his

screen instead of Kombothekra's. Surprised too. He listened to
what Gibbs had to say, keeping his replies to the absolute minimum, aware of Milward's eyes on him.

'Everything all right?' she asked, seeing him put his phone
back in his pocket.

Simon's best ideas always arrived in a rush, like a shot of
adrenalin to the brain. This one was no different. 'What came
first, Crowther's death or the mutilation of her mouth?' he
asked.

'The removal of the teeth was post-mortem. Why? What are
you thinking?'

'What about the weapons: gun, hammer, the knife used to cut
back her lips? Have you found any of them?'

Milward shook her head, as Simon had known she would.
The killer was hanging on to them, planning to use them again.
A killer who knew how to stage a production, who liked melo-
drama, who had perhaps killed before . . . 'You come across the
name Martha Wyers?' he asked.

'The writer?' Milward frowned. 'What's she got to do with
anything?'

'You've heard of her?'

'Only since about an hour ago. She and Seed were part of a
promotion that *The Times* and *Vogue* jointly—'

'I know about that,' Simon cut her off. 'Mary Trelease did a
portrait of Martha Wyers dead, with a noose round her neck.'

Incredulity flickered in Milward's eyes. Then she said, 'You're
not joking, are you?'

'No. Kerry Gatti was part of the same promotion—a comedian. He can't have been very funny, because he gave it up and
became a private detective. He's been following Ruth Bussey.'

Milward's eyes narrowed. 'On whose behalf?' she asked
eventually.

'No idea. Tell Proust to lift his ban and I'll go back to work
and find out.'

'We can find that out,' Milward said through clenched teeth.

'I've got to think this through: Mary Trelease painted a portrait of Martha Wyers? How did they . . .?'

'Have you interviewed her?'

'Mary Trelease? We're working on it.' Simon took this to mean that wherever Trelease was, she wasn't at 15 Megson Crescent.

Milward leaned forward. 'The witnesses who saw you outside Crowther and Elton's flat say they saw an old woman there, too, after you'd gone. Unfortunately they were too busy making notes about you to pay much attention to her, but the one thing they were certain of was . . .'

'Wrinkles and lines all over her face?' said Simon quickly.

Milward nodded. 'We've spoken to a bucketload of Mary Trelease's reprobate neighbours at Megson Crescent. All any of them wanted to talk about was how old she looks, how much older than her real age.'

So Trelease had been at Gemma Crowther's flat the night she was murdered. 'I don't think Martha Wyers' suicide was suicide,' said Simon.

Milward threw her pen down on the table. 'I don't know whether to have you lynched or offer you a job,' she said.

Neither option appealed. Simon didn't want to work for Coral Milward. He wanted to work for that treacherous bastard Giles Proust. 'Put me back where I belong,' he said. 'Let me help you as part of my team, helping your team—I know that's what they're doing, about a quarter as effectively as they would be if I was with them.' He hadn't meant to threaten Milward when he opened his mouth, but that was the way he seemed to be heading. Time to make it explicit. 'It's up to you,' he said. 'If you want anything else from me, you know what you need to do.'

Jan Garner didn't smile when Charlie walked into her gallery. 'I preferred it when the police didn't turn up every five minutes,' she said. 'None of you ever buys anything.' She was standing in the window, arranging artificial roses in a green glass vase—

pink, yellow and white ones. They had tiny clear beads stuck to their petals and leaves: fake drops of water.

'Any other police who've been here are nothing to do with me,' Charlie told her. 'They'd have been Met.'

'Can you tell me what's going on?'

'They've probably told me less than they've told you.' Charlie didn't stop to give Jan Garner time to dwell on the subtle dishonesty of her answer. 'The artist you told me about, the talented one who gave up painting after his first show sold out—was his name Aidan Seed?'

Jan nodded.

'That's why Mary Trelease chose you, this gallery,' Charlie told her, aware that she didn't have to.

'Mary knew Aidan?' Jan's shock appeared to be genuine.

'Not according to her. Did Aidan ever mention the name Mary Trelease, as far as you can remember?'

'I haven't spoken to him for eight years,' said Jan. 'I don't think so, no. Although . . . this'll sound daft, but when Mary walked in here last year and ordered me to frame her pictures, her name rang a bell. I put it down to one of those spooky *déjà vu* things, but maybe Aidan did mention her. It's impossible to remember after all this time.'

'What about Martha Wyers?' Charlie asked. 'Did he mention her?'

Jan looked surprised. 'That was the name of the dead writer Mary painted. You saying it jogged my memory. I don't remember Aidan talking about her, no. Ow! Thorn,' she explained, sucking her finger. 'Not real, but still sharp. People look down their noses at silk flowers, but I love them. They're not phoney, they're representations. I've always thought it odd that the same people who buy paintings of flowers to hang on their walls wouldn't give houseroom to man-made roses like these.' Was there a nervousness to Jan's chatter, or was Charlie imagining it?

'A couple of months before Aidan's exhibition here, he was

featured in *The Times*,' she said. 'In an article called "Future Famous Five".'

Jan was nodding. 'It was a huge coup, publicity-wise.'

'You don't remember the name Martha Wyers from that article?'

'No,' she said, after a brief hesitation. 'You mean . . .?'

'Martha was one of the five.'

Jan dropped the rose she'd been holding, pinched the skin of her neck between her thumb and index finger. 'Are you sure?' she asked. 'Of course you are. Stupid question. I couldn't tell you any of the names now, apart from Aidan's. I didn't keep the whole piece, only the bits about Aidan and TiqTaq. I keep anything and everything relating to my exhibitions.'

'Yesterday, you mentioned Aidan's private view,' said Charlie. 'That's like a private party for the friends and family of the artist, is it?'

'And of the gallery. Collectors, critics, other gallery owners. We all like to impress . . . Yes.' Jan stopped. 'You're right.'

Charlie had a feeling the question she'd been about to ask would prove unnecessary.

'A couple of them came to Aidan's private view, a couple of the future famous five. I remember him mentioning it. I'm not sure how pleased he was.'

'Why do you say that?'

'There'd been some kind of contretemps when they got together to have their photo taken. I don't think I ever knew all the details, but it was something to do with one or more of them calling Aidan pretentious. Which he wasn't,' said Jan defensively. 'He could be too intense and earnest at times, but there wasn't a grain of pretence about him.'

'So Martha Wyers might have been there, at Aidan's private view?'

Jan shrugged.

'Could Mary Trelease have been there too?'

'I suppose she might have been. It was a bit of a blur that

night—private views always are. I was madly busy and the place was packed. I don't remember individuals, only a big crowd of people, almost too big to squeeze in.'

'Did anything happen that struck you as out of the ordinary?' Charlie asked. 'Anything at all?'

'I don't think so. Two punters had a fairly predictable row about whether to buy a picture or not. A mother and daughter, I think. That's right, yes. I remember thinking I wouldn't have dared tell my mother how to spend her money, God rest her soul. It's amazing how tactless people can be—tussling in front of the artist like that. "It's not worth two thousand quid!" "Well, I think it is!" Usually I keep schtum, but on that occasion I butted in and told the daughter she was crazy.'

It didn't sound crazy to Charlie. Two thousand quid? Was there any reason for art to be so expensive?

'I don't mind if people genuinely can't afford it,' said Jan. 'But in this case, it wasn't about money. The daughter said the paintings were cold and unforgiving, that they had a "rotten soul"—I've never forgotten that. She was talking nonsense, and her mother looked upset by it, so I gave her a piece of my mind. Thank goodness Aidan didn't hear her.'

'Did Aidan talk to you about his personal life?' Charlie asked.

'Not really. Apart from jokingly.'

'What do you mean?'

'He once told me he had a stalker. When we were hanging his exhibition.'

Charlie tried not to look too eager.

'Oh, he wasn't worried about it or anything like that. He sounded almost flattered. He wasn't being entirely serious, I don't think.'

'Do you remember anything else he said?'

Jan's face creased in concentration. 'Something about having to let her have her way with him because she wouldn't take no for an answer. It was very tongue in cheek, though. I said something like, "It's a hard life when you're in demand," and he laughed. He referred to fate, too—fate kept throwing them together, something like that.'

Not many people would accept a stalker as part of destiny's grand plan, Charlie thought. *Odd*. 'Can you remember his exact words?' she asked.

Jan looked impatient, then tried to soften her expression to one of mock exasperation. 'It was eight years ago. Of course I can't.'

'And he didn't give his stalker a name?'

'Nope. Sorry.'

'You didn't take any photos or anything, did you? Of the private view? You said you kept a record of all your exhibitions.'

'That's an idea. I always take pictures. Want me to dig out the file?'

'Please.' It wasn't impossible that Mary Trelease or Martha Wyers or both of them might be in one or more of the photographs. And if they were? More evidence of a connection between the key players, but still nothing to indicate what they were players in, or how their individual stories fitted together. Had Martha and Mary been more than contemporaries at Villiers? Had they been friends?

Charlie recalled Mary's expression when she'd said, 'Not me.' Had Aidan Seed killed Martha Wyers? Hanged her? You murder one woman, then, years later, pretend you've strangled her friend. No—too bizarre. And why choose hanging as a way of killing someone? Automatically, Charlie's mind supplied an answer: *to make it look like suicide.*

'Could Martha Wyers have been Aidan's stalker?' she asked, not expecting Jan to know the answer.

'I've no idea. I suppose she could have been. Why?' Jan had pulled a manila folder out of one of her desk drawers.

'Martha published a novel before she died, *Ice on the Sun.* It's about a woman who falls for a man she meets at a job interview and pursues—'

'Oh, lordy.' Jan's mouth gaped open. 'Aidan told me he first met his stalker-woman at a job interview. It only came back to me when I heard you say it. He definitely did. I remember asking if he thought she'd fixated on him because he had the job she wanted.'

Charlie cautioned herself against getting her hopes up. Yet another connection; more unanswered questions. 'In Martha's novel, the man the heroine falls in love with is called Adam Sands—same initials as Aidan Seed.'

Jan was flicking through the file. 'Nothing here, I'm afraid. Look.' She handed Charlie several photographs. Seeing Aidan again in this context was almost shocking, though Charlie couldn't have said why. In the pictures, he was wearing a suit and was slimmer than he'd been when Charlie had met him. He was smiling for the camera, but there was a strain to the smile, as if he wasn't sure he could support its weight for much longer.

'Would you say he was a happy person?'

'Hard to tell,' said Jan. 'Sometimes he was jolly and chatty, life and soul of the party, but he could also be reserved, verging on morose. I had the impression life had been a struggle for him.'

'Why do you say that?'

'I was afraid you were going to ask me that.' Jan smiled ruefully. 'I don't know. Let me think about it.' She was silent for so long, Charlie started to wonder if she was waiting to be granted permission to think. 'It was the way he spoke,' she said finally. 'He expressed his opinions and pursued his ambitions so . . . assertively. As if he thought it was the only way to be heard. I used to wonder about his family. I know his siblings are much older than he is. None of them came to the private view, which I thought was rather odd; not one single relative of his came anywhere near the exhibition in the month it was on. That's almost unheard of.'

There was nothing remarkable about the photographs of Aidan Seed's private view. His paintings, from what Charlie could make out, were of interiors containing people, usually more than one. Charlie found herself staring for longer than she needed to at a painting of a staircase, with a middle-aged woman turning, halfway up, to look down at a younger man—almost a boy—who was looking away from her.

'Can you see how he uses almost stiflingly traditional painting techniques to create scenes that are aggressively contemporary?' Jan asked.

The picture was meticulously realistic; it could have been a photograph. Charlie was impressed, but she wouldn't have wanted it on her wall. It would make her tense. The couple depicted—if they were a couple—had evidently had a row, or were in the middle of one. It wasn't a peaceful painting. 'What's it called?' she asked, wondering if the title would offer any clues. If she'd painted it, she'd have called it 'These people are pissed off with each other because . . .' and then the reason. What was the point of a picture that told a story if no one could work out what the story was?

Jan had pulled a glossy card booklet out of the file. 'Here's the catalogue.' She handed it to Charlie. In the photograph, the stairs painting was labelled '12'. Number 12 in the catalogue was called *Supply and Demand*. Charlie was none the wiser. The picture had been reproduced in the catalogue, along with one other, of a fat man in a bath, his torso like a mountain.

'His titles are all . . .' The rest of the sentence withered and died in Charlie's mouth as she stared at the catalogue. Her hands shook. She'd been about to say that all Aidan's titles were evasive. They said nothing about what was happening in the picture.

Apart from one.

Painting number 18 was called *The Murder of Mary Trelease*.

17

Wednesday 5 March 2008

'Did you fall in love with Aidan the instant you saw him?' Mary asks abruptly.

'Yes.'

'So did Martha. Funny how that's used as a gauge of love's worth, isn't it? The more groundless it is, the more based on *nothing*, the more impressive it sounds. "I fell in love at first sight." We all want to say that—prove how passionate we are. And Martha was the worst kind of fool—a clever one. She was good with words and ideas, could make them serve her purpose, whatever it was. Within seconds she'd spun her reaction to Aidan, which was probably nothing more than sexual, into an irresistible narrative of love and enforced separation: the formalities of the occasion dictated that she had to walk into the interview room and he had to walk out of it while the chair of the appointment committee held the door open. Time for their eyes to meet, but nothing more. And their souls, according to Martha. She was an idiot,' Mary adds vehemently, as if afraid I might miss the point of the story.

She talks like no one I've ever known. I want to ask again about the eighteen empty frames, but she's already ignored the question three times. I know she'll continue to ignore it until she's ready, so I let her talk.

'The stupid cow made a virtue of it. If they'd exchanged even one word, she went round telling everyone, the perfection of that moment would have been ruined. There's no reasoning with someone like Martha. When the college phoned her to tell her she hadn't got the job, she claimed she'd known he'd got it before they told her. She was happier for him than she would have been for herself, she said. And she knew where she'd be able to find him, as of the first of October 1993: Trinity College, Cambridge. She didn't bother with the subtle approach—she wrote to him and told him she was in love with him. Any half-decent man would have read that letter and known straight away how vulnerable she was, but Aidan didn't care. He wrote back and told her he'd noticed her too. Noticed! She offers him unconditional love, and in return he tells her he's registered her existence! That was when I knew how dangerous he was for someone like Martha.'

'Dangerous?'

'He didn't say, "I feel the same way", he didn't say, "I'm sorry, I'm not interested". From his letter it was obvious he was one of those men who likes to reel women in, offering the illusion of intimacy with no substance behind it.' Mary is picking up speed, barely aware of my presence. 'He invited Martha to Trinity. She was so worried about being late, she got an earlier train and arrived in Cambridge an hour before she was supposed to. He'd told her where to find his rooms. When he opened his door and saw her there, he said, "You're early," and shook her hand. He didn't even kiss her on the cheek. She apologised and asked if he was busy. He said, "I'm painting." You know what he did then? Sat down at his easel and carried on. "I can talk at the same time," he said, not even looking at her. Martha had gone all the way to Cambridge to see him, and he made her wait while he finished filling in the red background of his painting with a tiny brush. She said it was like being tortured.'

Mary grabs a strand of her hair and puts it in her mouth, chewing it as if it's a curl of liquorice. 'When he'd finished painting, he took her for lunch. In college, surrounded by other people. He told her he was flattered, thought she was amazing, but didn't want to get involved with anyone—said he'd find it too stressful. He could have told her that when he wrote to her, saved her the trip, instead of leaving her to wonder if something about her in the flesh hadn't lived up to his memory of her. After lunch he sent her away. She wrote to him every day for a long time—her feelings hadn't changed—but he hardly ever wrote back. When he did, his letters were chatty, anodyne—as short as he could get away with. I also wrote to him once or twice: hate mail.'

Mary tries to smile. 'You know what I'm like when I get angry. I couldn't bear what he was doing to her. In the end she stopped writing to him and started writing a novel instead. All about him, and her obsession with him. It wasn't so much a book as a self-indulgent splurge, but apparently I was the only person who thought that. It got published. When it came out, she sent him a copy. She got his reply two days later—a card, thanking her for sending it, and quoting Gore Vidal. I suppose you know the famous quote?'

It's a few seconds before I realise she wants a response from me. Not giving her what she wants doesn't occur to me. 'No.'

' "Whenever a friend succeeds, something in me dies." '

'That's horrible.'

'Plenty of things are horrible,' she says impatiently. 'If they're true, it doesn't matter, but that's *not* true, not of me, anyway. I'd only want someone to fail if I disliked them. Wouldn't you?' She doesn't wait for my answer. 'Anyone else would have torn up Aidan's card and written him off as the arsehole that he is, but not Martha. Do you know what her take on it was?' When Mary laughs, it sounds as if she's choking, fighting for breath. She looks limp, like a doll that's had the stuffing pulled out of it. 'At least he thought of her as a friend.'

'What?'

' "Whenever a *friend* succeeds, something in me dies." Martha decided to minimise the hurt to herself by taking it as a declaration of friendship, something she'd not had from him before.'

I flinch. This is too personal a detail. I feel as if I'm invading Martha Wyers' privacy, ransacking the mind and heart of an unhappy dead woman. I ought to tell Mary to stop. I don't.

'She wrote him a few more letters, to which he didn't reply,' she resumes her toneless cataloguing of the facts. *As she sees them.* I wonder what Aidan would say if he could hear her telling the story. Would his version of it be different? 'Everyone told her to forget him, which was disastrous for someone like Martha—the very worst thing to say.'

'It supported her idea of them as doomed lovers, with the world against them,' I say. When Mary smiles at me, I feel something that's not easy to distinguish from pride, and it scares me. My desire to please others isn't safe. I wanted so badly to please Aidan. And Stephen Elton. For a while, I thought I had, did, both of them.

'What is it?' Mary asks.

I don't want to tell her what I'm thinking. I've surrendered too much of myself already.

'Don't you believe me?'

I nod.

'You don't, not entirely. You're not sure. It doesn't sound like the Aidan you know. That Aidan's kind and loving. On the other hand, you can't explain his recent behaviour, and you hope I can. You need me to be able to, so part of you wants me to be telling the truth. That part believes me.'

She's right. 'You make me sound schizophrenic,' I say, to hide my discomfort.

'There are divisions within every person. Especially those who are forced to bear unbearable pain. That's what trauma does—it divides you against yourself: the need to survive versus the desire for oblivion.'

One half dies. The other half lives.

I think I'm starting to understand. 'Did Martha hang herself because of Aidan?' I ask. 'Because he rejected her?'

'Yes. But that was much later, after they'd had sex,' Mary says. It seems not to occur to her that this might be hard for me to listen to. 'They met again in 1999. Someone decided to round up young, promising artists and writers and the like, and parade them in the press like performing monkeys. Martha and Aidan were both chosen. You can imagine what she made of that.'

'She thought fate had brought them together again.'

'She was right. Martha was Aidan's doom, and he was hers. Why do people assume fate has their best interests at heart?'

'I don't,' I tell her.

'You've got more sense than Martha, then. She tried to turn herself into the person she thought Aidan wanted her to be. She lost weight, changed the way she dressed . . .'

'Had he said he didn't like her appearance?'

'He'd said nothing! She made it up, the lot. All those years she'd been denied access to the real Aidan, she'd grown an alternative version in her mind, complete with all the preferences and attitudes she thought he ought to have. *That* was the man she was trying to please. And if he said things that didn't tally with what she wanted to believe about him, instead of letting them crush the fantasy, she denied her own feelings, brought them into line with his. Like when they were interviewed for *The Times* and asked which was more important to them, personal happiness or work. Aidan said—in front of Martha, knowing how she felt about him—that nothing could ever matter to him as much as his work. Martha said the same thing, to win his approval, even though she'd gladly have renounced not only her work but also her family, friends, everything, if she could have had Aidan.'

So would I, if I could have him how he used to be. Before London. I try to keep an even expression on my face so that Mary can't see what I'm thinking, but she's wrapped up in her own thoughts, not even looking at me.

'That was Martha's fatal mistake,' she says. 'If she hadn't told that one stupid lie, she'd be alive today.'

18

5/3/08

Charlie backed away, not wanting Jan Garner to see what she'd read. No wonder the name Mary Trelease had sounded familiar to Jan. 'I'm going to need to take this with me,' Charlie said.

Jan frowned. 'I haven't got a spare. I could have it photocopied if you want, let you have a copy.'

'I'll guard it with my life and bring it back as soon as I can.' Charlie wouldn't have been able to explain why a copy wasn't good enough. It wouldn't be the same as the catalogue, with its stiff, shiny pages. She had to show this to Simon. Dunning and Milward ought to see it too.

Aware that Jan hadn't yet agreed to let her take it, seeing the gallery owner's discomfort, Charlie held up her left hand. 'I'll leave you my engagement ring as security,' she said. 'You can keep it until I return the catalogue.'

'You can't do that,' said Jan. 'It's bad luck to take off an engagement ring. You're only allowed to take it off once—to put your wedding ring underneath it.'

'I take it off every night, when I go to sleep,' Charlie told her. 'I don't like wearing jewellery to bed.'

'That's terrible!' Jan squeaked. She too had a ring on the third finger of her left hand: a thick silver band with a milky pink stone set into it.

'I put it back on again every morning. I don't think it's bad luck.' Charlie felt herself tense up. 'Marrying someone who refuses to have sex with you, who's never said he loves you—that's my idea of bad luck.'

Jan looked confused. 'No one would do that,' she said.

'How well do you remember Aidan's paintings from this exhibition?'

'Better than I remember most shows. Why?'

'Were any of them violent? Women getting killed, that sort of thing?'

Jan recoiled. 'No. Nothing like that.'

'You're sure?'

'Absolutely. Aidan's work wasn't about violence. It was about awkward atmospheres between people, failures of communication.'

'I don't suppose you remember who bought what?' Charlie had to see that picture. Quickly. She crossed her fingers against it being in Auckland or Sri Lanka, the prized possession of a foreign collector who'd happened to be in London at the time of Aidan Seed's exhibition.

'I don't remember,' said Jan. 'But I don't need to. The sales list'll be in the file. It wasn't the usual suspects, though. Only three of the pictures sold at the private view, but the next day I had collectors coming in and ringing up, wanting to buy Aidan's work sight unseen. I didn't really believe in the power of word of mouth before Aidan. The entire show sold out in three days, and a lot of the buyers were clamouring for more—they wanted to know how quickly he could produce new work, and wanted first refusal as soon as he did. It was absolutely extraordinary.' Jan's eyes shone. Charlie suspected the exhibition had been the high point of her career as well as Aidan Seed's. She could feel her heart beating in the roof of her mouth. The information she wanted was in a file right in front of her. Any second now, she'd have her hands on it.

Jan pulled out two sheets of A4 paper, stapled together. Charlie waited for her to look, to notice the title of number 18, but she didn't. She held out the list for Charlie to take.

The first thing that leaped out was the name Wyers. A Mrs Cecily Wyers had bought number 4: *Routine Bites Hard*. Something snagged in Charlie's brain. Where had she heard that title before? The combination of those three words in that order was very familiar, but Charlie couldn't put her finger on why. She saw Ruth Bussey's face clearly in her mind. Was it something to do with Ruth?

From that unanswerable question, Charlie moved on to another: was Cecily Wyers a relative of Martha's? Could the two women who'd argued about whether or not to buy a painting have been Martha and her mother? Had Martha said in front of Jan Garner that Aidan's paintings had a rotten soul, and been admonished for it?

There was an address for Cecily Wyers beneath her name: Wynyates, Barnwell St Stephen, Hampshire. No telephone number. 'I'll need to take this, too,' Charlie said, turning the page.

Saul Hansard, Ruth Bussey's former boss, was listed as the buyer of picture number 10: *Six Green Bottles*. Number 18 was the last picture on the list, at the bottom of the second page. Charlie wouldn't have been entirely shocked to learn that Stephen Elton or Gemma Crowther had bought it. The unlikely had become so commonplace it no longer surprised her. Or at least, she thought it didn't, until she saw who'd bought *The Murder of Mary Trelease*. The name triggered a series of hard jolts in her brain, sending her thoughts running blindly, chaotically into one another.

The painting had been sold to a Mr J. E. J. Abberton.

19

Wednesday 5 March 2008

'Did you ever lie to please Aidan?' Mary asks.

'No. I don't think so.' I've only ever lied to protect myself, and Aidan.

'Martha did. If she'd stayed true to herself—told the truth *about* herself—she and Aidan wouldn't have formed their little bond against the others and gone off on their own. They wouldn't have gone to bed together—Martha might still have pulled back from the brink. It was the night they spent together that took her love for Aidan and the despair that went with it to a deeper level.'

'What happened?' I ask.

'The Five Future Failures went for a drink after *The Times* interview. They started talking about it again—the life versus work thing. Ended up having a blazing row. They all drank too much, and the friendly banter turned nasty. Aidan was the butt of everyone's jokes. What he'd said about living only for his work had sounded pompous even to Martha. If there's one thing Aidan hates more than anything, it's having people laugh at him. You've heard of Doohan Champion?'

'I've heard the name. Isn't he famous?'

'Very.'

'You said "The Five Future Failures".'

'Everyone fails eventually,' says Mary briskly. 'It takes some people longer than others, that's all. Doohan called Aidan a self-important wanker. Martha defended him. She told them they were a bunch of shallow losers—if Aidan was pompous, so was she, she said. She agreed with him, after all, or rather she pretended she did. By attacking Aidan's detractors, she finally fulfilled her only ambition: impressing him. They went off on their own, ripped the others' personalities and creative achievements, such as they were, to shreds over a curry in Soho, and ended up back at the hotel *The Times* had booked for them—in Aidan's room.'

'Do you know what the hotel was called?'

'The Conrad.' Mary gives me an odd look. 'In Chelsea Harbour.'

Not the Drummond.

'They had sex, according to the technical definition of the phrase.'

'What do you mean?'

'Penetration occurred, but that was about it. Aidan couldn't hack it.'

'Martha told you?'

'Later, after he'd packed her in, she started to tell everyone, even her parents, because she didn't understand. She had to understand everything, Martha. The world had to make sense, or she couldn't cope. At the time she hadn't minded the sex being bad because of what had gone with it. Aidan had told her he loved her, that he had ever since the day of the interview at Trinity.'

Mary jumps down from the windowsill where she's been sitting and starts to pace restlessly. There's excitement in her voice, as if this is the part she's been looking forward to. 'He told her exactly what she wanted to hear: that he'd known she was special, that he'd repelled her advances only because he was frightened of the strength of his feelings for her. He talked about the future, said he never wanted them to be apart again. He had to leave the hotel early the next morning to go to the National Portrait Gallery, where he was artist in residence. When he kissed her goodbye, he said, "I'll be in touch. Almost immediately."' Mary laughs. 'Martha was a writer. Words mattered to her. If she was certain that was what he said, then that was what he said.'

'He didn't get in touch.' My question comes out as a statement of fact. The story, though new to me, is eerily familiar. Aidan did the same thing to me: told me he loved me, proposed marriage, held me all night in our room at the Drummond Hotel, then became remote and distant immediately afterwards, withdrawing more with each day that passed. Even as he moved his things into my house, he was removing himself from my life.

'He didn't get in touch *at first*,' says Mary. 'Martha wrote to him and phoned him—nothing. No response. Finally, when she couldn't think of anything else to do, she waited outside the National Portrait Gallery for him. Every day for a week, but he didn't appear. She went in and asked about him, and they told her his residency had finished the week before. He'd moved too, and not given her his new address. That's when she started to tell the whole story to anyone who'd listen—waiters, barmen, taxi-drivers. She was a total embarrassment, but she didn't care. She wanted to know how it could happen: how can a man say he'll love you for ever one minute, then disappear the next?'

The smoke in the room is starting to get to me, even though the window's open and Mary finished the last of her cigarettes a while ago. I offer what seems to me to be the obvious answer. 'Men say that sort of thing to get women into bed.'

'No!' she snaps. 'Martha was already in bed with him when he said those things. She'd have done anything he wanted, whether he talked false romantic crap or not, and he knew it. He pretended to be in love with her for the sake of his own pride. Aidan's a perfectionist. He has to be the best at whatever he does. When he went limp inside Martha and couldn't do anything to salvage the situation physically, he realised he needed to start talking fast if he wanted to be impressive in any way at all.' Mary's eyes are hard, two grey stones. Bitterness underscores her every word. 'All his passionate whispering about everlasting love was a smokescreen, nothing more. He didn't mean a word of it. All that mattered to him was that Martha should think it was better with him than with anyone else. And she did. Like I said, Martha was a words person. She didn't care that the sex hadn't worked—he'd brought her fantasy to life with what he'd said. That night was the best night of her life, a night she spent with a lying, impotent—'

'Stop!' I can't stand to hear any more. 'Where did it happen? Where did she hang herself? Here?' I try not to think about how calm I felt when I first crossed Garstead Cottage's threshold—as if I was arriving somewhere that had always been my destination. *Somewhere I belong.*

'Downstairs,' says Mary. 'I'll show you. Come on.'

'No! Is that why you've brought me here? I don't want to see it!'

'What do you think I've got down there, Martha's dead body? It's nothing like that. It's an exhibition, that's all. You like art, don't you?' Before I have a chance to respond, she says in a sing-song voice that chills me, 'Aidan had an exhibition. He sent Martha an invitation.'

'You mean . . . before they spent the night together?' If I keep her talking, I won't have to look at whatever it is she wants to show me.

'After. A couple of weeks after, when Martha was struggling to come to terms with his failure to get in touch "almost immediately", as promised. She was getting ready to give up on him all over again, and then an invitation to his private view arrived via her publisher. No note with it, nothing personal, just the gallery's printed card. The stupid cow got her hopes up all over again. She was so sick of feeling miserable, she'd have latched on to anything.'

'Did she go?'

'What do you think? Her mother went with her, allegedly for moral support, though the secret plan was to put the Wyers financial muscle behind Aidan, make him do the right thing, as she saw it—make her daughter happy.'

'You mean bribe him?'

'Basically. In as subtle a way as possible.' Seeing my shock,

Mary smirks. 'Villiers families do it all the time—a crate of champagne to the head to secure a good reference, that sort of thing. Martha knew exactly what Cecily had in mind, and was desperate enough to turn a blind eye. She wanted Aidan, and she didn't care how she got him. At the private view, he barely looked in her direction. When she cornered him and asked why he'd invited her, he said, "You're interested in my work, aren't you? You always seemed to be. I thought you'd want to come."'

I find my voice and say, 'I don't believe he'd be so insensitive.' *No one would.*

'Yes, you do,' says Mary. 'You believe it because it's true. When Martha got upset, he sneered at her, called her a fake. Said he'd hoped she'd still want to support his work, even though things hadn't worked out between them personally. That was what he said—"hadn't worked out"—as if he'd tried his hardest. Martha lost it then, told him she'd been lying when she'd said her work was more important to her than a happy personal life. The others were right about him, she said—he was a self-important wanker. Bit awkward, when some of those others were also there, at the preview. Not as awkward as Cecily, though.'

Mary shakes her head in disgust. 'Martha had finally realised it was finished—the years-long fantasy died that night. He'd invited her *knowing* how she felt about him, *knowing* he didn't feel the same way, but hoping she'd buy one of his grim paintings all the same. She couldn't pretend after that. But her mother didn't know it was game over, so she started to wage her campaign: poured charm all over Aidan, told him she was Martha's mother, hinted at the size of the family fortune, dithered over which picture to buy and declared herself so unable to decide that she might have to buy more than one. Martha took her to one side and begged her not to buy anything, but Cecily wouldn't have it. She did agree to buy one picture, not two—she made that concession, but she didn't take Martha seriously when she said she wanted Aidan's show to be a failure. Martha often said things she didn't mean in the heat of the moment, and Cecily was used to her breaking down in tears immediately afterwards and taking it all back. She didn't see that this time was different.' Mary lapses into a brooding silence.

'Different because Martha had finally given up on him?' I say tentatively, knowing I will never give up on Aidan, though he might have given up on me a long time ago. I love him, no matter what he's done.

'Different because she hated him,' says Mary crossly, as if I'm lagging behind. 'She decided to destroy herself, and him, with one gesture: her suicide. Martha was a fan of the grand gesture. She invited Aidan here on the pretext of wanting to commission a picture from him. He said no at first—he worked from inspiration, didn't do commissions, all the predictable shit she knew he'd come out with. She put a stop to it by promising him fifty grand. The noble artist was willing to take a bribe, it turned out, as long as the bribe was big enough. Martha sent him a cheque for fifty grand the next day, along with directions to this place—her little writing hideaway.'

I can't disguise my shock. 'Fifty grand? She had access to that kind of money?'

'You haven't got a clue, have you? For people like me and Martha—for your average Villiers girl—fifty grand isn't "that kind of money". It's about the equivalent of what, I don't know, maybe five hundred pounds would be to you.' She raises her eyebrows. 'Sorry. I didn't mean that to sound quite as patronising as it did.'

'I can guess the rest,' I say, wanting it to be over. 'He came here, and she hanged herself in front of him.'

'She had it all set up. She was standing on a table. She'd left the cottage's front door open, put music on . . .'

' "Survivor," ' I murmur.

'Right. So that he'd know she was in, so that he'd walk in and look for her. He found her in the dining room, on the table with a rope round her neck, attached to the light fitting. He didn't say anything when he saw her like that, and she said only one thing to him: "You can keep the fifty grand. I won't be needing it." And then she jumped.' Both of us shift suddenly as Mary says the last word, conscious of how it would feel to fall through the air, your fall broken only by a sharp jerk that snaps your neck.

'Why were you there?' I ask, trying to banish the creeping hollow sensation Mary's story has left me with.

'Martha and I were inseparable,' she says, her eyes and voice flat.

'Until she met Aidan?'

'Even after that.'

'So . . .' I struggle to pin down what's niggling at me. Was Mary in the room when Martha put the rope round her neck? Did she egg her on? Did she stand by and watch, saying nothing. *Aidan and Mary, the two people closest to Martha, both artists.* 'Did Aidan know you were a painter too?' I ask.

'I wasn't. Before Martha died, I'd never painted anything in my life, apart from the bowls of fruit people put in front of me at school.'

Impossible, I want to say. 'But . . .' *You're too good for that to be true.*

'It's true,' says Mary. She kneels down in front of the dressing table mirror, lifts her chin and strokes her neck. 'Aidan was the one who made me start painting. We . . . both of us were there, when she died. Neither of us saved her. Afterwards, we were both complete wrecks. We only had each other to talk to about what had happened. No one else would have understood. Aidan told me painting was what he'd always done to get rid of his pain. He didn't say "pain". He called it "all the shit that's in my head". There was shit in my head too, plenty of it, so I took his advice. He helped me, told me I was good, properly good. He said I was better than him.'

She breaks off. 'There's no excuse for the way I . . . *forgave* him everything he'd done to her. He told me what it had been like for him, and it sounded so different. Not at all like what

Martha had told me. Even knowing how he'd treated her . . . As I said, there's no excuse.'

'Did you and Aidan . . .'

Mary snorts. 'We became friends, nothing more. Or rather, I thought we were.' She turns her head the other way, stares at her lined face, reflected. 'So, now you see how selfish I am. I don't hate Aidan for what he did to Martha. I like to tell myself I do, because it makes me feel better about myself, but it's not true. I hate him for what he did to me.'

I haven't got it in me to ask.

Mary rises to her feet. 'Come on,' she says. 'I'll show you.'

I follow her out of the bedroom. It's less smoky on the landing, though some of the smell has drifted out. We go down the steep staircase into the large kitchen, through an open-plan lounge-cum-study with a beamed ceiling. This leads through to a narrow hall, at one end of which is a closed door. Mary reaches up for the key that's balanced on top of the door frame. 'I keep it locked,' she says. 'What's inside is precious to me. No one's seen it apart from Cecily, Aidan and the police.'

'The police?'

'The various unlucky members of the Farnham constabulary who come round periodically, when I get paranoid, to check Aidan isn't hiding in the house with an axe. Except the one last night, he didn't ask to look inside. They're so sick of me by now, they don't check properly any more.'

She unlocks the door and pulls it open, standing aside so that I can see. The stench of paint fumes from the room is almost unbearable. At first I don't know what I'm looking at. An enormous pile of something: rubbish. *As if a skip full of some kind of debris has been emptied onto the floor.* The mess looks fluffy in parts, like feathers from many different birds, none of them matching, but I can also see wood, cloth, every colour I can imagine, and pieces of . . . is it canvas?

Abberton. Inside the outline of a person, this is what Mary stuck on to the picture: rags and rubble from this pile.

I see, all at once, dozens of tiny fragments: a painted smile, a fingernail, a patch of grey-blue sky, a patch of something flesh-coloured. A small chair, no more than a few centimetres high and wide, torn in half. 'Pictures,' I breathe. 'These were paintings, canvases. And frames, sawn into pieces. How many . . .?'

The mound is nearly as high as I am. Over it, someone has splashed several tins of paint, maybe even dozens, so that it looks as if it's been wrapped in multi-coloured string. Hard, dried pools of paint cover the floor. *As if someone stood next to the pile with a tin of paint and poured it in, so that it dripped all the way through and seeped out at the bottom.* The same colours have been splashed randomly over the cream and gold wallpaper, over the three large framed botanical prints on the walls: yellow, blue, red, white, green, black. At the back of the room there's a dining table, which has been pushed up against the large sash window, with more tins of paint on it, as well as a portable telephone lying beside its base, an ashtray, three un-opened tins of Heinz ravioli and a rusty tin-opener.

'Pictures,' Mary confirms. 'Frames. And stretchers—the wooden structures you stretch canvas around. I like the way that word sounds medical, makes you think of emergencies. It seems appropriate. If it hadn't been for an emergency, I'd never have picked up a paintbrush.'

I am transfixed by the size of the mountain of broken wood and shredded canvas, the glimpses I keep getting of landscapes and interiors, people's faces and clothes: an earlobe, a necklace, a jacket pocket. It's almost as if some pieces have been cut deliberately larger than the rest, to allow part of something to survive. I narrow my eyes, blur my focus, and it looks like a heap of multi-coloured precious stones. The pile stretches almost all the way across the room, leaving only a small gap on either side.

'Whose paintings are . . . were they?' I ask.

'Mine,' says Mary. 'All mine, now. I got them back.' She turns to me and smiles. 'Welcome to my exhibition.'

20

5/3/08

Charlie found Simon where he'd said he would be, in the bar at King's Cross station, surrounded by a large group of squaddies in uniform, all of whom looked younger than twenty and had foam moustaches from the pints they were not so much drinking as throwing at their faces. Simon was wedged into a small space between a table that looked sticky with weeks-old beer and a fruit machine that leaned to one side.

There was no second chair at the table, so Charlie pulled one over. She missed the days when pubs and bars were smoky. Devoid of the smell of cigarettes, they were life-size models, not the real thing. 'No drink?' she said.

Simon shook his head in irritation. *Shut up, I'm thinking.* Charlie knew the look well.

'Mine's a vodka and orange.' She perched on the cleaner half of the chair she'd grabbed, wishing she'd chosen more carefully. When he didn't move, she sighed and said, 'I hate London cabbies. They never shut up. You'd have thought seeing me with my phone clamped to my ear . . .'

'Who've you been talking to? I've been trying to ring you.'

'To say?'

'Gibbs phoned. He and Sellers were at Ruth Bussey's place.'

Charlie pressed her eyes shut. 'They saw the wall.' She tried to tell herself nothing bad had happened, nothing new. Sellers and Gibbs had known already. Everybody knew already.

'It's not as bad as you feared,' said Simon. 'She's not going to break into your house in the middle of the night and stab you. She admires you.'

'Admires me?'

'She collects self-help books. One of them's about building up self-esteem—I can't remember the title. I was in with Milward when Gibbs rang me. He said the book's got exercises in it, things you're supposed to do if you want to learn to love yourself. Techniques and tasks and stuff. Homework, I suppose you could call it. One of them's to identify someone you admire who's been through a tough time and come out stronger and wiser.' Simon shrugged. 'You get the idea. Oh—the book said it should be someone famous, so that you can collect stuff from newspapers and magazines about them. A celebrity.'

'You're making this up,' Charlie breathed.

'Does it sound like the sort of thing I'd make up? There was a receipt in the book—Bussey bought it from Word in September 2006.'

'Exactly when I was newsworthy,' said Charlie, trying to make light of it.

'Exactly when you thought the whole country wanted you dead, yeah. You were wrong. At least one person didn't. If she admired the way you—'

'Move on,' Charlie warned him. 'My self-esteem issues are my business—not yours and not Ruth Bussey's.' A sudden surge of emotion made it difficult for her to breathe. She looked down at her hands, picking at her fingernails. 'Did the book say to cover an *entire wall* with character assassinations of your chosen celebrity?' she asked. But there had been other articles stuck up alongside the hatchet jobs, she remembered—harmless ones about her community work, and pictures of her in uniform, smiling. Yes, there definitely had. Somewhere along the way Charlie had allowed herself to forget that because it didn't tally with her worst case scenario: that Ruth Bussey was revelling in her suffering, that the bedroom wall display was there for no other reason than to humiliate her all over again.

'Talk to Sellers or Gibbs if you want the details,' said Simon wearily. 'At first, yes, you put up everything you can find on whoever you choose, positive and negative write-ups, pictures of them looking their best and pictures of them looking like shit, all together. You look at it every day, if you haven't got anything else to occupy your time, and you . . .' Seeing Charlie's stunned expression, Simon snapped, 'Look, don't blame me if it sounds way-out. I'm only telling you what Gibbs told me.'

'Go on,' said Charlie. She wondered if Ruth had drawn up a shortlist. Which other disgraced celebrities had made headlines in September 2006? Not that Charlie was a celebrity. Still, she was curious to know if she'd had competition. 'You look at it every day, and?'

'You focus on how whoever you've chosen hasn't allowed their mistakes to defeat them, how they've bounced back, that sort of thing. The rest's predictable: you realise no one's perfect, everyone has their ups and downs, including you. Once you've got that straight in your head, you're allowed to take down anything that shows the person you admire in a bad light. In place of what you've taken down, you put up some of your favourite photographs of yourself, and there's your finished product: a wall-mounted display of you and the person you admire, both looking your best, having triumphed over all things nasty. I might have got a couple of details wrong, but that's the essence of it. The book even specifies that it ought to be a bedroom wall, so you can see it first thing in the morning and last thing at night.'

'Outrageous,' said Charlie. Still, she felt a little better. The idea of somebody thinking her admirable . . . Now she knew beyond doubt that Ruth Bussey was nuts.

'Bussey had scribbled your name on the relevant page and put a big fat tick next to it,' said Simon. 'You should be flattered.'

'Is she okay?' Charlie felt guilty for caring more now than she had before. So that's why Ruth had come to her last Friday.

If the person you most admire works for the police, and your boyfriend's scaring you out of your wits saying he murdered someone, the next step is obvious, surely—almost meant to be. *And when you see that the object of your admiration doesn't have a clue how to help you, what do you think then?*

'No one knows where Bussey is, Gibbs said. Same with Seed and Trelease.'

'She hadn't put any pictures of herself up,' Charlie said quietly. She looked at Simon. 'On the wall. Did the book say you're supposed to put up your *favourite* photos of yourself?'

'I think that's what Gibbs said, yeah.'

Charlie knew why Ruth hadn't got that far with the exercise: eighteen months after wasting her money on a self-esteem manual, she still didn't like any pictures of herself. Flattering or unflattering, it didn't matter; all images of her were images of a victim, someone to be reviled or pitied depending on your point of view. *Takes one to know one.*

'What? What are you thinking?'

'Nothing.'

Simon looked stumped. Charlie guessed he was wondering how hard he ought to try to make her talk about her feelings, and hoping that the answer was not at all.

'I'd live where I live now,' he said, after a few seconds of awkward silence.

'Sorry?'

'You asked me before—where I'd live if I could live anywhere.'

A quick glance told her he meant it. 'Where you live now? You mean Spilling, or your house?'

'My house is in Spilling. I mean both. I like where I am—why would I want to live anywhere else?'

'I'd live in Torquay,' Charlie heard her voice harden as she said it. No way was she moving into Simon's place after they were married. The kitchen was as narrow as a drainpipe and the bathroom was downstairs, behind it. The house was right on the pavement, too; people peered into the lounge as they walked past. And it was too close to Simon's parents. *No way.*

'I'd never live by the sea,' he said. 'It's one big, blue dead-end. I'd feel hemmed in.'

'You wouldn't be.' What other insane opinions was he harbouring that she didn't know about? 'You could take a boat.'

'Mary Trelease killed Gemma Crowther. To get her picture back—*Abberton*.'

There goes our intimate chat, thought Charlie. She added 'wouldn't like to live by the sea' to the list of what she knew about her fiancé.

'She was outside Crowther's flat on Monday night, when I was there—the same person who saw me saw her. She stayed after I'd gone. She knew Seed and Crowther were inside having a cosy evening together, with her picture up on the wall . . .'

'No one broke in, remember?'

'Trelease could easily have persuaded Crowther to let her in somehow, or maybe she used the gun from the off, backed Crowther into the flat at gunpoint, down the hall and into the front room where she shot her. She wanted her picture back— perhaps she was jealous, too. If she followed Aidan Seed to London, that suggests he was on her mind.'

'Maybe you were the one she was following,' Charlie suggested. 'Maybe you're the person she most admires in the whole wide world. No—that really is implausible.'

If she'd been trying to upset him, she didn't succeed. Usually Simon was easily riled. He only wasn't when he was in the grip of one of his fixations. Charlie knew the signs: verbal abuse rolled off him like rain off an umbrella. And that occupied look in his eyes, so that you could almost see his brain whirring . . .

'Trelease killed Crowther and made Seed go with her somewhere,' he said. 'She had a gun with her, must have had a car too. Wherever she took Seed, they went in her car, having first locked the painting in the boot of his, to make sure any suspicion fell on him.'

'Why must she have had a car?'

'She couldn't hold a gun to his head as they walked along the street, could she? If she had a car, she could make him drive, sit behind him and—'

'I don't believe this!'

'You said the picture hooks in Crowther's gums was a woman's touch,' Simon reminded her. 'Crowther was shot, then someone carefully knocked her teeth out with a hammer and replaced them with picture hooks. Compare that to Seed's description of strangling Mary Trelease—a killing at close range, her struggling, naked, right next to him, or under him, or on top of him . . .'

'So now he killed her while they were having sex? Another detail you've invented.'

'. . . Seed feeling his thumbnail pressing into his own flesh as he held his hands closed around her throat . . .'

'You forget, you're describing a killing we *know* didn't happen.'

'I think it did,' said Simon. 'Aidan Seed killed someone, exactly as he described to me. Not Mary Trelease—someone else.'

'Then why say it was Trelease?'

'That's what we have to find out. The first step's obvious.'

'Not to me it isn't,' said Charlie.

'Seed grew up in the Culver Valley on a council estate—that *Times* article said so. Megson Crescent used to be council-owned. Seed's in his early forties—let's assume he didn't kill anyone before he was eleven . . .'

'Did they start quite so young in those days?' said Charlie glumly.

'Mary Trelease bought 15 Megson Crescent only two years ago. Who else has lived in that house? Who's died there?'

Charlie stared at him. 'Bloody hell,' she murmured.

'We've been focusing on the name instead of the other details. Like the house.'

'But . . .' Charlie was shaking her head. 'Why offer a full confession—complete with an address, a description of the scene, the method of killing—and lie about the victim?'

'I can't answer that. Yet,' said Simon. 'It might not be as crazy as it seems, though. Some truth, some fiction: that's the mixture that makes for the best lies. Mary Trelease's death is the fictional part. She's alive—we know that.'

'And the true part . . .' Much as Charlie would have liked to laugh at his theory, she couldn't help wondering if there might be something in it. There wasn't a bed in the front bedroom of 15 Megson Crescent now, but before Mary moved in there might well have been. Most people put beds in their bedrooms.

'Aidan Seed killed someone in that house,' said Simon. 'Someone who used to live there. Years ago—just like he told Ruth Bussey.'

21

Wednesday 5 March 2008

'Aidan and I used to paint in this room,' says Mary. 'Together. For hours at a time, without speaking. After Martha died, I had a key cut for him, for the cottage. He often stayed overnight.' She turns to me. 'He slept in the spare room, where you slept last night.'

I make sure to keep my face neutral. There's something I don't feel quite right about in this room, but I'm not sure what it is. I stare at the pile of ruined paintings in front of me, barely able to believe it's real.

'Do you mind that I didn't tell you?' It dawns on me that Mary is talking about Aidan, the spare bed. 'It's only a room. I don't believe rooms retain memories of the past. There's no such thing as an atmosphere—it's in people's minds, like everything of any interest.'

'You had a key cut for Aidan?' Suddenly, it seems important to check all the facts. 'But it's not your cottage. You don't own it.'

Mary shrugs this off. 'So? I'm the one who uses it.'

'How did Martha's mother feel about Aidan staying here?' If I had a daughter who'd hanged herself after being treated badly by a man, I'd want him nowhere near me or any house of mine.

If I'd watched my best friend hang herself, or my lover, or ex-lover, the last thing I'd want is to spend any time at all in the room where it happened.

'I didn't tell Cecily,' says Mary. 'I didn't tell anyone.'

'Why didn't Martha's parents give up the cottage after Martha died?' I ask. 'Why do they carry on paying the rent so that you can use it—someone who's not even related to them?'

'I'm a leftover from Martha's life.' Mary smiles. 'Cecily doesn't think much of me, but she wants me around even so—a dog-eared souvenir of her precious daughter.'

My eyes return to the mound in front of me. 'How many paintings did you cut up to make . . . this?'

'I didn't count. Hundreds.'

'Whose were they?'

'Mine. I painted them and I owned them. Though for a while I thought I'd sold some of them to other people.'

I wait for her to say more.

'Aidan used to tell me when my paintings weren't good enough. He was always right, which made it worse. Eventually, with his help, it happened less and less often. He doesn't find it easy to give praise, but the criticisms stopped. One day he asked me if I felt ready for my first exhibition. He mentioned a gallery I'd never heard of, said he knew the owner. If I didn't mind, he said, he'd take my pictures to London for this guy to look at.' Mary barks out a laugh. 'Of course I didn't mind. I was thrilled. Aidan took the pictures—eighteen of them, there were. Came back the next day with the best news—the gallery wanted me. They wanted to give me a show.'

I watch the happiness and excitement drain from her face as she remembers what happened next. 'I don't know why I didn't ask to go to London with Aidan, see the gallery for myself—I did none of that, asked for nothing. Aidan kept saying, "Leave it to me," and I did. When I asked him when the private view would be, he told me there wasn't going to be one. This gallery never did them, he said. Now I know there's no such thing as an art gallery that doesn't do previews—they're crucial for sales, and publicity. At the time, though, I was new to the art world. Aidan was the experienced one, the one who'd had a sell-out exhibition and residencies at Trinity College, Cambridge and the National Portrait Gallery. I believed what he told me. I said I wanted to meet the gallery owner who'd liked my work, but Aidan advised against it. "They hate it when artists hang around," he told me. "Better to stay away, use me as a middleman to communicate any messages." He said the gallery owner was intrigued by the idea of me, and we needed to keep it that way by making sure I kept my distance. Like a fool, I fell for it.

'He brought me back an exhibition catalogue. Nothing fancy, just a few sheets of paper folded in the middle and stapled. But it had the titles of my paintings, the dates of the exhibition, some biographical notes about me. I was so proud of it.' Mary blinks away tears. 'Aidan went back and forth to London—or I thought he did—to check on how things were going. Well; it was going well, that was what he said whenever he came back. He seemed genuinely pleased for me. My pictures were selling— I couldn't believe it. One day Aidan came back and told me they were all sold. He even . . .' Her face screws up in agony. 'He had a sales list, so that I could see who'd bought what. There were nine names on it. I don't need to tell you what they were.'

I have no idea what she's talking about. How could I know who had bought her paintings?

'The first was Abberton,' she says softly. 'Don't say the others, please. I can't bear to hear them.'

A shiver runs the length of my back.

'Aidan took me out for dinner that night, to celebrate the sell-out. That's when I betrayed Martha.'

'You spent the night with Aidan.' I'd prefer to say it myself rather than have her tell me.

'No.' Her face sets in a mask of displeasure. 'Aidan and I have never had sex. Martha slept with him, and I knew what a failure that had been.'

'How did you betray Martha?' I ask.

'I told Aidan that if I had to choose between a happy, fulfilling personal life and my work, I'd choose the work. My painting. He smiled at me when I said it, and we both knew what it meant: that we were the ones, that Martha had never been like us. We'd discussed it, you see—Aidan told me Martha had admitted to having lied to the journalist who interviewed them.' Mary squints at me. 'Did I tell you about that?'

I nod.

'She pretended she'd choose her writing, when really she'd have given it up like a shot if she could have kept Aidan. He despised her for lying. He despised her shallow attitude to her work—he didn't want to be with someone like that. Martha didn't deserve Aidan, she never did.' Mary presses her hand against her mouth.

'Tell me about the exhibition,' I say. *Eighteen paintings. Eighteen empty frames on Aidan's walls.* But I don't know there are eighteen of them. I never counted.

'The day after our celebratory dinner, once I came back down to earth, I started to ask questions: when would I get the money? Was the gallery empty now, if my paintings had all sold? Aidan teased me for my ignorance, explained that the show stays up until the end of the final day, as planned. Buyers collect after take-down and that's when they pay. He'd made me inflate the prices in order to be left with a decent whack once the gallery had taken its commission. He joked about taking commission himself, since he was the one who set it up. I never stopped to wonder why he'd want to help me to that extent. He was spending more time on me and my exhibition than he was on his own paintings. If I'd thought about it, I'd probably have decided it was down to my talent, which had overwhelmed him.'

I hear the self-hatred that underlies the casual sarcasm.

'I knew how good I was. I could see it. Aidan was an artist—artists should care about art more than anything. I believed he did. Until I found myself in London one day visiting a friend, and decided to disobey his orders.'

'You went to the gallery?'

'I couldn't resist.' Mary turns on me. 'Would you have been able to? I thought it couldn't do any harm, as long as I didn't go in. I was going to look in the window, nothing more, just to

catch a glimpse of my work in that strange, exciting setting—a
real gallery. I wanted to see the red sold stickers on the labels . . .' Her words peter out. A solid, paralysing silence de-
scends on the room, one I'm afraid to break.

'Mary? What did you see?'

She doesn't answer. I ask again.

'He should never have told me the name of the gallery. Or he
should have made one up—how hard is it to make up a name?
He's got no imagination. That's why I'm a better artist than he
ever was. Artists need imagination. Connaughton.'

'What's that?'

'The gallery. Connaughton Contemporary. My pictures
weren't there. The man there had never heard of me. I rang Aidan, and when I told him what had happened, what I'd seen—
not seen, rather—he told me to come back to the cottage. His
voice sounded so . . . unwelcoming, so flat, nothing like the person I thought I knew. It was as if he'd been possessed by some
remote, horrible stranger, and the old Aidan had been wiped
out. That's when I remembered that the old Aidan had driven
Martha to suicide. I'd allowed myself to ignore what I knew
about him in my desperation to latch on to someone after Martha's death. We'd experienced the horror of it together—for a
while, that was all that mattered.'

I shut my eyes and think about London, when Aidan's behaviour towards me changed. *Whenever a friend succeeds, something in me dies.* He'd written that in a card to Martha Wyers,
after she sent him a copy of her published novel. Did he set
Mary up for a fall because he was jealous of her talent as a
painter? I wish he was telling me the story instead of Mary, to
help me understand why he did what he did.

'I came back here,' she says quietly. 'The door was open. I
called his name—nothing. So I started looking. I found him in
here. On the floor next to him was a pile—like that one, except
smaller. I had no idea what it was. It just looked like a mess,
although I could see little familiar things, colours and shapes I

recognised, but I didn't grasp the truth until Aidan told me straight out.'

She starts to walk slowly around the mound of detritus. 'He was so proud of his plan to destroy me—he described it as "genius". There was no exhibition, never had been. No one in London had seen my work. Aidan took my paintings—I let him take them—and he destroyed them one by one. Thanks to my trip to London and my lack of self-control, I found out early. He'd been planning *this* . . .' She kicks the heap and lets out a low groan that startles me, as if the pain inside her has a voice of its own, deeper and more raw than hers. 'Planning my *surprise* for the end of the exhibition, when I'd have been expecting a cheque from the gallery.'

'I'm sorry,' I say, understanding at last why she doesn't sell her work, why she keeps it all in her home and entrusts it to no one.

'I stood where you're standing now, sobbing, begging him to tell me why. He said he had another surprise for me. It was an exhibition sales list—not the one he'd given me already, the one he'd faked, but a real one, from his exhibition at TiqTaq. The names, Abberton and co? They were *Aidan's* buyers. Not mine, never mine. All the people I'd imagined loved my work—all along it was Aidan's work they loved.'

'The paintings,' I say, more to myself than to Mary. 'Outlines of people with no faces—because they weren't real.' That's how Aidan knew, how he could predict the series, what Mary would call the eight paintings that followed *Abberton*.

'The ones who bought Aidan's paintings were real enough, I suppose,' she says, off-hand.

'Why? Why would he do something like that?'

'He never told me. That was almost the worst thing. He bragged about what he'd done to me, but he wouldn't explain. As always, he avoided talking about his reasons or his feelings, apart from to say he'd been pleased when we went out for dinner and I said what I did about choosing my work over a happy personal life. It sounds so pompous—I'd barely been painting for a year, at that point—but already it was my life's work. It was all I wanted to do. It still is. When I told Aidan that over dinner, he knew he'd picked the perfect way to damage me beyond repair.'

Seeing my confusion, perhaps mistaking it for disbelief, Mary says, 'Oh, I can give you reasons if you want them. They were clear enough when he threatened me. Before he walked out of this room and out of my life, he put his hands round my throat and squeezed so tight I thought I was going to die. He said, "You're never going to paint another picture. Understand? And you're never going to tell anyone what happened when Martha died. If I find out you've done either, it'll be you swinging from the end of a rope next time."' Mary shudders. 'No one was going to ruin his career, he said. He was going to be a star, and Martha and I couldn't do anything to stop that happening.'

'But . . . Martha committed suicide,' I say numbly.

'He could have saved her,' says Mary. 'By the time he tried, after he'd phoned the ambulance, it was too late. He couldn't risk that becoming public knowledge. Think of it. What a thing to be known for—an act of cowardice that caused the death of a promising young writer who had her whole life ahead of her.'

'But you hadn't said anything so far, and if he hadn't destroyed your pictures, you'd have had no reason to . . .'

'He hated me anyway, long before Martha died. He'd never forgiven me for the letters I sent him when he was at Trinity, messing Martha around. I could see through him, all the way through. I knew he was scared and damaged, too gutless to deal with his problems, preferring to make other people suffer instead. I can prove how much he hated me. Look.' Mary runs from the room. I follow her up the stairs to her bedroom. It's covered in discarded clothes, with no visible floor-space, and stinks of cigarettes. Every drawer in the scratched mahogany chest gapes open. Mary pulls something out of the bottom one. 'This is the sales list from Aidan's exhibition.'

It's handwritten but clearly legible.

'Look at the title of the last painting on the list.'

'*The Murder of Mary Trelease*,' I read. 'He called one of his pictures that?'

'That was the first threat. He took great pleasure in telling me the painting didn't even have me in it, or a murder. He said he liked titles that kept people guessing. Now does it make a bit more sense to you—him confessing to the police that he killed me? It's part of a game he started years ago.'

Her question barely registers. My eyes have fixed on a name I wasn't expecting to see: Saul Hansard. Saul bought one of Aidan's paintings. Abberton, Blandford, Darville, Elstow—they're all there too, under the heading 'Buyers'. Cecily Wyers also bought one of Aidan's paintings, as did someone called Kerry Gatti (Mr).

'You understand why Aidan wants to kill me,' says Mary in a lifeless voice. 'I didn't stop painting. He did. He can't allow that to go unpunished.' She starts to cry. 'I took such care to make sure he never found out. I didn't exhibit my work, didn't sell it—I did everything I could to keep my painting a secret, but he still found out. Thanks to you.' She puts her hand on my arm. 'I don't mean that the way it sounds. I know it's not your fault.' Her fingernails dig into my skin. 'For years, after what he did to me, I painted nothing but him. Over and over again, from memory: how his face looked when he told me what he'd done. Each time I finished a picture of him, I destroyed it immediately and added it to the pile. My exhibition,' she says sadly. 'The only one I'll ever have.'

My heart beats as if someone's bouncing it against the wall of my chest. I stare at the names and addresses of the people who bought Aidan's pictures, picture I've never seen. If I had them in front of me, would it make anything clearer? Would they take me closer to the person Aidan really is? I try to tell myself they wouldn't, but it's useless. The need to see them swells inside me—a physical craving, beyond rationality. It's obvious where I ought to start: with my friend, Saul Hansard.

I look up, catch Mary's eye. I don't even have to ask. She knows. She understands. 'I'll call you a cab,' she says.

22

5/3/08

'If we work on the assumption that Aidan Seed strangled some-one—an unknown woman—in the front bedroom at 15 Megson Crescent, that means he can't also have killed Crowther,' said Simon. He'd been to the bar and returned with a pint for him-self and one for Charlie, though she'd told him twice that she wanted a vodka and orange. 'The methods are too different.'

'The situations might have been different,' she pointed out. 'One might have been spur of the moment, one planned.'

He was silent for a few seconds. Eventually, he said, 'I can't say you're wrong, because I've got nothing solid to back it up. But . . . I don't know, I've never killed anyone, but I doubt kill-ing's like cooking, where you might do it one way one time and another way another time: today you might microwave your baked beans, tomorrow you might heat them on the hob. I reckon for a lot of killers, there's only one way they'd ever kill, either because the method's part of a ritual that's important to them, or because only that one way feels possible. Someone who'd lose his temper and strangle a woman in anger wouldn't kill coldly and dispassionately with a gun—take away the heat of the moment and he couldn't kill at all. A shooter wants to guarantee absolute control. He wouldn't be able to face some-thing as risky as a strangling, in case his victim overpowered him, or—'

'Maybe,' Charlie cut him off. 'Maybe all this is true of most killers, but there could be one—let's call him Aidan Seed—

who *has* killed in more than one way. And who says you have to lose your temper to strangle someone? That could be planned, too.'

'Milward said Seed wasn't their suspect,' said Simon. 'At least admit it's possible: Trelease killed Crowther either because Seed was spending time with her, or because he'd given her *Abberton*, or a bit of both. We know Trelease likes to keep her paintings to herself, doesn't like the idea of other people getting their hands on them. We also know she attacked Ruth Bussey, Seed's girlfriend—maybe she's even killed her by now.'

Charlie groaned. 'You're going to say Mary Trelease is obsessed with Seed and she's killing the other women in his life. That's wild speculation even for you.'

'Do you think we can assume Adam Sands in Martha Wyers' novel is Seed?' Simon asked.

'Definitely. I phoned Trinity College, Cambridge. Martha Wyers applied for the job there that Aidan got. They met at the interview, like Adam Sands and the fictional version of Martha.'

'Then I'm right,' said Simon, as though this were a plain fact. 'Trelease murdered first Wyers and then Crowther because she saw them as rivals for Seed's affection. She'll kill Ruth Bussey for the same reason, if she hasn't already.'

'How does *Abberton* fit in?' Charlie asked.

'I don't know.'

'And where's Seed now? You're saying Trelease made him drive her car somewhere at gunpoint . . .'

'She's killed him.'

'How convenient,' said Charlie drily. 'Everyone I mention, you tell me Mary Trelease has killed them. Evidence? None, which is why you're saying it to me and not to Milward or Kombothekra.'

'Milward's in no mood to listen to me. I fucked up.' He glared at Charlie, daring her to criticise him. 'She was coming round to trusting me, and I threatened her. She as good as threw me out on the street. As for Kombothekra . . .' Simon sighed heavily. 'He rang me before, wanting to give me an update. I called him a coward.'

'A coward?' Charlie was confused.

'This situation—us being out of the loop, him breaking rank and drip-feeding us information—the way I saw it, it was win-win for him. He keeps us up to speed and buys our loyalty—no way we're going to serve him up on a plate to Proust once he's stuck his neck out for us, right? He can tell us as much as he wants without risking anything. The more he leaks, the more grateful we are, the more we return the favour by protecting him. To us, it looks like he's going out on a limb because he's on our side. To the Snowman, he's the good boy who never puts a foot wrong.' Simon shrugs. 'Easy way for a yes-man like Kombothekra to look like he stands for something. That's what I thought until Gibbs phoned.'

'And now?'

'I was wrong,' said Simon. 'Seems Kombothekra's support for us is more public than I gave him credit for. Sellers and Gibbs know he's been in regular contact with us, and he's been doggedly fighting my corner with Proust, too. None of which I knew when I laid into him.'

'Sam doesn't hold grudges,' said Charlie. 'Tell him you're sorry and tell him your overblown theory. For what it's worth, I think Seed's a hundred times more likely to have killed Crowther than Mary Trelease is. He's got a *real* motive—Crowther spent three days torturing his girlfriend.'

Simon was shaking his head. 'Seed's not the sort to take revenge. Nor to harm anyone deliberately—which is how I know that, whoever he strangled at 15 Megson Crescent, it wasn't planned.'

'*What?* Where are you getting all this from?'

'Have you heard of George Fox?' Simon asked.

'No.'

'Born 1624, died 1691. He was the founding father of Quakerism, pretty much invented the whole thing single-handedly. Gemma Crowther rated him.'

'How do you know?'

'I went to an internet café when Milward chucked me out. You don't have to charm information out of computers, or thank them afterwards.'

Or make love to them, thought Charlie. Maybe Simon would prefer to marry a Toshiba Equium M70. Charlie only knew the name of that particular model because she owed her sister one.

'Crowther's written about George Fox on at least four Quaker websites, quoting his words of spiritual wisdom like she thinks the sun shines out of his arse. On one of the sites, some-one's posted a comment with the heading "Cobblers", taking her to task, someone with a not-so-high opinion of Fox. Guess who?'

'Aidan . . . oh. Len Smith?'

Simon shook his head. 'Seed used the name Len Smith for the Quaker meetings, when he was pretending to be Crowther's friend, but online he used a different alias to pour scorn on her views: Adam Sands.'

Charlie's eyes widened. 'He called himself after the character in Martha Wyers' novel, the one based on him?' *As if, after all these years, he wanted to endorse her version of him.* Was it guilt, Charlie wondered, because she loved him enough to take her own life and he didn't love her at all?

'George Fox was an arrogant twat who wouldn't be told anything by anyone,' said Simon. 'He was a tyrant—smug, rude, tactless, intolerant, *unforgiving*—remember that, it's important. Worst of all, Fox dismissed the inevitability of sin.'

'That sounds complicated,' said Charlie, wondering what any of it had to do with Aidan Seed.

'The idea that human beings regularly fuck up and need to ask God's forgiveness when they do,' Simon explained. 'I grew up with the idea of sin. It was as much a part of my childhood as illicitly watching *Grange Hill*. That's a Catholic upbringing for you—saying your Hail Marys every time you think a bad thought or lie to your mother.'

'So saying Hail Marys is like writing lines, is it? Ten, fifty, a hundred, depending on how bad the sin?'

'Pretty much,' said Simon. 'I hated it—still hate the idea of it—but I can see now that it had one thing in its favour: the emphasis on the difference between right and wrong, the idea that wrongs need to be put right. You have to say sorry, make amends. Basically the set-up is that God's the boss, the Pope's next after him, your parish priest's next, then your parents, and you're a piece of kindling waiting to be dropped into the flames of Hell.'

'Sounds great,' said Charlie. 'What a carefree childhood you must have had.'

'I'm not talking about me,' said Simon, blushing, though he manifestly had been, unless Charlie was confused and it was George Fox who'd been watching *Grange Hill*. 'Fox claimed he had the light inside him and was therefore incapable of sin—that's tantamount to claiming he was God. Other people sinned, lesser beings, and when they did he withheld his forgiveness. Adam Sands had a story to prove it. I'll show you the website, you can read it. There was another prominent Quaker, a man called James Nayler, who got himself in trouble for allowing some of his adoring women disciples to fawn over him in public once too often. He was accused of blasphemy, of parodying Christ's entry into Jerusalem.'

Charlie rolled her eyes. 'Some people really need to get over themselves,' she said.

'Nayler suffered a range of hideous punishments for what was seen as his blasphemy—he was imprisoned, branded, pilloried, whipped. Fox distanced himself from Nayler when Nayler was at his lowest point, and when Nayler got out of prison, a broken man, when he publicly repented and renounced his follies in several statements, wanting nothing more than to be reconciled with Fox, Fox rebuffed him.'

'You sound like you're quoting,' said Charlie. ' "Rebuffed"?'

'That was the word Adam Sands used. From his tone, he

seemed pretty incensed that the founder of this enlightened, peaceful religion that promotes tolerance and forgiveness was a shithead hypocrite—guilty of the very same self-aggrandising attitudes he couldn't forgive Nayler for. As Sands, Seed ended his contribution to the website by saying, and I quote, "Without contrition and forgiveness, there's no hope for any of us. How can you want to be part of anything set up by a shitbird like George Fox?"'

'Did Crowther reply?' Charlie asked.

'Only in the words of Fox himself—a long quote, something about the New Jerusalem and how it's only available to those who don't vex and grieve the spirit of God. Those who do are beasts and whores, and they're covered over by the spirit of error and dispatched to Babylon.'

'Lovely,' Charlie muttered. 'I think I'm starting to get an inkling of what attracted the likes of Crowther and Elton to Quakerism.'

'Now can you see why I don't think Seed's a revenge-motivated killer? If you're going to murder someone, why not just do it? Why pretend to be their mate and argue with them on internet discussion forums first?'

'Here's a question for you,' said Charlie. 'If Seed didn't kill Crowther and was never planning to, and if he wasn't her friend or a Quaker either, what the hell was he doing hanging round with her at all? Why did he give her *Abberton*?'

Simon's expression darkened. 'Not a clue,' he said ungraciously, enraged as always by his ignorance.

Charlie opened her bag, pulled out the exhibition catalogue Jan Garner had given her and put it in front of him, wondering if he was in a fit state to pay attention. She could have boasted that, unlike him, she'd made real progress, but she'd have felt too cruel and, besides, it was about to become obvious.

'*The Murder of Mary Trelease*,' Simon read aloud. 'Oil and watercolour. £2,000.'

Charlie passed him the sales list. 'That's two thousand quid eight years ago, don't forget. J. E. J. Abberton mustn't be short of a bob or two. Only one problem: his address, as listed there, doesn't exist.'

'Are you sure?'

She tried not to take the question as an insult. 'I spent what felt like hours on the phone to 118118, checking and double-checking. There were eighteen paintings in Aidan Seed's exhibition. Three were sold to real people with real addresses: Cecily Wyers, Saul Hansard and Kerry Gatti.'

'You reckon Cecily Wyers is Martha's mother?'

'Seems likely, based on what Jan Garner said about a mother and daughter fighting over whether to buy a picture.'

Simon nodded his agreement.

'Cecily, Gatti and Hansard bought one picture each, leaving fifteen. Those were sold to our old friends, the gang of nine.' She read the names aloud, out of the alphabetical order she was used to. 'Mrs E. Heathcote, Dr Edward Winduss, Mr P. L. Rodwell, Sylvia and Maurice Blandford, Mrs C. A. Goundry, Ruth Margerison, Mr J. E. J. Abberton, E. & F. Darville, Professor Rodney Elstow. The Darvilles bought four pictures, Rodney Elstow three and Dr Edward Winduss two. The others bought one each.' Charlie paused to take a quick breath. 'The addresses Jan's written down for these nine buyers don't exist. Or rather, eight of them don't exist at all, and one—'

'They're not ex-directory?'

'Nope.'

'I don't suppose it's possible none of the nine has a telephone,' said Simon.

'How likely is that? Anyway, no. I rang the post office once I'd finished with directory enquiries. They don't exist, Simon. Apart from Ruth Margerison's.'

Simon looked down at the list. 'Garstead Cottage, The Avenue, Wrecclesham . . .'

'Villiers is in Wrecclesham, the boarding school Wyers and Trelease went to. While I was on to the post office, I asked for the school's postcode and full address, and guess what also turned up under the "Villiers" listing? Ruth Margerison's address and postcode.'

Simon frowned. 'I don't follow.'

'Villiers' grounds are so vast, they cover several postcodes. There are about twenty school buildings in total, all listed individually. One of them's Garstead Cottage. It's even on The Avenue, which must be the name of a road within the grounds. I rang Villiers, asked to be put through to Ruth Margerison at Garstead Cottage, and was told nobody by that name lived there.'

'Did you ask who did?'

'Yeah, and I got nowhere. Every time I ring that place, I get tight-lipped politeness and no help whatsoever. No one wants to talk about Martha Wyers.'

'We need to get down there.' Simon drained the dregs of his pint. 'We're the police—they have to talk to us. They don't know we're unofficially suspended.'

'I rang Jan Garner in the cab on the way here,' said Charlie. 'Asked her if she had records of how all these people paid for their pictures. She didn't, not that far back, and she couldn't remember. All that's on the sales sheet for each painting is a tick, to indicate the buyer's paid. She says at least one paid in cash—she remembered that because it was so unusual.'

'If the addresses don't exist, maybe the people don't either,' said Simon.

'One thing Jan did remember: most of them she didn't meet in person. She said only three of the pictures sold at the private view.'

'Cecily Wyers, Kerry Gatti and Saul Hansard?'

'She couldn't say for sure, but she said it was possible. Most of the others rang up later. Payment and merchandise were exchanged by post and courier.'

Simon frowned. 'Is that usual?'

'Jan says not. She took it as a mark of how far word had

spread about Aidan's work—that people were buying it without having seen it. Two of the nine, Elstow and Winduss, said they wanted first refusal on any paintings Seed did in the future—Jan made a note of it on the file.'

'Bit gullible, isn't she? All these buyers she's never laid eyes on . . .'

'She was making money, selling pictures—she's hardly going to question that, is she?' said Charlie. 'The most successful exhibition she's ever had.'

'Villiers.' Simon stood up, picked up his book. 'That's my next port of call. Coming?'

'Shouldn't we take this to Milward first?' Charlie asked.

'You can if you want,' said Simon. 'I'll bow out. If I see her again, I'll end up decking her.'

Charlie couldn't imagine Milward would be interested in a catalogue from a years-old art exhibition. 'No,' she said. 'I'll head back home. One of us needs to talk to Kerry Gatti and it looks like that one's going to have to be me.' She sighed. 'My lucky day. Yet another one.'

23

Wednesday 5 March 2008

I jolt awake to the sound of a loud voice, a man's, talking about traffic. The radio. I'm in a car I don't recognise, with grey leather seats and a small tree hanging down from the rear-view mirror, like in a cab. Slowly, my brain puts the pieces together: this is the taxi Mary ordered to take me to the station.

'Why are we on the motorway?' I ask the driver. Through the gap between his seat and his headrest, I can see a patch of pink neck, white hair so neat and even it looks like a carpet, ending in a perfect straight line at the base of his skull. All three lanes of traffic are stationary. We're in the middle one. Ahead, a few people have climbed out of their cars and are stretching, or leaning in through open windows to talk to other drivers. I wonder how long we've been here, how long I was asleep. It's getting dark outside.

'You want Spilling, don't you?'

'I was going to get the train,' I tell him. 'I thought you were taking me to a station.'

'I was told to take you all the way, miss.'

'No.' I push away the desire to drift back into sleep's comforting oblivion. 'I haven't got enough money for . . .'

'You won't be needing any,' he says, twisting the mirror so that we can see one another. His eyes are grey, with pouches of skin above and below them, and heavy white eyebrows that sprout forward instead of lying flat against his skin. 'It's on the account. All I'll need from you's a signature when we get there. If we get there,' he adds cheerfully.

'The account?'

'Villiers.'

'There's been a misunderstanding,' I tell him.

'No misunderstanding, miss. I was told to take you to Spilling. Looks like we might be in for a long haul, though. There's been an accident two junctions ahead and they've closed traffic down to one lane. Are you thirsty? There's some water in the freezer-bag back there. I'd have told you before, but you were out for the count.'

To my right, in the footwell, there's a squat blue case. I undo my seat belt, lean down and unzip it. There are eight unopened bottles of mineral water in its chilled interior.

'Help yourself,' says the driver. 'They're for you, not for me.'

I'm confused. How can they be for me? Why would I need eight bottles of water? 'I'm fine, thanks,' I say, uncomfortable with him watching me. 'Really, I'd prefer it if you dropped me at a station.' There's a leather pocket attached to the back of his seat, with the top of a glossy, red-covered magazine sticking out of it: *The Insider.*

'New to Villiers, are you? You look too young to have a daughter there. Job interview, was it?'

'I was visiting someone.'

'First time? That explains why you're not used to the Rolls-Royce treatment. If you were a parent or a teacher, or even one of the girls, you'd expect nothing less. Between me, you and Barney McGrew, it's nice to meet someone who doesn't take too much for granted once in a while. Not a Villiers girl yourself, are you?'

'No.'

'I can tell you're not. Villiers is our main account—we're the only firm they use, and that's why: for the service we provide. Would you like the radio on now that you're awake? Sorry if it disturbed you before. I was keeping it on to hear the traffic bulletins.'

'I don't mind.' Talking is using up energy I can't spare. I need to think about what I'll say to Saul. Having refused to face him in person for so long, I have no right to turn up without warning and fire questions at him. Knowing he'll be delighted to see me, that he'll answer them willingly, only makes it harder.

I thought Saul had shown me all the art he owned. Why didn't he show me Aidan's picture? Before the day Mary attacked me at the gallery, we used to have dinner together from time to time, either at Saul's house, with his family, or at mine, where it would be only me and him; I felt bad about that, but Blantyre Lodge is too small for a proper dinner party. The main point of those evenings was to show each other new paintings we'd bought. We joked about our 'collections'. Saul used to say, 'You and I are the taste-makers of the future, Ruth. Once all the pickled baby skeletons and diamond-studded skulls and unmade beds have been seen for the shams they are, you and I will be there to lead the way. True art will once again reign supreme.'

Does Saul know where Aidan is? Does he know why Aidan called one of his paintings *The Murder of Mary Trelease*?

'Radio Two all right for you, miss?' asks the driver. 'Or would you prefer a ditty or two? I've got some CDs.'

The word 'ditty' makes me think of *It's a long way to Tipperary* and *Pack up your troubles in your old kit bag*—songs I was forced to learn at school and hated. 'The radio's okay,' I tell him.

'There's a copy of the school magazine in the pocket behind me,' he says. 'Latest issue. You're welcome to have a decco if you get bored. Get a glimpse of how the other half lives.'

One half dies. The other half lives.

I pull *The Insider* out of the leather pouch and start to flick through the pages. There are photographs of schoolgirls in yellow blouses and maroon blazers, standing in lines, smiling. Each picture represents an achievement—money raised for charity, a victory in an independent schools' public-speaking competition. On the next page there are more pictures of Villiers girls, this time in yellow tracksuits and swimwear, holding up trophies. I see Claire Draisey, the woman I met last night, also in a yellow tracksuit, and find out from reading the caption that as well as being Director of Boarding, she coaches the netball and synchronised swimming teams.

On the opposite page there's a picture of a modern-looking building, a white-walled hexagon with large windows on every side. I'm about to pass over it when the name 'Cecily Wyers' catches my attention. The building has been named after her. I read the paragraph beneath the photo. It quotes Martha Wyers' mother, an old Villiers girl, as saying she's always been passionate about the arts, which is why she and her husband donated most of the money that turned the school's dream of its own dedicated theatre and drama studio space into a reality. I stare at these five lines of text long after I've finished reading them, as if they might tell me something about Martha that I don't already know.

Odd that Cecily didn't think to name the building after Martha instead of herself.

I'm about to close the magazine and put it back in the pocket behind the driver's seat when my eye is drawn to another name, at the bottom of the last page. *No. It can't be.* I look at it, half expecting it to disappear, but it doesn't. *Goundry.* The name is there, but the context makes no sense. A prickly sensation starts to creep along my arms, up my back and neck and behind my knees, as if I've got pins and needles in my skin.

I re-read the paragraph. Goundry's not a common name. If it were Wilson or Smith, I wouldn't have noticed. I drop the magazine, open my bag and pull out the sales list Mary gave me. There's the name again: Mrs C. A. Goundry. An address in Wiltshire. My heart judders an irregular, drawn-out beat as something else leaps out at me from the page. I didn't read the addresses before; I was too stunned by the nine names being there, looking so innocent and not at all mysterious—the people who bought paintings from Aidan's 2000 exhibition.

The address given for Ruth Margerison, who bought a painting called *Who's the Fairest?*, is Garstead Cottage, The Avenue, Wrecclesham. Mary's cottage. I stare at the handwritten list. I know that writing, the curly 'M' of Margerison . . .

Disorientated and panicky, I clear my throat. 'Excuse me?'

The driver turns off the radio. 'Yes, miss?'

'There's something here about a talent contest. In the magazine.'

'That's right. They have it every year, first Saturday after Valentine's Day. There's a lot of pressure on Villiers to go co-ed, but the head and the board are determined not to. All the statistics show that it's easier to educate girls when there are no boys around, but try telling the girls that. And some of the parents—a lot of them take the attitude, if their daughter wants boys, they expect boys to be provided, like good school lunches and private bedrooms in the dorms.' He laughs. 'I reckon I get to hear more of their complaints than the head does. Not a lot I can do to help them—I'm only a cabbie. Most of them assume they can buy anything, and normally they can, but the board have dug their heels in over the single sex issue. They know who'd get an earful the minute the results took a dive.'

I want to scream at him to get to the point.

'Valentine's Day tends to bring the bad feeling to the fore, as you can imagine,' he says, scratching the back of his neck. 'The contest's a bit of fun, designed to make the girls forget about the cards that never arrive because hardly any boys know they exist, tucked away in the middle of the countryside. It's a shame, really. But they all love the contest—it's the only one where the boarding houses go up against each other, you see. Usually the competitions are against other schools and the girls have to present a united front. They have that drummed into them from their first day: Villiers is one big happy family, and it demands absolute loyalty. And it is happy, to be fair. I wouldn't have minded sending my daughters. Not much chance of that.'

The boarding houses. I read the paragraph again: 'This year, for the first time since our Valentine's Day Talent Contest was launched in 2001, Goundry was the winning house, with a massive total of 379 points. Well done, Goundry! The traditional slap-up victory breakfast will take place on Saturday 1 March in

Goundry's dining hall, and we'll have no girls (or house mistresses or masters) from other houses trying to sneak in, thank you very much—we know that's gone on in previous years and this time we're cracking down!'

It's crazy, but I'm going to ask him. 'You don't happen to know how many boarding houses there are, do you?'

'Course I do. There's not a lot about Villiers I don't know. I've been—'

'How many?' I focus on his pink neck, try not to think beyond it.

'Let's see, now.' He starts to tap the steering-wheel. I count the taps, feel a numb disbelief take hold of me when they stop at nine. 'Nine in total.'

'What are they called?'

Amiably, as if reeling off his children's names—the daughters he couldn't afford to send to Villiers—he begins to list them, unaware of the horror that burrows deeper into my mind with each one. 'Abberton, Blandford, Darville, Elstow, Goundry—that's the house that won this year's talent contest. Caused an uproar, that result. Goundry's a sporty house. Darville and Margerison are more intellectual. Winduss is your drama and your singing, so of course they expect to win every year.'

Knowing what was coming did nothing to prepare me. New sweat sticks my shirt to my back. *I don't know who they were. They never told us. Isn't that funny?* I'd forgotten Mary saying that until now. 'Us': the pupils. The girls weren't told who the nine boarding houses were named after. Real people, presumably.

'Where did I get to?' says the driver. 'Oh, yes. Goundry. Then there's Heathcote. Margerison, which I mentioned—one of the more academic houses. Rodwell and Winduss—or Luvvies, as it's known unofficially—those are the last two.'

The traffic has started to move, slowly but picking up speed all the time. The gaps between the cars are growing wider. 'Looks like we're on our way,' he says.

'Stop. Please,' I say shakily. Everything has changed in the time it took him to list nine names.

'This is a motorway, miss. I can't stop. Are you all right?'

'Can you pull over?'

'I can do, if you want me to.' For the first time, he leans out of his seat and turns to look at me. The skin of his face is as pink as the back of his neck, puffy around his mottled cheeks. He has a white moustache that covers the whole space between his mouth and his nose, and a grey beard. His would be a good face to paint; it has more colours and textures than most.

My mind swings back to Mary's portrait of Martha Wyers, to the different textures and colours death gave her face: the white-encrusted lips, the blotchy chin . . .

I pitch forward and grab the headrest in front of me, breathing fast and hard as certainty rushes in. The picture of Martha . . . *oh, my God.*

'Are you all right, miss?'

'Not really. Can you stop on the hard shoulder?'

'It's a bit dangerous, is that. There's services coming up. I'll stop there for you.'

The discoloured patches on Martha Wyers' chin. I assumed they were bruises, or some kind of bodily fluid that had come from her mouth—vomit or blood. I shied away from the specifics because they were grotesque.

Maybe there was some blood or bruising, but there was something else as well: a pale brown smudge below Martha's lower lip, shaped like a child's drawing of a dog's bone. A birthmark.

I think of the paint splashed over the pile of cut-up paintings, of the cows mooing in the fields beyond Garstead Cottage. Mary walking in a slow circle around the heap of debris in her dining room, letting out a low moan, an animal sound . . .

'Do you have a mobile phone?' I ask the driver. 'I need to borrow it. I can give you some money.'

'Don't be silly,' he says. 'You're welcome to it.' He passes it through the gap between the driver and passenger seats. 'Don't you have one? I thought everyone had one these days.'

'Not me,' I say. Not Aidan either. It was one of the many things we found we had in common early on; both of us hated the idea of having our privacy invaded by ringing wherever we went.

I dial directory enquiries, and, lowering my voice, ask to be put through to Lincoln police station. I expect to hear a recorded greeting, but a woman answers. 'Good evening, Lincolnshire police. How can we help?'

I ask for PC James Escritt, steeling myself for bad news: his shift ended an hour ago; he doesn't work there any more; they have no idea where he is now.

I can only ask him, no one else. If he isn't there . . .

'Hold the line,' says the woman, and a few seconds later I hear a voice I haven't heard for years. He sounds no different.

'It's Ruth Bussey,' I tell him, knowing he hasn't forgotten me any more than I've forgotten him.

I wait for him to ask me how I am, make small talk. Instead, he says, 'I've heard the news.'

'News?'

'Gemma Crowther's death.'

'I didn't kill her,' I tell him. The taxi swerves slightly to the left.

'I know that,' says Escritt.

'I need to ask you a favour,' I say. And then, not caring how odd it sounds, either to him or to the man whose phone I'm using, I ask if he'd be willing to check my gardens. Not all of them—there are too many for that. Only the ones that appeared in magazines, the ones I won awards for. There are three of them. I give him the addresses. After a short hesitation, I say, 'And Cherub Cottage.'

Escritt doesn't ask for a reason, or quibble about the strangeness of my request. 'What am I looking for?' he asks.

'I want to know if any of them have been interfered with in any way. Destroyed.'

'You mean by new owners?' he says. 'Ruth, you can't expect—'

'No, that's not what I mean. I'm talking about attacks on the gardens. Have any of the owners reported any criminal damage last year or this year?'

There's silence as Escritt wonders why I think anyone might want to vandalise work I did years ago. He knows my answering silence means I'd prefer not to explain.

'I'd say no to most people,' he says eventually.

'Thank you.'

'It might take me a while. Can I reach you on the number you're calling from?'

'For a bit. I'm not sure how long, but . . . yes. I know it's a lot to ask, but can you try to be quick? If anything *was* reported . . .'

'I'll ring you,' he says curtly.

I clutch the phone. The driver doesn't ask for it back. He doesn't say anything. I pull my diary out of my bag and find Charlie Zailer's number. After my conversation with James Escritt, I want to talk to someone else who knows who I am, who will call me 'Ruth' instead of 'Miss'.

There's no ringing, only a recorded voicemail message. She must be talking to someone else, or have her phone switched off. 'It's Ruth Bussey,' I say. 'Ring me back as soon as you get this message. The number's . . .' I break off.

'07968 442013,' says the driver. His voice carries no trace of his former bonhomie. It's full of apprehension, or disapproval; I can't tell which.

I repeat the number and press the 'end call' button, then lean forward and drop the phone onto the passenger seat. 'Thank you.'

'Services coming up. Are we still stopping?'

Say no. Go back to Spilling. Go home. Let the police deal with it.

'We're going back,' I say. 'To Villiers. Drive along the hard shoulder if you have to—just get me there as quick as you can.'

24

5/3/08

Charlie had hoped things would be winding down by the time she got to the Spilling Gallery, but the party seemed still to be in full swing at nearly nine o'clock. The lit interior was dark with bodies, and she heard the noise as soon as she got out of her car: laughter and clashing voices.

She'd rung Saul Hansard at home first, having found his number in the phone book. His house was listed by name: The Grain Store. That's right; she remembered him mentioning the dilapidated building he and his wife had bought and converted. Charlie knew Saul from an initiative she'd been in charge of last year to combat business crime. Most of the local shop-owners had been involved; Saul had been among the least obnoxious and demanding.

Tonight there was a private view at the gallery, Breda Hansard, Saul's wife, had told Charlie. The windows were so heavily misted that you could hardly see the pictures on display. As Charlie walked in, she was hit by the competing smells of wine and sweat. Now she could see the paintings; they were of local scenes, made prettier by unrealistically bright colours and what looked like pieces of gold tin-foil stuck to each one to represent the sun, or yellow flowers growing beside the road. Twee. Just the sort of thing the people of Spilling were bound to love.

Saul saw Charlie, and broke off from the group of people he was talking to. 'I'm glad they sent you,' he said. 'Let's go through to the back.'

'Glad who sent me?' Charlie pulled off her coat and draped it over her arm. The gallery was uncomfortably hot with the thick, moist heat that could only be generated by too many people crammed into too small a space.

Saul hadn't heard her, so Charlie repeated her question.

He looked puzzled. 'You're not here because I phoned?'

'No. Who did you phone?'

The back turned out to be a large room that might have belonged to an inspired but undisciplined child with artistic leanings. Marker pens were scattered everywhere, on every surface and on the floor; Charlie's foot rolled on one as she walked in. There were large sheets of white cardboard with paint splashes on them leaning against walls, paintings both framed and unframed in tottering piles, aerosol paint cans with dried paint dribbles down their sides that had spilled on-to the table, tissue paper, mainly torn, occasionally screwed up into uneven balls, wood shavings, glue . . .

'I wanted to talk to someone,' said Saul, fiddling with his red braces, the same ones he always wore. 'I've had all sorts of police in and out yesterday and today, asking me questions. They wouldn't answer any. I was worried. I think some people I care about might be in trouble, or missing, and . . .'

'Would those people be Ruth Bussey, Aidan Seed and Mary Trelease?'

Saul looked satisfied, briefly, then anxious. 'You're also here to ask about them?'

'Unofficially.'

'Mary Trelease isn't a person I care about,' he said thoughtfully, as if reluctant to declare himself unconcerned. 'Though of course, I wish her no harm. She's a very strange lady. Difficult. I lost Ruth because of her. You know Ruth used to work for me?'

'Ruth told me about her row with Mary. It happened here, didn't it?'

Saul nodded.

'Did you see it?'

'Only the end of it. That was bad enough.'

'What exactly happened?'

'Wait a minute. Sorry.' Saul seemed agitated, pressing the thumb of his right hand into the palm of his left as if trying to drill a hole in it. 'Can you at least tell me if Ruth and Aidan are all right? Both are . . . well, I couldn't bear to think of either of them being in any trouble.'

'I don't know if they're all right,' Charlie said, feeling awful when she saw the effect it had on him. 'You're better off asking whoever you've been dealing with from London.'

'London? I haven't spoken to anyone from London.' Saul was growing twitchier by the second. 'The policemen who came here were local. I've seen them going into the Brown Cow. And coming out, sometimes, very much the worse for wear. I've seen *you* with them. I can't remember their names. One of them was tall and . . . large-ish, with a northern accent.'

'Was the other short and dark, with a face like a vindictive rat?' Charlie asked. *Sellers and Gibbs.* Coral Milward's little helpers. They must have been beside themselves with glee when they'd found their former skipper's misfortunes plastered all over Ruth Bussey's bedroom wall. Charlie remembered how Milward had taunted her about those same misfortunes, and rage flared inside her. 'Tell me about Ruth's fight with Mary,' she said.

Saul looked caught out. 'I thought you said she'd told you.'

'Mary brought in a picture to be framed, Ruth wanted to buy it, Mary didn't want to sell?'

'That was the essence of it, yes. Mary's the only artist I've ever met who refuses to sell her work. She doesn't even like people to see it. She once told me she'd prefer it if I could put the frames on without looking at the pictures. I told her it was impossible. Knowing what she was like, I'd never have dared to ask to buy anything, though she was extremely talented. I should have warned Ruth.' He pressed his thumb harder into his palm. 'Has Mary hurt Ruth again? I'll never forgive myself if she has.'

' "Again"?' said Charlie. 'What happened between them exactly? How badly was Ruth hurt?'

'No bones were broken, if that's what you mean. The damage was mainly psychological. Mary pushed Ruth up against a wall, took a full cylinder of red paint and sprayed it all over her face. After which Ruth completely withdrew into her shell, wouldn't come to work, wouldn't speak to anyone.'

'What aren't you telling me?' Charlie inclined her head, forcing him to meet her eye. 'Listen, Ruth came to me for help last week. I think she might be in danger. Anything you tell me, anything at all, might make the difference between me finding her and not finding her.'

'This won't, I promise you.'

Charlie had assumed Saul would be a pushover, but he seemed to have taken a stand. Which made her all the more determined to break him down. 'You can't possibly know that,' she said. 'Please. I wouldn't ask if I didn't have to.'

Saul stared at the floor. 'Ruth wet herself, all right? It was horrible. It must have been awful for her. In front of Mary and me, and the couple who'd walked into the gallery a few seconds before, hoping to see a few nice pictures on their way round town, not a sobbing woman with red paint all over her face, standing in a pool of her own pee!' He sighed. 'I shouldn't have told you. How would you like it if someone repeated a story like that about you?'

'People know worse things than that about me,' Charlie told him abruptly. 'Have you heard the name Martha Wyers before?'

Saul's forehead creased. 'Martha . . . Yes. She's a writer, isn't she? Aidan knew her. They were both part of an arts promotion some years back. I seem to remember they had their pictures in the papers. Glamorous, young, sexy artists—you get the idea.'

'Did you ever meet her?'

'Yes, I think I did. Aidan had an exhibition at a gallery in London.'

'TiqTaq.'

'That's right.' Saul looked surprised that Charlie knew. 'I think Martha Wyers came to the private view. I can't remember her face, but the name rings a bell. Aidan might well have introduced us. Any rate, I seem to remember her being there.' He picked up a marker pen from the table and spun it round as he thought back several years. 'With her mum, possibly. Yes, that's right, because the mum told me about Martha's book.'

'*Ice on the Sun*.'

'I have no memory of the title, I'm afraid. But Mum was rather full of her daughter's achievement, as I recall, and Martha found it embarrassing.'

'Do you remember seeing Mary Trelease at Aidan's private view?'

A tremor passed across Saul's face. 'Why would Mary have been there?' he said. 'Mary doesn't know Aidan.' When Charlie didn't contradict him, he muttered, 'Please, don't tell me they know each other. I'd never have sent Ruth to Aidan if I'd known he had any connection with Mary.'

'When did you first start framing for Mary?' Charlie asked him briskly. People who were determined to blame themselves did so even when others advised them not to—that was Charlie's conclusion, based on her own experience. Better to move on and distract him from his concerns rather than allow him to dwell on them. She was meeting Kerry Gatti in a pub in Rawndesley at half past nine; she couldn't waste time.

'A while ago,' said Saul. 'A good three or four years, I'd say. I'd offer to check, but I doubt I'd be able to find anything dating back that far.' As if to prove his point, he lifted a piece of paper from the table, stared at the scarred wood beneath for a few seconds, then replaced the paper in an almost identical position.

'When Mary first came to you and told you her name—Mary Trelease—did it sound familiar?'

'No. Why? Should it have?'

Charlie saw no reason not to tell him, since he'd attended the private view and could easily have seen it for himself. 'In Aidan's exhibition at TiqTaq, there was a painting called *The Murder of Mary Trelease*.'

Saul looked appalled. 'What? But . . .'

'You didn't see that title?'

'The gallery was a scrum that night. I don't think I looked at all the titles, but I'd have noticed, surely, if there'd been a picture of a murder? There wasn't.' His face had turned pale. 'Has Mary been . . . killed?' This time he didn't wait for an answer. 'I saw her as recently as last year,' he said, shaking his head. 'Aidan's exhibition was in 1999 or 2000 or something like that. The timing . . .'

Charlie fought the temptation to tell him she was as baffled as he was, had been since last Friday when Ruth Bussey had dragged her into something that made no sense, chronologically or in any other way.

'You bought a picture at Aidan's private view,' she said.

'Yes. If you're going to ask to look at it, you can't. I had it for less than a week.'

'How come?'

Saul flushed. 'I suppose this is something else you'll say I need to tell you if I want you to find Ruth.'

'I'll be discreet,' Charlie promised.

'I sold it. A few days after I picked it up from TiqTaq, I got a phone call from an art collector. I regard myself as a collector too, but I'd never call myself that the way this chap did. For me it's purely a pleasure. He was evidently a big cheese in the art world, and he wanted to know if I'd be willing to sell him Aidan's picture, the one I'd bought. He knew what I'd paid for it, and offered me four times that amount.' A pained look spread across Saul's face.

'You accepted his offer,' Charlie guessed.

'I felt terrible about it, but yes, I took the money. This place wasn't as established then as it is now. Even now, I constantly have cash flow problems. Strange thing was, I didn't really like the painting. I never admitted it to Jan—Jan Garner, that is. She runs TiqTaq, she's an old friend of mine.'

Charlie nodded.

'She thought Aidan was the best thing since sliced bread, but I didn't take to his work at all. I liked him enormously as a person—I'd offered him a job by that point—but there was something about his paintings that left me cold. They were too . . . abrasive, somehow. Looking at them closely made me want to squirm.' Saul shrugged. 'So, no doubt that contributed to my decision, but it didn't make me feel any better about it— worse, if anything. A courier arrived the next day and took the picture away with him.'

'What about the money?' Charlie asked.

'Oh, I had that almost immediately. Within a couple of hours of our first phone call it had appeared in my bank account. Eight thousand pounds.'

'Not to be sniffed at,' Charlie agreed. There was no picture she wouldn't sell for that amount, apart from ones she knew she could get more for, obviously. The *Mona Lisa*, or Van Gogh's *Sunflowers*. Those were the only two famous paintings that sprang to mind.

'I honestly thought Aidan would be better off with his work in a real collector's collection, not up on my wall at home,' said Saul. 'I never told him, though—I kept meaning to, but I couldn't bring myself to do it. Which meant I could never invite him back for dinner, all the time he worked for me.'

'I don't suppose you remember the name of this collector, do you?' Charlie asked, not holding out much hope.

'I do, as a matter of fact. I'm from Dorset originally, and he had the same name as my village of origin, a place no one's ever heard of unless they were born there. Or rather, he had half of its name. I don't suppose you've ever heard of Blandford Forum, have you?'

Charlie hadn't. Still, she knew which half was the collector that had made Saul the offer he couldn't refuse. A man with a wife called Sylvia, and a home on a street that didn't exist.

'His name was Blandford,' said Saul. 'I wouldn't swear to his first name, but I have a feeling it might have been Maurice. Maurice Blandford.'

The Swan in Rawndesley was as hot and packed as the gallery had been. Charlie pushed her way to the bar and ordered a pint of lime cordial and soda, feeling the need to rehydrate. She could see Kerry Gatti sitting at a table with two women, reading a hardback book, but he hadn't seen her yet. She was late, but he wasn't looking out for her. Didn't care if she turned up or not. She took her drink and elbowed her way over to him, spilling some of it on the way.

'Kerry.'

'Jesus,' he said, looking up. 'Did you ask the barmaid for a urine sample?' One of the women at the table turned her chair away from him. The other gave Charlie a look that made it clear he was nothing to do with her.

His book was by Stephen Hawking, *A Brief History of Time*. A bookmark was sticking out of it suspiciously close to the front cover. Kerry had probably read all of five pages.

'Is it having a girl's name that makes you so unpleasant, or your failed career as a comedian?'

He laughed. One of the most irritating things about him was that he seemed to enjoy being insulted. 'I'm not the only one with a failed career. Yours is about to go down the tubes, from what I hear. And your fiancé's.'

'How did you know I was engaged?' Charlie asked lightly. You had to pretend not to care with Kerry. That was the trick. The more he saw he was getting to you, the more he stuck the knife in. On the plus side, you got to throw as many knives as you liked in return. He was the only person Charlie knew who required and deserved nothing in the way of tact and consideration.

'I make a point of following your progress,' he said. '*Regress*. Don't tell me you're seriously going to get hitched to that humourless pillock Waterhouse?'

'That's the plan,' Charlie told him.

'A damn poor one, if it's true. I for one don't think you'll do it. You want all the razzmatazz of an engagement, but you'll save yourself at the last minute. I bet you've not set a date yet.'

Charlie took a deep breath. 'Whether we have or not, it's no skin off your diary. You're not invited. Sorry.' She flashed him a false smile.

'Don't be,' said Kerry. 'I couldn't come anyway—I'd be too embarrassed for you.'

'You've never spoken to Simon, have you? He wasn't sure who you were.'

'Yeah, well, I'm sure who he is. A brain in a vat. Walk-on-water legend as a detective, non-starter as a husband. Does he know about us?'

Charlie laughed. 'Yeah. He knows about *us*, as in me and the several hundred men I fucked before I got engaged to him. One of whom happened to be you.'

'Ouch,' Kerry squealed. 'Momma, you're the dirtiest.'

'If you're asking does he know about you *specifically* . . . As I said, he's not even sure who you are.'

'He will be. I've done the two of you a favour, because I'm that kind of guy. When you find yourselves sacked and skint, ring Seb at First Call. I've told him Waterhouse is good. I lied and said you were too, for old times' sake. He'll find jobs for you both if you ask him nicely. Not that this'll put you off, but you probably won't have the pleasure of working with *moi*. I'm handing in my notice any day now, giving the comedy another go.' Kerry shrugged. 'I'm a funny guy. You've got to make the most of your talents in this world. I'm sorry to hear you've been neglecting yours since you got engaged. I'd heard calls to the Samaritans had been on the up recently—now I know why. You provided a valuable public service in your heyday.'

'You know Aidan Seed,' said Charlie. 'You went to his private view at TiqTaq in 2000.'

'Did I?'

'You bought a painting. A few days after you collected it, you got a call from someone who wanted it enough to offer you more than you'd paid for it. A lot more.'

'I never liked Seed and I liked his creepy pictures even less,' said Kerry. 'I wouldn't have bought one if I hadn't had too much to drink. He seemed to be going places, and I thought it'd be a good investment. As it turned out, I got to cash in sooner than I'd expected.'

'You sold the picture you bought to a man called Maurice Blandford. Or perhaps that wasn't his name. It might have been Abberton, or . . .'

'You were right the first time. Maurice Blandford. Suck his cock, did you?'

'No. If he exists, if he has a suckable cock, then no—I didn't.'

'All cocks are suckable,' said Kerry. 'Trust me, as the proud owner of a fine specimen.'

'I assume you're referring to a spare you keep in a jar somewhere, for special occasions?'

'You said it.'

Damn. She should have thought ahead. She'd asked for that one.

'Did Aidan Seed hire you to follow Ruth Bussey? To find out about her background?'

'It's the same rule for you as for Neil Dunning esquire.' Kerry took a sip of a drink that looked like port before smiling sympathetically at Charlie. 'Worse for you, since you're in no position to come back in the morning with a warrant. Face it: you're out in the cold. This'll tickle you: Dunning asked me if I thought you and Waterhouse could be trusted.' He grinned, genuinely pleased to be delivering the news. 'Don't worry, I stuck up for you. If it makes you feel any better, Dunning'll get nothing from me, warrant or no warrant, so you can't accuse me of not playing fair.'

He looked serious for the first time since Charlie had arrived. 'I'm not the Salvation Army, sweetheart. I help people only after money's changed hands. Outside of that, I don't tell and I don't ask. I'm not curious, see. That's the most important asset some-one in my delicate position can have, let me tell you. Have I asked you who Maurice Blandford is?' He licked his finger and tapped the air, awarding a point to himself.

'Did you meet Blanford?' Charlie asked. 'Or did he send a courier for the picture, and transfer the money directly into your bank account? He did, didn't he? Did that strike you as odd at the time?'

'The only thing striking me as odd are your questions. And Dunning's. Putting it all together, I'd say Aidan Seed's mixed up in the suspicious death Dunning's fretting about, and maybe Maurice Blandford is too, but I don't know how, and I don't care. Like I say, money has to change hands.'

'I don't suppose you've still got the bank statement with the account name and number on it? From the transfer?'

Kerry snickered. 'This is what I love about you: that faint whiff of desperation—your signature scent.'

Charlie persisted. 'How much did Blandford give you for the picture? Was it something in the region of eight thousand pounds?'

'If you're waiting for me to ask how you know all this, you're in for a long wait,' said Kerry. 'I don't pry, in case it leads to a conflict of interests.' He raised his glass, clinked it against Charlie's. 'I've got my sponsor to think of, my early retirement. My name in lights outside comedy clubs . . .'

'Sponsor?'

He patted her hand. 'It all comes down, in life, to whose side you're on. You're on Simon Waterhouse's side—that's why your career and love life are going down the pan. Me? I'm on the side of my clients, because, at the end of the day, they pay the bills.'

'You said "sponsor" singular.' Kerry looked put out. Charlie licked her finger and notched up a point to herself. 'Money seems to like you, Kerry. First you buy a painting by a guy you can't stand for—what, a grand? Two? And a stranger offers you eight for it when you've had it less than a month.'

'I talked him up to ten, actually,' he corrected her. 'And it was less than a week.'

Charlie believed him about his lack of curiosity. She also knew that, like most men, he had to prove he knew more, had to be the one steering things. 'Then you get yourself a client who pays over the odds,' she went on, hoping she'd guessed right. 'She pays you so much, you can think about giving up work and wasting the rest of your life antagonising tiny audiences in dingy pubs and clubs all over the country. Your sponsor. Not Aidan Seed. You said you didn't like him, so it can't be him who's bought your loyalty. It's Mary Trelease, isn't it? She's the one who paid you to tail Ruth Bussey.'

Mary, with her refined accent and her Villiers education, so out of place on the Winstanley estate. Who else could it be? 'Or Gemma Crowther,' Charlie added, just in case. 'Which one's funding your comedy comeback? Mary or Gemma?'

'Neither.' Kerry looked smug. 'Unless one of them left a will I've yet to hear about.'

'What did you say?'

'You're barking up the wrong tree.' He pronounced each word slowly and carefully as if he was talking to an imbecile.

Pretend you know already. Pretend you know what he knows, or thinks he knows. 'Did Aidan Seed kill Gemma Crowther? Did he kill Mary Trelease?'

Kerry's eyes narrowed. He looked like a smug cat. 'I'll give you this much: you're one step ahead of your Cockney counterpart.'

'Dunning didn't know Mary Trelease was dead,' said Charlie, aware of her pulse charging beneath her skin.

'He seemed a mite confused,' Kerry agreed.

'He talked about her as if she was still alive. Asked you if you knew her.' Charlie didn't know where she was going with this, but it felt right. She wished Simon was with her. 'Did you tell him she was dead?'

Kerry held up his hands. 'Not my responsibility to set him straight. If he comes back with his warrant tomorrow as promised, he'll get no illumination from me, nor from my pristine office. I don't tell anyone anything.'

'Unless cash changes hands. I know,' said Charlie impatiently. 'All right, then—how much? Name your price for telling me everything you know that relates to Aidan Seed, Mary Trelease . . .'

'Charlie, sweetheart, don't demean yourself. You're not going to be able to claim it back on expenses, you know.'

'. . . and Martha Wyers.'

That wiped the smile off his face.

'Dunning didn't ask you about her, did he? Come on, name your price.'

'I'm out of your league,' said Kerry. 'Financially speaking. Unless you're offering payment in kind.' He stared at Charlie's chest and ran his tongue along his bottom lip. 'I might be persuaded.'

'Yeah, right. Is your bedroom still covered in fake leopard skins?'

'Leopard skins are sexy, señorita.'

'Not when they're covered in spilled Weetabix, they're not.' Saying this reminded Charlie of who she was talking to. *He'll get no illumination from my pristine office.* Nothing about Kerry Gatti was pristine. He was the same self-satisfied slob he'd always been. There was an open briefcase at his feet. He'd wedged it between his legs.

Charlie pushed her lime cordial and soda over to him. 'I'm going to get a real drink,' she said. Kerry opened his book as she stood up. Maybe he really did want to read about black holes. If only he would fall into one.

At the bar, Charlie showed her police ID to two young men standing beside her. 'For twenty quid each, I need you to start giving me a hard time,' she told them. 'Loud enough for the whole pub to hear. Accuse me of pushing in.'

''Ey?' said one, slow on the uptake.

'Let's see the money, then,' said his friend. Checking Kerry was busy with Stephen Hawking, Charlie gave them each a £20 note. They started laughing.

'Is that the best you can do?' she said. She didn't need Oscar-winning performances from them, only a bit of high-volume aggression. They looked the sort who ought to be able to manage it. In the end, Charlie had to threaten to nick them for theft—taking her money under false pretences. Finally, one of them—the marginally brighter one—started yelling at her. Too loud, really hamming it up, but it didn't matter. Charlie let him insult her and threaten her for about half a minute, then backed away from the bar, saying, 'Look, forget it. I don't want any trouble.' As she walked back to the table, he shouted obscenities after her. *Earning every penny, the fucker.* Charlie heard the barman threaten to bar him if he didn't pack it in.

'What was that about?' Kerry looked amused. 'Where's your drink?'

'Not worth it,' she said tersely.

'Liver going by the name of Lily these days, is it? I'd heard as much. Come on, give us your money, I'll go for you.'

'I'm not giving you fuck all.' Charlie restrained herself from asking what he'd heard. Was he referring to her transferring out of CID? Did people think that was down to fear? 'If you want, you and your sponsor can buy me a vodka and orange.'

As soon as he'd gone to the bar, she put both her feet around his open briefcase and pulled it over to her. Inside, there was a copy of a book called *Voice and the Actor*, season two of *The Wire* on DVD, an iPod, some CDs—Rush, Pink Floyd and Genesis—and two thin blue envelope files. Charlie opened one and saw the name Aidan Seed. She froze for a second, unused to having things happen the way she wanted them to.

She slipped both files under her shirt and folded her arms

over them as she walked to the stairs that led to the ladies. Instead of following the drunk girl with the chunky calves and mud-dipped stiletto heels up to the next floor, Charlie carried on to the end of the passageway. Beside the door of the gents' there was another one marked 'emergency exit'. She pushed the silver bar and it opened on to a yard full of empty crates and recycling skips.

She ran round the side of the pub, through the car park at the front and on to the road. Her Audi was parked half on the pavement, under a street light. Pulling the files out from under her shirt, Charlie pointed her key-fob at the car and pressed the unlock button. Nothing happened. 'Come *on*,' she breathed through gritted teeth. She pressed again. Nothing. And again. And again. *Shit*. She looked over her shoulder. No sign of Kerry. Yet.

She unlocked the car manually and set off the alarm. The noise, an ee-aw-ee-aw screech, sounded like an amplified saw cutting through metal. People on the street were giving her dirty looks, mouthing things at her that she couldn't hear and wasn't sorry to miss.

Sweating in spite of the cold, Charlie jabbed the unlock button several more times with her thumb. Useless. She tried the lock button, also to no effect. The battery was beyond resuscitation. Without a new one, she assumed there was no way of turning off the alarm.

She looked behind her again and this time she saw Kerry. He was in the car park, looking left and right. She ducked down behind the wall that separated the pub from the street, then raised her head in time to see him run round the back of the Swan. She knew he'd be back soon, having failed to find her there.

With no time to think, Charlie abandoned her wailing car and ran across the car park, up the front steps of the pub and back inside, clutching the files tight so that nothing fell out. He wouldn't look inside. Knowing what she'd done, he wouldn't think she'd be stupid enough to come back.

Charlie ran up the stairs to the ladies', pushed a couple of indignant drunk teenagers out of her way, and locked herself in a cubicle.

She didn't open the files straight away. She was too busy breathing, which felt like something she hadn't done for a while. She could still hear the sodding car. Once her head had stopped throbbing and she could see an immobile, much-graffitied toilet cubicle rather than one that pulsated and warped in front of her eyes, she was ready to read what she'd taken from Kerry's briefcase.

There was a file on Aidan Seed and one on Ruth Bussey. Ruth's told Charlie nothing much that she didn't already know: evangelical Christian parents, garden design business, three BALI awards. Most of the information Kerry had gathered had to do with Gemma Crowther and Stephen Elton. There was a lot about the court case. Charlie imagined how he must have congratulated himself on sniffing out that juicy morsel.

She opened the other file. Here were things she didn't know about Aidan Seed: details of his education, his father's death from lung cancer. She skimmed the pages, looking for anything that stood out. Aidan's mother's cancer—also in the lungs. His stepfather . . .

Charlie cried out in shock. *Aidan Seed's stepfather*. This was it. She pulled her phone out of her bag and rang Simon. Voicemail. *Shit*. Where was he? He never ignored his phone; he was too neurotic. To him, each missed call was an opportunity for ever lost. It was one of the things Charlie took the piss out of him for, along with getting more calls from his mother than from anyone else.

Someone flushed the toilet in the next cubicle. Charlie waited until the gurgling of the cistern had stopped, then rang Simon again. This time she left a message. 'Seed's stepfather—his name's Len Smith. He's in an open prison, Long Leighton in Wiltshire, serving a life sentence for a murder he committed in 1982. He strangled a woman.' Kerry had written nothing in his report about whether the woman was naked or in bed when she died, but Charlie knew. She did a quick calculation in her head. Aidan Seed had been thirty-two when *The Times* feature was published in 1999, which made him . . . fifteen in 1982.

'Smith murdered his partner in their home,' she told Simon. 'I don't need to tell you the address: 15 Megson Crescent. They lived there with Smith's three stepkids, Aidan and his brother and sister.' In case Simon was as full of disbelief as she was, Charlie added, 'I'm not making this up. Aidan lived in that house until he left home. The woman Len Smith's inside for killing—her name was Mary Trelease.'

There were photocopies of photographs from newspapers: grainy, but distinct enough for Charlie to be able to see that the Mary Trelease Len Smith had killed looked nothing like the Mary Trelease Charlie had met. *Met in the same house the first Mary Trelease had lived and died in.* She held the clearest of the pictures close to her face. She'd seen this woman before, but where? It wasn't possible. The first Mary Trelease had been dead for twenty-six years. Smith was seventy-eight now, Kerry had noted. He'd been denied parole on several occasions.

Charlie was about to put her phone back in her bag when she noticed a small envelope symbol on its screen. A message. How long had it been there? How long since she'd checked? She pressed '1' to play it, expecting to hear Simon's voice, and heard, with a jolt of surprise, Ruth Bussey's instead.

25

Wednesday 5 March 2008

'Wait here,' I tell the driver, halfway out of the cab as it draws to a slow halt outside Garstead Cottage. 'Keep the engine on.' I run past the cardboard cow with the yellow earring and pound on the cottage's back door. Mary's 'Survivor' song is playing. She opens the door and squints at me, as if I'm a bright light and she's been in the dark for a long time. She wasn't expecting me back. 'You've got to get out of here,' I tell her. 'No time to explain. The taxi's outside. Go somewhere, anywhere. Go to Martha's mother's house.'

'Cecily?' She looks down at her bare feet, doesn't move. She's wearing torn jeans and a black shirt with paint on it. I want to grab her, pull her outside and out of the way. 'What's going on?' she asks.

I'm going to have to tell her something. 'I rang the police in Lincoln. Two of the gardens I designed have been vandalised—turf torn up, plants pulled out of the earth. One last summer and one in the early hours of Tuesday morning.' *Not more than six hours after Gemma Crowther was murdered.*

Mary's eyes widen. 'Cherub Cottage?'

'No. Two of the three I won awards for.' I can't understand it, not really, and I don't want to try. For someone to attack something as beautiful and natural as a garden, something so irreplaceable—it's beyond my comprehension. The owners will replant and reseed, but it won't be the same. No two gardens are ever the same.

I can't let the sadness in, not now, when I need to stay alert.

Mary grips the door frame. 'He did it to you as well.'

'Look, there's no time. He's coming here. Go.'

'I'm not leaving you to—'

'You have to! I can't explain now. You have to trust me, like I trusted you. Give me your mobile number—I'll ring you as soon as I can.'

'I need a few minutes,' Mary says, disappearing inside.

The seconds drag. The taxi-driver turns off his engine and I gesture at him to switch it back on.

When Mary comes outside she's got shoes on, a jacket and a khaki hold-all. 'Mobile number's on the kitchen table, with the phone. Here are the keys.' She puts them in my hand. 'Ring me.' She's fumbling in her bag, moving too slowly. I want to scream at her to hurry. 'Why don't you come with me?' she says. 'We could both—'

'I can't. Go to your parents' house and—'

'My parents?' She blinks at me in the darkness.

'Go to my house.' I pull my keys out of my bag and throw them at her. 'Ring the police, ask them to wait with you.'

At last she gets into the taxi. 'Ring me,' she says before closing the door. 'Take care of yourself.'

I watch as the cab turns and drives down the long path, over the discreet speed bumps that look like small hillocks in the concrete, and out through the school gates. Once it's gone, I run back to the cottage. Mary left the door open. The music's still playing. I run to the dining room and turn the door handle, but nothing happens. I turn it the other way. Nothing. Locked. I reach above the door frame for the key, but there's nothing there. Frantically, I sweep my fingers all the way along the tiny ledge. The key's gone.

I run back to the kitchen, where I've seen other keys hanging from small hooks on the underside of a wooden cabinet. Yes—five metal hooks, screwed into the wood. More than five keys. I try them one by one, sprinting between the two rooms, but none of them's the right one. I'm going to have to smash the window.

I run past the kitchen table, where Mary has painted her mobile number in blue on the wood; there's a thin blue-tipped brush next to the cordless phone. Outside, there's no one around. I can see lights in some of the windows of the main school building in the distance, the one with the square tower, but they seem a million miles away.

At the back of Garstead Cottage it's darker than at the front, without the lights on either side of the path. There's a window that must belong to the dining room—it's the only one that's the right size. I bend to pick up a large stone from the ground and find myself rearing back. I can't pick up a stone and throw it. *I can't.* What else can I use? My shoes aren't heavy enough, nor is anything in my bag.

The bikes at the front. I sprint round the side of the house and find, near the bikes, something even better: a metal tyre pump. I grab it and run back to the dining room window.

I'm about to smash the glass when the music stops. I hesitate, listening to the intense silence all around me. Less than five seconds later, the noise starts up again: the same song, endlessly repeating. 'Help!' I scream into the empty, muffling air around me. 'Somebody help me!' *Nothing.*

I drive the bicycle pump into the windowpane, putting all my weight behind it. The glass smashes. Most of it falls into the room. I use the pump to scrape away the jagged pieces still sticking out of the frame. Then I climb in through the window and push the heavy floor-length curtains aside. The air in the room is full of what I think at first are small, coloured feathers, floating, but they're not. They're pieces of canvas, lifted from the top of the pile by the gust of wind that's blown in through the smashed window. There it is in front of me, an enormous, flaking, shedding growth that looks as if it's sprouted from the floor: the mountain of destroyed paintings. And the paint that's been thrown over it, pooled on the floor . . . I bend, touch a puddle of blue with my fingers: it's still wet. *More paint, even since I left.* I bring my fingers to my nose and sniff.

This isn't the sort of paint anyone would use for pictures; the smell's too strong, too chemical. I look over at the dining table. The tins of paint, the same ones I saw last time I was in here, with Mary, are round and wide. *Dulux.* For painting walls, not pictures. *For disguising a worse smell underneath.* It didn't occur to me before. None of the walls in Garstead Cottage are this shade of blue. Or yellow, or green. *Or red.*

My heart pounding, I bend to touch a pool of red. The texture is different. I smell my fingers and cry out. Blood.

I dive into the pile and start to tear at it, pushing its mass to one side, shovelling fragments aside with my arms, tunnelling my way in. I burrow down, spitting pieces of canvas out of my mouth as I go. Every few seconds I lift my face to breathe. I keep delving and pushing until I hit something hard and cold, something I know can't be a painting, or part of a frame.

I close my hand around it and pull it out: a hammer. On its silver-coloured head, I can see where the blood has dried in smears. I throw it across the room, hating the feel of it against my skin, and carry on digging, combing with my fingers. *I've got to be right. I've got to be . . .*

I'm touching a hand.

A painted smile, a fingernail, a patch of grey-blue sky.

I saw a fingernail when Mary first brought me in here. I thought it was a cutting from a painting, but it wasn't. It was real.

I sweep wildly with my arms, attacking what's left of the canvas mountain until it breaks up, falls away to one side or the other, and I see him. 'Aidan!' I sob. *I'm sorry. I'm so sorry.*

His eyes are half closed. There's a square of shiny brown tape over his mouth. I yank it off, hoping he'll move or make a sound. *Nothing.* I'm terrified to look at his still, white face, in case it stays still for too long. He was alive last night, earlier today. *The cows, mooing in the fields outside . . .* I thought one of them sounded as if it was in pain. *The low groan I thought came from Mary* ... It was Aidan I heard, Aidan moaning in agony, his life spilling away in blood that I mistook for red paint on the cream carpet. *Why didn't I see? Why didn't I know?*

Beneath his right shoulder there's a dark hole in his shirt. Its edge is black, as if the fabric's been burned. *Shot—he's been shot.* His mouth is slack, open, and I can see something inside it, something flesh-coloured, too big to be his tongue. I touch it, then, as gently as I can, I pull it out. It's a peach-coloured bath sponge, similar to the one Gemma used to gag me. She also used parcel tape to keep my mouth closed and the sponge in place. The exactness of the recreation paralyses me for a moment as ice-cold terror floods my body. I thought that once I had the truth, the fear would end, but it hasn't. It's worse.

Aidan didn't destroy my gardens, or Mary's pictures. She lied. She told me there were eighteen paintings in her exhibition that never was, the one Aidan invented. Did she forget she'd said that, when she showed me the sales list from Aidan's TiqTaq show? It wasn't the real list, it was one she'd written out herself. I recognised her 'M' from her signature on *Abberton*. Eighteen pictures in Aidan's exhibition, eighteen empty frames on his walls, each one a tribute to a painting that had been viciously dismembered.

She switched places with him in her story, reversed their roles. Made him the destroyer, herself the victim.

I lied too. Did Mary believe me, that I wanted her to leave Garstead Cottage for her own safety? Was I convincing?

Panting hard, I drop the sponge and wipe my hand on my trousers until the skin smarts.

I must call an ambulance. Not the police—the police are for when it's too late and it isn't, it can't be. I run to the door, forgetting it's locked and I have no key. When it won't open, I head for the window instead, skidding on the feathery mess that's all over the floor, ready to throw myself out onto the grass.

'Hello, Ruth,' says a tremulous, distorted voice from outside, and I scream, as if the night itself has spoken to me.

A form appears from the blackness, moving closer. A thin, lined face that sags under the weight of its triumphant smile, like someone trying to hold aloft a trophy that's too heavy. *Mary.* Wearing an expression of such manic, barely controlled elation that it makes me scream again, even before I see the gun that's in her hand.

26
5/3/08

Kate Kombothekra had the car keys ready when she opened her front door. 'Here you go,' she said, thrusting them at Charlie.

'You sure this is okay? I don't know when I'll be able to bring it back.'

'It's fine. The boys and I'll walk to school tomorrow. It'll do us good, though don't tell Sam I said that. When he said it to me I nearly throttled him. One thing: if you could avoid smoking in it . . .'

'Do my best,' Charlie shouted over her shoulder.

As she slammed the driver door, she heard Kate yell, 'Or at least open the . . .' Charlie beeped the horn. Steering with one hand, she pulled her phone out of her handbag on the passenger seat and pressed redial. 'Villiers,' said the voice that answered after three rings. 'Claire Draisey speaking.'

'Hello, it's me again, Charlie Zailer. Any luck?'

'I'm afraid not. There's been some kind of emergency here, and the deputy head's in a meeting. I've rung round everyone I can think of, and no one's seen hair nor hide of a Simon Waterhouse. Are you sure he's here?'

'Not absolutely. It's where he said he was going, that's all I know.' Charlie had rung the school when she couldn't reach Simon on his mobile, and got a recorded message, tacked on to the end of which was an emergency out-of-hours number—Claire Draisey's, as it turned out. Draisey had told her few mobile phones could get reception in Villiers' grounds, which made Charlie all the more inclined to think that was where Simon was.

'Look, I'm going to have to free up this line,' said Draisey, sighing. 'You're from the Culver Valley, did you say?'

'That's right. So's DC Waterhouse.'

'Right. Then you're nothing to do with the London police.'

'London police?' A burst of adrenalin set off Charlie's internal antennae.

'Yes. A colleague said they're on their way here. Look, I don't know much more than you do at this stage. A group of our girls went on a trip to the Globe Theatre tonight to see *Julius Caesar*. I've just checked the car park, and the minibus isn't back yet, which it certainly ought to be, and we're all rather anxious in case . . .'

'I wouldn't waste your time if this wasn't important,' said Charlie. 'Are you sure you've checked everywhere?'

'No, I haven't,' said Draisey bluntly. 'I didn't say I had. I've spoken to those members of house staff that I could get hold of, and that's all I can do, I'm afraid. I'm not traipsing round the grounds at this time of night looking for your missing colleague. Do you have any idea of the size of our empire?' The last word was loaded with sarcasm. 'It'd take me most of the night.'

'What about Garstead Cottage?' Charlie asked.

'What about it?' Draisey said curtly. 'It's rented to a private tenant who I'm not about to disturb. Now, if you'll—'

'Wait,' said Charlie. 'I got a message to ring somebody—someone I think might be in trouble. When I rang her back on the number she gave me, I got through to a taxi-driver: Michael Durtnell, his name is. He works for a firm called N & E Cars.'

'Newsham and Earle,' said Draisey. 'That's our taxi firm—the one the school uses.'

'Right.' Charlie let out the breath she'd been holding. *Progress.* 'He said he'd left Garstead Cottage twice today, each time with a different woman passenger. Both women then decided they didn't want to go anywhere, and asked him to take them back to Garstead Cottage. He said both were behaving strangely. I think one of those women is the person who phoned me. DC Waterhouse might already be—'

'Sergeant Zailer, if I could stop you for a moment?' Draisey sounded exhausted, her voice fainter than it had been previously. 'I should have realised when you said you were from Culver Valley Police. I don't suppose I'm thinking straight, with the minibus missing and rumours of London coppers beating a path to our door. I know for a fact that the current resident of Garstead Cottage has a friend staying with her at the moment— a female friend.'

It had to be Ruth Bussey.

'I also know, as perhaps you don't, that she's in the habit of pestering the local police, summoning them when there's absolutely no need and generally making their lives a misery. Sounds like tonight she's decided it's your turn. She has another house in your neck of the woods, I believe.'

'What's her name?' asked Charlie, driving too fast in her excitement.

'If you don't know, I don't think it would be appropriate for me to—'

'Mary Trelease?'

A heavy sigh. 'If you know, why are you asking me?'

'I'm on my way to you now,' Charlie told Draisey. 'When I get there, I'll need you to—'

'I'll either be too busy to help you, or I'll be asleep,' came the firm reply. 'I'd strongly advise you to save yourself the trip. You're not the first police officer I've said this to, and you won't be the first to wish you'd listened to me when you've wasted a good night's sleep for absolutely no reason. Good night, sergeant.'

'Mary Trelease died in 1982,' Charlie shouted into her phone, but Claire Draisey was gone.

Charlie drove at twice the speed limit all the way to the motorway. Once she was on it, she rang the number Coral Milward had left on her voicemail. When the DS answered, she said, 'It's Charlie Zailer.'

'Where the fuck are you? Where's Waterhouse? Anyone'd think we weren't all on the same side here. Who the fuck do you both think you are, treating me like I don't exist?'

'I think Simon's at Villiers,' Charlie told her. 'I'm on my way there now.'

'You're on your way to my office is where you're on your way to.'

''Fraid not,' said Charlie.

'They should have got rid of you two years ago—I would have done, if you'd been one of mine. They're sure as hell going to wish they did once they've heard what I've got to say about you. Once a fuck-up, always a fuck-up. I'm going to take your career and your future and every fucking thing you've got and stick it up my big fat arse before shitting it out again. You'd better—'

Charlie switched her phone off. On the same side? Funny, that was never the impression Milward gave. She'd said nothing about having dispatched anyone to Villiers. Despite what Claire Draisey had told her, Charlie had no way of knowing if anyone from the Met was on their way to the school. She decided to stick with her original plan and head for Garstead Cottage, even if it meant losing her job. Ruth Bussey and Mary Trelease were there—hadn't Draisey said so?

She turned on Kate's car stereo and heard what sounded like a live gig—raucous applause and cheering, electronic music almost drowned out by hands and voices. When the clapping died down, a man started to speak. He didn't say who he was, but Charlie guessed he was Kate's sons' headmaster, or one of their teachers. This was a school concert on CD. He was thanking something called the Wednesday Club Ensemble for its synthesised rendition of 'Ten Green Bottles'.

Hearing the title jolted something at the back of Charlie's brain. She breathed in sharply and turned off the stereo. *Six*

Green Bottles—that was the name of a painting in Aidan's TiqTaq exhibition. Surely . . . no. If it was true, it would be crazy. She forgot to steer, and drifted halfway into the next lane as, suddenly, several other things clicked in her mind, then swerved to get herself back on track, ignoring irate beeps from other drivers. It was crazy, no doubt about that, but she was right. She had to be.

She'd seen several unframed paintings on the walls at Mary's house. One was of a man, woman and boy sitting round a table covered with empty wine bottles. Green bottles. Charlie hadn't counted, but she was willing to bet there were six of them. She'd also seen a picture of a woman looking in a mirror, the same woman from the bottles picture. *And from the photographs in Kerry Gatti's file.* That's why Charlie had recognised the face— she'd seen it before, on Mary's walls. The first Mary Trelease, the one who died in 1982. *A woman looking in a mirror . . .* Another of the titles Charlie had seen on Aidan's TiqTaq sales list was *Who's the Fairest?* Mirror, mirror, on the wall, who's the fairest of them all?

And the picture Ruth Bussey had described to her that had been in one of the downstairs rooms at 15 Megson Crescent, of a boy writing 'Joy Division' on a wall—that had to be *Routine Bites Hard*, another of Aidan's titles. The first line of Joy Division's best known song, 'Love Will Tear Us Apart', a song Charlie had heard thousands of times, contained those words, that phrase. She sang it under her breath, trying to assemble the bizarre chain of events in her mind.

In 1982, Len Smith had killed his partner, Mary Trelease, according to the official version of events. In 2000, Aidan's first exhibition at TiqTaq had been a huge success, after which, unusually, he'd decided to give up painting. Charlie thought of the photograph Jan Garner had shown her of his *Supply and Demand*, the picture that had been reproduced in the exhibition catalogue: a woman at the top of the stairs, looking down at a boy. Charlie hadn't focused on their faces, but she knew they were the same woman and boy she'd seen in the unframed pictures on Mary's walls: the first Mary Trelease and . . . it had to be the young Aidan. And the older man—Aidan's stepfather, Len Smith? Smith had two other stepchildren, Aidan's brother and sister—could it be them in the painting Charlie had seen upstairs at Megson Crescent, the fat, dark pair with eyebrows that dominated their faces? Yes—had to be. Thinking about it, there was a resemblance between them and Aidan.

Mary had copied the pictures from Aidan's exhibition. *No, they're not mine.* That's what she'd said. Then, only moments later, she'd admitted to painting them. Now Charlie understood. Mary had repainted Aidan's pictures herself, the exact same scenes, though the paintings couldn't have been more different from Aidan's muted, painstakingly realistic ones. Charlie smacked the steering wheel in triumph as she realised she had the answer to another question: the copies, Mary's versions of Aidan's pictures, were unframed because they had to be. The people who framed for Mary—Saul Hansard and, later, Jan Garner—had seen Aidan's exhibition; they'd have spotted what Mary was doing if she took her copies in to be framed, and she didn't want them to know.

Why? Why paint someone else's pictures?

Charlie lit a cigarette, her brain on overdrive. The nine buyers: Abberton, Blandford, Darville, Elstow, Goundry, Heathcote, Margerison, Rodwell and Winduss. Their addresses didn't exist and neither did they. Ruth Margerison of Garstead Cottage didn't exist. Garstead Cottage belonged to Villiers, Mary's old school.

And Martha's. Martha Wyers had also been a Villiers girl.

An unpleasant sensation, like the brush of cold fingers, crept up Charlie's spine. What sort of person was she dealing with here? What sort of mind? Could it be that Mary had bought all the pictures from Aidan's exhibition, using false names? Apart from the three paintings bought by Saul Hansard, Cecily Wyers and Kerry Gatti, and Charlie knew that at least two of those had been sold on to Maurice Blandford shortly afterwards.

The story, when Charlie told it to herself, seemed too outlandish to be possible. Mary Trelease was killed at 15 Megson Crescent in 1982. In 2008, another woman, also called Mary Trelease, lives in the very same house. That alone was chilling enough. Not everyone, thought Charlie, would be capable of first dreaming that up and then putting it into practice. Everybody enjoyed a good scary story; hardly anyone knew how to bring one to life.

And in between 1982 and 2008? How did the story bridge a gap of twenty-six years? A job interview, at which a woman falls in love with a man she doesn't know. She writes a book about him. Later, she meets him again when they both have their photographs taken for a feature in *The Times*. It must seem to her as if fate has reunited them. A little later still, she attends the private view of his first art exhibition. She studies his work carefully, being obsessed with him. She sees a painting called *The Murder of Mary Trelease*. She thinks nothing of it, not until some time has elapsed, time during which her obsession has intensified. She hires a private detective who tells her the man's father is in prison for killing a woman called Mary Trelease, and, of course, she remembers the picture. But the picture says something different about who committed the murder. Not in an obvious way—there's no graphic depiction of violence—but subtly, so that the woman, our heroine, thinks she's the only one who knows the truth.

Anyone who cared about stories would know that only the most important character gets to be in that position: knowing everything while everyone else knows nothing. That would be good for the ego, thought Charlie, though ultimately not good enough to restore an irretrievably contaminated specimen to health. This was a woman who, after a failed suicide attempt, painted herself dead, with a noose round her neck. As she wished she could be, or as she thought she deserved to look?

Charlie thought about Ruth Bussey and her self-esteem exercise, her failure to put up flattering photographs of herself alongside the pictures of Charlie, in spite of the book's orders. For the past two years, Charlie had avoided looking at images of herself; she'd avoided being photographed as far as possible. How much more must you have to hate everything you are, were and might ever be to pour all your energy into painting yourself contorted and defeated by death?

Was that the story in her head? Charlie wondered. A woman who loathes herself, in spite of having all the money in the world to buy art, the services of private investigators, whatever she wants? In spite of her immense talent, and everything she could achieve if she looked forward instead of back? She can't, though, that's her tragedy. Her only story's an old one, yet she's terrified of it ending. That's why she plays games, withholds the truth in a way that lets you know she's keeping something from you, forcing you to play hide and seek with her. She has to make it last, because once the game's over, there's nothing left for her.

He seems to have got hold of the idea that he killed you.

Not me.

A woman who knows about leaving you wanting more, about making up people and names that don't exist. Someone who, no matter what she calls herself, no matter what she does with her time, will always be first and foremost an inventor of stories.

Martha Wyers.

'My understanding was that DC Dunning would be coming in person, and bringing a warrant with him,' said Richard Bedell, Villiers' deputy headteacher.

'He will, on both counts,' said Simon, who had been less than frank and done nothing to correct Bedell's assumption that he and Dunning worked together. Bedell was younger than him, and wore faded jeans, a cream fleece and loafers. Simon had to keep reminding himself that he wasn't talking to an unusually confident sixth-former who'd been left in charge of his father's office. The room was the size of most schools' assembly halls. Simon was trying to sit comfortably on a lumpy plum-coloured chaise longue, and found he kept needing to raise his voice to make himself heard across an expanse of beige carpet that was set into a border of hardwood flooring, perfectly even on all sides.

Bedell's oversized desk was covered with piles of exercise books at one end—red and dark green, some thin, some fat with paper inserts, all bedraggled—and telephones and mugs at the other. He had three phones, none of which was a mobile, and twice as many mugs, two of them navy blue and yellow, bearing the school's logo. On the carpet beneath his desk was a coil of black wires from the telephones and his computer, printer and fax machine that looked as if it would take many years to untangle.

'All I'm asking is to be pointed in the direction of Garstead Cottage,' said Simon. 'If Ms Trelease doesn't want to talk to me, she doesn't have to. We'll wait for Neil Dunning to arrive with his warrant. I'd like to try, though. As I explained before, I'm concerned about her safety.'

'And as *I* explained before, DC Waterhouse, I've already established that Mary doesn't want to see or speak to you or any of your colleagues, or have you in her home. She became quite hysterical at the prospect, and I can't afford . . .' Bedell broke off. His chin puckered as he swallowed a yawn. 'Let me spell it out for you,' he said, as if granting Simon a special favour. 'Egan and Cecily Wyers have been extremely generous to us over the years. Villiers isn't like Eton or Marlborough, or most of the public schools you might have heard of—we haven't got vast reserves of capital to fall back on when times are hard. If our numbers fall, as they have recently, and there's less coming in from fees, we're in trouble. Frankly, we need the support of parents like the Wyerses—it's thanks to them alone that we've got a brand spanking new theatre building.' He threw up his hands, a gesture that invited Simon to contemplate the narrowly avoided catastrophe of the school's having to go without this particular asset. 'Our part of the bargain is the cottage, providing a safe haven for Mary where she can get on with her work in peace. In view of which, I'd like to ask you what I asked DC Dunning: is a warrant and all it entails strictly necessary? Because, I won't lie to you, it's not going to go down well with Egan and Cecily.'

'Do Mr and Mrs Wyers have a particular interest in Mary Trelease?' asked Simon.

Bedell's face dropped, losing all its expression. 'Pardon?' he said.

Simon repeated his question.

'Don't you detectives communicate with one another? I explained the situation to DC Dunning in all its irregularity.'

Simon was considering how best to respond to this when Bedell said, 'I'm going to give him a quick call, if that's all right. He said nothing about you turning up, and . . .'

'You've seen my ID,' said Simon. He was getting into that cottage, even if he had to tie Bedell up with telephone wire. 'Did Dunning tell you he wants to speak to Mary Trelease in connection with a murder?'

Bedell closed his eyes. Left them closed for a good few seconds. 'No, he didn't. This is a disaster, a complete disaster.'

'I take it you mean for the murder victim,' said Simon. 'Gemma Crowther, her name was. She was shot in her home on Monday night. The killer then knocked her teeth out and hammered picture hooks into her gums.'

Bedell winced and rubbed the bridge of his nose. He stood up. 'Listen, I'd appreciate it if you'd take my word on one thing. Mary has her problems, I won't deny that. Genius has its price. But she certainly hasn't killed anybody. That's taking it too far, to accuse her of that.'

'I'm not accusing her of anything,' Simon pointed out. 'We want to ask her a few questions, that's all—her and several other people. We're a long way off charging any of them.'

Genius has its price. A despicable motto, if ever Simon had heard one. Was the price payable in human teeth, for fuck's sake?

'Why don't I ring DC Dunning, see how long he's going to be?' Bedell suggested, picking up one of the phones on his desk with a heavy sigh. 'I knew something like this would happen one day.'

'You knew Mary Trelease would become involved in a murder investigation?'

'No, of course not. That's a rather crass thing to say, isn't it? I knew there'd be trouble—that's all I meant. I inherited the situation: Mary and the cottage. If I'd been around at the time, I'd have spoken up strongly against it. Some money's simply not worth the price. As it is, we could find work for a full-time member of staff dealing with parents' complaints. There'll be a shit-storm—pardon my French—if this latest piece of news gets out.'

Bedell's words made little sense to Simon, who knew only that he didn't like the picture that was building up. Bedell looked down at his desk, half-heartedly moving a few pieces of paper around. 'What's Dunning's number?' he asked irritably.

'I left my phone in the car,' Simon lied, patting his pockets. He'd had no reception since he arrived at Villiers. It made him nervous, as if his being uncontactable might be causally linked to catastrophe for those he cared about. He imagined his mother's anguished voice: 'We tried to telephone, but you didn't answer . . .'

'I know where I put it,' said Bedell. 'Wait a second.' He left the room, pulling the door to. Simon heard his shoes squeak as he walked down the corridor, then the sound of a door opening and closing. As soon as Bedell spoke to Dunning, Simon would lose any chance he had of getting into Garstead Cottage. He couldn't afford to wait.

He went out into the corridor and down the stairs opposite Bedell's office door, then down two more flights. He unbolted the door he and Bedell had come in through, went outside and pulled it shut behind him. A long path stretched ahead into the distance, with lantern-style lamp posts and a row of large square brick buildings on either side. How hard could it be to find a cottage? There was nothing that fitted that description in front of him for as far as he could see.

Bedell had left his curtains open when he'd taken Simon into his office. Through the window, Simon had seen a lit courtyard surrounded by long, single-storey prefabricated huts with dark wooden sides that had looked almost oriental. Perhaps Garstead Cottage was one of those.

He walked round to the back of the building, where he found another path that led to what looked like a signpost about 200 metres away. It was much darker here, almost too dark for Simon to read the signs when he reached them. Several rigid rectangles of painted wood with arrow-shaped ends protruded from a pole. One said, 'Cecily Wyers Theatre'. Another said, 'Main Building', but it was the third one Simon read that made him grab the pole and trace the letters with his fingers: 'Darville'. Beneath it, pointing in the same direction, was a sign that said, 'Winduss'.

As far as Simon knew, these names belonged to people who'd bought Aidan Seed's paintings. *Who lived at addresses that didn't exist.* For a few seconds, standing alone in the darkness and the silence in front of this strange object that looked a bit like a white tree, its branches at right angles to its trunk, Simon felt like an idiot who didn't know what to do, or what to think.

There were five paths to choose between. He strained to see as far as he could along each in turn, which wasn't far at all. Each one disappeared into blackness. There was no sign of the prefabricated huts he'd seen from Bedell's window. In the end he decided to follow the sign that said, 'Stable Block', on the off-chance that Garstead Cottage might once have housed whoever looked after the horses. It was as good a guess as any.

He crossed a field, after which the concrete walkway narrowed and gave way to a dirt track. Definitely still a path, though. Simon followed it through a cluster of small trees and into another field. When he started to feel wetness at his ankles, he looked down and saw that he'd been walking on grass. Where was the dirt track? Had it run out or had he strayed off it? He saw dark shapes ahead and made his way towards them. The stable block. He'd assumed, when he'd read the sign, that this would be a conversion: a languages or science laboratory, or living space for the pupils, but as he approached he both heard and smelled evidence of the presence of horses. There was no Garstead Cottage, not here.

He was about to turn back when he heard what sounded like a stifled scream coming from behind the stables. He ran round the squat cluster of buildings, looked in all directions and saw nothing. 'Hello?' he called out. 'Anyone there?' This time he heard a giggle, and walked in the direction it had come from. He'd taken only a few paces forward when something that felt like hard netting pushed him back. A fence, as high as his waist. 'Fuck,' he muttered. More giggles followed. Then he spotted something that stood out because, unlike everything else around him, it wasn't dark: three small orange dots that seemed to be attached to a mass of trees nearby. The glowing ends of cigarettes.

Keeping his eye on them, Simon made his way over to the trees. When he was still too far away to see faces, he heard a voice. 'Oh, man, sir, we're *really, really* sorry. We totally know there's no *way* we're not going to be in, like, pure trouble . . .'

'I think you should punish us?' another girl said, making the statement sound like a question. 'That way we won't make the same mistake again?' A fit of giggles followed this unlikely sounding assertion.

'I'm not a teacher,' Simon told the disembodied voices. 'I'm police. Smoke yourselves stupid for all I care.'

'No way! Oh, man! What's, like, a policeman doing creeping round Villy in the dead of night?'

'This is outrageous,' said the third girl.

Now Simon was closer and could see their faces. They looked about sixteen, and were wearing pyjamas with nothing over them, no coats or anything. They shivered in between fits of hysterical laughter. 'I'm looking for Garstead Cottage,' he told them.

'What are you doing over here, then?' one of the girls said scornfully.

'He's better off over here. You don't want to go to Scary Mary's, Mister Policey-man.'

'Tasha!'

'What? He doesn't. She's, like, a pure nightmare.'

'You're talking about Mary Trelease,' said Simon.

'Oh my God, she's probably his girlfriend or something!'

'Maybe he's come to, like, arrest her?'

'Where's the cottage?' he tried again. 'Can one of you show me?'

A peal of scandalised giggles greeted this suggestion. 'Yeah, *right*! Like we wouldn't be so dead if our house master caught us wandering round at night in our jarmies.'

'She's frightened of Scary Mary. I'll take you, soon as I've finished my ciggie.'

'Flavia, you're *such* a liar! Like you wouldn't be totally too scared.'

'Right back at you, babes.'

'What's there to be scared of?' Simon asked, hoping Neil Dunning wouldn't choose now to arrive with his warrant and find Simon lurking amid the trees with three scantily clad teenage girls.

'Oh my God—he doesn't know!'

'You, like, *so* won't believe us if we tell you?'

'She cuts Villy girls' throats and drinks their blood.' This prompted more giggles.

'I don't believe she exists? I've never seen her, and I've been here since I was thirteen?'

'No, seriously, though, she *doesn't*—drink blood or anything like that. But she *does* only come out at night.'

'That's totally understandable? I'd be too ashamed to come out in daylight if my face looked like that.'

'She starved herself, right, and once all the fat had gone from under her skin, her face collapsed and she was left with the face of, like, an eighty-year-old hag. That's pure truth, man.'

'She's a Villy *legend*.'

'The oral storytelling tradition,' one of the girls said in a mock deep voice, and they all screamed with laughter. Simon guessed they were aping one of their teachers.

'Shut *up*, poo-brain! If I lose my exeat privs thanks to you, it'll be pure tragedy.'

'No way are we getting curfed for helping a policeman.'

'Shut up and let me tell him. He hasn't got time to waste listening to you two infants. We don't know for sure . . .'

'We so do. I heard Miss Westaway and Mrs Dean talking about it.'

'It might all be scurlyest rumours.'

'You mean scurrilous. Scurlyest isn't a word. I apologise on behalf of my intoxicated housemate,' said the girl nearest to Simon. 'It's so not a rumour—it's the scandalous truth. Scary Mary had a boyfriend who dumped her, right, and she was so miz she tried to kill herself. Hanged herself in Garstead Cottage.'

'And he was there too, the boyfriend,' one of the other girls chipped in.

'Oh, yeah, I forgot that bit. Yeah, she made him go round for the whole *closure* thing.' The girl Simon thought was called Flavia—unless he'd got mixed up, and she was Tasha—drew invisible quote marks in the air. 'And when he got there, she was standing on the dining table, with a rope round her neck, attached to the light or something . . .'

'A chandelier! It was a chandelier!'

'Yeah, right. In a cottage?'

'I heard it was a chandelier.'

'What*ever*. So, like, he called an ambulance and she was rushed to hospital, but on the way there in the ambulance, she *died*—like, majorly *died*. And she had no heartbeat or oxygen going to her brain for three whole minutes . . .'

'It was ten minutes . . .'

'No one comes back to life after *ten minutes*, babes. I've seen Scary Mary—she's odd, but she's not a veg. What was I saying? Oh, yeah: the ambulance people brought her back from, like, beyond death, and she was supposed to be brain damaged, but she wasn't. She was, like, totally fine. Except she wasn't, because that was when she turned into Scary Mary. She changed her name.'

'Stop,' said Simon. 'What do you mean? Changed it to what?'

'Mary Trelease.'

'Scary Martha would have sounded rubbish—it doesn't rhyme.'

'Martha?' If the girls' confidence and state of undress hadn't made him feel so uncomfortable, he'd have asked more forcefully.

'Martha Wyers—that's what she used to be called. But after she died and came back to life, she wouldn't let anyone call her that any more, because, like, Martha Wyers had died?'

'Gross! This story's a pure freak-out, every time,' one of the girls said, wrapping her arms round herself.

'She lashed anyone who called her Martha. Even her mum and dad had to start calling her Mary.'

'Lashed?' Simon interrupted. He had to ask.

'What? Oh, it's, like, an expression?'

'Translation for Villy outsider: she got really angry with anyone who called her Martha.'

'And she lost weight when she turned into Mary. She was a pure tubber before.'

'She was pining, wasn't she, for her one true love?'

Simon couldn't think clearly with the girls chattering at him. 'Do you know why she chose the name Mary Trelease?'

They looked at one another, silent for the first time. 'No,' said one shirtily after a few seconds, annoyed to have been caught out. 'What does that matter? A name's just a name, isn't it?'

'Yes it is, Flavia *Edna* Seawright.' More giggles erupted.

'Her name's not the only thing she changed after her *resurrection*, I know that,' said Flavia, in an attempt to divert attention.

'Oh, yeah—how weird is this?'

'She used to be a writer—she had a book published.'

'Yeah, there's a copy in our house library.'

'She must have been in Heathcote, then.'

'No, Margerison.'

Simon understood the signs he'd seen. *Boarding houses.*

'What house she was in is so, like, trivial? She was a writer, but after she hanged herself and it didn't work, she never wrote another word—she took up painting instead. Not me personally, but loads of Villy girls have seen her wandering around at night, smoking, covered in paint . . .'

'Didn't Damaris Clay-Hoffman stop her and ask her if she had a spare ciggy?'

'Damaris Clay-Hoffman's such a rank liar!'

'Where's her cottage?' asked Simon. 'Don't come with me, just tell me where,' he said to the girls. He wanted to approach quietly, not with a screeching chorus around him.

As Flavia Edna Seawright pointed to her left, a loud noise, like a small explosion, burst out of the night. 'Oh, my God!' she said, grabbing Simon's arm. 'I'm not even joking any more, man. That sounded like a gun.'

27

Wednesday 5 March 2008

'A stupid mistake,' says Mary. 'You said "Go to your parents' house". You meant Cecily's house, didn't you? I could see from your face that you knew. You're a bad liar.'

Pain burns all the way through me. There's a bullet inside me, metal in my body. I saw it coming towards me, too fast for me to move. I'm lying on the floor. I reach out for Aidan's hand, but he's too far away.

'You're a . . . good liar,' I manage to say. 'You're Martha.'

'No. Martha died. Her heart stopped. Her mind stopped. You can't die and be the same person afterwards. I'm one of the few people alive who knows that's not possible.'

'Abberton . . . the names . . .' I try to raise my head, to look down at my body, but it hurts too much. I can't move and think at the same time, and I have to think.

'What about them? What about the names?'

'Aidan didn't destroy your . . . paintings. You did it to him. You bought . . .' I can't go on.

She looks down at me. I feel light; not a person any more but a weightless flow of pain. My mind starts to hum; it would be easy to fall into that comforting sound, allow it to roll me away. 'He did it,' Mary insists. 'He took all my pictures and he cut them to pieces.'

'No.' I gasp for air. 'The names . . . boarding houses . . .'

'No!' Mary raises her voice. 'I'd never do that. He did it. He did it to me.'

'You bought his pictures using those names.' Each breath is a struggle, but without the struggle there would be nothing, no energy to stay alive. 'You . . . made him come here . . .' My mind fills with words that would take too much effort to say. *He didn't want to see you again, but you bribed him: fifty grand for a commission.* 'He stopped painting because of what you did.'

Scenes from the story Mary told me drift back into my mind. *One half true, the other half lies.* The cottage door left open, as she said. Aidan walking in, looking for her. Finding her standing on the dining table with a rope round her neck, his ruined paintings on the floor in front of her. Did she tell him what she'd done and then jump? Two shocks for him, locked together in one moment for devastating impact. That's why he couldn't move at first, why he didn't rush to save her life. He was traumatised, paralysed.

'My gardens.' Every word wrings sweat from me. 'Not Aidan. You did it. One last summer, to punish me for . . . Saul's gallery. I frightened you. You hate not . . . being in control.' *The second after Charlie Zailer spoke to you on Monday and told you I was Aidan's girlfriend. You'd given me* Abberton *as a gift, without knowing: another loss of control. Another punishment.*

'What about your dead boyfriend?' says Mary impatiently, leaning over me. 'What about what he did?'

I close my eyes. I know what he didn't do. He didn't lie to me. Not until later. Even then, he didn't lie outright. To the police, yes, but never to me. 'He killed Mary Trelease,' I breathe. 'Years ago.' He was telling the truth when he told me that, at the Drummond Hotel. It was before I mentioned *Abberton*, before his confession had made me freeze, when he trusted me without reservation.

The woman I can only think of as Mary bends over me, using the gun to push her hair away from her face. 'What Mary Trelease are you talking about?' she asks. 'Who do you mean?'

'I don't know.'

'Exactly. None of this involves you. You should have gone

away. I *sent* you away.' I hear this as an accusation of ingratitude. She's appalled by me. 'Whatever you think you know, you're wrong.'

Anger kicks in, as intense as the pain. 'I know everything but who she was. She lived at 15 Megson Crescent. Aidan killed her there.' In the front bedroom. Her naked, in the centre of the bed, Aidan's hands round her throat . . .

'He killed her, and let his stepfather take the blame,' says Mary patiently, putting her face in front of mine so that I can see her telling me. 'His stepfather's been in prison for twenty-six years, and Aidan's left him there to rot, never visited him or written to him, not once. How do you feel about him now, now that you know that?' Her words drift past me without taking root.

'The house,' I say, my lungs aching with the effort. 'That's why you bought it. Why you changed your name to hers.'

Mary points the gun at my face. I close my eyes, wait for her to shoot, but nothing happens. When I open them, she hasn't moved. Neither has the gun. 'Why?' she says.

I can't answer. I don't know how much blood I've lost, though the sensation of losing it is constant. I feel transparent. Hollow.

'It's up to you. You can talk or you can die.'

'No! Please, don't . . .' I try to turn my head away from the gun.

'Did you think that was a threat?' She laughs. 'I meant that if you talk, if you start to tell a story, you won't let go until you get to the end. For your mind to keep working, your heart has to keep working. You have to stay alive.'

She's right. Not everything she says is a lie. The story of Aidan and Martha, right up until the point where she hanged herself, that was all true. Except . . . yes, even the part about Mary writing to Aidan, berating him for treating Martha badly. Not literally true, but symbolically accurate, as accurate as she could be without revealing her true identity. *There are divisions within every person. Especially those who are forced to bear unbearable pain.* The Mary who wrote angry, accusatory letters to Aidan—though she wasn't called Mary then—was the intelligent part of Martha Wyers, the part that could see the truth: that the relationship was going nowhere, that Aidan didn't love Martha the way she loved him.

No surprise that he didn't. Hard to love a woman who proclaims undying love one minute then savages you the next.

'Tell me the story you think you know about me,' says Mary. She sits down beside me and draws her legs up to her chest, balancing the gun on her knees. If I could move my right arm, I could grab it.

I worked it out, put it all together in the taxi on the way back here. I have to do it again now, force my brain to keep going. 'Phone an ambulance,' I say. 'You can't let us die.'

'Aidan's been dead for a while,' she says matter-of-factly.

'No,' I moan. 'Please. It might not be too late.' Martha came back to life. Aidan can't be dead. I won't believe it.

'Look at us. One bleeding body, one corpse, and a husk who's been half dead for years. No one who took an objective look at this room could think it was anything but too late, Ruth. For all of us.' She twists her hair into a spiral.

'Private detective,' I whisper. 'Told you . . . Aidan's stepfather . . . in prison for killing Mary Trelease. You'd seen the painting . . .' No. Can't get it wrong, can't waste words or breath. 'You'd bought it—*The Murder of Mary Trelease*. Bought it and . . . destroyed it, like you did all of them.'

'No.' Mary's voice is firm. 'I'm an artist. I don't destroy art.'

In my head, I see a picture of a man and a woman in a bed. Naked, or the woman is. The man's hands round the woman's neck. The man recognisable as Aidan, so that Mary—Martha—knew Len Smith wasn't the killer.

'Why did he kill her?' I mouth the words, not sure if I'm making any sound at all. I feel deathly cold all over my body. Like ice.

'He'd have told you if he wanted you to know.' Mary smiles.

'Martha. Wasn't. Alone. Any. More,' I exhale one word at a time. *I can do it.* I can get to the end. 'An ally ... another woman Aidan had ... hurt. Mary Trelease.'

Mary puts the gun down behind her and leans back on her hands. 'Show me anyone who's survived an ordeal and I'll show you a shrink in the making,' she says. 'Ally is a good word. What about you, Ruth? Aidan's hurt you too, hasn't he? Playing games with you, messing with your head. And Stephen Elton hurt you.' She pulls a packet of Marlboro Reds and a lighter out of her pocket, lights one. 'All women whose lives have been ruined by men are my allies. All of them. If we organised ourselves, we could be the world's most powerful army.'

'You called yourself Mary Trelease. You bought ... house ...' I have to talk, to stop myself thinking about my own helplessness.

'Shall we speed this up?' says Mary impatiently. 'I moved to Spilling when I found out Aidan lived there. What sort of man moves back to the town where he spent his miserable childhood? You might want to think about that.' I turn my face away from her cigarette, breathing is hard enough without the smoke. 'Fifteen Megson Crescent is the house he grew up in. I had to have it, obviously, so I bribed the owners out.'

'You called yourself Mary Trelease.'

'I changed my name legally. I *am* Mary Trelease.'

'You started painting because painting ... was *his*,' I murmur, pulling my mind back as it starts to drift. *Get to the end.* 'Wasn't ... enough that you'd destroyed his work. Everything that ... had been his ...'

'What? Ruth!'

She's patting my face. 'I'm still here,' I say. Reassuring her. She wants to hear the story. 'Painting. You ... took it away from Aidan. Made it yours. You were good at it. Better.'

'Yes,' Mary stresses the word. 'I was better than him. He gave up. I never give up. You only need to look at our backgrounds to understand why. The shrink I saw, the one who told me to write my story in the third person—you know what else she told me?'

I try to shake my head, but it won't move. My body is numb, detaching from the pain. I can't feel anything but my thoughts: frail, flickering threads I'm trying hard to hold on to.

'Ninety-five per cent of her work is undoing psychological damage done to people in childhood, by their parents. *Ninety-five* per cent.' Mary sounds angry. 'Can you believe that? I was in the other five per cent, the tiny minority. I started from a position of safety and happiness: an adoring mum and dad, before I disgraced them and brought suicide and madness to the family. Money, and the best education it could buy. I've always believed in my own talents and abilities. Aidan never has. His childhood was an eighteen-year prison sentence.'

'Why?' I fight to stay conscious.

'I suppose it wasn't so bad before his mum died. Even then, they were dirt poor and lived in a slum. You've seen the house— it's a slum, right? You wouldn't keep animals there, let alone use it to house human beings. Aidan's stepfather, Len, the one in prison—he was drunk all the time, violent. The sort of person you'd expect to find on a council estate—all my Megson Crescent neighbours are versions of Len Smith, or his family.' I hear her laugh. 'Knock on any door and there's someone waiting to sell you a gun and teach you how to use it. From the day Aidan was born, he was in danger from his surroundings. That's why he gives up so easily. That's why he's dead and we're not.'

'No . . .'

'He gave up as soon as Gemma Crowther let me into her flat. Saw me and gave up.'

'You shot her. Not Aidan.'

'She had my picture. He gave her my picture.'

I force my eyes open, aware that what I've just heard is an admission.

'I'm afraid I forgot all about you when I saw it,' says Mary.

'You and her, I mean—the history. I remembered too late, once she was already dead, that she ought to have suffered, ideally, instead of dying straight away. You'd have preferred her to suffer, wouldn't you?'

There are some punishments no one should have to endure, not even Gemma Crowther. Death. Torture. No one deserves those things. No one has the right to mete them out.

'No?' Mary sounds irritated. Her face is a blur; I can't see her properly any more. 'In that case, you'll be relieved to hear that she didn't feel a thing.' She giggles, high-pitched, like a little girl. 'I did my best for you, anyway,' she says. 'Or, rather, I gave Aidan instructions and saw to it that he complied. He's the framer, not me.' She laughs, a low, raw noise from deep in her throat. 'There's nothing wrong with wanting and taking revenge. It's the most natural thing in the world. Do you know what Cecily said? She and Martha had a huge row on the way home from Aidan's private view, after Cecily had bought one of the paintings. Not that she got to keep it for long. It met with an unfortunate accident. Before Martha worked out how she was going to put a stop to Aidan's success, she told Cecily she wanted him to fail. She wanted none of his pictures to sell, not a single one. She wanted him to fail more than she wanted to succeed herself. That's the question the journalist from *The Times* should have asked, not life or work. Your own success or someone else's failure.' In the short silence between 'Survivor' finishing and starting again, I hear the faint crackle of Mary's cigarette as she inhales.

'Cecily quoted some famous writer or other who'd said that writing well was the best revenge. "You've got your writing, Martha. Aidan's talent doesn't threaten yours. You don't need him or his failure to prop you up. You can succeed without him." That's what she said. Have you ever heard anything so stupid? Writing well, the best revenge? What a load of shit! Is it a better revenge than killing someone, or fire-bombing their house? I don't think so.'

Eighteen empty frames. Aidan made frames for the paintings he'd lost, the ones Mary destroyed. Why won't she admit it?

'I know why,' I tell her.

'What? You know why what?' I can feel her face close to mine, her breathing. I twist my mouth into a smile. I want to hurt her.

I can only say it in my head, not out loud. I can tell the story to myself. Mary's painting might have been a way to get revenge on Aidan at first, to prove she could beat him at his own game, but it came to mean more to her than that. She was good at it—not just good; brilliant. It gave her something she recognised, even in her misery, as being valuable. After a while—maybe months, maybe years—cutting up painting after painting of Aidan and adding it to the pile wasn't enough for her. She could see she was getting better. Painting wasn't Aidan's talent any more, it was hers. She stopped feeling as if she was attacking Aidan when she carved a canvas to pieces with a knife, or hacked at it with a pair of scissors; she was attacking herself, her own work. She didn't want to do that any more. Something had to change.

She started to paint other pictures that weren't of Aidan, ones she kept. The ones I saw in her house, of the family who used to live on her estate, and the *Abberton* series. Those might not have been of Aidan, but they were about him. About what she did to him. They mattered to her. They were the story of her life.

'You . . . got scared.' I stop, try to fill my lungs with the air I need to carry on. 'You understood . . .' I want to tell her I know how she felt.

'What? What did I understand?' She shakes me, and I let out a howl of pain. My body throws out a last spurt of energy to fight it. I use it to get more words out. 'You understood . . . how it would feel to have your pictures . . . destroyed. The worst thing . . . what you'd done to Aidan. You felt guilty.' *That's why you won't admit it. The guilt, once you felt the full horror of what you'd done, was more than you could bear.*

'I don't believe in guilt,' says Mary quickly. 'My therapist said it was an unproductive emotion.'

I see how it must have happened: her guilt and shame transmuted into paranoia, that Aidan would find out about her—where she was living, what she was doing. That he'd do to her what she'd done to him. She couldn't risk it. The only way to make sure it never happened was never to sell any of her paintings, to maintain absolute control. She was terrified of what Aidan might do to her, of the punishment she felt, deep down, that she deserved from him. At the same time, she couldn't resist the impulse to close in on him, once she knew where he was—to infiltrate his life, lurk on the edges of it, where he might just notice her.

She took her paintings to Saul to be framed, knowing Aidan had worked for Saul, that Saul had bought a picture from Aidan's exhibition. Mary had to have whatever had been Aidan's, including Saul's support.

You're not a shrink.

I could be. Easily. I don't believe I'd need any training whatsoever. All I'd need is experience, which I've got, and a brain, which I've got.

I know I'm right. Mary set out to steal Aidan's life as a punishment, because she believed he'd stolen Martha's. She moved to the same town, lived in his old house, did the work he used to do, mixed with people who had been his, like Saul—all without him realising. It was about proximity as much as punishment; she wanted to be close to him. Her plan worked perfectly, until I ruined it, until Saul sent me to Aidan to ask for work. That was when the past and the present crashed into one another. She must have known they would, eventually.

What was supposed to happen? I want to ask her how she imagined her and Aidan's story would end, before I came along and disrupted her plans, but my tongue has sunk to the floor of my mouth like a lead weight. Something else has changed, too. The song has stopped: 'Survivor'. Stopped for good. It's still playing inside me, the lyrics and music imprinted on the dark walls of my mind, like gold letters left on the night by sparklers.

How can it have stopped? Mary hasn't left the room. She doesn't seem to notice the silence.

'Stand up slowly and raise your hands above your head.'

Stand? I can't move at all. Then I realise it was a man's voice I heard, not Mary's. He was talking to her.

Help. He's going to help me.

I drag my eyes open and at first see nothing but Mary's hair spread across her back. She's turned away from me. Then she growls and lunges and I see him crouched down in the corner of the room. He's got the gun. He knocks Mary to the ground.

Waterhouse. DC Waterhouse. He speaks to me without taking his eyes off Mary. 'It's all right, Ruth. There's an ambulance on the way. You're going to be fine. Just hold on.'

Mary crawls across the room like a spider, grabs the hammer that's lying near Aidan. I blink at Waterhouse, my eyes watering until I can hardly see.

'What are you planning to do with that hammer, Mary?' He sounds calm. I like hearing his voice. 'Put it down.'

'No.'

'If you try to use it on anybody, I'll shoot. Without hestitation.'

A few seconds later I hear a crunch of bone. All I can see is greyness.

'There. I used it on myself, and you haven't shot me. You were lying. Shall I carry on? I've got nine other fingers: Abberton, Blandford, Darville, Elstow, Goundry, Heathcote, Margerison, Rodwell, Windus.' She giggles hysterically.

'Try to accept that it's over, Mary,' says Waterhouse.

I hear footsteps, too heavy to be Mary's, then her voice. 'I wouldn't bother. If he's got a pulse now, he won't have for long.'

My mind clears in a flash. Why did she say that? She told me Aidan was dead. Was she lying?

I wait for Waterhouse to say the words I'm desperate to hear, but he says nothing, and I'm too weak to ask.

If he's alive, then he's about to die. Mary thinks he'll die. This might be my last chance.

I don't blame you for not trusting me, Aidan. I don't deserve your trust.

If I pretend he and I are the only people left in the world and force my words into his mind, maybe he'll hear me.

In London, when you told me about Mary Trelease, I didn't say what you needed to hear. I didn't say I loved you no matter what, even though you'd said it to me. And then the next day, when I told you I'd seen the picture: Abberton, *by Mary Trelease, dated 2007 . . . I told you you couldn't have killed her. I'd met her. I described her, described Martha Wyers. You recognised the description—the hair, the birthmark under her mouth—and you knew. In that instant, you must have seen it all: that Martha had assumed the name of the woman you'd killed. It had to mean she knew what you'd done. She knew, and she was in Spilling, she'd been to Saul's gallery. She was moving in closer. You thought I might be hers, not yours—I might have been part of her plan. Another trick. Like your sell-out exhibition, the success you'd believed in until she showed you the truth.*

You'd seen the lengths she'd go to in order to destroy you. What if she went to the police? And now you'd confessed to me—someone you no longer trusted. What if, between us, she and I could send you to prison for murder?

It won't have taken you long to see the problem with that theory: it was too simple. Mary hadn't gone to the police, not so far. She couldn't have—the police had shown no interest in you. I didn't go to them either, after what you told me in London, not straight away. And I loved you: you could see I loved you. You could feel it. You started to hope that maybe it wasn't an act, maybe I was telling the truth. Was it a test, sending me to her house for the painting? If I was innocent, if I wasn't con-

spiring with her against you, then surely I wouldn't be able to get my hands on it—was that what you thought? When I came back with Abberton, *what did you think then? That it all seemed a bit too easy: the artist who'd refused to sell me her painting suddenly decides to give it to me as a gift? Even then, you couldn't bring yourself to believe I was on her side, because you loved me.*

Was it revenge you had in mind at first? Do what she'd done to you? Did you want to get your hands on her picture so that you could obliterate it? Or did you only want to see it? You hadn't known she was a painter until I told you. Did you want to see her work, see what it was like? Whether she was any good? Did you fantasise about killing her when you heard she'd called her painting Abberton? *She was taunting you. You knew that, Mary being Mary—being Martha—she'd see it through to the end, that* Abberton *would be followed by* Blandford, Darville, Elstow *and the rest: the buyers who'd never existed and never bought your work, named after the boarding houses at her school.*

What you said to me at the workshop after Waterhouse and Charlie Zailer left, about seeing the future: that if you hadn't killed Mary Trelease already then maybe you were going to— was that the threat Mary took it for? Did you want me to tell her you'd called her a bitch and said she should get out of Spilling, go somewhere you wouldn't find her? No, it was more than that, even if that was part of it. Waterhouse had just told me how the real Mary Trelease died—strangled, naked, in a bed. You never wanted me to know the terrible details of what you'd done. I think that was the moment you realised: if I stuck around, if we stayed together, I'd end up finding out the whole truth. You wanted to protect me. You knew I'd be terrified if you started talking about seeing the future—you wanted to drive me away so that I wouldn't be sullied by you or your past crime. And maybe you wanted to frighten me because you were angry, too. I didn't trust you enough to tell you the full truth about so many things. I told you I went to the police, but I didn't mention that it was Charlie Zailer I'd spoken to, the woman whose face is all over my bedroom wall. I never told you why I stopped working for Saul, not really.

You didn't need to try to scare Mary, if that was your intention. She was afraid of you anyway, obsessively so. She called the police to Garstead Cottage regularly, made them check you weren't hiding in there, waiting to take your revenge. She couldn't believe retribution wasn't lying in wait for her, couldn't conceive of a world in which a person might get away with a crime as serious as hers. She doesn't care two hoots about what she did to Gemma Crowther—that, in her eyes, was justice. It's what she did to your paintings that she can't bear. That's why she can't stand to hear me say the nine names, why my asking 'Who's Abberton?' at Saul's gallery had the effect on her that it did.

At the art fair, at your insistence, I described the picture I'd seen on TiqTaq's stand: the outline of a person, not recognisable as male or female, stuffed with what looked like scraps of painted cloth. Pieces of your pictures: that's what she used to fill in the human form. Did you want me to get Abberton for you to prove I wasn't lying about having seen it, or because it had those pieces in it and you wanted your pictures back, even in shreds? Maybe both. I think you wanted to have the scraps of your work rather than let her keep them.

I hear another bone-splitting crunch.

'Don't do that,' says Waterhouse. 'How can you do that to yourself?'

'Easy. I don't paint with my left hand.'

When I told you Saul had given me Mary's address, the look on your face . . . you hadn't realised until then that she was living in your old house, where you killed the real Mary Trelease. You must have been able to see that I was telling the truth, that the address meant nothing to me, but it's hard to banish doubt once it's crept in. You didn't believe my love for you was unconditional, not after the way I'd reacted to your confession. And

Mary—Martha—knew what you'd done. You knew that eventually she'd use that knowledge, use the power she had over you.

'Hold on for the ambulance, Ruth. It should be here any minute.' Waterhouse is talking to me. All I want is to know if Aidan's alive or not. Why won't he tell me that?

'You're not as clever as you think you are,' I hear Mary say.

'How clever is that?'

'I followed you to London. You were following Aidan. You didn't see me, did you? You took me straight to Gemma Crowther's flat.'

'You killed her,' says Waterhouse.

'Not me. Aidan.' She knows I'm too weak to contradict her. She's enjoying it: lying in front of me, knowing I can't stop her.

'You're holding the hammer you used to knock her teeth out and hammer nails into her gums,' says Waterhouse.

'Aidan did those things. Why would I kill her? He wanted revenge for what she did to Ruth. Anyone would.'

'If he was the one holding the gun on Monday night, how come he ended up getting shot?' There's a pause. 'You've got no answer for that, have you?'

'I'm not saying I didn't shoot *him*. I'm saying I didn't shoot Gemma.' He's made her angry. 'You're no Sherlock Holmes, are you? It's okay, you don't need to be. I can tell you what happened.'

'Go on.'

'Where do you want me to start? Aidan had to find out about Gemma and Stephen for himself. Ruth told him nothing—can you believe that? No communication whatsoever. A relationship like that can't last. If Ruth didn't want him to know, she shouldn't have kept so many trauma keepsakes. That's very common, to do that. Did you know that?'

'No.'

I feel as if I'm hearing the conversation from a distance. It's like listening to a far-away radio. I could so easily drift out of the range of the voices.

'Aidan found a box full of souvenirs under her bed, every-thing she'd kept from Gemma's trial.'

When? I want to ask. I can guess the answer: after the art fair, after he moved in with me. He searched my house, looking for evidence that Mary and I were in league against him.

'He looked Gemma and Stephen up on the internet and found what he expected to find,' Mary tells Waterhouse. 'Their attack on Ruth, all that. But the name Gemma Crowther kept coming up in another context too—on Quaker websites. That's how he found out which meeting she went to. He started going too. He wanted to find out if she was the same Gemma Crow-ther who'd nearly killed his girlfriend.'

'Told you all this at gunpoint, did he?'

'He didn't have to say anything he didn't want to. Neither do I. I'm telling you because I want to, no other reason.' Mary's voice is full of scorn.

'Did he find out, then?' Waterhouse asks. 'That she was the same Gemma Crowther?'

'Not at first. Not until she mentioned that she used to live near Lincoln. Then he knew. He asked her why she moved to London. That was the test: to see if she'd changed. If she had, he said, she'd have told him the truth: what she'd done to Ruth, and that she was sorry, that she was a different person now. At the very least she'd have mentioned having been in prison, even if she didn't say what for. But she didn't. She lied—made up some story about wanting a change of scene and career. He knew she was a fake when she told him that.' Mary laughs. 'She was a healer, did you know that? What a fucking hypocrite! No loss to the world, that's for sure.'

'Why did Aidan give Gemma Crowther your painting?' Waterhouse asks.

Silence. Or else they're talking but I can't hear them any more. When I hear Mary's voice, I'm relieved. 'He said they de-served each other. Gemma and the picture.' She's crying. 'As if a painting's a moral agent, as if it can *deserve* anything. Monday night was going to be the last time he saw her—he told me. He wanted nothing more to do with her, or me. He was going to leave *Abberton* with her because it seemed *appropriate*, he said. And then he'd be rid of us both for ever, me and her.'

'Makes sense,' says Waterhouse. 'That's why you made him lock *Abberton* in the boot of his car before forcing him at gunpoint to drive here. It wasn't only about framing him for Gemma's murder, was it? It was symbolic. You wanted to show him he couldn't shake you off so easily.'

He's right, isn't he Mary? You wanted the police to find something of Aidan's and something of yours together: his car, your painting.

Aidan knew he couldn't shake you off. That was one lesson you didn't have to teach him. It's why he went to the police and confessed, as soon as he saw I was planning to involve them. Thinking about it, I'm sure he followed me that day. I told him I was going to the dentist, but I'm a poor liar. He was right not to trust me. He'd confided in me and I betrayed him. Not straight away, but eventually, when the uncertainty became too much for me. He'd been convinced I would, ever since our night in London—it was only a matter of time. And when the time came, he was ready with his official confession. It was the only way he could keep control of the situation.

He as good as sent the police straight to your house, Mary, to see if you'd tell them. If you were going to ruin his life again, he wanted you to get it over with. He was trying to force your hand. You could easily have told Waterhouse or Charlie Zailer the truth: that your name used to be Martha Wyers, that Mary Trelease was the name of a woman Aidan had killed. You could have told them about the painting in his exhibition, The Murder of Mary Trelease.

What was in that picture, Mary? I know you remember. How annoyed you must have been when you found out from your private detective about Mary Trelease's death. You'd had, in that painting, evidence of Aidan's crime—had it and destroyed it.

How good was it, as proof? What story did the picture tell? I'm surprised you didn't have a stab at recreating it yourself, since by that point you'd started your new life as a painter. You must have remembered it detail for detail. Did you do a sketch of it and put it somewhere safe, so that you wouldn't forget what you'd seen and what you knew?

No answers come. No one can hear the questions going round in my head.

What was in the picture, Aidan? Nothing obvious. You'd only have risked calling it The Murder of Mary Trelease *if it wasn't too much of a giveaway. It can't have been a painting of you strangling her in which you were recognisable as the killer— people like Jan Garner and Saul Hansard would have asked questions. So what was it?*

You told the police you'd killed Mary, told them how and where you did it. But the woman you described was Martha— the woman you knew they'd find alive at 15 Megson Crescent. That was the point where you can't have been sure. It was a gamble: either she'd tell them everything, produce whatever proof she had, or she wouldn't. She'd say nothing. And the police would dismiss your story as the ravings of a deranged man, a man who could look them in the eye and insist that he's murdered somebody who isn't dead. You wanted them to think you were crazy. You didn't want to go to prison.

You regretted telling me you'd killed Mary Trelease as soon as the words were out and you saw the horror on my face. But you couldn't take it back, not something as big as that. You couldn't say you were joking. I wouldn't have believed you. I could see the state you were in. Your only hope was to turn your confession into one you knew could be disproved—disproved by the existence of a woman calling herself Mary Trelease.

As much as you wanted to protect yourself, you also wanted to confess. And you did: finally, you went to the police and told the truth. Even when you had to lie, when you had to withhold so much of the story that you ended up telling a different story

*altogether, you were still able to say the main thing that was
true: that you'd killed Mary Trelease, that you'd strangled her in
bed, in that room. It must have felt good to say it, after so many
years of guilt and silence. Unburdening yourself, but with a
safety net in place to give the lie to your confession—the presence of a real live Mary in the house where you told the police
they'd find her body.*

*She didn't tell them what she knew. That would have meant
handing control over to them, and there was no way she'd do
that. You saw she hadn't done it—no detectives came back to
you to ask about the other Mary Trelease, the real one. But it
still wasn't over. Martha Wyers wasn't going to disappear; you
knew how doggedly clingy she was, how determined she was to
latch on to your life as if it was rightfully hers. She was still
there, at 15 Megson Crescent. She still knew what you'd done. It
would never have been over, not unless you'd killed her, and you
couldn't do that. You weren't a killer. I don't know why you
killed a woman years ago, but I know you're not a killer.*

'Me, frame Aidan? He's a murderer—a cold, calculating murderer. He strangled a woman—he told you so himself and you
were too stupid to listen.'

*Martha's right: you wanted to know if Gemma Crowther
was sorry for what she'd done to me, if she'd changed. You can't
change unless you face up to what you've done. That's what you
tried to do in London, at the Drummond Hotel. Maybe you'd
have succeeded if I'd given you the support you needed instead
of letting you down.*

*You wanted Gemma to show you she'd changed so that you
could believe that sort of change was possible. If she could re-
deem herself, so could you. You must have wondered about
Martha, too. Yes. That's why you told her about Gemma, about
wanting to see if she regretted what she'd done. Did you hope
Martha would apologise for the terrible thing she'd done to you,
even while she had a gun pointed at your face? Yes. I know the
way a victim's mind works, being one myself. You can accept*

*that someone has damaged you beyond repair, and maybe that
they will again. What you can't accept is a total absence of regret.*

*Martha didn't say she was sorry. Of course she didn't. Did
you know then that you were better than her? Or did you start
to wonder if anyone, any human being, was any good at all?
Maybe you were as bad as Martha and Gemma—a killer who
hadn't had the guts to face up to his crime, who'd let someone
else take the blame. Did you say whatever you needed to say
after that to make Martha shoot you? Was it a relief when she
did?*

'Which woman did Aidan kill?' Waterhouse's voice swims
under the surface of my consciousness. 'Mary? You said he
killed a woman. Which woman?'

'Me! He killed me!'

'Simon!' A third voice. Not mine. A woman's. I have to open
my eyes again. When I do, I see Waterhouse turning, Charlie
Zailer at the window, Mary lunging for the gun. *No . . .*

She's got them both now, the gun and the hammer, one in
each hand. There's something wrong with the way she's holding
the hammer.

'Bussey's alive, Seed's dead,' Waterhouse says.

I breathe in, breathe out. I think to myself that I ought to
stop if I want to die. *Suicide: a sin.* Does it count if all you do is
stop breathing, when breathing's so hard? If there's a God, does
he have a view on that?

'Aidan's not dead,' Mary says quickly. 'If he were dead, I'd be
dead, and I'm not.'

'Put the gun and hammer down, Mary,' Charlie Zailer says.
'There's an ambulance outside. This has to stop now.'

'Aidan's not dead! Check.'

I hear movement; then, a few seconds later: 'She's right.
There's still a pulse.'

Relief washes through me. *There's an ambulance outside, Aidan. Just hold on a little bit longer.*

'Stay away from me!' Mary growls like an animal. She's behind Waterhouse, pressing the gun against his head. Her hand is shaking, her finger wobbling the trigger. 'I'll kill him if you come any closer.'

'That's my fiancé you've got there,' says Charlie. 'Did you know that? Remember, we talked about him? You wondered why I wouldn't choose to paint him, if I had to paint somebody.'

'I don't care who he is. Stop where you are, or I'll shoot him. I mean it!'

'I love him. We're supposed to be getting married, even though everyone we know thinks it's a really bad idea.'

'Shut up!'

'It isn't a bad idea, though, because I can't be happy unless I'm with Simon. And after what I've been through, I think I deserve to be happy. You know all about what happened to me, right? You told me you did. I'm just like you, Martha. My life was in pieces, all because of a man . . .'

'Don't call me that!'

'. . . but I was lucky enough to find a way out of my despair. I've got a chance to be happy now, and . . . well, the thing is, Simon and I haven't actually been happy together yet, even though we've known each other for years. All we've done is waste time.'

Mary swings the gun round, points it at Charlie. The hammer falls from her left hand. That's right: she broke her fingers.

'Put the gun down, Mary,' says Waterhouse.

'Keep quiet!' Her voice is shaking so much, I barely recognise the words. 'Or I'll shoot you so you die, like Gemma. Not like these two. I never wanted to kill them. Ruth's my friend.'

'You didn't want to kill Aidan?' Charlie says. 'You shot him in the chest.'

'I shot him in the shoulder. I . . . I meant to aim higher. I didn't want to shoot him at all, but he wouldn't . . .'

'Wouldn't what?'

'He wouldn't admit that he loves me.'

I hear a series of noises that are painful to listen to: shrill one minute, rasping the next. Can they all be coming from Mary? They don't sound human.

'The medics need to come in here and help Aidan and Ruth,' says Charlie gently. 'You're going to let them do that, aren't you, Martha?'

'Martha's dead!'

'You said you didn't want to kill them . . .'

'If I do what you're asking, what will happen to me?'

'Prison. You know that. You're not stupid. You'll be able to paint there, though. Or write, if you want to. I'll make sure of that. I'll look after you, but first you've got to put the gun down.'

'What about my paintings, the ones in my house? What will happen to them?'

There's a pause. It seems to last a long time.

'Nothing. They'll be waiting for you when you get out. And you will get out. You've got to trust—'

'How long?'

'I don't know exactly. With extenuating circumstances taken into account, perhaps five years.'

'You're lying!' Mary waves the gun in the air as if she can't decide who to aim for. 'Five years for a murder and two attempted murders? That's too little. How long? Tell me the truth.'

'You'll be allowed to keep some of your paintings with you on the inside,' says Charlie. I hear fear in her voice for the first time. 'I'll do everything I can to make sure—'

'I wouldn't be able to take them all with me, would I? All my pictures?'

'Hand the gun to me and I'll make sure they go with you, every single one of them.'

'You've seen how many there are.' Mary's voice shakes. 'They won't fit in a prison cell. I can't not have them with me.'

'There are prisons that have other kinds of accommodation, not only cells. Women's prisons especially. Some prisoners have their own rooms, or they share with one other person, but the rooms are a decent size.'

'Sounds like a Villiers dorm.'

'It's true, Mary,' says Waterhouse. 'We'll make sure you have the space you need for your paintings.'

'You're lying, both of you,' she says, sounding calmer. 'That's okay. I won't hold it against you.' She lifts the gun, holds it to the side of her own head. When she speaks again, I can hear that she's smiling, even though her face is turned away from me. 'Now, Martha,' she says. 'No mistakes this time.'

'No!' Charlie screams.

'I think yes,' says Mary, and pulls the trigger.

28

12/3/08

'The CPS won't touch it with a bargepole unless we can do better than this,' said Proust. His 'World's Greatest Grandad' mug lay on its side. He rolled it back and forth on his desk, smacking the handle against the wood every few seconds. 'It doesn't help that Aidan Seed's in the habit of confessing to killings that never took place. He still hasn't offered a satisfactory explanation for why he did that—why tell us he'd killed one woman when in fact he'd killed someone altogether different?'

'He's still in bad shape, sir,' said Charlie. 'Ruth Bussey's explained it in Seed's presence. I was there. I saw him confirm her explanation as best he could. Seed regretted having told Bussey he'd killed Trelease. He got cold feet about facing up to the truth after all these years, and by that time he knew Martha Wyers was calling herself Mary Trelease, so he decided to turn what he'd originally intended to be the beginning of his true confession—"I killed Mary Trelease"—into an easily disprovable false one.' Charlie shrugged. 'I know you don't like it, but it does make sense, sir.'

'If that's your opinion, Sergeant Zailer, then you have my condolences.'

'We've been through this,' said Simon impatiently.

'Not everyone's mind works in exactly the same way yours does, sir.'

Proust gave Charlie the look he reserved for despicable traitors.

'Even if we accept Bussey and Seed's explanation and a revised confession from Seed, it's going to be an uphill struggle if Len Smith sticks to his story,' said Sam Kombothekra.

'The CPS don't do uphill struggles, sergeant. You know that as well as I do. They prefer gentle strolls down country lanes.'

Sam nodded unhappily. 'In their eyes, Smith's a killer, yes, but he's not a liar.'

'He isn't a killer,' said Simon. He wasn't interested in other people's eyes and the things they saw that weren't there. After last week he was less interested than he'd been before. Most people were idiots, even those whose rank and years of experience might suggest otherwise. Coral Milward had been so determined to nail Stephen Elton for Gemma Crowther's murder that she'd wasted God knows how much time trying to break down what she'd called Elton's 'suspiciously solid' alibi. It was solid because he'd been telling the truth.

Elton, Simon had heard from Colin Sellers, was a habitual user of prostitutes, both male and female. ('No droughts for him, lucky sod. World's his oyster—both hemispheres.') After helping to clear up at Friends House on the night Gemma was murdered, he'd paid a visit to one of his regulars, a sixteen-year-old called Sharda who shared a bedsit in Seven Sisters with three other illegal immigrant sex workers. Elton's alibi was also his motive: Gemma Crowther had known about his habit and regularly threatened to expose it to their Quaker friends if he didn't follow her orders to the letter. Effectively, he was her domestic slave. Elton had been foolish enough to admit to Milward that he'd frequently fantasised about killing Gemma, and only didn't because he loved her. 'You've got to admit, though, that's a good reason,' Sellers had remarked this morning to Simon, entirely without irony.

Mary Trelease hadn't been interviewed at all, despite a long and elaborate description she'd given Ruth Bussey of an encounter with a detective from London. All lies. Dunning had called at 15 Megson Crescent several times and got no response. When he finally got round to entering the premises by force, Trelease and Ruth Bussey had already left for Garstead Cottage. Simon had found this out from DC Kevin Prothero, the newest member of Milward's team, the one to whom she'd assigned the task of dealing with some of the more awkward loose ends. Two of these were Simon and Charlie.

Milward had spoken to Simon once since last Wednesday, on the telephone. Without apologising, she'd explained how wedded she'd been at first to Stephen Elton in the role of chief suspect, and given Simon her reasons, in the manner of someone who'd forgotten she'd been proved wrong. Her 'thank you' had been distant and non-specific. Simon would have preferred one that came firmly attached to a mention of he and Charlie having risked their lives and put Milward's case to bed for her in the process.

'Look at what we know,' said Proust. 'Smith's been in trouble with the law for most of his life. An alcoholic, a wife-beater, a gambler. Seed's got a clean slate.'

'Which is why anyone with a brain'd believe him over Smith,' Simon pointed out. 'Len Smith had no reason to kill Mary Trelease.' He hadn't expected this, not on his first day back at work. To be in the thick of things, as if he'd never been gone, arguing his case, as he always did; an unpopular case, as it always was. Proust wasn't a fool; by now he was surely aware of the extent to which Simon and Charlie had gone this one alone—reporting to no one, with no official authorisation.

When they'd been summoned to the Snowman's office, neither of them had been in any doubt that a bollocking was coming. Nothing official—Proust wouldn't want to put his name to the suspension or sacking of anyone the tabloids were calling heroes, and neither would the Chief Super or the Chief Constable—but something that, nevertheless, would let Simon and Charlie know that they would be paying for the sins of their over-inflated egos for a long time to come.

They'd rehearsed their resignation speeches all the way to

Proust's glass cubicle. Sam Kombothekra had looked as surprised as they had when the Snowman had started to talk as if it was business as usual, as if Simon and Charlie had been in the loop all along.

'Smith had a reason to kill her, Simon,' Kombothekra said now. 'She'd been sexually abusing his stepson for nearly a year. I know what you're going to say: Smith's own abuse of Aidan started long before Mary Trelease came on the scene . . .'

'Making him something of a hypocrite if he subsequently killed her for what he himself had been doing for years,' Proust interjected.

'He wouldn't see it that way,' said Kombothekra. 'Aidan was his, simple as that. No one else had a right to touch him. Mary Trelease was also his, and she'd made him angry. I can see exactly why he might strangle her.'

'Except he didn't,' said Simon.

Kombothekra carried on as if he hadn't spoken. 'Trelease would wait for Smith to pass out, which he did reliably every night, and she'd start on Aidan. In Smith's eyes, what he did was justice. He's proud of it. "I'd kill anyone who laid a finger on one of my kids"—that's what he told me, and it's what he's been saying to anyone who'll listen to him since he's been banged up.'

'The men who come out with that shit are the ones who don't give their kids a second glance from one year to the next,' said Charlie. 'They want to talk about killing, that's all—next best thing to doing it.'

'If Smith didn't and doesn't care about Aidan Seed, why is he willing to do time for a crime Seed committed?' asked Proust.

'He cared,' said Simon. 'Lots of abusers love their kids.'

'Shame,' said Charlie. 'Pure and simple. Seed's brother and sister both say Smith went to pieces after their mum died. He was a classic insecure bully. Once his punch-bag was gone, he couldn't handle being on his own—the drinking got worse, and he moved Seed into the master bedroom, into his bed. Mary Trelease was strangled in that bed in the middle of the night. How could Smith explain to the police that his stepson was in bed with him and his girlfriend? A man like him'd rather go down for a murder he didn't do.' She shook her head in disgust. 'Aidan was twelve when Pauline Seed died. Can you imagine what it must have been like for a boy of that age—forced, under a constant threat of violence, to share a bed with your stepfather?'

'The brother and sister can't say for sure, but both reckon Smith started abusing Seed as soon as the mother died,' said Simon. 'Neither did anything to stop it, though, because they didn't know for sure if there was anything to stop, and they both lived in fear of Smith. Luckily for them, they were older, and only had a few years to sit out before they could leave home.'

'Aidan wasn't so lucky,' said Charlie. 'And those bastards left him there to rot—their own little brother. Of course Smith was sexually abusing him, and even if he wasn't, they knew what sort of life he was forcing on him. Aidan wasn't allowed out, apart from to go to school—even that, only sometimes. More often than not, Smith kept him off school, for company. He wasn't allowed to bring friends back to the house—that was while he still had friends. Once he started to withdraw into himself, they gave up on him quickly enough.'

'He wouldn't have wanted to bring anyone back,' said Simon. 'Would you want your mates to see that you shared a bedroom with your stepfather, if you were a twelve-year-old boy?' He knew all about not wanting friends to get even the smallest glimpse of one's home life. In his case, it was pictures of the Virgin Mary and painfully uptight parents he'd been ashamed of.

'Whatever Smith's done or not done, there's no doubt Seed means a lot to him,' said Kombothekra. 'Even though Seed's never visited him in any of the prisons he's been in, Smith's clinging to the hope that one day he might. Every time I speak to him, he asks me to pass the same message on to Seed. He never mentions his other two stepkids. I think he's forgotten they exist. Sir, if you look at it from Simon and Charlie's angle, the message might be Smith's way of letting Seed know he's going to carry on lying for him. I mean, even if he's really lying for his own sake, he'd want Aidan to believe otherwise, wouldn't he, if he's hoping for a reconciliation?'

'Is your head that easily turned, sergeant?' Proust snapped. 'That's not what you were saying before Waterhouse and Sergeant Zailer turned up. "Tell Aidan I'd never let anyone hurt him—I never have and I never will"—you and I agreed, did we not, that Smith was referring to the murder of Mary Trelease?'

'Why not take his words literally?' Simon suggested. '"I never have"—all right, granted, that might be a reference to Smith having strangled Trelease, though it's more likely to be a reference to his having covered for Seed and taken the blame. But what about "I never will"? Smith's nowhere near Seed's life now, is he? How can he stop people from harming him? He didn't stop Martha Wyers from putting a bullet in Seed, did he? "I never will" is Smith's way of letting Seed know that he's going to carry on lying to protect him.'

'We're talking about a Neanderthal inebriate, Waterhouse. Precision of language is unlikely to be his primary concern.'

'Actually, Smith hasn't had a drink in more than twenty years, sir,' said Kombothekra, causing the Snowman to bang his mug handle harder on the desk.

'I think you're wrong, sir,' Simon told Proust. 'I think Smith's message to DS Kombothekra was very precisely worded: to let Seed know he'd continue to keep their secret, while on the surface seeming to mean only that he'd killed Mary Trelease—the meaning you took from it. You can't say that just because he's from a council estate he's incapable of deliberately making a statement that has two possible meanings.'

'But now that Smith knows Seed's confessed, that he wants the truth to come out, wouldn't that give him pause?' asked Kombothekra. 'I've heard the way he talks about Seed.' He looked around the small office apologetically. 'I'm the only one of us who has. Heard it first-hand, I mean. Seed's all he's got. I mean, I know he *hasn't* got him, I know Seed wants nothing to do with him, but in Smith's mind, Seed's his life, the only thing he's living for—the hope that one day they'll be reconciled. Simon's right, Smith's not stupid. He knows there was no need for Seed to confess after all these years. Why would he keep up his so-called protection, knowing it's unwanted?'

'The last twenty-odd years of his life, banged up in one miserable, stinking hole after another, have been about protecting Seed,' said Simon with feigned patience that he knew everyone in the room could see through. 'Okay, maybe there was an element of self-interest—he was ashamed to admit he'd shared a bed with his stepson—but all these years sitting in his cell? He'll have dreamed up a different story, a better one—himself as the self-sacrificing hero. Both the brother and sister have said how much Smith loves Seed—too much.'

Kombothekra nodded. 'That's what they told me, and they told Kerry Gatti the same thing.'

'Gatti's a fucking liar,' said Charlie in a stony voice. Simon hid a smile behind his hand. She'd been furious to discover that according to Gatti's version of events, he had willingly handed over two of his files to her. He'd also denied another of Charlie's claims: that he hadn't known, when she'd met him at the Swan pub in Rawndesley, that Martha Wyers had changed her name legally to Mary Trelease. Gatti wasn't any more prepared to lose face than Len Smith was.

Simon said, 'If Smith tells the truth now and Aidan takes his place in custody, what's it all been for?' He looked at Kombothekra. 'You've got kids. Don't you ever stop them doing something they're gagging to do because you think you know what's best for them and they don't?'

'Maybe Smith wants it to be true,' said Charlie. 'That he killed Mary Trelease. Better for his pride: he strangled his girlfriend when he caught her trying to force herself on his teenage stepson. In that version of the story, Smith gets to come out a hero, in his eyes and, for sure, in the eyes of most of the guys he's been swapping stories with since the early eighties. I'd bet everything I own that Smith *did* sexually abuse Aidan. Maybe he couldn't help himself, and hated himself for it—if he genuinely loved Aidan, he might well have done. If he tells the world and possibly himself, too, that Mary Trelease was the abuser, and that he put a stop to the abuse by killing her, he's redeemed, isn't he?'

'Exactly,' said Simon. 'Think about the other version of the story: for years, he sexually abused the stepson he loved because he was lonely and desperate and fucked-up after his wife died. Then he got a new girlfriend—Mary Trelease, a cinema usherette whose own two kids had been taken into care, an alcoholic and a heroin addict. Smith brought her into the family home, into his bed, but even then he couldn't let Seed go. He made Seed sleep in the bed with them . . .'

'Aidan was his comfort blanket,' said Charlie.

'Whatever he was, Smith wasn't willing to do without him. Maybe he stopped abusing him once he had Trelease to take care of his sexual needs, but Seed still had to lie there every night, listening to the two of them having sex.' Simon kept his eyes on Proust as he spoke. He knew Charlie thought talking about sex made him uncomfortable, and he hated the way she studied his behaviour. It made him feel like an alien under a microscope.

'You've read the brother and sister's statements, sir,' she said. Her less confrontational tone made Simon aware that he'd been raising his voice. *Keep your cool. First, find some from somewhere, then when you've got it, keep it.* 'Aidan used to creep out on to the landing to get away from Smith and Trelease, but Smith would come out of the bedroom stark naked—he'd actually interrupt sex with his girlfriend—to drag him back in. If he was in that bed, Aidan had to be in it too: house rule. The brother and sister each witnessed it on more than one occasion. Both said that, as well as being aggressive, Smith was clearly scared.'

'According to both siblings, Smith claimed he couldn't sleep if Seed wasn't in the bed with him,' said Kombothekra, looking down at his notes. 'Said he had panic attacks. Maybe he felt the same even after he got together with Trelease.'

'Pity we can't put Seed brother and sister behind bars,' Proust muttered. 'For presenting themselves as victims of equal status as much as anything else. By the time Mary Trelease appeared on the scene, they were both about to leave home. They couldn't have gone to the police once they'd left? No, not them—they opted to drop in for tea and cake every so often instead, witness one or two horrors, then be on their way.'

'I think the tea and cake would have been more like cheap cider and smack, sir,' said Charlie.

'We're getting sidetracked,' said Simon. 'Of course Smith isn't going to tell the truth: that he ruined his stepson's life, then brought in a woman who'd already been judged unfit to be around children to ruin it a bit more. Smith might have loved Seed—he might have needed him as a comfort blanket—but that need placed Seed directly in the path of Mary Trelease, and he knows it. Night after night, she'd wait until Smith was out of it and force herself on Seed. Eventually, he got so desperate that he closed his hands around her throat and put a stop to it once and for all, for which I don't at all blame him, and what was Smith doing when that happened? Sleeping off a bottle of whisky at the far edge of the mattress, drooling onto his sweat-soaked pillow? Do you think anyone'd want to tell that story about themselves? Smith's going to cling on to his lie for dear life, whatever he thinks Seed might or might not want him to do.'

'Which is why we find ourselves in a predicament,' said Proust, righting his empty mug. He knew exactly how pleased everyone was that the knocking noise had stopped; Simon could see it on his face. 'Thank you, Waterhouse, for defining things so clearly. Len Smith will cling to his story. Aidan Seed, as soon as he's strong enough to do any clinging, will doubtless cling to his, and the CPS will cling with equal ardour to their right to finish work on the dot of three o'clock, after which time they get a nosebleed if they remain at their desks, as we all know.'

'Have you told him about the painting?' Charlie asked Sam.

'I wouldn't rely on Sergeant Kombothekra to transmit information if I were you. Considerable time and energy could have been saved if his initial searches, which he assured me were exhaustive, though perhaps he meant exhaus*ting*, had brought to light a twenty-six-year-old murder.'

'I was looking in unsolveds, sir,' said Kombothekra. 'There's no database of victims' names. How was I supposed to . . .?'

'What's this about a painting?' Proust asked Charlie.

Simon swallowed a sigh. Hopeless; why was she even bothering?

'I don't know it exists, sir, but if it does, it might help to clarify things.'

'I see,' said the Snowman, wanting her to see he was sickened by what he'd heard. His sickened look was similar to his despicable traitor look; one suggested disgust provoked by stupidity and the other disgust inspired by treachery, but that was the only difference. 'So we're in the realm of rubbing lamps and waiting for genies to appear, are we?'

'Aidan Seed painted a picture called *The Murder of Mary Trelease*. Martha Wyers destroyed it along with all his others, so obviously we don't know what it depicted, but Ruth Bussey thinks there was something significant in it, and I'm inclined to agree with her. There must have been something, so that when Wyers found out from Kerry Gatti that Aidan's stepfather was banged up for killing a Mary Trelease, she thought she knew that he hadn't. Seed isn't yet strong enough to answer all our questions, and I'm not sure when he will be, but . . .'

Charlie paused; looked at Simon. He nodded. She'd got this far—might as well let the Snowman hear the rest.

'After Trelease destroyed all Aidan's pictures from the TiqTaq exhibition, she painted her own versions of them.'

'We've found seventeen of these in her house,' Kombothekra chipped in. 'Only one's missing. You can guess which.'

'I'm almost certain that once Mary—sorry, once *Martha* realised that one of the pictures she'd destroyed was possible proof that Aidan had committed a murder, she immediately painted a version of that picture herself, from memory. Why wouldn't she? She painted copies of the other seventeen pictures from his TiqTaq show.' Charlie paused for breath before saying, 'Ruth Bussey agrees with me, sir.'

'Well, then.' Proust's voice was granite. 'What more could I hope for in the way of verification?'

'Sir, if we can find that picture, maybe show it to Len Smith . . . I mean, I know a painting doesn't exactly prove anything, but we could maybe use it as leverage, to get him to talk . . .'

'Remember when you and I sat in a noisy café in town, sergeant, and you told me you weren't good enough for CID? I'm inclined to agree. I wasn't then, but I am now. You're talking about a painting that might not exist. Have you asked Martha Wyers' parents about it?'

'They couldn't help us, sir,' said Kombothekra.

Cecily and Egan Wyers were embarrassed by everything to do with their daughter's paintings, which they'd already decided to sell as a job lot as soon as a decent amount of time had elapsed. Simon found that shocking, no matter what Martha had done. The word Mr and Mrs Wyers had used most often in connection with their daughter since her death was 'mortified'. Egan Wyers, in particular, was furious that Martha had enlisted the help of his domestic staff in order to get her hands on the paintings from Aidan's exhibition, and bought their silence afterwards with money he'd given her. He appeared to be angrier about that than about the murder Martha had committed. Every time his wife shed tears over the death of her only child, he shouted at her that there was no point, that nothing could be done about it now.

'There's no picture that fits the bill at Garstead Cottage,' said Kombothekra. 'Or at Villiers. I spoke to Richard Bedell, the deputy head, who as good as told me that even if the school did have any paintings by Martha Wyers, which they don't, they'd be binning them round about now. I got a pretty heated earful from Bedell about how the Wyers family had done unimaginable damage to the school's reputation. Apparently Martha used to wander round the grounds crying and accosting girls, telling them she'd died and come back to life. A lot of the pupils found it scary, and others became so obsessed with Villiers' own resident loony that it distracted them from their work. There was nothing the school could do, though, because of the Wyers' generous sponsorship. They had to let Martha have the cottage.'

'Their greed was their downfall,' said Proust. 'I'm not going to lose sleep on their behalf. Villiers is still standing and still rich. The same can't be said for Martha-Mary-Wyers-Trelease or whatever her names were.' Seeing the others looking at him oddly, he added with relish, 'And I won't be losing sleep for her either. Now, do we have any other ideas about how to proceed? Ones that don't involve us relying on the rumour of a copy of a painting?'

'What if we could persuade Seed to go and see Smith in prison?' said Kombothekra.

'Absolutely not.' Simon turned to Charlie, sure of her support until he saw her face. 'Don't tell me you think it's a good idea?' he said. 'After what that evil bastard put him through, we're going to persuade him to pop in for a chat?'

'It might be good for Aidan to see Smith face to face,' said Charlie. 'To tell him the truth and ask him to tell the truth. Look where lies and avoidance have got him. Ruth Bussey's certainly in favour of having everything out in the open—he might listen to her, even if he's reluctant at first. Why don't we explain the problem to Aidan instead of trying to protect him as if he's a kid?'

'And if he can't talk Smith into telling the truth? Then he

feels like a failure on top of everything else he's had to go through, and it's our fault.'

'I think it's a reasonable idea,' said Proust. He'd avoided the word 'good', reluctant to pollute Kombothekra's mind with praise. 'Don't worry, Waterhouse. It won't be down to you to do the persuading. I think Sergeant Zailer might manage that without your clodhopping assistance.'

'I don't work for you any more, sir. I work for—'

'No,' said Simon. 'If it's got to be done, I'll do it. I know I'm not . . .' He paused.

'The list is endless, isn't it?' said Proust. 'The list of what you're not. Top of it is this: you're not going to be concerning yourself with Aidan Seed from hereon in.' Proust opened his desk drawer, pulled out what looked like a large book. Except it wasn't. It was . . . oh, shit, it couldn't be . . .

'Yes, Waterhouse. Brand new, with shiny cover and unbroken spine. The Automobile Association's latest road atlas of Great Britain. I bought it with a ten-pound note I found in the bin by the photocopier shortly after our last tête-à-tête.'

'Sir, you can't . . .'

'There are two categories of people in this world, Waterhouse: those who admit to the mistakes they've made and attempt to compensate, and those who correct them retrospectively in their own minds by pretending they never happened. If something succeeds, they were behind it all the time. If it fails, they never supported it in the first place.' Proust leaned back and folded his arms across his belly. 'I like to think I belong in the first category. If I get something wrong, I put my name to it and do my best to atone for my mistake.'

Simon, Charlie and Sam Kombothekra stared at him, dumbfounded.

'On this occasion, I'm pleased to say I couldn't have behaved better and therefore have nothing to atone for,' the Snowman went on. 'Whatever our colleagues in London had to say about you, Waterhouse, I stuck resolutely to the view that you were reliable and would be proved to be so. While others doubted, I always knew you'd be back here where you belong. How would it have looked if you'd returned to discover that I'd reassigned Mrs Beddoes and her multifarious misdemeanours to Sellers or Gibbs? I did no such thing. I fought off many attempts, on the part of colleagues who shall remain nameless . . .'—Proust scowled at Kombothekra—'. . . to purloin work that was rightfully yours. You all know I have my faults, but I'm happy to say disloyalty isn't among them.'

He held out the road atlas for Simon to take. 'Happy travels, Waterhouse. May the prevailing winds be with you.'

29

Tuesday 1 April 2008

'Do you think he's all right in there?' I ask Saul for about the twentieth time. We're in Sam Kombothekra's car in the car park at Long Leighton prison, waiting for Aidan, Charlie and Sam to come out.

'I think he's more than all right,' Saul says, as he has twenty times already. 'What about you? Can you face what might happen?'

'If Aidan can, I can.' Yesterday I donated my entire collection of self-help books to Word on the Street, where I'd bought most of them. This morning I took down my Charlie Zailer wall. None of that was real. The progress Aidan and I have made since that night at Garstead Cottage—that's real. Substantial.

Saul pats my hand. 'I'm going to tell you something Aidan made me promise not to,' he says.

'What?' My heart dips. 'We agreed no more secrets. When did he . . .?'

'He's going to ask you to marry him. Later today, whatever happens in there. He's got an engagement ring in his pocket. What will you say?'

I feel faint with relief. 'Yes. Obviously.'

'Good. I knew that would be your answer.'

'Then why tell me and spoil the surprise?'

'There have been enough surprises already,' said Saul. 'With any luck, there won't be any more for a good long while.'

I open the car door, seeing Charlie walking towards us across the car park. Something's not right. She's looking purposeful, walking too quickly. 'I need you both to come inside,' she says.

'I don't want to see him,' I tell her, panicking. 'Aidan doesn't want me to . . .'

'You won't see Len Smith. You'll be nowhere near him.'

'Is Aidan all right?'

'He's doing fine. He's doing brilliantly.'

'Then what . . .?'

'It's better if I show you. I'm assuming neither of you's got your passport or driving licence with you.'

'No.'

Saul shakes his head.

'Then leave everything in the car—wallets, bags, the lot.'

'But . . .'

'Be quiet and listen. Until we get back here, your names are Tom Southwell and Jessica Whiteley. You're both here for a job interview—English teacher, education department. You handed over your passports this morning—they've got them—and you've just nipped out for lunch. Right?'

I'm about to tell her I can't do it when I hear Saul say, 'Right.' I make a face at him behind Charlie's back, but he doesn't notice. He's busy mouthing, 'Tom Southwell' to himself.

When we reach the glass-sided hut that's set into the high wire-mesh fence, Charlie says her name with confidence, for our benefit as well as that of the uniformed guard inside. 'You've got my ID already. There I am.' She points to her name on his list. 'Oh, it wasn't you before, was it? Sorry.'

'No probs.'

'Same with us,' says Saul easily. 'Tom Southwell and Jessica Whiteley.'

'In you come,' says the guard. He has to unlock three gates for us. Charlie tells him we know where we're going and he leaves us to it.

'Where *are* we going?' I ask.

'Patience, Ruth,' says Saul. I give him a look. He's the one who's supposed to dislike surprises; he's all talk.

'To the education department,' says Charlie.

'I don't want to teach English in a prison,' I tell her. 'What's going on?'

Eventually, we come to a wide corridor with green-painted walls. I think of the last time I followed Charlie down. It feels like a lifetime ago. Like that one, this one has pictures on the walls, the prisoners' artwork, some of it excellent. Charlie stops in front of a picture, and when I look at it, my heart surges up to fill my throat.

'Her,' I say, feeling the same horror I'd feel if she were to materialise in front of me, back from the dead. I'd recognise her style anywhere. I recognise the picture, too, from Aidan's description.

'We were right,' says Charlie. 'I'm sorry. I know it's a shock, but you had to see it. I couldn't not show it to you. We were right, and my boss was wrong. Ex-boss,' she corrects herself.

'*The Murder of Mary Trelease*,' I say. 'So she did do a copy. But . . . how did it get to be . . .?'

'She visited Smith in prison,' says Charlie. 'It occurred to me on the way here that she might have. Why wouldn't she? She wanted to get close to Aidan in any way she could, as long as it wasn't too risky. She knew Aidan didn't see Smith or have any contact with him. She couldn't resist.'

'You mean . . . you asked Len Smith . . .?'

Charlie shakes her head. 'Sam and Aidan are with him. I haven't seen him. No, I asked one of the wardens if I could see a list of Smith's visitors. There was a Martha Heathcote on the list. Heathcote was her house at Villiers. I checked. The warden I asked was very helpful. He remembered Smith being extremely distressed after the visit. It's the only visit he's had since he's been here—everyone thought he'd be delighted but he wasn't. The opposite. Ms Heathcote brought him two presents, both of which he wanted nothing to do with. He told the prison staff to burn them. One was this picture. The other was a book.'

'*Ice on the Sun*,' I murmur.

'Yes. Which is now in the prison library,' says Charlie. 'Resources are finite, here like everywhere else. They weren't about to throw away a book that could go in the prison library or a painting they could stick on the wall.'

'It's not signed,' I say, staring at the picture. Aidan has described it to me, but seeing it—or rather, seeing Martha's replica—is something altogether different. The painting is of a bedroom at night. The room's dark, but some light's coming in through the curtains. It looks as if it might be the early hours of the morning. There are three people in the bed: an older man, asleep, wearing a sweat-stained vest, turned on his side, a yellowing pillow beneath his head, a dribble stain by his mouth. Then there's a naked woman in the middle of the bed. Her eyes are wide open and there are faint bruises on her neck. I'm not sure anyone would say with certainty that she was dead unless they knew. On her other side, there's a young man, or an old boy, wearing a T-shirt and a pair of shorts, sitting up, hugging his knees and crying, looking at the person looking at the picture. *Aidan*. She's captured him perfectly: how he must have looked, how he must have felt.

'He needs to see this,' I say. 'Can he use it to prove what happened if . . . if his stepfather won't . . .'

Charlie's shaking her head. 'He won't need to, though. Smith will do what Aidan wants him to do. It'll be okay, you'll see.'

'It will,' Saul echoes, squeezing my arm.

'Even if she'd put the right title on it . . .' says Charlie.

'What do you mean, the right title?' I look carefully, but can't see a title anywhere. There's no writing at all on the picture.

'I thought she'd have called it *The Murder of Mary Trelease*,' says Charlie. 'I can't understand why she didn't. It's as if she hasn't quite got the courage of her convictions.'

'What did she call it?' asks Saul, leaning in close to the wall to look at the back of the picture. Of course: that's where the title would be, if it were anywhere.

Carefully, with both hands, Charlie lifts the painting off the wall and turns it round so that Saul and I can read the label on the back. Tears spring to my eyes as I read Mary's handwritten words, words that make no sense to Charlie or to Saul, and won't to Aidan either.

Words that make sense only to me. Four, in total.

The Other Half Lives.

Acknowledgements

During the writing of this book, I received a lot of help and inspiration from the following people: Lisanne Radice, Jenny Hewson, Anneberth Lux, Mark and Cal Pannone, Guy Martland, Tom Palmer, James Nash, Steve Mosby, Wendy Wootton, Dan Jones, Jenny, Adèle and Norman Geras, Susan Richardson, Suzie Crookes, Aimee Jacques, Katie Hill, Dominic Gregory and Rosanna Keefe, Nicky Holdsworth, Vikki Massarano, Chris Tulley, David Welsh, Anthony, Susan and Ben Rae, Jo Colley, Rebecca Hossack, Ana Finel Honigman, Fiona Harrold, Jill Birch, Christine Parsons, Morgan White, John Silver, Nicholas Van Der Vliet, Alison Steven, Nat Jansz, Anne Grey, Debra Craine, Adrian Searle, Neil Winn, Tony Weir, Swithun Cooper, Paula Cuddy, Hannah Pescod, Will Peterson.

I am particularly grateful to my superb agent Peter Straus, and my fantastic and lovely publishers, Hodder and Stoughton, especially Carolyn Mays, Kate Howard and Karen Geary, without whose expertise and support I hope never to find myself, and Alasdair Oliver whose jacket designs are to my books what Gok Wan is to frumpy women.

Finally, I'd like to thank all the readers who have written to me—your letters, more than any other inducement, keep me motivated to write the next book.

The 'Future Famous Five' article took its inspiration from a real newspaper feature with the same title written by Imogen Edwards-Jones and published in *The Times* in 1999.